Love
&
Other
Disasters

Love & Other Disasters

ANITA KELLY

FOREVER

NEW YORK   BOSTON

This book is a work of fiction. Names, characters, places, and incidents are the product of the author's imagination or are used fictitiously. Any resemblance to actual events, locales, or persons, living or dead, is coincidental.

Copyright © 2022 by Anita Kelly

Cover design and illustration by Hattie Windley. Cover copyright © 2022 by Hachette Book Group, Inc.

Hachette Book Group supports the right to free expression and the value of copyright. The purpose of copyright is to encourage writers and artists to produce the creative works that enrich our culture.

The scanning, uploading, and distribution of this book without permission is a theft of the author's intellectual property. If you would like permission to use material from the book (other than for review purposes), please contact permissions@hbgusa.com. Thank you for your support of the author's rights.

Forever
Hachette Book Group
1290 Avenue of the Americas, New York, NY 10104
read-forever.com
twitter.com/readforeverpub

First Edition: January 2022

Forever is an imprint of Grand Central Publishing. The Forever name and logo are trademarks of Hachette Book Group, Inc.

The publisher is not responsible for websites (or their content) that are not owned by the publisher.

The Hachette Speakers Bureau provides a wide range of authors for speaking events. To find out more, go to www.hachettespeakersbureau.com or call (866) 376-6591.

Library of Congress Cataloging-in-Publication Data has been applied for.

ISBNs: 978-1-5387-5484-9 (trade paperback); 978-1-5387-5485-6 (ebook)

Printed in the United States of America

LSC-C

Printing 1, 2021

For Meryl & Rosie

Love
&
Other
Disasters

CHAPTER ONE

Dahlia Woodson might have been shit at marriage, but she could dice an onion like a goddamn professional.

The first even slices, the cross hatching. The comfort in how logical and perfect it was. Dahlia had put in the work, onion after onion, until she could create consistent knife cuts every time. Until she trusted her hand, her knife, without having to think about it at all: fast and efficient and right.

When Dahlia stepped onto the set of *Chef's Special* in Burbank, California, on a Tuesday morning in late July, she thought about onions.

She certainly couldn't focus on the mahogany floor under her feet, how it positively *gleamed*. Or how high the ceilings were, far higher than she had imagined, than seemed necessary. Like some sort of sports stadium. For food nerds.

And the lights—sweet holy Moses.

It felt like walking into an airport terminal after a long cross-country flight: everything too fast, too loud, too full of *new*.

Except the set of *Chef's Special* wasn't new, not exactly. Dahlia had seen it before, back home on her TV set.

But it was different in person. More overwhelming, more surreal.

She approached the soaring wooden archway that marked the rear edge of the set. It was majestic and unmistakable, like the doorway of a cathedral, if a kitchen could be a church.

She shuffled around it, staring in awe, dazzled by the shining lights above. And a second later, smacked herself right into a solid wall of person.

A person who released a displeased grunt at Dahlia's face implanting into their chest.

Dahlia bounced back a step, a rubber ball of embarrassment, tongue sticking to the roof of her mouth. Blinking up, she watched as the other contestant ran a freckled hand through their strawberry hair. It was buzz cut on the sides, longer on top, and when their hand released, a flop of it fell back over their right eyebrow.

Dahlia cleared five feet, but barely. And this person was *tall.* That eyebrow hovered what felt like a full floor above her.

But it was cute, the strawberry hair. It made Dahlia think of leaves changing color in the fall, and Anne of Green Gables, and sunsets reflected off of still water. They hadn't moved since her face met their chest, and the nearness of another body felt grounding somehow, like when your eyes lock onto someone in Arrivals you recognize, the cacophony of the airport finally settling around you.

And so maybe it was the sunset hair or the simple proximity of another sentient human being, but Dahlia opened her mouth and—

"Oh, god. I just ran right the fuck into you. I am so, so sorry. I am just so nervous. Like, I think the last time I was this nervous was my fourth grade spelling bee, when I forgot how to spell *whistle* and everyone laughed at me and I maybe peed my tights, just a little. God, wearing tights is the *worst*."

Dahlia sucked in a breath. She could see, from the corner of her eye, the other eleven contestants milling around, waiting to be herded to their assigned cooking stations by a producer named Janet. Strawberry Blond Hair kept standing there, staring at her with a blank look on their face. Dahlia felt awkward ending the conversation here, but she didn't know how to transition smoothly from fourth grade urination—although, for the record, she stood by her assessment of tights—so she simply barreled on, her brain scrambling to find a more relevant way to finish this horrifying minute of her life.

"Anyway, this is weird, right? That we are going to be on TV. That this is real. All I can think about is onions, which is so dumb because everyone else is probably thinking about, you know, veal and foie gras or whatever. Although I'm also thinking about how I'm probably going to trip over someone's feet the first time we all run into the pantry. And how I will likely forget how to cook as soon as the timer starts." She paused to laugh a little at herself. "A veritable parade of positive thinking, right here."

Dahlia pointed to her head. Attempted a charming smile.

Strawberry Blond Hair blinked.

"Cool, okay, so, great. Good talk. Bye."

Dahlia turned to pivot around their shoulder right as a pale hand landed on her arm.

"This way, honey."

Thank the goddesses above. Producer Janet was saving Dahlia from herself. If such a thing was even still possible.

Swallowing, Dahlia tried to take it all in as Janet led her through the curving maze of cooking stations that took up the majority of the floor space in the cavernous set. But mainly, all she could focus on was how much she liked the bright red frames of Janet's glasses, and the small pulse of warmth that had pushed into her pounding heart when Janet called her *honey*.

They stopped at the very front of the semicircle of stations, all the way to the right.

"Here you go, Miss Woodson. This is you."

And with a reassuring smile, Janet whirled away to direct the next contestant.

Here were all the details Dahlia had seen on TV for the last seven seasons of *Chef's Special*: the deep greens and golds and sparkling turquoise scattered throughout the set in pops of colored glass. How the dark wood of the walls and the floor contrasted against those lighter hues.

She had always thought the set resembled an old Scottish castle on the moors, only recently been paid a visit by *Queer Eye*. Cozy and strong all at once, its foundations invoking a sense of time and honor—and here and there, some bright splashes of cheer.

Dahlia stared down at the shining, stainless steel counter-top of the station. *Her* station. She recalled the blank look on Strawberry Blond Hair's face a few minutes ago, as she made a fool of herself within minutes of stepping onto set, and resisted the urge to lean down and smack her forehead against that stainless steel a few times.

Instead, she closed her eyes and breathed in through her nose, like that yoga class she went to once a year ago had taught her.

Onions. The scraggly brown bits on the top and bottom. The pure white of the insides, firm yet pliant. The reliable structure of layers. So many recipes started with the basic building block of a finely diced onion.

Dahlia was learning, in her new life, to take things one step at a time. If she started with basic building blocks, focused on each small step, she could accomplish things.

Dahlia's eyes blinked open as a tall white man with dark hair ambled over to the workspace next to hers. He was looking down, furiously scribbling in a small notepad. Oh god. People were taking notes, and Dahlia felt like she'd barely heard half the words coming out of Janet's mouth this morning. And Janet was loud.

"Hey," the tall dude said, finally looking up. He stuck his pencil behind his ear, all cool like, and held out a hand. "Jacob. Looks like we're tablemates."

Dahlia shook his hand. She thought she maybe said her name. She was thrown by how confident he seemed, when all she could think about, aside from onions and that embarrassing scene under the archway, was how gassy she suddenly was. Her stomach was making alarming gurgling sounds. She glanced around the room. All the other contestants were making idle chatter, smiling at each other. They ranged from cocky and attractive, like Jacob, to a short older woman in the opposite corner, her salt-and-pepper bob shaking as she nodded vigorously at the Black woman next to her.

Wait. Dahlia recognized that bob. She had met that bob on the shuttle to the hotel from the airport two days ago. A grandma from Iowa, Dahlia remembered now. She was exactly what you would expect from a Midwestern grandma: kind, but sharp. Like you knew she made a mean apple pie, but also wouldn't let you get away with any of your shit. Dahlia had loved her immediately. Barbara! That was her name.

A small spark burst to life in Dahlia's veins.

If Barbara could do this, so could she.

But when Dahlia's eyes glided away from Barbara, the faces of everyone else blurred at the edges.

She took another deep breath. Peppers. She liked chopping peppers too. Not as satisfying as an onion, but so aesthetically pleasing. Exquisite, vibrant colors, colors that were almost hard to imagine emerging from nothing but seeds, sunshine, dirt.

All you needed were building blocks.

"Hello, contestants of season eight!"

Dahlia swiveled back around.

Holy leapin' lizards.

Sai Patel. Sai Patel was in front of her. Standing in the middle of the Golden Circle, where the contestants would be called at the end of each Elimination Challenge to greet their glory or their doom. Dahlia was suddenly disconcerted that her cooking station was so close to this circle, this space which would spike her anxiety and determine her future. It would, in fact, never escape her vision.

Everything was fine.

"I know how nervous you are right now." Bless Sai Patel, and his mussed dark hair, and his shirt with the top button unbuttoned, for saying this out loud. "But remember—we chose you, out of thousands of possible contestants, for a reason. You've already gotten through the hardest part. You're here! And now? This is when the fun starts."

As Sai Patel grinned out at the thirteen contestants of

season eight, Dahlia could see with her very own eyes that one slightly crooked canine she had observed so many times from the comfort of her couch back in Maryland. It was even more perfect in person, Sai Patel's smile, and the fact that one of the most famous chefs in the world was standing in front of her, appearing genuine and encouraging and fully invested in this whole thing, began to soothe Dahlia's nerves.

He was right, after all. She had made it through the auditions in Philly for a reason. *Chef's Special* was for amateur chefs; thousands of people tried out each year. It meant something that she had been one of the thirteen out of all those thousands to make it here. She had worked hard. Her new tablemate Jacob and his dumb pencil behind his ear weren't any better than her. She could do this.

She could win $100,000.

Janet swooped in as soon as Sai departed, her voice somehow sweet and commanding all at once.

"Here we go, folks! We've got a busy day ahead of us."

Dahlia steeled her spine, forced her head to clear. She understood she had to listen to Janet now. About how they were going to leave the set and walk back on again, for real this time, with the cameras rolling. They were to hold their heads high, smile brightly, show they were ready to get this business started.

And Dahlia was not going to vomit. Or release gas. She was going to think about onions and peppers, or perhaps the calming, repetitive motion of chopping cucumbers, summer squash, carrots. Slice, slice, boom. Trusting the rhythm of your wrists.

What she ended up picturing, though, as she walked out

on set again, was garlic, smashing them out of their papery shells with the flat blade of a knife. She felt it in her palms, the competent smack of her knife, the power of it. A fragrant, essential building block crushed beneath her fingertips.

Her mind focused, her tunnel vision fading away. Sai was in front of her again, now joined by the other judges, Tanner Tavish and Audra Carnegie. The table behind them was tall and imposing, the wall behind it made of polished hickory with a huge gold circle in the middle, a near reflection of the one on the floor. *Chef's Special* was splashed across the circle at an angle in forest-green letters, off-center, a fast, carefully lazy script.

Dahlia felt the cameras watching her, and there were a few things she knew.

She knew it had been a foolish, rash thing, quitting her job for this.

She knew she could fail spectacularly. Fall flat on her face.

But there were other things, too. Things she hoped to be true.

Like maybe she was made to create delicious, magnificent things.

Like maybe this was her chance to prove it. That she could be *good* at something. Really, truly good at something, something she chose, something that was for herself and no one else.

Sai Patel's voice boomed once again from inside the Golden Circle, his voice effortless in its masterful projection, his dimples and twinkling eyes radiating charisma, the scruff of his facial hair a level of sexy that bordered on rude. Dahlia had to make a conscious effort to not stare at his forearms, those experienced muscles peeking out from his rolled-up sleeves.

And then the cameras stopped, because apparently Audra

Carnegie's skirt wasn't lying exactly right, and some of the contestants weren't smiling hard enough. Dahlia breathed out and glanced around her again, taking in more of the set—the abstract Chihuly glass sculptures, all perfectly lit in hues of green and blue, that dotted the clear wall between the cooking stations and the pantry. She could just glimpse the pantry through them, and her pulse ticked up at all the fresh produce on display, the just-visible corner of the refurbished library card catalog she knew held every spice she could imagine. Dahlia could not wait to get herself inside that pantry.

It was when she turned her head to see what lay on the other side of the set that her eyes landed on that strawberry blond hair again. And a face, she saw more clearly now with the increased supply of oxygen to her brain, that was generously dotted with freckles. Their hazel eyes were staring straight at her. At least, Dahlia thought hazel was the right word: an arresting greenish-gray, with flecks of gold and flashes of darkness mixed within. The hue of their hair seemed even brighter here, under the full effects of the stage lights, like they were cast in a heavenly glow.

If heavenly glows also included grumpy scowls.

If cool, lean Jacob next to her was a jaguar, Strawberry Blond Hair was a lion.

They were at the station directly behind hers. Dahlia's face warmed again at the recollection of their interaction earlier, but creeping rays of confidence were seeping into her now. She could make this better, too.

She worked up a friendly smile. "Good luck," she whispered. Which was a much more normal thing to say to a fellow

Chef's Special competitor than, you know, talk of fourth grade spelling bees.

They looked at her, unmoving, for a second longer. She thought, maybe, she saw their jaw clench. And then they grunted.

Again.

Except this was a *purposeful* grunt. They *thought about* this one.

They grunted at her, and then averted their eyes.

So. That would be a *no* as to whether they had found Dahlia's freak-out charming.

Dahlia turned back to her station. She glanced at Jacob, who was staring straight ahead, arms crossed at his chest, standing in a wide power pose.

Fine. You couldn't win them all. She still had the prospect of friendship with Barbara from Iowa, at least. Screw these people; grandmas were awesome.

It took far longer than Dahlia had anticipated, but finally, *finally*, over an hour and many surprisingly specific instructions later, it was time to cook.

The first challenge was always simple, open ended. Each contestant cooked whatever they wanted to showcase their personal styles, their signature skills. Everyone knew this, had time to plan for it for weeks.

She in fact didn't trip on the mad dash to the pantry. As soon as Dahlia got her hands on some limes, she felt calm. Back at her station, she swept her dark hair onto the top of her head as the red clock embedded in the judges' table clicked away, and she made a game plan. She was vaguely aware that Jacob was making filet mignon, that Strawberry

Blond Grunting Face behind her was making lamb. She knew it would be this way.

On every cooking show she'd ever watched, everyone always jerked off to proteins she hardly ever cooked with. All of that stuff cost money. Money a single, recently divorced copy editor didn't have.

Honestly, the only protein Dahlia could *really* afford, if she ever stuck to her budget, was canned tuna. But she preferred vegetarian dishes anyway. One could do some pretty amazing things with fresh produce, flour, grains, eggs, and a shit ton of spices. Perfecting homemade pasta was the first true balm to her soul last year after she moved out of the house she had shared with David, to be truly on her own for the first time in her life.

Vegetarian dishes didn't win *Chef's Special*.

But. Dahlia had grown up by the rocky shores of New England. She currently lived by the brackish waters of Chesapeake Bay. She knew seafood, too.

Not that fish tacos were really a signature of either New England or the Chesapeake. But whatever, who wanted to mess with crabs and lobsters, which had always seemed to her like more work than they were worth? She could have her way with a slab of cod and still have fun with all the other stuff. Marinade to mix, fresh tortillas to grill, cabbage to chop, jalapeños to mince. Colors, flavors, juices. The brighter and saucier the food, the more joy Dahlia took from it.

She had no idea whether fish tacos would be too basic for the judges or not, but she knew they would taste good and they would look pretty, and those were the only building blocks Dahlia had to work with.

So she juiced, she mixed, she grilled, she chopped, she cooked. She made a plan and followed it. She smiled at the judges and answered their amiable banter when they stopped by her station. She tried not to think about the cameras, tried not to look at the judges' faces as they sampled her food. Tried not to think about lamb or steak.

And even though this first day of filming had already seemed to take a million hours, the sixty minutes they had to cook truly did fly by. Somehow there were only five minutes left, and Dahlia felt tense but good, this rush of adrenaline wiping all other thoughts from her mind. Her hands were steady as she plated. She even had an extra minute to tidy her station.

When Tanner Tavish yelled, "Time's up!," her arms fell to her sides. Her feet took a step back.

And that was when Dahlia started to shake.

Which she hoped wasn't noticeable in all of these high-definition cameras, or to the judges in front of her, who had been around the world and cooked in Michelin-starred restaurants. Who walked around set like they owned the joint. Because they did. At worst, she hoped her trembles were only noticed by Freckled Grumpypants behind her, whose opinion of her probably couldn't get any lower at this point anyway.

There was a brief break, as Janet and the production assistants and the judges huddled and pointed and discussed who knew what. Contestants' plates were adjusted slightly, perfected for the cameras. Contestants ran to the bathroom, laughed nervously with each other. Dahlia stood in place, biting her lip.

And then they were back.

And Audra Carnegie said her name.

Seriously?

She would be the first to have her food judged?

Dahlia had no idea whether this was a blessing or a curse. But she did know her nerves were still recovering from sixty minutes of hyper-focus.

Closing her eyes for just a second, she took another yoga breath. She placed her hands underneath her plate. She stepped away from her station. She rounded the table.

And she tripped.

The world went in slow motion, a torturous horror film. From outside of her body, Dahlia saw Sai Patel rush forward, hands outstretched, brown eyes wide. She thought she heard someone curse. Had there been something in her way? An up-turned snag of electrical tape? Or had she, Dahlia Woodson, for the love of all that was holy, really tripped over her own feet after she had made her very first meal on national TV?

Oh dear lord. She was going to literally fall flat on her face.

Somewhere, in the recesses of her brain, she thought, *Well, naturally*, before her mind went numb. The studio lights were blinding as starbursts of rice, ribbons of purple cabbage, and a playful dash of lime crema took flight moments before her body slammed onto the floor.

CHAPTER TWO

L ondon just needed a moment to themself.

They had stepped into this dim hotel bar to find it, escaping to this grimy table in the corner, crumbs and drink rings littering its surface. Just one moment to themself. They could have continued up to their hotel room to decompress after this entirely too long first day of filming. But their hotel room didn't have bourbon.

The first taste had felt so good, burning the back of their throat in exactly the way they desired. Cold, strong, a kick of home. It cleared their mind, just a touch. Another glass, and they might clear this whole funky headspace entirely. They had performed well today, but that was likely only because they had practiced making that lamb approximately ninety-eight times.

Tomorrow, the real *Chef's Special* started. Face-Offs. Ingredient Innovations. Elimination Challenges where they didn't have weeks to prepare. Real World Challenges. They had to get their mind in order, as soon as humanly possible, if they wanted to succeed.

And maybe they were only here because they got too drunk

with Julie last Christmas, when they saw the ad about *Chef's Special* auditions coming to Nashville. Julie had dared them to try out, and they had never once in their life said no to a dare from their twin sister. But now that they were *here*, it was real. And the more London thought about what they would do with that prize money, the better they felt about it.

London wanted to succeed at this more than anything.

So they spent the next two sips of bourbon clearing their head and preparing for tomorrow, for the next day, for every challenge to come.

And then a bag slammed into the empty chair across from them.

The surprising bag was followed by an equally surprising woman, whose wild dark hair framed a face that declared she had had quite enough of the day, thank you very much. She stuck her hands on her hips, visibly huffing, and glared at them.

"Dahlia." London winced, recalling her spectacular trip on set, which had occurred hours earlier at this point but was still imprinted on their mind. Because how could it *not* be. It had been...epic. "I am so, so—"

"Oh, shut up." She waved a hand. "Everyone is so sorry for me. I know. Believe me, I'm sorry for me, too. I don't want to talk about that."

London gripped their liquor, unsure what in the world they and Dahlia Woodson had to talk about, if they couldn't talk about that.

But Dahlia apparently knew.

"Why didn't you say good luck back?"

London blinked.

"Or even smile!" She continued, booming with anger when London didn't respond. "You didn't have to say anything, but you could have at least smiled back. Or said literally anything to me, after I embarrassed myself at the beginning of the day. All I was trying to do was be friendly. Look for a little reassurance before the most terrifying thing in my life commenced. Why be such a jerk?"

London was too stunned to reply. Or to even take another sip of bourbon. Which they sorely needed.

Dahlia crossed her arms over her chest.

"Did I do something to you?"

London could feel it now, see it in her eyes as Dahlia attempted to bluster on, how the heat was going out of her. Her anger was quickly giving way to sadness, or fatigue, or something else. And while the anger had been startling, no part of London had any room for this stranger's sadness. By the time she pushed out her last question, she only sounded tired. "Or are you just one of those people who indiscriminately hates everyone?"

London frowned at this characterization, even if it had been weakly thrown. "I don't hate you. That's not...no." They took a breath. Fine. They'd put an end to this thing. "I'm sorry I didn't say good luck back."

The truth was that London remembered Dahlia saying good luck to them. They remembered their brain registering that they should reply, and the command not quite reaching their mouth. They remembered pretty much everything about Dahlia Woodson from today, from the moment they walked on set and first got a glimpse of that hair.

It was mesmerizing. Thick, almost black, unkempt. But

the thing that left London slightly gobsmacked was simply how much of it there was. It cascaded in waves all the way to her waist. It was ridiculous, was what it was.

The season eight cast had met last night for a meet-and-greet cocktail hour and dinner at some swanky restaurant in Burbank. There was so much going on, so many hands to shake and names to remember and fake smiles to plaster on, that London hadn't kept track of the other contestants as closely as they knew others were, scouting each other out, looking for signs of weakness. But when London saw that hair today, they knew they would have remembered it. That hair had not been at the meet and greet. And now it appeared that it would be in their direct line of vision for the entirety of filming. Or, at least, until one of them was eliminated from the competition.

"Hey," London had asked Ahmed, their tablemate, when they huddled behind the archway, waiting for the go-ahead to officially enter the set on camera this morning, right after she had run her face into their chest. "Do you know who that woman is, in front of us? Next to Jacob?"

"With the hair? Name's Dahlia Woodson. I think."

"She wasn't around last night, though, right?"

"Nope. I only think that's her name because I heard Janet say, 'Where the hell is Dahlia Woodson?' at some point."

"Huh."

London simply didn't like being thrown off, was the thing. It was *fine*, of course, that Dahlia had apparently blown off the meet and greet, that she was stationed in front of them. But it was unnecessarily distracting, really, that all of that hair was down, completely untamed and uncontained. Like, was she actually planning on cooking like that? Because for starters, it was completely unsanitary. It would never fly in a professional kitchen.

But hairnets weren't sexy on-screen. Maybe the producers had asked her to keep it down? But no, a quick glance around set had revealed several other people with their hair up. The more London had stared at it, the more infuriating it became.

London had been so distracted by it when they first saw it that they had simply stood there, like an idiot, as Dahlia whirled up to them under the archway, a tiny hurricane of energy, and smashed into them. And proceeded to be... adorable.

Her hair was up now, drawn into an enormous, slanting bird's nest on top of her head, the mechanics of which, honestly, London couldn't compute.

When she collapsed into the seat across from them, unceremoniously shoving her bag onto the floor, a few more strands escaped, floating around her face, her tanned skin. She looked exhausted, but somehow that skin still seemed to glow anyway, even in this dim bar lighting. Which was, London thought, scratching at the back of their neck, scraping across their own ghostly skin, extremely unfair.

"Can I get something for you?" A petite waitress, the roots of a fading dye job clear in her sloppy blond bun, stopped by the table. There was an orange stain on her left shoulder. She, too, looked exhausted.

It was a real party in this hotel bar tonight.

Dahlia jutted her chin toward London's glass. "What's that?"

"Bourbon." London still felt tongue-tied, trying to process this whole interaction, but their brain remembered this.

"Yeah, that. That sounds good."

The waitress nodded and walked away.

Dahlia sighed, rubbing a hand over her face. She was wearing a loose knit purple dress over leggings, and when she'd sat down, the scoop neckline of said dress had slipped over one of her shoulders, revealing a black bra strap and a delicate stretch of collarbone.

London had barely talked to this woman, and they already felt like they knew too much about her. That she had peed her pants—but just a little—in the fourth grade. How vulnerable her face looked after falling on national TV, a bit of crema on her cheek. That she was wearing a black bra. That she had been nervous today.

London hadn't actually felt that nervous, somehow. Only generally disgruntled.

The waitress returned, slipping the glass into Dahlia's hands before disappearing. Dahlia took a good slug, and London cleared their throat. They weren't quite sure why Dahlia was still here, why she had decided to sit down, but if London smoothed this over maybe she'd leave faster.

"I didn't mean to be rude to you today, if I was. I've, uh, had a rough couple of days."

Dahlia looked at them over the rim of her glass, freezing for just a moment.

And then she slammed the glass on the table and began to laugh.

With every passing second, she laughed harder.

London couldn't do anything but stare.

"You," she said eventually, wiping at her eyes. "You made lamb that was so, quote, magnificently cooked that it looked like Audra Carnegie wanted to kiss you, *and* you managed to not spill your entire plate while busting your ass on national television, but sure, you're having a bad day. All right." Dahlia rolled her eyes, gathering her breath back after her laughing fit. She took another massive slurp of bourbon.

London felt their cheeks flame, even more so than usual.

"Audra Carnegie did not want to *kiss* me," they said. "And they liked your fish tacos, too. After they let you reassemble them," they added, more lightly, scratching the back of their neck again in an attempt to dispel their secondhand embarrassment.

"Yeah, well." Dahlia finished her bourbon with another eye roll.

She shouldn't be that put out, really. The judges had already sampled her tacos before she made her dramatic on-screen tumble. Filming the judging portion of the show took so long that the food normally got cold. So most of the judges' assessments came from taste testing they did throughout the actual cooking process. This had been one of the first things Janet had told them. Dahlia's feat of aerodynamics had been impressive, but it didn't actually threaten her spot on the show. London had watched her make those tacos. They could tell they were good.

"Hey, can I get another one of these?" Dahlia called out to the waitress as she was about to fly by their table again, motioning to her empty glass. The waitress raised an eyebrow, likely at how quickly the glass had been drained, but it was clear Dahlia didn't much care. She scanned a greasy placard that was at the edge of the table. "And…some chips and guacamole! Yeah, awesome. That would be awesome."

"Awesome," the waitress repeated, deadpan, before floating away.

London felt much the same.

"Just to clarify," they said, leaning slightly forward. "Are you mad at me?"

London understood that *Chef's Special* was a competition. That they should not care what Dahlia Woodson thought of them. They had spent the last few years of their life working hard at not caring what people thought of them.

But it felt wrong anyway, that they could make a stranger angry so quickly, for reasons they still didn't one hundred percent understand. For some reason, they didn't want Dahlia to be mad at them, however strange she might be.

"Nah." Dahlia shrugged a shoulder. "Honestly, I'm not that good at being angry, in general. Whenever I'm angry about something, I always end up getting sad in the end instead, so I try to avoid it. And…that was too much information. Yikes, I need food in my system." She paused. "It was a valiant effort, though, right? At being angry?"

"You called me a jerk," London affirmed.

Dahlia grinned. "See? That felt weird coming out of my mouth, but I said it anyway! Look at me." She reached out and grabbed London's glass. "Why are you not drinking this?" She took a long sip and winced, as if it had hit her throat too fast, before pushing the glass back across the table. "Anyhoo, so I'm done. Now tell me about your horrible day."

She really just…did that. She drank London's bourbon.

Dahlia Woodson was a real piece of work.

The chips and guacamole arrived before London could think of what to say, along with Dahlia's second bourbon on the rocks. She crunched into a chip the moment the waitress placed them on the table, and her eyes went wide. "Oh man. Oh wow. They do not have chips like these on the East Coast. You should have some."

London did not reach for a chip, but they finally took a sip of their own bourbon again. They felt harried, like they were constantly one step behind in this conversation, like they never knew what Dahlia was going to say or do next, and they had no idea how to extricate themself from this sad, poorly lit bar.

"So, your bad day. I'm all ears." Dahlia prompted again as she dug into the guacamole, chomping on another chip, smiling now, like she was suddenly having the time of her life.

"Why weren't you at the meet and greet yesterday?" London asked instead.

Her smile drooped, and she looked slightly shamed. "Oh. The whole idea of that gave me supreme social anxiety. I told a PA I was having bad cramps."

"Are you serious?" London burst out, incredulous, their mouth suddenly working again. "It gave *all* of us social anxiety! This entire show is like, an exercise in surviving social anxiety! And you used *cramps* as an excuse?"

"Hey!" Dahlia frowned. "My menstrual cramps are *really bad*, okay! When I have them! Don't judge me."

But London *was* judging her. In fact, they were pretty angry at *her* now, irrationally or not. Because they were going to have to come out to her now, to get it over with, and if she had just shown up for the dumb meet and greet, they wouldn't have to do this again. If she just had some control over her fucking hair, London would have said good luck back hours earlier, or reacted in whatever way Dahlia found acceptable, and she wouldn't be here, right now, ruining London's moment of peace.

They took a breath.

"Last night, at dinner, I came out to everyone as non-binary, so everyone would know my pronouns, which are they/them. I thought it would be good for everyone to know right away, so there wouldn't be awkward misgendering, and I could actually just be me on this thing. But some people didn't take it great, which I should have expected, but it still threw me off a little, because I had been too optimistic, so I was a little off today. There. Okay? Are you satisfied?"

London motioned to the waitress for another drink. Dahlia was quiet now, which made London feel smug, but smug in a way that didn't actually feel good at all.

"Who didn't take it great?"

London glanced at her. Her face looked different, but they couldn't read it.

"It doesn't matter."

"No, it really does. I want to make sure I don't accidentally befriend someone who's actually an asshole."

London sighed. They were so tired that they wouldn't truly contemplate Dahlia's reaction until later, how steely her voice had turned. "It was mainly Lizzie."

"Remind me, which one is Lizzie again?"

"Frizzy blond hair. White woman, fifty-ish, maybe."

Dahlia's brow furrowed in concentration. She looked so *serious* all of a sudden. "Glasses?"

"Yeah."

She nodded. "What did she do?"

"Oh, you know…" London waved a hand, not wanting to rehash it. Coming out to so many strangers like that, all at once—it had been terrifying, but they figured it was the most efficient way. It had been one of the tensest moments of London's entire life, attempting to announce it to the table quickly and casually.

But they thought they'd gotten away with it. A white woman with dark hair hidden underneath a backward baseball cap named Cath had leaned forward, her voice deep and comforting when she said, "That's cool with me. Thanks for telling us, London." And then she'd given this little nod, which London had immediately accepted as a Fellow Queer Nod of Approval, and they had let out some of the breath that had been pent up in their lungs. Others at the table nodded too, smiled at them.

Until Lizzie had cleared her throat, dabbed the corner of her mouth with a napkin, and said, "I'm sorry, but what do you mean?"

And London's stomach had clenched all over again. It was exhausting, on an ordinary day, having to constantly explain and defend your existence. And it had been a long plane ride here from Nashville, their nerves already frayed from embarking on this strange journey.

They decided to be direct, basic, repeating more slowly what they'd already fucking said. Nonbinary. They/them pronouns. The end.

Lizzie had squinted her eyes at them, like they were speaking in Klingon.

"But that doesn't make any sense."

Janet's chair scraped loudly against the floor.

"You really want us to refer to you, a singular person, using *they*?"

"Yup." London shoved their fists in their pockets, gritted the single syllable between clenched teeth. The rest of the table seemed frozen, staring determinedly at their plates, their sweating glasses of water.

Janet placed a hand on Lizzie's shoulder. Lizzie looked around the table. "Oh, come on," she said, her voice turning derisive, "I can't be the only one who thinks this is a bunch of malarkey. There's no such—"

"*Lizzie.*" Janet's voice was firm. Not even Lizzie could fight that voice.

Janet had led her swiftly away from the table, Lizzie muttering under her breath, and then they were out of the room, and the table descended into painfully awkward silence. It was likely only a few seconds until Cath said something that broke the tension, but London couldn't hear what it was through the ringing in their ears. They had taken two bites of their food and departed shortly thereafter.

Making others uncomfortable by being honest about their identity was a skill London already had familiarity with. They just hadn't experienced it on quite as grand a scale before.

"Yeah," Dahlia said now, softly, and London's mind returned to this dark hotel bar. "I know."

Even though London had not actually described any of last night's events out loud.

"Let me know if there's anything I can do," Dahlia added. "If Lizzie's being a bitch to you, or anyone else."

London frowned. "It's fine. I just needed a day to process

it. I don't need to be..." They waved their hand again. "Your queer charity case."

"No, I'm not..." Dahlia's mouth opened and closed, color hitting her cheeks. She leaned back in her chair. "My older brother Hank is trans. He started transitioning a few years ago. So I know the things people can say. That's all."

She took a sip of bourbon.

London hadn't expected that. They didn't know how to respond.

"I'm sorry I wasn't there," Dahlia said after a moment, in that same quiet tone she'd used before. And then she stuffed two chips in her mouth. But London could tell she wasn't enjoying them.

London was sorry she wasn't there, too. A little pissed about it, actually.

Not because they thought Dahlia automatically understood them now, or that she could have magically saved the situation somehow. There were a million ways to be trans, and just because she loved her brother didn't mean she knew London.

But now they knew she was at least an ally. And when London let go of even a shred of their irritation, they could picture it, suddenly, knowing how oddly honest Dahlia Woodson was. She probably would have cut Lizzie off even before Janet did. She would have said something weird and funny and it would have made things slightly better.

Maybe.

But she had been hiding in her room pretending to have cramps, so.

"Are you planning on being out on the show, too? Like to viewers?"

"Yeah." London cleared their throat. "I was going to share my pronouns in my first solo interview, but then we ran out of time today filming, so I didn't even get to do that right."

They grabbed a chip. And of course Dahlia was correct. They were fantastic.

"That's... that's big. Hank will be so excited. He'll cry, probably, when he watches it. But that loser cries about everything." Dahlia smiled, but it was smaller than before, when she'd been laughing at them, when she'd tasted her first West Coast tortilla chip. It was a no-teeth smile now.

Something had flared in London's chest when she said that about Hank, though. They knew it shouldn't matter, that they should only be doing this for themself, but... it was reassuring. This confirmation that them being out on this thing could mean something.

They felt they should say something, give something in return for this small gift.

"The chips are very good."

Although they couldn't stop themself from adding: "The guac is just fine, though. I could make better."

Dahlia's smile grew, just a fraction. "I bet you could."

London glanced at her, unsure whether she was making fun of them or giving them a compliment. Her eyes looked genuine. They were a shade of brown that was right smack in between the darkness of her hair and the tan of her skin, making her face, in general, a perfect palette.

Just a pure bourbon observation.

"Can I ask what you would do?" Dahlia asked, looking at them. "If you won?"

Finally, an easy question.

"I would use the money to start a nonprofit. For LGBTQ kids, back in Tennessee."

"You're from Tennessee?"

London nodded. "Nashville."

Dahlia smiled again, but she looked down at the table as she did it. She readjusted her dress, dragged the purple material back up over her shoulder. London ignored the tiny spark of loss that dragged under their skin.

"Hank has always wanted to go to Nashville. He loves country music. Named himself after Hank Williams."

London watched her pick up a chip, place it on its edge on the tabletop. She held it there with her fingertips, making no move to bring it to her mouth.

"That's really noble," she said. "The nonprofit thing."

"I mean, I have no idea how to actually start a nonprofit," London said automatically, embarrassed. Because Jesus, they didn't want to be seen as *noble*. That felt gross. "But...yeah, I'd like to try."

"That's great."

London had never seen a sadder tableau than Dahlia Woodson staring at that chip, unmoving.

"Hank should go," they said, deciding suddenly to make a real effort. At not being a jerk. At drawing Dahlia back out from wherever she had disappeared in the last five minutes. "To Nashville. It's a great place."

"Yeah," she said, half-heartedly.

"What would you do with the money if you won?" London asked.

If it was possible, Dahlia became even more still.

"I have a lot of debt," she said finally, shrugging. "It turns out divorce is expensive. And I have student loans, and..." She trailed off. "I don't know. Some money would be nice."

Wait. This woman was divorced? She couldn't be much older than London, and they were only twenty-six.

Maybe London, in fact, knew very little about Dahlia Woodson.

"Anyway, I should probably go. Sorry for interrupting you."

Dahlia stood abruptly, draining the last of her bourbon as she went, leaning down to grab her bag. She dropped some bills on the table and then paused, fiddling with the strap of the bag.

"So, this is embarrassing," she said, not meeting their eye. "But I'm not one hundred percent sure. It's London, right? There were so many new people to meet today, and I was nervous, and—"

"Yeah. It's London." And then they added, dumbly, like they were reciting roll call in school, "London Parker."

She smiled, just a little.

"I'm Dahlia."

"Yeah. I know."

"Oh. Right. Okay. Sorry again. See you tomorrow, London Parker."

London felt strange after she left, a little lonely, maybe, even though they had come here to be alone. They chugged the rest of their bourbon before paying their tab, not caring to linger in this bar any longer, too close to the knowledge of how much they liked the sound of Dahlia's voice saying their name.

CHAPTER THREE

Janet's hand landed on Dahlia's shoulder the next morning, five minutes after the cameras turned off for a break.

"Dahlia, honey," she said. "Time for your first interview."

The frames of Janet's glasses were purple today. She smiled reassuringly.

Dahlia took a breath. She had just lived through her first Face-Off challenge, where each contestant squared off against another to complete a basic culinary task. The winners of each Face-Off gained advantages for later challenges.

Dahlia had lost her Face-Off. To Lizzie, of all people. Which sucked. It sucked real hard.

And she had a slight bourbon headache.

Still, she hadn't fallen on her face so far today.

And she hadn't made a further fool of herself in front of London Parker. Dahlia was determined to look like less of an idiot in front of them from this moment forward.

She was trying, in other words, to have a positive outlook.

But as Dahlia followed Janet toward the back corner of the set, Janet's curly hair bouncing in a loose knot as she walked, Dahlia curled her fingers into the hem of her tank top. Her humiliations of the past twenty-four hours, including the California rolls Lizzie had just crafted faster and more artistically than Dahlia had, dropped away as a different anxiety settled in her gut.

Dahlia had been thinking about this moment since she'd learned she made the cut for the show a month ago.

When the contestants introduced themselves in their first solo interview, they only had to state a few basic facts about themselves. Where they were from, their jobs back home, what they hoped to get out of the show.

But even trying to think of answers for these simplest of questions made Dahlia feel inadequate and confused these days.

She was *from* New Bedford, an old whaling town in southern Massachusetts next door to Rhode Island. It was New England who had raised her.

But she lived in Maryland now. Her ex-husband David had commuted to DC and she commuted to Baltimore; they had lived between the two in suburbia for the six years of their marriage. She had contemplated moving to Baltimore proper when she moved out last year, but she ended up sticking to what she knew. Because everything, from getting up in the morning to feeding herself, had felt hard, and sticking to what she knew felt like the only option. She found a small apartment in their same dull town, even though she no longer felt any real allegiance to it, to its string of mini-malls and chain restaurants. She wondered, at times, if she ever had.

David had moved to Arlington.

So at least she didn't have to worry about running into him at the Food Lion.

The small set where the *Chef's Special* contestants would film their solo interviews was tucked in a back corner of the sound stage, beyond the wooden archway, next to craft services. A thick, marbled window lit from behind and made of stunning turquoise glass took up the entire back wall. It was beautiful, and it soothed Dahlia immediately when she walked in the room, even if it didn't give her any better ideas of what to say.

She sat on a stool. She blinked while the camera focused on her, while PAs adjusted the lights. The young woman behind the camera with short, tightly curled hair peeked out at her and smiled, full of friendly vibes.

"Hey, Dahlia. I'm Maritza. Remember, we just need the basics here. Start with your name, age, location. Good to go?"

Dahlia nodded numbly. Wordlessly, Maritza counted off with her fingers and then gave the signal.

"My name is Dahlia. I'm twenty-eight and originally from Massachusetts."

Her mind blanked.

Maritza bopped out from behind the camera again. "Okay. Something about your career, and why you're here?"

Right. Sure.

Except Dahlia didn't *have* a career.

She had worked as a copy editor at a small Baltimore paper for the last four years, and enjoyed it for the most part. She had always liked writing and editing, and the work was interesting sometimes. More and more of the paper was simply canned from larger news wires, but the local beats their reporters still got to cover felt important. She liked her co-workers, especially Josh, who covered their online marketing and social media, who made her laugh and had always treated her with respect.

But she'd become restless these last couple of years after so many days in the same cubicle, never moving on to something bigger, better, more challenging.

Dahlia had dreams, but vague, blurry ones, dreams that held no concrete value. Seeing the world. Doing something she was passionate about, something meaningful. She simply had no idea what that something *was*. She worried that if she made cooking her career dream, she'd lose the joy in it. And sometimes, this last year, it felt like that joy was all she had.

Dahlia didn't want to own a restaurant, or even work in one, but cooking meant something to her now, something primal and important. When her mental health and her marriage started to break down two years ago, far before she fully understood either of those things was happening, it was cooking that calmed her. Made her feel productive and useful.

Cooking made her mind focus on something other than herself.

And then, as she started getting better at it, as she started cooking more not because she had to but because she wanted to, she started to stray away from strict recipes to rely on instinct and knowledge alone. And that? That made her feel creative and powerful—two adjectives she had forgotten to associate with herself. And then it wasn't just a distraction. Cooking held the possibility of helping Dahlia Woodson find herself again.

She was still working on that part. Finding herself again.

Because other than being really good at chopping vegetables

and making homemade pasta, other than knowing she wanted to get the hell out of Maryland suburbia, Dahlia understood who she was less and less with each passing year. Like she was growing up wrong.

But she couldn't say any of that to the camera. She couldn't talk about her student loans.

So Dahlia swallowed, tried to smile, and said the most generic thing she could think of.

"I only started cooking seriously a few years ago, so I'm really excited for all I can learn here."

Maritza nodded. "Good." Her head swiveled to another PA as she checked notes on her phone. "AJ, can you go get Khari next?"

Dahlia left the room, worried, with a mortifying rush of shame, that she might cry.

She had never wanted to be a generic person.

She walked to craft services and shoveled down ten grapes without tasting a single one.

Dahlia was acting differently today, and London didn't like it.

Maybe they didn't have the right to judge how Dahlia Woodson did or did not act, considering they had barely known her for twenty-four hours. But they had spent at least eight of those hours yesterday staring at the set of her shoulders, the angle of her neck as she leaned forward in concentration at her station, the way she unconsciously shuffled her weight from one foot to the other when she was anxious. The way her cheeks swelled when she smiled.

They knew the way her face looked when she laughed, how her eyes beamed out joy when she tasted something she loved.

She was wearing a cheerfully bright yellow tank top today. But the Dahlia Woodson on set now seemed diminished. Quiet.

Most likely, it had nothing to do with London, or their conversation last night. Even if London had spent more minutes than they cared to admit contemplating whether they actually had been a jerk yesterday. Or thinking about the look on her face when she talked about money, her debt, how they wished, somehow, that they could erase it.

Not that, again, it was any of their business.

Dahlia was probably just quieter today because her nerves were settling down, because she was getting focused. Like London should be doing.

They were wandering through the pantry, waiting for the Ingredient Innovation to finally start, while Janet pulled contestants aside for solo interviews and the judges shot cheesy B-roll for the show's corporate sponsors. The Ingredient Innovation was the most creatively demanding segment of the show, and London was antsy about it. The judges presented an oddball or lesser-used ingredient, and the contestants had to produce a small plate—usually a side dish or a simple dessert—that featured the ingredient and didn't taste like garbage. London had always been good at following recipes with precision, at improvising with ingredients they were familiar with, but the element of surprise stressed them out. They knew the Elimination Challenges were the big cooks that really counted, but the judges took into account the skill and creativity shown during the Ingredient Innovations, too, before they made their final decision at the end of each episode. London had to get their head in the game, if they wanted to keep landing on the right side of those final decisions.

And yet—as if the universe was determined to put Dahlia Woodson in the way of London's focus—there she was, standing stock still in front of the card catalog of spices in the pantry, clutching a tiny notebook to her chest. London watched her for a moment, intently inspecting the card catalog, which had been painted seafoam green before being repurposed to spice storage. It was pretty cool. But there was a lot of cool stuff on this set.

Dahlia was transfixed.

And for some reason, instead of turning and walking the other way, London stepped closer. "Hey," they said. "You okay?"

Dahlia's eyes didn't stray from the card catalog, but she nodded.

"I just," she whispered, "I just love it so much."

Something about the way she whispered this was so cute that London knew, with a twinge of helplessness, that they were no longer mad at her, really, for faking cramps.

"Yeah," they agreed. "Me too."

They stared together at the card catalog in silence for a minute more.

"I really wanted to beat her," Dahlia said suddenly.

"Lizzie?" London had felt bad when they saw Dahlia hadn't won her Face-Off this morning. But the Face-Offs weren't even that big a deal. Sometimes the advantages were pretty helpful, especially later on in the competition, but they were mainly just dramatics.

Although they had been glad, if they were being honest, that it was Dahlia who had to face off against Lizzie today, and not them. That they had had the good fortune of being paired with Cath. Who had kicked their ass in the Face-Off, assembling her California rolls way faster—London had been too concerned about being neat with them—and punched their arm in victory when the timer buzzed. Their arm was still a little sore, actually, but it had made them laugh.

It was true, though, what they had told Dahlia last night about Lizzie. They just needed some space to get over the meet-and-greet dinner. You couldn't let transphobes keep you down forever.

"Yeah." Dahlia nodded, her brow furrowing. "She was so *nice* to me." She was still hugging her notebook to her chest. "It was irritating."

A small smile crept onto London's face.

"I know what the first secret ingredient is, for the innovation challenge," Dahlia said a few seconds later, changing subjects abruptly. London was almost getting used to it now, never knowing what Dahlia was going to say next. "I saw a crew member moving some stuff around."

"Really?" London turned to her. "What is it?"

If Dahlia were a smart competitor, she wouldn't even be telling them this. But she opened her mouth without hesitation. "Spam."

"Huh." London turned back to the spice cabinet, their mind already whirring. "That seems like a bit of a softball. Spam's easy."

"Yeah, I know."

They stood for another few moments in silence, until

London started to feel awkward. "All right, I'm going to head back out there." They motioned behind their shoulder with their thumb. "You just going to stand here staring at this thing until they call us back?"

Dahlia nodded. "Yep."

London stuck their hands in their pockets and tried to hide another grin. On a whim, they turned back to her once they'd reached the pantry doorway.

"Hey, Dahlia?"

"Yeah?" She finally tore her eyes from the card catalog to look over at them.

"Good luck."

They only allowed themself the briefest of glances at her smile before they turned and walked back to their station.

Where they had the misfortune of overhearing a conversation between Jacob and Jeffrey, who were standing at Dahlia's station in front of them.

"This is what I'm saying." Jeffrey, a balding white man from Texas, was gesturing emphatically. "America needs to get up to speed on the insect scene. We're entirely too cocky about our proteins here."

"Exactly," Jacob said. "When I was in Brazil last year, I had these beetles…"

London glanced back toward the pantry, wondering if they should go back and ponder the spice cabinet with Dahlia a minute more.

London agreed, honestly, about eating more insects. But it was the way these people talked. All around them, all morning long, London had overheard other contestants boasting to each other about cooking accomplishments they'd already achieved, the most exotic dishes they'd ever prepared, the places around the world they had dined in. London had grown up around people like this, people who overvalued their own importance. Had grown tired of them, long ago.

A part of them daydreamed about dragging Dahlia to the side of the set. Complaining about everyone else in the room together. Did she also hate Jacob? Because the dude seemed like a real drag. London had lucked out, they thought, with Ahmed as a tablemate.

The set felt surprisingly like high school, all this posturing around strangers. Ahmed and Cath were the only people London felt comfortable around so far, the only people they'd want to sit with in the cafeteria.

Along with, they admitted to themself, the woman with the infuriating hair who had declared them a jerk.

They couldn't exactly explain it. But it had felt, for a moment last night, and for a minute just now in the pantry, like maybe they were on the same side. Made for the same lunch table.

And London longed, suddenly, to see Dahlia roll her eyes at someone who wasn't them.

They shook their head, mentally blocked out the voices of Jacob and Jeffrey.

This wasn't high school. It was a competition. One that was televised, and London had to start really paying attention now. Dahlia was a competitor, not a science project partner. She could stay in the pantry. London would keep their grumbling to themself.

They took out their notebook from their back pocket.

And started to make some serious plans for Spam.

CHAPTER FOUR

Dahlia felt the tiniest bit guilty about the excitement that poured into her veins when she walked onto set the following morning and saw the poor things: their gaping, airless mouths, their bug-eyed, frozen faces.

Jacob gagged next to her as they approached the feast of fish laid out on a table in the middle of the Golden Circle. It did smell godawful.

It also smelled *familiar*.

Today was their first Elimination Challenge day, and finally, it felt like a day that would go right from the start.

The funny thing was Dahlia wasn't even super into fish, not really. But she had gone to a class run by some fishmongers in Baltimore last year, right on Inner Harbor, that had deepened her knowledge of the slippery creatures. Dahlia had learned most of her cooking skills from YouTube or blogs or, occasionally, if she was feeling fancy, real live cookbooks. But when she found classes or seminars that weren't too expensive, like at the fishmongers, they were always her favorite. It was different to see things hands-on, to be able to ask questions. This was what she had been looking forward to on *Chef's Special* the most, the ability to get hands-on advice from the best of the best. The ultimate leveling up.

She had her notebook at the ready when Audra Carnegie stepped to a smaller table set up next to the pile of fish for a demonstration.

The contestants jostled around each other to get a good view of Audra and her fillet knife, a large, shimmery rainbow trout laid out in front of her.

Dahlia, of course, jostled herself right into a shoulder wearing an army-green T-shirt, one that revealed freckled forearms dusted with strawberry blond hair.

Dahlia straightened, rooting her feet to the floor, and clicked open her pen. She stared determinedly over Barbara's shoulder at the trout, like a professional-ass chef about to take some professional-ass notes.

She did feel a smidge better about her relationship with London now, after their brief interaction in the pantry yesterday. She still wouldn't call them *friends*, but it appeared they had moved past whatever weirdness she had created in the hotel bar. Which was a plus.

Another plus: Audra Carnegie looked hot as hell, gutting and filleting this fish in front of them like a boss. Her dark skin shone under the studio lights, her braids swirled into an intricate knot on the top of her head. She went slowly and spoke calmly, but she never hesitated with her knife, with her skillful hands.

"After you make your incision behind the gill plate, we're going to look for the spine. Remember, again—always, always keep your hand *behind* your filleting knife."

Dahlia was delighted Audra was doing this demonstration

instead of Sai or Tanner. She'd always felt like Audra got the shaft on this show, only thrown in for her feminine touch, her advice on plating, salads, baked goods.

But girls could break down a fish. They could scoop out innards with their bare hands. By the time Audra had two perfect trout fillets in front of her, Dahlia was ready to give her a resounding high five and begin smashing the patriarchy of the food world together.

But before Dahlia could get to patriarchy smashing, the thirteen contestants of season eight were sent back to their stations.

"Now that we all feel confident about breaking down a trout," Sai Patel said with a smile, "there's a small twist. Winners of yesterday's Face-Off, please come to the Golden Circle."

Lizzie, Cath, and the other Face-Off winners did as asked.

"Now, each contestant will be assigned a different fish today." Sai gestured with an arm to the cornucopia of fish on the table. "And your advantage, Face-Off winners? *You* get to choose which contestant is assigned which fish."

Intrigued murmuring ensued, and then Lizzie and company were let loose to decide the losers' fates. They walked around the table, whispering to each other and making notes, until handing a final list to Sai.

Dahlia ended up with swordfish, which was significantly larger, and hence more difficult, than rainbow trout. She was happy with it, though. Such a funny and badass creature, the swordfish.

Dahlia leaned down and tapped its intimidating bill.

"I'm sorry I'm going to slice through your anus and tear your guts out through your throat," she whispered. She could practically feel Jacob's eye roll next to her, and she didn't care. She felt good today. "I appreciate you. Thank you for your sustenance," she concluded, with one more loving tap, before straightening. Jacob was staring at her.

Oh! She could use some of those peppercorns she'd seen yesterday in the pantry. They were so pretty, a dazzling mixture of black, gray, burgundy, and hunter green. Dahlia could already hear them popping in her pan, the sizzle of the swordfish in butter. Lemon peel, parsley, garlic. Something simple for a side. She started stacking the building blocks in her head, and anticipation buzzed in her toes.

"Ladies and gentlemen!" Tanner Tavish raised his arms dramatically from the middle of the Golden Circle. "Prepare yourselves for your first Elimination Challenge. Your hour of fish filleting and cooking is about to begin."

London groaned, both at the dead fish lying on a thick black mat on their station, and at Tanner's *ladies and gentlemen.* Both, at the moment seemed equally irritating.

London had never actually gutted a fish before, which in hindsight seemed like an embarrassing skill to miss. Their assignment of halibut was a relatively common white fish whose meat London had cooked with before. But they had apparently never actually…*seen* a halibut. It looked nothing like a rainbow trout, London knew now.

"Careful with this one," the crew member who had flopped it onto London's station had said. "Its scales are tiny and hidden in the skin." And then he had smiled and floated away.

Fantastic.

It was also rather…flat. And had strange fin things on the top and bottom. Were they called fins?

London should have tried harder with their California rolls.

"And your time begins…" Tanner leaned forward, drawing out the pause. "Now!"

The red numbers at the judges' table clicked from 60 to 59.

London picked up a knife.

Things went smoothly for a while, or as smoothly as a slippery, unwieldy piece of protein could go. Scales were indeed sons of bitches, but once London had sliced their first fillet from the spine, they started to breathe easier.

And then they made the mistake of looking up.

Dahlia's swordfish was already done, somehow, and her fillets looked flawless. She was currently helping Jacob, with Tanner Tavish observing, likely to make sure Dahlia didn't help *too* much. She was gesturing with one hand, holding Jacob's knife along his catfish with the other. Her body looked fully relaxed, so different from how she had looked yesterday and the day before. London could tell by the way her shoulders were no longer bunched, by the smile on her face, by the way she leaned her hip casually against the station.

"Yes," Tavish was saying. "Exactly. Excellent technique, Dahlia."

Before Dahlia returned to her swordfish, she pointed to the now semi-mangled head of the catfish on Jacob's station. She motioned to her own chin, surely saying something about the horrifying, slimy whiskers on the fish, although London couldn't hear exactly what she was saying over Ahmed's frustrated cursing next to them.

London flipped their first fillet over—slightly hacked, but intact, not bad for their first try, they thought—and started on the halibut's other side.

From the corner of their eye, they saw Dahlia hold Jacob's catfish up to her face, bug out her eyes, and make a loud sound to the effect of *"Bleeuuurrrrgh."*

London started to laugh.

Their hand slipped. And then everything happened very fast.

Somehow Dahlia was there in a flash, reaching out to grab London's hand, bunching up a corner of her apron and wrapping it around their thumb. She was applying pressure to the wound before Ahmed even looked over or Tanner Tavish had time to hustle around to their station.

"Medic!" she yelled, eyes laser focused on London's thumb, which was currently leaching blood through her yellow apron.

"Miss Woodson, what are you *doing*?" Tavish hissed, laying a hand on her shoulder. "Get back to your station. Seriously, you're ruining your apron."

"Oh, whatever, it'll come out with some hydrogen peroxide. Which I'm sure the medics have. Hey, guys." Dahlia smiled at the two EMTs who had hustled over, only stepping away when they took over.

London felt it acutely, the moment her fingers left theirs.

Ten minutes later, London sliced a lemon. They had no idea if this was the next logical step in their carefully formulated plan, but the lemon was there, so they sliced it.

Their thumb ached, pulsing behind the lumpy gauze the medics had applied. Good god, London could not believe they had done that. After Audra had cautioned the contestants no less than ten times to keep their hands *behind* their filleting knives. London deserved to get eliminated for this, probably. In the very first week. Mortifying.

This was why London was upset. Because they were a competitive person who wanted to win this thing, and they'd made a truly dumb mistake. Because cooking with a huge wad of gauze around your hand was a real pain in the ass.

It had nothing to do with Dahlia Woodson's fingers squeezing theirs. Or the way she had said *oh, whatever* to Tanner Tavish, who was, by all accounts, the scariest person on set.

London picked up another lemon.

It matched the color of the tank top Dahlia had worn yesterday perfectly.

She was wearing a raspberry-colored sweatshirt and floral-patterned shorts today. The sleeves of her sweatshirt had been pushed up her forearms when she reached back to grab London's hand, but the fabric had still brushed their arm for a second, soft and comforting. Her hair was up in that ridiculous bun. She'd put it up right before she started taking notes during Audra's demonstration. An escaped ribbon of it had fallen over her eyes when she'd leaned over to examine London's thumb. London had wanted to reach out and tuck it behind her ear.

Oh god.

London wanted Dahlia Woodson.

They sliced a third lemon, for no good reason at all.

They had wanted her, probably, from the moment they

first saw her, but the last twenty minutes had really slapped them across the face with it, and this was dumb. London couldn't remember the last time they had wanted someone real, someone beyond thirst traps on the internet, and now they were in lust with this woman who stood less than ten feet away from them, who they might not ever see again if they were kicked off today anyway, who was recently divorced, from a dude probably, who was a distraction they did not need.

Dumb, dumb, dumb.

London hadn't dated since they first came out as nonbinary three years ago. Dating while nonbinary felt confusing and intimidating, even though they knew there had to be some dating apps out there with trans-friendly options available. Right? Right. But they still felt so messy inside, most of the time, and on a related note, London hated halibut.

They cooked it anyway. Grudgingly.

Once the hour was up, the cameras turned off for a brief break, and Dahlia turned around.

"You doing okay?" she asked.

London felt a surprising urge to grunt at her again. God, they *were* a jerk.

"Sure," they said.

She stepped toward them. "It was the rib cage, right?"

They nodded, feeling their cheeks flush.

Dahlia held out her palm, traced a white line that ran right near her left thumb. "The first time I tried to gut a fish." She smiled. "Tricky bastards."

London wanted to lift that hand and run their tongue along that scar. And then move to that mouth, smiling and red and full, her lips the same color as her sweatshirt, the teeth behind them blinding.

They swallowed.

"Yeah. It was a pretty big mistake, though."

"Whatever. It doesn't matter if your food's still good. And it looks great."

She nodded at London's plate. She was lying. It did not look great. Her face looked great.

"Thanks. For, you know." London lifted their bandaged hand. Although they didn't know why they were still talking. They wished for this conversation to end, desperately, so they could return to stewing about the other contestants and not talking to anyone ever except maybe Cath and Ahmed and definitely only thinking about food and food only.

"Oh, of course." Dahlia smiled again. And then that old woman, Barbara, was at her side, chattering in her ear, and Dahlia turned away, and London let out a breath.

Judging began shortly afterward, and god, but judging was boring. London admired the judges' ability to continually eat cold food, but their feet started to go numb after so much standing around and waiting. The only upside was watching Dahlia's dish get judged, how glowing the reviews were. And even though London couldn't see her face as Sai and Audra and even Tanner complimented her, they watched her hands behind her back, squeezing each other until they were white.

And they could see, too, as she walked away from the Golden Circle, how she was trying to school her features and act calm, but the corner of her raspberry-colored mouth kept twitching, her eyes bright.

She caught their eye as she rounded the corner to her

station. London should have grunted at her again, probably—they understood this immediately a second later—but they were an idiot. They smiled at her.

And her face exploded. Like when she had tasted the tortilla chips for the first time in the bar, but better. Jesus, those teeth.

And then she faced forward again, and London bottled it inside of them, that smile.

The judges' reviews of London's dish were not as stellar, but to their surprise, they weren't awful, either. When it came time for winners and losers, London was solidly in the middle of the pack. They had never felt more grateful to be mediocre.

The judges always called the top three contestants to the Golden Circle first, before choosing the bottom three. Dahlia, Khari, and Ayesha were the top three today, but it wasn't really a question. Dahlia won.

She was happiness personified, and London could barely look at her. After a poor guy named Mason was the first contestant eliminated, after the cameras turned off, after they confirmed with Janet they weren't needed for any more solo interviews, London slipped away into the smoggy midsummer air of Los Angeles. It was still surprisingly warm out, even as the sun slipped away at the horizon. They got their phone out of their pocket.

Why the fuck didn't you make me learn how to gut a fish, they texted Julie as they walked back toward their hotel room, a space that was cold and soulless and safe, completely lacking in any charm whatsoever.

CHAPTER FIVE

L ondon did not body-slam Jacob out of the way, exactly. It just *happened* that Jacob was slow and lazy and London was impatient to get on the bus. It just *happened* that pushing past Jacob ensured London's butt ended up in the empty seat next to Dahlia Woodson.

Complete coincidence.

"Oh, hey." She smiled at them, and London cursed themself. They had spent all of last night texting everyone they knew in Nashville, followed by reading Twitter for hours, to distract themself from any thoughts of blinding smiles or shoulders exposed by yellow tank tops or fingers wrapped around their thumb. They hadn't even left their room, for fear of running into her. They had discovered two nights ago, when they'd both been returning from a late-night snack run, that her room was only a few doors down from theirs.

And yet. One glance of that hair this morning, and they were back on their bullshit already.

"Hey. Congratulations on the win yesterday."

Dahlia blushed. "Thanks. How's your thumb?"

"It's good. Healing already."

As London wiggled their thumb at her, they were aware of how ridiculous this was, their desire to be next to this woman, to see her smile. Even aside from Dahlia being way out of their league, they'd heard her tell Barbara she lived in Maryland. Which was, the last time London checked, pretty far from Nashville. Either of them could get kicked off at any time. And London still knew barely anything about her.

"Where do you think we're going?"

"I hope somewhere exciting." Dahlia looked out the window, but London could see the smile in her profile.

London had been surprised *Chef's Special* was throwing a Real World Challenge at them so early on. These off-set challenges were normally interesting, even if they were almost always group challenges, and group challenges were the worst. Whichever group lost today would return to the set on Monday for another Elimination Challenge, while the winning team got immunity and a day off. You really wanted to be on a winning team for a Real World Challenge.

"Hey." Dahlia turned back toward them. "Did you ever get to record your first solo interview? Introduce your pronouns?"

London nodded. It had been surprisingly easy, talking to a camera instead of a table full of strangers. They were choosing, consciously, to not think about the fact that that camera would be broadcasting their words to millions of people. Because that still seemed surreal. "You get to do yours?"

Dahlia shrugged. "Yeah. It was boring." The warmth in her eyes dimmed. The bus lurched suddenly out of the studio parking lot. And as the silence between them stretched, just as in the hotel bar, London again felt that desire to bring her back.

"So I've been thinking," they started, scratching at their neck. "Whistle. It's a pretty hard word to spell."

She blinked at them.

"I keep thinking about it, and it's like when you stare at a word too long and it starts to look weird, you know? I've started questioning whether I know how to spell it, now, let alone in fourth grade."

Dahlia laughed, loud and bright, and London's body began to relax.

"I know! But"—she bit her lip—"I was a TAG kid. I should have known how to spell it."

"TAG?"

"Talented and gifted." She rolled her eyes. "And I *did* know how to spell it. I did!" She smacked London in the arm, as if they had implied she didn't, and it shocked a laugh out of them. Women kept hitting them in Los Angeles, and they felt strangely okay with it.

"W-H-I-S-T-L-E," Dahlia spelled now.

"Good job," London said, smiling.

"Shut up," she said immediately. And then, sounding serious, "My mom was so disappointed."

"About a fourth grade spelling bee?"

She looked out the window again. "Yeah."

And before London could say anything else, the bus stopped.

"All right, kids, time to head out!" Janet shouted from the front of the bus.

"Wait," Dahlia said. "What? We were on the bus for like, two minutes."

"Yeah." London leaned over her slightly to peer out the window, not at all noticing that she smelled like peppermint. "Are we seriously here already? Oh. Oh god."

Outside the window, the sounds of screaming preteens grew louder with each passing second. They jumped up and down, waving. London was...not ready for this.

But when they looked over, of course, Dahlia was smiling.

"Sweet," she whispered. She waved back, causing the kids closest to their window to squeal even louder.

London leaned back in their seat and exhaled.

They had arrived at their first Real World Challenge.

It was a bar mitzvah. On the plus side, Adam Abramovitz was definitely going to be the coolest kid in his middle school for at least a week.

On the down side, Jeffrey was Dahlia's group leader.

To be fair, she didn't know Jeffrey that well. She still didn't know anyone that well.

But sometimes you had gut feelings about people. And Dahlia had a gut feeling that Jeffrey was a giant jerkface.

"Dahlia." He pointed at her once the twelve remaining contestants were broken into two teams of six and six. "You're on hummus."

"I'm on...hummus," she repeated, her pen paused over her notebook. She did not need to take notes on how to shove chickpeas into a food processor.

"And whatever other appetizers you want to make. You're the snack table. Make it pretty. All right, now, Ahmed—"

"Wait," London, next to her, interrupted. "You saw Dahlia win the challenge yesterday, right? The fish challenge?"

Their group's assigned main course today was salmon. Which almost made Dahlia laugh, when she saw the ingredients laid out on the temporary set the crew had constructed behind this fire hall. It was like she was living in a pescatarian hell.

"Yeah, and luckily she didn't fall on her face yesterday. I'm not going to have our main course scattered all over the floor." Jeffrey raised a condescending eyebrow. "This isn't just for the judges; this is a real event."

"What the—" Dahlia elbowed London lightly in the ribs to stop them. She was glad London was on her team, and appreciated them standing up for her, but now Jeffrey had actually embarrassed her, and she just wanted everyone to move on.

"Anyway, I believe I'm the team leader here." Jeffrey glared London's way, and from the corner of her eye, Dahlia saw their jaw clench. "Dahlia's on apps. London, you're on desserts. Now, Ahmed and Beth..."

Whatever. She could make a kickass hummus. She loved apps.

"Remember to take this seriously," London muttered to her, scribbling in their own notepad. "This is a *real event*. For thirteen-year-olds."

Dahlia suppressed her snort.

After Jeffrey had finished his orders, London and Dahlia both bolted for the table at the back of the temporary set, like rushing to get the back seat in a school bus, claiming it before heading over to collect their ingredients.

The reality of a challenge like this set in pretty quickly once the judges had given their spiels and the cooking actually got underway. The food didn't necessarily need to be Michelin-star quality; you simply needed to make a shit ton of it in a short amount of time. Dahlia was all for it. Just building blocks, over and over. Consistency was her jam.

Plus, she felt a small thrill at the idea of making food that was going to be consumed by actual people, not merely sampled by three judges before being thrown away. Whether those actual people were thirteen years old or not.

And, she discovered, there was something calming about working next to London. They were a solid worker, both chill and efficient. The more they worked together, the more she felt like they had gotten the best deal. Appetizers and desserts? That was the good stuff.

They spent the first twenty minutes in comfortable, productive silence.

Dahlia's good vibe started to wane, however, by the third time Jeffrey had stalked over to criticize her. "Come on, Dahlia!" he had shouted the first time, followed by "You haven't even *started* the hummus yet?"

She hadn't. Because Dahlia was simmering the chickpeas in baking soda and water first, to help remove the skins. This would make a smoother hummus. She'd been working on dough for fresh pita and roasting red peppers while the chickpeas simmered. Her building blocks were stacking up perfectly. She knew what she was doing.

Still, Jeffrey returned ten minutes later with a "Step it *up*, Woodson!" and an aggressive hand clap in her face, for no apparent reason. It was a bit over the top, honestly. Maybe Jeffrey was looking to get some acting gigs out of *Chef's Special.*

But even though Dahlia knew he was being ridiculous, it didn't feel great, being humiliated on national TV. She thought she'd gotten that over with already, during her fish taco tumble. Was this how she was being pigeonholed? The bumbling, incompetent one?

"Hey," London said, jolting Dahlia out of her reverie.

They were holding the rolling pin they'd been using on their rugelach dough.

"There has to be some way to accidentally smack Jeffrey over the head with this, right?" They tilted it in their hands. "We could make it look smooth somehow. Would probably only result in a minor concussion."

Dahlia nodded, trying to tamp down her smile.

"It would make for some good TV," she concurred.

"We would merely be doing our part for the ratings."

"Or maybe..." Dahlia glanced around the counter and picked up a crostino. "We start with some light torture, work up to concussions? Just crush a bunch of these and stuff them into his socks, make him walk around on it. Like Legos."

London tilted their head, considering. "I like where you're going with this, Woodson."

"Or..." Dahlia's eyes snagged on the bowl she had just put her muhammara dip into. "You could hold him down, and I could rub some peppers on his eyeballs?"

London leaned forward a bit, smothering a half cough, half laugh in their fist.

"That is...yes. Of course," they said.

"Make him swallow cinnamon?" she pondered, thinking about the rugelach. She shook her head. "No, too cliché."

Dahlia drummed her fingers on the table, fully invested in this game now.

"Oh!" She grabbed the bowl of walnuts farther down the table, waiting to be crushed and wrapped into the rugelach dough. "I got it." She turned to London, holding the bowl up to her chin. "Crushing crushed nuts *into his nuts*."

Except at the exact moment this triumphant idea came out of her mouth, their entire corner of the set seemed to settle into a magical hush, making her words ring out, loud and uncomfortable. Like that one time back home at her office when everyone somehow decided to shut their mouths seconds before she had decided to let out a covert fart.

Ahmed and Beth, at the table in front of them, along with, Dahlia couldn't help noticing, the nearest camera, all slowly turned to look at her.

"We could just slip them into his underwear…" Dahlia murmured, for some reason, as if it was important to finish explaining the plan to London. She cleared her throat as their neighbors continued to stare. And some tiny part of her brain whispered *fuck it*.

"Just, you know," she said, voice a bit louder, "discussing… foodie kinks."

London burst out laughing. It was the first time Dahlia had actually heard London laugh, for real. It was high pitched and wheezy. She loved it.

Dahlia tried to ignore the stares, dumping the walnuts onto the table and picking up a knife.

She kicked at London's foot under the table. "You started it."

So maybe *Chef's Special was* a little like high school.

Ahmed and Beth eventually turned back around, and London looked down at their hands, shaking their head. They tried to calm their face, refocus on their tasks.

"Knives," they said quietly, after a moment.

"Huh?" Dahlia looked over at them, eyebrows raised.

"For our torture. We could probably get a lot done with knives."

"London." Dahlia blinked. "Damn. You are getting *dark* with this."

"Look, I'm doing what I can to get my brain away from *foodie kinks.*"

"Fine. Killjoy." Dahlia paused her walnut crushing to reassess the table once again. Her eyes went wide. "But listen, if Jeffrey *was* into some weird food stuff, just imagine how many things here he could—"

"Miss Woodson."

London jumped as Tanner Tavish appeared in front of them, breaking London's half-horrified, half-turned-on anticipation of whatever Dahlia was about to say next.

Tavish planted his hands on their table, leaned in disturbingly close to Dahlia. She straightened, sobering. London clenched their fists.

"I'm intrigued to see that this competition is so entertaining for you." London noticed a cameraman closing in behind Tavish's shoulder. "But the time is ticking, and the work you do today affects your teammates as well. I might also remind you both"—his eyes flickered London's way before refocusing on Dahlia—"that you are miked while you are on set. If you can't take this competition seriously, or conduct yourselves with professionalism, I assure you there are countless other amateur chefs across America who would be happy to take your place."

With that, he turned on his heel and marched away.

Dahlia looked down, face beet red. She wiped some scraps from the table onto her palm, dumping them into the trash. Picking up a rag, she busied herself with cleaning their already clean counter.

London scowled, their short fingernails digging into their palms. If they were getting the work done, what did it matter if they were having fun?

Because London had been, they realized. Having fun.

"I'm sorry," they said quietly. Dahlia glanced at them, mustering a smile before a flash of uncertainty flickered in her eyes.

"They can't really kick me off the show for that, can they?"

London shook their head. "I don't think so. If they can, I'm going down first. You're right. I started it."

"Nah," she said. "All those nonbinary kids in Tennessee need you."

London was quiet. They didn't know what to say to that.

"Seriously, though," Dahlia whispered. "You don't think they'll air any of this conversation, right?"

"Do I think they'll air us talking about torturing a fellow contestant? No, Dahlia, I don't." London paused. "It would be funny, though, if they did."

"They'll probably air my trip on the first episode, though."

London grimaced. "Yeah. They'll probably air that."

Dahlia was quiet a moment. Then she laughed a little. "Wow. I am really bad at this."

"No, you're not. I thought we already established this. Your swordfish yesterday—"

"No, no." Dahlia waved them off again. "Not cooking. Being on TV. I am bad at being a human adult on TV."

"Oh." London considered this. The spectacular trip and Tanner Tavish getting up in Dahlia's face would make for good TV, sure. But London mainly thought about how her skin would shine on camera, how radiant her smile would be.

"Maybe," they said.

They started chopping mint and dill for Dahlia's tzatziki. The two of them had somehow started working together on each other's dishes, without talking about it.

"They'll air me almost slicing my finger off, too," London said after a minute. "So until you shed some blood, you can really get over yourself, Woodson."

Dahlia brushed olive oil over slices of pita. She smiled, small and quiet. She dropped sea salt and pepper over the pita before popping them in the oven.

"How did you know?" London asked. "That I had hurt myself yesterday? I don't think I even made a noise."

"Oh, yes, you did." Dahlia's face perked up. "You hissed. Like, *eeeeeeessshhh*." She stretched out her mouth, her neck contorting in a surprisingly unattractive manner.

"I did not."

"Believe me, you did. Hank was an absolute klutz growing up, always hurting himself. I'd recognize that hiss of pain anywhere."

"I think I would have remembered hissing."

"Of course you wouldn't. You were in shock. Is it bothering you, cooking today?"

She reached out and touched London's thumb.

It was barely a graze, just where the bandage ended.

But London's tongue felt oddly heavy in their mouth anyway.

"It's fine," they managed. Dahlia nodded. She moved her hand, popped a slice of cucumber in her mouth.

London and Dahlia got back to work. They were good at working together, moving around each other, borrowing tools, handing each other ingredients with ease. London tried not to dwell on Dahlia's fingers on their hand, on the sounds she made when she sampled something that particularly pleased her palate.

They thought, *This is a good day.*

Elsewhere, however, all was not well on Team Jeffrey.

Ahmed and Beth were having some serious issues over the salmon. Exactly what, London couldn't tell, but there was a lot of tension five feet away. Jeffrey strode toward them, his face set on supervillain-who-just-realized-they're-going-to-lose mode, with Sai Patel not far behind.

"Yikes," London muttered.

"Should we help?" Dahlia worried her bottom lip.

"What the fuck is wrong with you two?" Jeffrey yelled.

"Fuck you," Beth responded.

"Seems like they have it under control," London said.

"Oh, absolutely." Dahlia nodded quickly.

London dipped a slice of orange bell pepper through Dahlia's hummus.

"That's some damn good hummus."

Dahlia beamed. "Thanks, friend."

"How long did you cook this?" Sai Patel sputtered.

"I tried to tell Jeffrey that these pans—"

"Your rugelach, though. Truly spectacular." Dahlia snagged a bite fresh out of the oven. London tried not to stare at how she licked her fingers after, and utterly failed.

"Thanks, friend," London repeated.

As it turned out, the salmon was overcooked and rubbery.

"We probably should have helped," Dahlia whispered an hour later, as they worked on breaking down their stations. The judges had seemed genuinely pissed.

"Oops," London said.

Their team lost.

When the contestants finally collapsed on the bus for the return trip to the hotel, the daylight was draining from the sky, a stripe of hazy purple hovering at the horizon. London turned to Dahlia after they plopped down into the same seats they had taken before. She leaned her head back against the headrest, holding her elbows across her stomach, her eyes closed. London's mouth hung open, ready to say something foolish, but the sight was so arrestingly intimate that they stopped.

Dahlia must have sensed their stare anyway.

"What?" She cracked one eye open, lifted an eyebrow.

"I had a good time. Cooking with you today."

London felt their neck turn pink.

Dahlia smiled. "Me too. And you know what?" she added after a minute. "You haven't grunted at me in two whole days. It's like I don't even know who you are anymore, London Parker."

CHAPTER SIX

A week later, the contestants of season eight piled onto another bus at the crack of dawn. When Dahlia felt someone drop into the seat next to her, she turned, a grin already growing on her face. She'd had a horrible night, and she needed aimless banter with London Parker more than ever before.

But familiar strawberry hair did not greet her today.

Lizzie touched the corner of her glasses nervously.

"Hello, Dahlia."

Dahlia groaned internally, turning back toward the dark window, working to keep her exhausted, cranky sigh contained.

"Lizzie," she acknowledged.

Dahlia, somehow, had learned more than she ever needed to know about this woman over the last week and a half since their Face-Off. She had learned that Lizzie's husband's name was Chance, that he was a long-distance trucker. That Lizzie was a dental hygienist who had harbored a dream of opening her own bakery for years. That they lived in San Diego. That her two sons' names were Billy and Lucas. That Billy was in the Navy. That Lucas was graduating from high school this year and planning to attend a local community college and live at home next year to save money.

Dahlia did not ask for any of this information about Lizzie and her seemingly decent, hardworking, middle-class family, but Lizzie simply spilled it anytime Dahlia was around her. She was unflappably nice to Dahlia, even when Dahlia tried her darnedest to ignore her, and Dahlia felt worse and worse about it with each interaction. She did not want niceness that was only granted because she appeared to fit into the boxes deemed acceptable by society.

With a shudder, the bus pulled away from the lot. Lizzie was blessedly silent for a peaceful ten minutes.

And then she cleared her throat.

"So, Dahlia," she started, her voice low, confidential. "I've noticed you've become friends with London."

Oh, dear lord. Dahlia closed her eyes, willing herself strength from whatever deities were up there.

From what Dahlia had been able to tell, Lizzie and London avoided each other like the plague on set. London hadn't mentioned anything else about her since that first night in the bar. Dahlia had been hopeful that meant Lizzie wasn't bothering London too much, and that London accordingly hadn't wasted too much of their brain space on her.

"And I just worry," Lizzie went on now, "that they might have told you some inaccurate things about me."

Except Lizzie didn't say *they*.

Dahlia's eyes popped open.

"I know we didn't get off to the best start, but honestly, Dahlia, I'm just trying to look out for—"

"Lizzie," Dahlia interrupted, working hard to keep her voice equally low. How hard was it, really, to use the right word? Dahlia wanted to throw the last twelve hours of her life into a dumpster and set it on fire. "I'm going to stop you right there, because it's way too early, and I'm tired, and honestly, if you want to be friendly with me, or whatever it is that's happening here, you can start by not misgendering my friend in front of me. Or anywhere, actually, ever."

Even in the low light of the bus, Dahlia could see Lizzie's face pale, her mouth scrunching into an ugly pucker in the middle of her skinny, wrinkled face. She reminded Dahlia of her elementary school nurse, Ms. Tucker, who never believed Dahlia when her stomach hurt.

"Misgendering," Lizzie repeated back, voice sour.

"Yeah," Dahlia replied tightly. "Google it."

"Well!" Lizzie tittered, her voice rising now. Dahlia glanced around the half-sleeping bus, panic beginning to bubble in her veins. There. London was four rows ahead of them. If Lizzie made this into a *scene* with London four rows away, then Dahlia would... would... Dahlia would have to do something untoward. "Well," Lizzie huffed again. "Here I was, just trying to talk. They call *us* the intolerant ones. I swear."

Lizzie shook her head, muttering, and reached underneath her chair. Noisily, she grabbed her bag and stomped to her feet.

"Thanks for the chat, Dahlia," she said testily, before making her way up the aisle and finding a new seat next to Khari.

London wasn't the only one who swiveled around to look at Dahlia.

Ugh.

She slunk deep into her seat, knees propped up in front of her.

She could have handled that better. Hank wouldn't have liked it. He was all about opening hearts and minds, the big soft dummy, and Dahlia had just ensured that Lizzie's heart and mind were slammed shut to her now.

She wiped her palms on her jeans and took a deep breath. She was sleep deprived and disoriented, and feeling just a tad sick of people.

People like Lizzie, being disappointingly shitty.

People like David, sending disconcertingly nice emails.

She had stared at it for too long when it hit her inbox last night. Had it practically memorized by now.

Dahls,

Hi.

This is probably the most awkward email I've ever sent, but...I wanted you to know. I've started seeing Megan McCombs. She was a year ahead of us in school. Not sure if you remember her. I just wanted to tell you before you heard it from someone else, or saw it on Facebook, or something awful like that. I don't know why I felt like I should tell you, but...anyway. There it is.

Of course Dahlia remembered Megan McCombs. Megan had been part of student government in high school, helping lead pep rallies and Veteran's Day assemblies. She was a star volleyball player. She had also always been genuinely nice. A naturally likable person.

Dahlia wanted this to be okay. David deserved someone like Megan. If anything, it surprised Dahlia that he had taken this long to get back out there again.

Dahlia, for her part, only let herself consider dating again on her darkest, loneliest nights. When she missed having someone to talk to, when she longed to be touched. Her mind wandered, especially, about the options that were open to her now. Dahlia had known since college that she was queer. But since she'd only ever been with David, she'd never truly been able to explore that part of her, at least not in the way she sometimes fantasized about. Dahlia considered, on those lonely nights, throwing on something slinky and driving into DC or Baltimore. Finding a queer bar. Kissing whoever she happened to find attractive up against dirty bathroom walls. Having one-night stands.

Or, even, signing up for the dating apps everyone in the world other than her knew how to use.

And then she'd wake up the next morning and remember that she still felt too guilty and sad to do even that. That she wanted to reassemble herself first, on her own, before she brought someone else into the mix of her confused heart.

And so she'd watch another YouTube cooking tutorial and practice her knife cuts instead.

It made sense, though, that not only would David be dating again now, but that he would have waited until he found someone solid. That he would stick with someone they knew in high school. Someone who was sensible and successful. Dahlia had no idea what Megan McCombs was up to these days, but she assumed she was successful.

Most of all, Dahlia knew in her gut that she would make very nice babies. That Megan McCombs would be a great mother.

> I hope you're doing well on Chef's Special. I still can't really believe that's happening, but I'm happy for you. I haven't decided yet if I'll watch. I don't know if it would be good for me. But I'm proud of you. I really do hope you're doing well, Dahlia.
>
> Okay. That's all. Don't feel like you have to respond to this.
>
> David

Dahlia closed her eyes and leaned her temple against the cold glass of the window. The bus wheels rolling over cracked asphalt vibrated through her skin, rattled her brain inside her skull.

What had David wanted Dahlia to feel when he sent that email?

The confirmation that he was absolutely decent?

Dahlia watched the LA scenery fade away outside the window, stretch into dusty hills, the emerging morning light casting a thin golden light over the landscape. And she thought, *How nice that must be, moving on. Not feeling angry at me anymore.*

"Hey." London scraped the toe of their sneaker against the gravel of the parking lot as they approached Dahlia's side. She stood with her arms crossed, staring stonily across the fields of Graham Family Farm. "You okay?"

Dahlia glanced at them, and her eyes softened. She dropped her arms. "Yeah."

London stuffed their hands in their back pockets. A part of them was dying to know what had happened between her and Lizzie on the bus, but a larger part of them had exactly zero desire to ask.

This was their fifth day of filming in a row this week, and London was feeling it today, the exhaustion heavy in their limbs. But their mind felt good. Limber. They were ready for this second Real World Challenge today. They had done well this week, including a win during yesterday's Elimination Challenge. Talking to Dahlia on set had become easy, after Adam Abramovitz's bar mitzvah, even with their continuing attraction to her, which they were working on tamping down. London was precariously close to having a surprisingly good time with this whole *Chef's Special* thing.

"This view isn't bad," they ventured after a few moments of silence. The eight other remaining contestants milled around behind them, waiting for the producers and crew to finalize logistics. "The farms in Tennessee are better," they added. "But this one's okay."

"You've spent a lot of time on farms?" Dahlia asked, her shoulders relaxing. "I thought you were from Nashville."

"My roommate Eddy is on the board of this local co-op, and he got me involved in it. I tried to work at the storefront a couple times, but I was not the best at...customer relations."

Dahlia grinned. "Ah."

London shot her a defensive look. "I *can* be quite friendly, you know. These co-op customers are just…special. So now I help with runs to local farms a couple times a month, transporting stuff back and forth. Most of the farms do their own deliveries, but if we have a special order, or sudden demand…" London shrugged. "Some of the farmers are old and cranky, but a lot of them are young, actually, doing really cool things. Although I like the old and cranky ones, too."

A pang of homesickness hit London's gut.

"I like them. The farmers. So sometimes if I'm bored, or whatever, I'll go to some of the farms to help out. They always need help."

They paused, aware they were rambling. Even still, they felt compelled to add a minute later, "It feels good. Seeing where your food comes from." And then they blushed, at how earnest this came out, and they finally did shut their mouth.

Helping out the co-op, working on the farms meant a lot to them, though. For the last few years, London had made a conscious effort to give back, to be a more useful person. It was why they felt so invested in this LGBTQ nonprofit idea, if they won *Chef's Special*.

Their family had always been well off. London's parents both worked in pharmaceuticals, each in different capacities: their mom on the science end, their dad on the business side. They had grown up in a large house outside Nashville, with a nanny and private tutors, housekeepers, and landscapers. The house was surrounded by a spacious, lusciously green yard with rolling hills beyond, which London could gaze upon from the small balcony off their bedroom. The Parkers kept a boat on Percy Priest Lake and took vacations every summer, to locales both near and far.

London had loved almost everything about the external parts of their childhood. And they realized now how lucky and privileged they had been.

The internal parts of their childhood, of course, had been trickier. Julie had always been their steadfast best friend, and they'd had other friends, too, a couple of relationships in high school. But London had always felt . . . off. Painfully awkward. Never quite fitting in, at least not exactly, not the way they wanted to. They figured all teenagers felt a little strange in their skin. It wasn't until college that London realized not all teenagers felt quite like them.

"Huh." Dahlia was smiling now. "Interesting. So why are Tennessee farms better than this one?"

London looked out at the soft hills on the horizon. They seemed to leap from the flat earth out of nowhere, breathtaking in their own way. They were also entirely devoid of trees, and strikingly, undeniably, brown.

"Isn't it obvious?" London swept their arm over the scenery. "Tennessee is *green*."

Dahlia thought this over. "Sure. This is pretty too, though, right? In a . . . less green way."

"No, it is. It is. I just could never live here year-round."

"Really?"

"You could?" London lifted a brow. "I mean, you're from the East Coast, right? Could you imagine living in a place that didn't have real seasons? Where the leaves didn't change colors in the fall?"

"I do like seasons. But . . ." London waited, watching Dahlia's

Thoughtful Face. The one she got when she was planning out a recipe, her eyes slightly narrowed, her mouth pinched on one side. "California does have palm trees. And you have to admit, palm trees are spectacular."

"I do not have to admit anything. They freak me out a little, to be honest."

Dahlia gasped. "Are you serious? Oh my god, I *love* them."

"They look like an alien species." London shook their head. "Like...they make no sense."

Dahlia shook her head back at them. "You're wrong. They're fantastic."

They stood in amiable silence for a few minutes. The morning was still cool, and London liked the breeze, the lightly sweet scent from the wildflowers that lined the parking lot.

"You really like Tennessee, huh," Dahlia said eventually, a funny half question, half statement, but London answered anyway.

"I do. Nashville, in particular. It's not too big, not too small, even if it is gentrifying fast. You really should visit, with Hank. It's famous for great food and great music. And there are seasons. What more could you want?"

"You think you'll live there forever?" Dahlia asked.

"Probably. Yeah." London shrugged.

"And it's where you've always lived."

London shot Dahlia a curious glance. She was still staring out at the horizon, but she was asking these questions strangely, slowly, like London enjoying where they were from was a recipe she didn't understand.

"Yeah."

"Huh," she said again.

"Okay, you lot, look alive!" Janet clapped her hands and called them to attention before London could find out further what was actually happening behind Dahlia's Thoughtful Face. Janet stood on a log across the parking lot, the early-morning sun shining through her bronze curls. "You'll be getting all of your instructions for today from the judges as we film, so be on your toes. We've never worked with this farm, so"—she shot laser eyes out at all of them—"don't embarrass us in front of these people. And make sure you look jazzed about all this nature shit. Okay! Eyes on Audra."

A PA counted down, and the cameras were on.

"I am extremely pleased," Audra began, "to lead you to your lovely companions for episode five of season eight."

And she did look pleased. She was wearing a light green and blue flannel over dark jeans. London had never, not once, seen ultrafeminine Audra Carnegie dress like a lesbian before, and they were pleasantly surprised by it.

She spun on her heel and walked toward a rustic barn at the far end of the first field. The contestants followed, dust kicking up beneath their shoes.

Once they arrived, Audra shoved aside the barn door with a dramatic flourish.

"Oh no," London muttered, their good mood dropping down to the soles of their feet.

"Oh my god," Dahlia whispered, grinning from ear to ear. As if to counterbalance London's unease, whatever mood she'd been in when they departed the bus had officially disappeared. "*Yes.*"

And then she actually clutched London's arm. Which would have been a much more exciting moment for London had they not been surrounded by the pungent, nefarious aroma of bovines.

"They are *so cute*."

Dahlia seemed to realize what she was doing a second later, and quickly dropped her hand from London's arm, her cheeks flushing slightly. London stared at her.

"Cows are not cute. They are dangerous."

Slowly, purposefully, Dahlia turned her body to face London fully.

"Dangerous," she repeated.

"Yes," London huffed, crossing their arms, trying to ignore how they could still feel the spot on their bicep where Dahlia had touched them, about to explain that cows were of course dangerous, when Sai Patel interrupted them.

"Graham Family Farm has been producing food for the greater Los Angeles area for over three generations, providing produce and dairy products to local restaurants, stores, and food banks. The first thing you need to know is that we will not be doing any cooking challenges here. Today is about education and appreciation of the systems that sustain us.

"We *will*, however, be gathering some of the ingredients you will use for your next challenge back at the studio. We will also closely observe how seriously you take today and how well you complete the tasks we ask of you, and our observations will factor into our decision during the next Elimination Challenge.

"Your first task today is one that the Graham family and their employees have to complete twice a day, every day, here on the farm: milking a cow."

Barbara clucked to herself from Dahlia's other side as the cameras stopped and the judges conferred with a broad-shouldered man in the corner. "Milking a cow was a basic skill where I grew up. Easy peasy."

London disagreed, just a tad.

"I can't believe they're having us do this," they whispered to Dahlia. "What if someone gets hurt?"

"Um," Dahlia said, and London knew she was laughing at them, and they did not care. "I'm pretty sure they'll be in those stall thingies, and we'll be outside those stall thingies, so I think we'll be all right."

"Stanchions," Barbara supplied.

"Right!" Dahlia's eyes lit up. "They'll be in stanchions. It'll be okay, little buddy." She patted London patronizingly on the shoulder, her smile stretching practically to her ears.

"They move suddenly sometimes," London stated. Dahlia was so tiny. "They could crush you."

"So you're saying that, in all your time volunteering on Tennessee farms, you've never milked a cow."

"Of course not," London scoffed. "Seriously, there are machines for this." A second later, "Wait, have *you* milked a cow before?" It would track that fish-filleting-master Dahlia would also have mastery of large farm animals. London had learned you never knew what to expect with Dahlia Woodson.

"No." She shook her head. "But I'm excited to."

"Good god, *why?*"

"London," Dahlia said seriously. "I have not asked much of you, in our less-than-two-week-old friendship, but I must insist that you tell me, right now, exactly what happened in your past between you and the cows."

"Nope." London shook their head. "Never." And that was a promise.

You smoke weed with your cousin Oliver in high school one time...

The cameras were rolling again.

"If you've ever used even a dab of butter in one of your cooks," Sai Patel was saying, "you will appreciate the existence of that butter more after today. Gather 'round, please, and pay careful attention as Randy demonstrates the proper technique..."

Begrudgingly, London took meticulous notes on washing, stripping, holding, and squeezing teats. Jacob, beside them, snickered every time Randy said *teats*, and really, this was all a bit much. For anyone, London thought, except for, apparently, Dahlia Woodson.

She raised her hand when Randy asked for questions.

"Do your cows have names?"

Randy gave her a long, serious farmer stare.

"No," he finally said.

"Well, *that's* clearly a lie," Dahlia muttered, scribbling furiously in her notepad.

"What are you even writing down?" London couldn't help but ask. Even though they knew.

"Possible cow names. *Obviously.*"

London peeked over her shoulder. Her handwriting was big and loopy, messy. It fit her perfectly.

"Margaret?" they asked skeptically.

"I mean, look at her." Dahlia gestured to the cow behind Randy, freshly milked. "She is clearly a Margaret."

"You know, I agree, love," Barbara piped up.

Dahlia beamed back at London. "See?"

It disturbed London, how close Dahlia's pure delight in this moment pushed them toward feeling almost glad to be in this barn.

Which, for the record, they still were not.

Which was confirmed when their name was called in the first lineup of milkers. While Graham Family Farm had more than enough cows for each contestant, *Chef's Special* did not have enough crew onsite to film them all at once. Which meant that when London approached the black-and-white beast assigned to them, Dahlia was right behind, watching, waiting for her own turn.

Swell.

"Dahlia, you'll have to back up a bit to get out of the shot." Maritza motioned from behind her camera.

London sat on the stool outside the stanchion. They put on gloves. It was cold in the barn, and flies buzzed around their head. They tried to pretend this wasn't happening.

And they were pretty successful at it, for the first minute of filming. They washed down those teats like a champ. Arranged their thumb and forefinger around the base of one, as Randy had shown, ready to squeeze.

And then the damn cow moved.

As London's hands were jostled, panic caused them to squeeze wildly, and the beast emitted a loud, annoyed moo.

"Oh my *god*," Dahlia breathed.

London felt it before they saw it. The surprising hit of warmth. The earthy smell of dirty cow juice.

With dread, they looked down.

At where they had just squirted milk. All over their crotch.

For a moment, they were speechless.

And then they said, "I fucking hate cows."

Dahlia exploded into giggles.

"London, try not to curse on-screen," Maritza said, and they could hear it in her voice, too, how hard she was trying to hold in her own laughter.

"Huh," Randy said, because of course Randy was there, and of course he wasn't laughing. "Interesting one, there. Remember, you're not actually pulling on the teat. That's a misconception. You're just gathering up the milk and then squeezing. Downward. *Away* from you. Into the bucket."

"I—I wasn't pulling; it just—" But Randy was already walking away.

"Oh my god, London, if you hurt Maisie, I will never talk to you again."

London turned to Dahlia. "Maisie."

"How did that even *happen*—" Dahlia covered her mouth, flapping her other hand around, tears in her eyes.

Maisie flicked her tail.

It swung and smacked London right in the head.

"Fucking—"

Dahlia and Maritza couldn't even make coherent sounds now, they were both giggling so hard.

London rubbed their ear. "I suppose you don't care that that actually *hurt*," they muttered to themself.

"Okay, London." Maritza's voice was high-pitched from wheezing as she stood up. "You actually have to finish the milking now."

Of course they did. London took a deep breath and re-focused, which was hard to do, what with a wet, weirdly warm crotch. Maybe they could bribe Maritza somehow, to make sure Sai Patel never saw this footage. By some small blessing, the three judges were all busy watching over other contestants.

"Wait," Dahlia said suddenly. "Oh my god. Oh my *god*."

"*What?*" London gritted out, exasperated, turning to look at her when they heard a soft *plop*. This time, they smelled it before they saw it.

"*London,*" Dahlia breathed. "Maisie just took a gigantic dump."

London closed their eyes and counted to ten. "I can *see* that, Dahlia."

They heard rustling on their other side. Opening their eyes, they watched Maritza sink onto her haunches, hand on her mouth, face red.

Until Tanner Tavish appeared out of nowhere and asked, "How are things going over here?"

Maritza straightened. Dahlia choked on a snort.

"Fine. Things are going just fine," London said between gritted teeth. They shoved their hands around Maisie's teats, squeezing her blasted milk into the goddamn bucket.

CHAPTER SEVEN

It took twenty-four hours and two showers to get the cow smell off London's skin.

And during those showers, they found themself humming the inane song Dahlia had made up while she milked her own cow, which of course she had handled flawlessly.

This should have been irritating, Dahlia's cow song being stuck in their head. But instead, throughout that whole blessed Saturday off, London kept catching themself smiling.

While catching up on social media, when her laughter randomly burst into their frontal lobe, how she couldn't stop giggling the whole bus ride home.

After they decided to take a dip in the hotel pool, lying on a chaise underneath the bright sun to dry off, when they closed their eyes and all they could see was Dahlia's face, shining and open, when she found the perfect artichoke in the fields of Graham Family Farm.

All of which made it especially confusing hours later, when London ran into Dahlia in the lobby of the hotel and her face was pinched and closed off, her eyes red and blurry, like she'd been crying. London had a hard time remembering the cow song then.

They had been watching a movie in their room, had come downstairs to get junk food from the gas station across the street.

"A.m./p.m. run," London said, after they stopped in front of each other and a second of awkward silence passed. They tilted their head toward the door. "Want to come?"

Dahlia seemed to think about it. London shoved their hands in their pockets to prevent them from touching her. Eventually, she nodded.

London opted for silence as they picked out white cheddar popcorn, Reese's peanut butter cups, and powdered-sugar doughnuts. Dahlia followed quietly behind. London almost cheered when she finally uncrossed her arms to pick up a pack of peach gummy rings.

"It's been a long week," she said as they stood in line to check out. "Sorry. I'm tired."

"That's okay." London shrugged.

Dahlia made a vague noise in her throat and looked down. She was wearing a fitted pink T-shirt today, a black polka-dotted skirt, and sneakers. She was one of those girls who could really pull off skirts and sneakers. Probably because her legs were so damn pretty. Probably because she could pull off anything.

London scratched at the back of their neck as they walked back toward the hotel. They had never been very good at being comforting. Whenever they wanted to make Julie feel better, they just made fun of her until she yelled at them. Yelling at London always made Julie feel better. But they didn't think that strategy would work here.

They paused when they reached the sidewalk outside the hotel. Something at the corner of the building caught the edge of London's vision. Out of simple desire to not leave Dahlia yet—they feared as soon as they walked back inside the lobby she would scurry away like a very cutely dressed mouse—they followed it.

Golden light and muffled noise spilled out from a tall window on the first floor. London peeked through the narrow slit where the heavy drapes of the window parted, offering a glimpse of a ballroom.

Dahlia waited silently behind them. London watched the swarm of bodies inside for a minute more.

And then they made a decision.

"Dahlia." They swiveled back around to face her. Her head was cocked to the side, her eyes tired but curious. "Did you happen to have any plans this evening?"

"Um." Dahlia bit her lip. "Sleeping?"

"Or"—feeling suddenly bold, London gripped her shoulders—"come crash this wedding with me instead."

Dahlia's eyebrows shot up into her forehead.

"Come again?"

"Crash this wedding with me."

Dahlia shook her head. "What?" And then, "We'd get in trouble."

"I don't think so. Look at them." London pointed their now-healed thumb behind them at the window. "This is clearly a huge wedding, and everyone's trashed. Like, they are duh-*runk*. No one will even notice us. Look at that bride! She would probably give us a hug and thank us for our years of friendship at this point."

Dahlia stared at them. London, a complete fool, kept their hands on her shoulders. Because it was the weekend, and because it felt good.

And then a ghost of a smile appeared on Dahlia's lips.

"Are you a frequent wedding crasher?" she asked.

London shook their head. "But there's a first time for everything, right?"

"A first time for everything," she repeated.

One of them could get kicked off next week.

But right now? It was Saturday. They'd survived a long week. And London had almost turned Dahlia Woodson's frown upside down.

Whatever happened from here on out was worth it.

"We'll have to get changed." Dahlia's face turned thoughtful now, plotting. Damn, but London loved that Thoughtful Face. "Do you have wedding attire?"

London hadn't thought this far. "Maybe I have a bow tie? I don't know. I'll fake it."

"I have...a dress," Dahlia said slowly, like the existence of it was precarious, and London's stomach flipped, imagining the possibilities of this dress.

"Okay." Dahlia stepped away, nodding. Her smile was shaky, but it was there. "Okay, let's do this thing. I'll meet you at your room in fifteen?"

London nodded.

And now she was really smiling. "All right, London. Go make yourself dapper."

Dahlia's head tilted to the side.

"Are you listening to Tegan and Sara?"

"Is that weird?"

London glanced at Dahlia once before retreating back into their room, picking up their phone to stop the music. They couldn't spend any longer than that brief second staring at that dress. It was a silky black thing with a severe neckline that dropped between her small breasts, practically down to her navel. Jesus Christ, it was indecent and incredible. No wonder she had paused before she mentioned it.

It was the first thing that sent flares up in London's brain that perhaps this had been a bad idea.

"No, I guess it's not weird," she said. "I just expected you to listen to like...a lot of hip indie rockers I'd never heard of, or something."

London *did* listen to hip indie rockers Dahlia had probably never heard of. But when they were nervous, they retreated to their playlist of early-to-mid-2000s music they and Julie had grown up listening to when they were just kids: Tegan and Sara, The Shins, Modest Mouse, Death Cab, stuff they listened to before they could even understand the lyrics. Being twins, they and Julie fought constantly, especially in elementary school. But as the two of them grew into adolescence, music had started to tether them to each other. It likely always would. This playlist always made London feel grounded and calm.

"Okay. I'm ready." London approached the door again, where Dahlia was still standing. She didn't move, forcing London to stand there awkwardly, waiting. They tried for dear life to hold on to their Tegan-and-Sara calm.

Dahlia reached forward and straightened London's bow tie. "You look cute."

London was ready to crash this wedding, but they did not think they looked cute, and they certainly didn't expect Dahlia to say they looked cute. A printed button-up accompanied by the bow tie and dark jeans was the fanciest thing they could conjure up. Even if London had accepted it more in the last few years, had worked to make it feel more comfortable, they still thought they had a weird body: lumpy in places it shouldn't be, like their stomach and hips; too narrow in others, like their shoulders. They looked like an Oompa-Loompa compared to Dahlia.

She had put on makeup, too, her eyes even darker than normal, her lips redder than before. She was unequivocally gorgeous.

For a second, while getting ready, London had considered putting on some makeup, too. The desire to mess around with makeup was a pull they experienced maybe once or twice a year. They'd gone so far tonight as to pull out mascara from a bag stuffed in their closet. But then they'd remembered that the only person who could make makeup look semi-decent on them was Julie. And the few times they'd let Julie do it, they'd been drunk. They didn't even know why they'd brought it here to LA.

Anyway, even if London did look cute, did they want Dahlia to think they were cute, specifically? Cute was for puppies. For babies.

London cleared their throat and walked forward, forcing Dahlia to back up so they could close the door.

It was time, clearly, for alcohol.

"I'll take a rosé, please." Dahlia flashed that bright white smile at the bartender five minutes later, after they had slunk into the ballroom like they belonged there. Or rather, London had watched Dahlia slink. She was into this now, London could tell, and she was a far better slinker. London mainly walked awkwardly with their hands in their pockets and tried not to look at Dahlia's exposed torso.

"And...for you?" The bartender looked up at London, and London recognized it immediately—the pregnant pause, the way the bartender looked at them for a beat too long, trying to puzzle out whether they were a man or a woman. London hated that pause, but appreciated the bartender all the same for leaving out the *sir* or *ma'am* they'd heard him use with his previous customers.

"What kind of whiskey do you have?"

"Is whiskey all you drink?" Dahlia asked. Somewhat judgmentally, London thought.

"I happen to enjoy a wide variety of alcoholic beverages, thank you very much," they replied. "Whiskey is simply... better than all the other things."

Dahlia laughed as London approved a neat glass of Balcones.

"It's certainly better than *rosé*," London added as they stepped away from the bar. Dahlia rolled her eyes and tapped her glass against theirs before bringing it to her lips, taking a long sip and making a dramatic *mmmmmmm* noise for emphasis.

London knew Dahlia didn't mean for this noise to sound absolutely filthy, but they had to take a long sip of their own drink and avert their eyes anyway.

"All right," Dahlia said decisively. "Let's dance."

London looked over and realized her hips were already moving, her feet already shuffling, to what they believed were the sonorous tones of Usher. She was throwing back her rosé entirely too fast—although with rosé, London supposed, it didn't matter whether one consumed it properly or not—and London barely had a moment to appreciate the way her neck bobbed when she swallowed before she was depositing the glass on an empty table and grabbing London's hand.

"Oh," they said, clearing their throat again. "Right. I don't really dance."

"London Parker." Dahlia put her hands on her hips, squinting at them. "You invite me to a wedding, and then you tell me you don't dance?"

"Well, I—" London sputtered. "I was mainly thinking of the free alcohol." *And I wanted to make you happy.* "Speaking of, I'm going to get another drink." They clanked their empty glass down on the table next to hers, not wanting to be outdone.

And by the time London had acquired their second glass of whiskey, Dahlia had jumped headlong onto the dance floor by herself, throwing her hands in the air and smiling at everyone around her.

She fit right in. As expected.

London drank this whiskey slower, tracking Dahlia with their eyes around the room. Each shake of her hips and bounce of her shoulders seeped into their system, vivid and dangerous. She was so...fluid.

The DJ was making a few decent selections, the beats pounding the air harder and harder in London's ears as the whiskey hit. Eventually, for better or worse, London couldn't help but want to join in.

Dahlia beamed at them as they made their way to her, her smile so bright it lit something on fire in London's chest. Or maybe it was just the whiskey that created the small, shiny ball of light suddenly taking up residence in their rib cage.

Light that faded two minutes later, when Dahlia started laughing at them.

"London," she breathed between giggles. "Oh my *god*."

"I know," London said with a frown before she could continue. "I told you I don't dance."

"Listen. Just...bounce on your feet less. Use your hips more. And whatever you are doing with your hands, oh my god, just stop." Her hands curled over theirs, which had been balled into fists. Fists that London had aimlessly been flailing in front of their chest.

"What am I supposed to do with them, then?" they asked helplessly, both needing Dahlia to move her hands from theirs and dreading the moment she did. Which was two seconds later.

"I don't know! Just...relax your fingers and move them around your body more. Or in the air." Dahlia demonstrated, her palms pushing toward the ceiling in rhythm to the music as she danced in a circle.

When she turned to face London again, they attempted to replicate the move, their hands rocking around above them as they spun. Dahlia laughed when they faced each other again, the effort dipping her forward toward them, her hands suddenly on London's sides. "Yes! That's better. That's an improvement."

London's arms stayed frozen above their head. They looked down at Dahlia, their chest already heaving slightly from the exertion, a light sweat permeating their neck. It would be impossible to lower their arms without wrapping them around her. Dahlia seemed to realize this at the same moment and stepped away, removing her hands.

"Sorry," she said quickly, with a small smile, and London wished she wasn't.

After fifteen more minutes of dancing that proceeded without any further touching, a slow song started, introduced as the second-to-last song of the night. Before London could panic fully about the horrifying, synthesizer-filled love song blaring through the sound system, Dahlia nodded her head toward the corner of the room.

"Bartenders have abandoned their posts. Come on!"

London waited, catching their breath, as Dahlia peered behind the counter.

"Do you want white or red?" She held up two bottles of wine.

"Dahlia. You must know that white wine is, objectively, not good. Right?"

Dahlia rolled her eyes before shoving a pinot noir into their chest. "Oh god, you're one of *those*. Of course." Carrying a bottle of white in her right hand, she grabbed London's free hand with her left and scurried them out a side door to the courtyard at the back of the hotel.

London felt light, weightless, happy to let Dahlia lead them through dark ballrooms and abandoned courtyards for the rest of their life.

They sat shoulder to shoulder on a bench against the wall

once they were outside, a shimmery lighted fountain in front of them, the night air around them cooler than before, drying the sweat on their skin.

"Wait. How are we going to open these?" London held up their bottle of wine.

"Already on top of it." Dahlia dug around in her small purse until she unearthed a small Swiss Army multitool, smoothly extracting a corkscrew from within it.

"Wow," London said, genuinely impressed.

"Never leave home without it." Dahlia popped open her bottle. "And," she added, "yours is a twist-off."

London looked down at their pinot and laughed. "So it is."

They sat in silence for a few minutes, taking inelegant slugs from their respective bottles, listening to the night around them, all the drunken voices behind the wall screaming along to "Don't Stop Believin'."

As the wedding guests started to disperse into the hotel, the air settled into quiet.

"So," London said eventually. "You're really divorced?"

Because that was the way to break the silence.

Dahlia didn't move beside them, didn't flinch or stiffen or make a move to get away. Yet with each second that passed that she didn't respond, London kicked themself a bit harder. It was just, their head was full of whiskey and mediocre wine, and they had just been at a wedding, and . . .

Dahlia sighed. "Yeah. As of last year, officially."

"I'm sorry, if you don't want to talk about it. You just seem so young," London babbled, digging the hole deeper. "And I can't imagine anyone wanting to divorce you."

Right. Okay. London probably hadn't needed to add that last sentence. They took another sip of wine.

"No, it's okay. Actually, you know what?" Dahlia took another sip of wine too. "I want to talk about it." Except then she didn't. She just stared straight ahead at the fountain, doing her disappearing thing again. But London had time. They waited.

"David and I met in high school. Started dating my junior year." Abruptly, Dahlia sat up straighter on the bench and launched into it. "I had never dated anyone before, never had anything other than silly crushes, and David was so handsome, so kind, so everything. I thought we were soul mates. Because you probably always believe that, when you're in high school. But sometimes it's true, you know?"

Her face looked wistful for a moment. London wanted to run their knuckles along her cheek.

They also knew, with sudden clarity, that they had made a mistake.

It wasn't that London didn't want to know about this. All right, sure, maybe they didn't exactly want to hear about how in love she and this David had been, but they were here for whatever Dahlia wanted to talk about.

Except for some reason, when London had asked Dahlia about her divorce, they thought she'd laugh and say something like, "Yeah, life's a bitch, huh?" Not...launch into her life story and start to sound sad. They had no idea why they'd thought that. Clearly they were an idiot. But they had crashed this wedding so they could see Dahlia laugh and dance, not ruminate on her failures. With each sentence she spoke, London cursed themself.

"David convinced me to go to the same college as him, George Washington in DC, even though it's expensive as hell and my family couldn't really afford it. But it's a good school, and I got in, so..." Dahlia trailed off.

So *cool*, now London was reminding Dahlia about her heartache *and* her financial problems. Killing it.

London's parents had been able to pay for their college education at Belmont in full.

They took another sip of wine.

As they watched Dahlia in the moonlight, the refraction of the fountain's light making shadows dance on her face, London became infuriated anew that Dahlia couldn't use $100,000 to take herself on a vacation to Fiji, or Patagonia, or wherever she wanted to go in the entire world, whatever she wanted to do. London pictured her on a sailboat, flying across the open sea, that hair blown back in the wind like a piece of art.

"David always knew he wanted to work in DC, for the government. He made me watch a lot of *West Wing* reruns in high school."

"I've never actually watched that," London interrupted, for no good reason other than they suddenly hated this guy, a little, who got to binge-watch TV shows with Dahlia in high school.

"Eh, it's good, you know, for political fantasy. Smart writing, but they treat women like shit on it. Anyway." Another slug of wine. "He proposed to me on Christmas of our sophomore year at GW. At home, in Massachusetts, where we're from. I was a little shocked, honestly, that he couldn't wait until we were done with college. Like, that felt weird? But of course I said yes. Of course I wanted to marry David. Also, what a way to ruin Christmas for everyone, if I had said no."

Another pause.

London did not point out that ruining Christmas for other people was not a resounding reason to say yes to a marriage proposal.

"What did you major in, in college?" they asked instead, to distract her.

"Communications." Dahlia rolled her eyes again. "I didn't really know what I wanted to do. Still don't. What did you major in? If you went to college?"

"I did. I majored in audio engineering technology at Belmont, in Nashville."

Dahlia stared at them.

"And that's what you do now? Audio…"

"Audio engineering. Yeah. I work on podcasts right now, but the goal is to get into a music recording studio, one day."

"Huh." Dahlia turned away from them, staring out at the fountain and taking another drink.

London had no idea what this *huh* meant. It was a similar *huh* to the ones she'd given at the farm, when they'd talked about the co-op. Had they sounded pretentious just now? London knew sometimes they could sound pretentious when they talked about audio stuff. They just really liked it.

London bounced their knee. "So, you and David," they prompted, even though they didn't want to. They didn't really want to hear more about David, this past that had caused Dahlia pain. If only because they knew knowing this Dahlia, the one who looked weary and vulnerable next to them, would change things. At least for them.

But they also knew her story wasn't over yet.

"Right. So he proposed. I did make him wait to have the actual ceremony until we had both graduated. So that's what happened. College graduation, wedding, real jobs, house together in the suburbs, boom."

"The American dream."

"Yeah."

"Except you hated it," London filled in after a moment. Because...that American dream didn't really sound like Dahlia at all. At least the Dahlia London knew. The one who imitated catfish and sang to cows.

"I didn't *hate* it." There was another long pause.

Looking at Dahlia more closely, London realized her eyes were glassy. Fuck. If she started crying for real, London would...do something. Hold her hand. Make her tea and wrap her in a quilt and never let her go. London didn't have a quilt, or tea, but they would find some.

"I loved David. I really did. He's a genuinely good person. We were lucky to both find jobs right away. I worked at a small paper in Baltimore—kept working there, actually, until I quit right before coming here. I didn't hate that either; I just...didn't *love* it." She looked down at her hands before looking directly at London. "I want to *love* something, you know?"

"Yeah," London said, and their voice came out raspy. Probably because their throat was constricting, almost painfully.

"Anyway. We were doing okay. We had friends; I was starting to pay off some of my loans; I liked decorating the house. Hank started to transition, and David was really supportive of the whole thing, which made me love him more."

Maybe David wasn't a *total* asshole.

But London still didn't trust the guy.

"And then a few years ago . . . we started having The Talks, you know?"

London shook their head slowly. "The last serious relationship I had was in college. I don't know what The Talks are."

Dahlia sighed. "The future. Family. Kids."

"Oh." London could see where this was going now.

"We had both always assumed we wanted kids. Because we fucking talked about it all the way back in high school, and I said I wanted them!" Dahlia's voice projected across the courtyard. "Because when you're eighteen, when you're twenty-two, that's what you feel like you're supposed to want, especially as a woman. But . . ." Dahlia sighed again. "While David and I were settling in to marriage, I watched all my other friends travel, and stay up too late in New York City, and teach English in Japan, and be drunk and adventurous, and . . ." Dahlia let the sentence fade away.

"You realized you didn't want kids," London said.

"I realized I was sad."

With horror, London watched a tear fall down her cheek. They reached up to brush it off with their thumb without thinking. Dahlia didn't react, and London let their hand fall back to the bench, feeling useless.

"And yeah, I didn't want kids. Maybe I will, eventually, but David wanted them, then, before we were thirty. He came from this big family, and he wanted a big family too, and he was always real type A and had a plan and . . . We started fighting all the time. It was awful. I felt like shit."

"I'm sorry."

"Don't be sorry. *I* was the asshole, don't you get it?" Dahlia turned toward them, eyes flashing, her voice getting louder, angrier. "I just *changed my mind*. Of course David was confused. Of course he was angry. He wanted kids before thirty, and we ended up with a divorce before thirty instead. I fucked up his whole life."

"Dahlia." London shook their head. They went to raise their hand to her cheek again, but then stopped themself. "It's okay to change your mind. That kind of thing happens a lot, as people grow up. We change our minds. It's okay."

Dahlia squeezed her eyes shut. "People change their minds about their favorite vegetable, not a fundamental part of your goals in a relationship. And the fucked-up part is I still don't even know what I want! We got divorced, and I still worked the same job I didn't love, still lived in the same Maryland suburb that didn't feel like home anymore. I'm not having the adventures I longed for when I was so unhappy with David. I broke a good person's heart, and now I'm just boring and unhappy alone. Way to go, me."

London had witnessed Dahlia's shifts in moods, the way her eyes lost their joy, her mind scurrying away. They always knew it wasn't to someplace good. But this was still hard for them to swallow, this frustration and self-deprecating anger. That hidden behind yellow tank tops and blinding smiles, Dahlia Woodson was sad. It wasn't right.

"You got onto *Chef's Special*," London said after a moment. "You quit your job and hopped on a plane to Los Angeles to be on a TV show. If that's not adventurous, I don't know what is."

Dahlia gave them a sad smile.

"You just crashed a wedding," London added.

"It was your idea," she rebutted.

"But you still did it. I—" London sighed, feeling irritated at the world. "I think you're chock full of adventure, Dahlia Woodson."

Dahlia's smile grew a bit. She turned her face toward her lap, messing with the label on her wine bottle. London felt, for perhaps the first time all evening, like they had said the right thing.

They were quiet then, lest they ruin it.

The fountain bubbled pleasantly; the traffic behind the wall of the courtyard was a quiet, comforting whir. The sky was midnight blue, the horizon smudges of orange and gray haze.

London thought they could feel Dahlia lean her shoulder, just an inch or two more, into their own.

After many long minutes, she said, "Okay. Enough of that. Let's talk about food."

Dahlia put her bottle down on the ground and turned fully on the bench to face them.

London glanced at the bottle, which was almost empty. They still had at least half of theirs. Damn. That…was not good.

"Food?" London raised their eyebrows, trying to adjust to this abrupt change in topic, resisting the need the pull her and her secret sadness into their arms. "Isn't talking about food all day enough?"

"No, because we don't get to talk about the food we want to talk about! We just have to do what the judges tell us, and can I tell you, I don't even really like fish?"

London laughed at that. "Okay. What do you want to talk about?"

"What's your favorite bad food to make when you're sad? When you only want the most comforting thing you can think of?"

"Barbecue," London said immediately. "I love everything about barbecue."

"What? No, that's not a good answer." Dahlia shook her head.

"Excuse me?" London lifted their head from the concrete wall, now also turning on the bench to face her, their knees bumping into each other. "What are you talking about, barbecue isn't a good answer? It is literally America's comfort food!"

"But it takes so *long*!" Dahlia said dramatically. "All that marinating, and getting the grill going, and cooking and smoking and then you have to have sides and—"

"The sides are the best *part*!" London exploded. "Wait, no, that's not right. The meat is the best part! But it's *all good*! That's why barbecuing is so good!"

"I know barbecuing is good, London; Christ, I'm not a fascist! It's just a lot of work."

"You know what else I love about barbecue?" London kept going, on a roll now. God, it felt good to talk about this, something they knew how to talk about, to be on common ground with Dahlia again. "I love that it's different everywhere. I love that Carolina barbecue is different from Memphis, from Texas, from St. Louis. You know? So much of food in America is homogenized, the same from California to Virginia, but barbecue is the one thing where the places that care about it are like *no*, this is fucking *ours*."

"Oh my god, you are such a *nerd*." Dahlia rolled her eyes. "Also, there's differences across America in pizza, too."

London waved their hands in frustration. "No, there's Chicago style and New York style and then everyone else trying to imitate one or the other. That's it. And it's just one dish. It's not a whole experience. It's different."

Dahlia shook her head, unconvinced, but she was smiling. London loved that she was smiling now. They had no idea why they had ever brought up divorce. Clearly, they should have been talking about food all night. They were an asshole.

"Okay, let's refocus," Dahlia said. "Barbecue is delicious, I concede, but I'm looking for *one thing*, one simple thing you can whip up in thirty minutes or less, when you're so sad you can hardly leave the couch."

London stopped again at that. At the thought that Dahlia apparently got so sad sometimes she could hardly leave the couch.

London was frustrated and confused and angry a lot, about a lot of things, but they didn't know if they ever got that sad.

But Dahlia was still smiling right now, even as she talked about her sadness. So London played along.

"Brussels sprouts," they said eventually.

Dahlia lost her damn mind.

"Are you *serious*?" she boomed, shoving London in the chest. It hurt a little. "You eat Brussels sprouts when you're sad?"

"*Yes,*" London said indignantly, rubbing at their chest. "You roast them with garlic and butter until the leaves turn brown, and then they're so crispy and—"

"*Rice Krispies treats!*" Dahlia shouted, so loudly they stared at each other in shock for a second. And then they both started laughing. "Rice Krispies treats," Dahlia repeated between laughs. "I make Rice Krispies treats when I'm sad. *That* is an acceptable answer."

London smiled. "I'm sticking with Brussels sprouts. They're good."

"You are the worst." She smiled back at them until London's heart started beating too emphatically and they had to look away. "Or muddy buddies," Dahlia said after a minute. "Muddy buddies are also good in a pinch."

"Please don't push me again when I ask this, but what the hell are muddy buddies?"

"Oh, you know. Maybe you call them something different. When you take melted chocolate and peanut butter and powdered sugar and mix it all together with cereal in a bag? I don't make them as much because I literally can't stop eating them until I've eaten the whole bag and then I feel sick."

London squinted in thought. "Maybe my nanny made those once or twice when I was a kid."

Dahlia looked at them. "You had a nanny?"

Shit.

"Uh, yeah." London scratched at their neck. "She's the one who taught me how to cook, actually." In fact, other than Julie, their nanny had been London's best friend for a majority of their childhood. Her death London's sophomore year of college was still the greatest loss they'd ever experienced.

"Oh." Dahlia nodded. "That's cool."

London felt, with slight panic, something slipping away from them again in Dahlia's face. Fucking money. "How did you learn to cook?" they asked, desperate to divert the conversation back to her.

She shrugged. "I started getting really into it a couple of years ago, when my marriage was starting to crumble. It was a good distraction, you know? It calmed me down. Made me focus on something I could understand. I watched a lot of YouTube videos."

"Wait." London stared at her as this sank in. "So you only really started cooking a couple of years ago? And you just taught yourself?"

Dahlia frowned. "Yeah? Is that bad?"

"No, Dahlia, that's *amazing*. You are so good. Most of the people on this show have been cooking since they were kids. Some of them have had professional training. Jesus. You're really talented."

Dahlia looked over her shoulder toward the fountain. "I don't know about that. We've only done a few challenges, London. I mean, remember last week? I was assigned *hummus*. Anyone can make hummus."

"Come on, that was just because Jeffrey was an asshole. And I should add that you made really good hummus. And you've been in the top three and *won* and—"

"Ugh, London, I don't want to talk about the show right now, okay?"

"Okay." London bit their lip, looked at her looking across the courtyard. The light from the fountain was still casting faint blue shapes across her face, strangely pretty and ethereal. Her hair was up, and her neck was right there, long and elegant, and London ached for it. To touch it. To taste it. To reach out their fingertips to her arm, mere inches away, and—

"We should probably head upstairs. It's getting cold."

Dahlia stood up. And sat back down. "Oh." She looked over at London. "I am very drunk."

London smiled. "Yes, I know."

She pressed her palms to her eyes. "I might need your help."

London stood and offered her their hand. Once Dahlia accomplished a standing position, she released London's hand so she could clutch their entire arm instead. All ten fingers wrapped around London's bicep and they felt drunk, too, and it was hard to say whether it was from the mediocre wine or the heat of Dahlia's body, so close to them now. Intimately close.

"Oh my god," Dahlia groaned, leaning her forehead on their shoulder. Fuck, her hair smelled good. "I didn't even realize how messed up I was until I stood up. I felt totally fine before. God. Bodies are so weird."

"This is what I've been saying for years," London said ruefully.

"Our rooms are so far away. Can you even believe this fountain? Oh my god."

London patted one of her hands as together, they hobbled their way back toward the door.

"Remember when Tanner Tavish yelled at me last week?" Dahlia asked as they walked inside. The bar mitzvah felt like so long ago—years, it must have been—that London felt their own bout of hysteria bubbling under their skin. "He was so *mean*. Do you think he's that mean in real life, or just for the cameras?"

"That mean in real life." London nodded decisively, dragging Dahlia through the empty ballroom. "For sure."

"No." She shook her head, and then moaned with regret at

the motion. "I bet he lives with a bunch of cats. And they're named like, Sugar Biscuits. I bet you he writes fan fiction! What *kind* of fan fiction, though, is the question. *Supernatural? Downton Abbey? Yes*, yes, that's it." Dahlia smacked London's arm. "He writes super-dirty *Downton Abbey* fan fiction. By candlelight. While wearing bunny slippers and a silk nightgown. And can I tell you, London?" London really wanted Dahlia to shut up. So they could kiss her. "He *really* loves his grandma. Aw, jeez. I think I love Tanner Tavish."

"Okay." London patted her hand again. It was soft and made them think delirious things.

"Oh my god. London. The *cows*." Dahlia stopped in the middle of the hallway, doubling over in laughter. "I can't believe I got drunk with you and I didn't even get you to tell me your deal with cows."

"Dahlia." London struggled to get her upright again, to keep her moving. Awareness was filtering back into their system, and they feared she might need access to a bathroom soon.

Dahlia gasped as they entered the lobby.

"Barbara!"

Tearing herself away from London's arm, Dahlia scuffled across the floor to the small couch where Barbara sat, knitting a scarf.

"London!" she shouted over her shoulder. "It's *Barbara!*"

"Right." London stuffed their hands in their pockets as they made their way across the lobby. "I can see that."

"Barbara, what are you doing here? It's like one a.m."

Barbara's calm blue eyes glanced between Dahlia and London and back again. Dahlia's dress shifted as she leaned toward Barbara, and London could see the soft underbelly of one of her breasts.

That bright ball of light was back in London's chest again, migrating dangerously to other places.

"I could ask the same of you two," Barbara answered.

"Oh, we crashed a wedding in the ballroom," Dahlia said casually. "Are you making a scarf?"

"Yes. I have unfortunately developed a bit of insomnia in my old age, to answer your question."

"Oh, Barbara, you are not *that* old."

Barbara glanced down at Dahlia's dress, and then reached over to pat her arm. "Yes, sweetheart, I am. Anyway, I find myself getting lonely up in my room, so I've been coming down here, watching people come and go. It's been quite interesting, actually."

"Barbara!" Dahlia yelled. "You could totally hang out with us if you get lonely!"

Barbara looked up at London then. They blushed.

"No," she told Dahlia. "Thank you for the offer, but that's quite all right."

"Are you making the scarf for one of your grandkids?" Dahlia leaned even closer still to Barbara, examining the handiwork in her lap. "Aileen maybe?"

Barbara smiled widely at Dahlia then. "Bishop, actually."

London gaped at the two of them. Of course Dahlia knew the names of Barbara's grandkids.

"That's so nice." Dahlia leaned her head on Barbara's shoulder and closed her eyes. "Barbara, wouldn't it be great if you could be my mom? I mean, I have one already, but you could be like, a secondary one, you know? One who actually *likes* me."

Barbara froze before looking up at London quizzically. London shook their head, raising their eyebrows. Their heart pounded, quietly but persistently, behind their temples.

"I think it's time for you to go to bed, sweetheart." Barbara gently pushed Dahlia away from her shoulder. London swooped in to help Dahlia stand. She swayed into them, her head bobbing onto their chest. London was overwhelmed. They wanted to wrap their arms around her. They didn't know how to act in front of Barbara. They needed to sleep.

"Take care of that one, okay?" Barbara nodded at London, her brows furrowed in concern.

London nodded back, hoping they looked sober, responsible, steady. "I will. Good night."

Slowly, quietly, they slipped an arm around her waist. They navigated the elevator. They walked Dahlia to her door.

Dahlia paused, key card in hand. London waited, a step behind her, hands back in their pockets. They were unsure what was going to happen here. If she was about to be sick. If she was about to invite them inside. If she had just forgotten how to open a door.

She twirled toward them and poked them in the chest.

"I just want my life to be *big*, you know?"

Dahlia's brown eyes were unfocused.

"Like...like the way your favorite song feels, when you're sixteen. I want my life to feel like that. I want to feel *big*. I want to do messy, wild things, things I'll remember, things that are *interesting*." She bit her lip. London wasn't sure if they were breathing. "Maybe Hank will have kids one day, and I can be that kooky aunt with lots of stories, you know? I'll wear chunky jewelry, like Janet, and say funny, inappropriate things. And they'll be like *oh, that Aunt Dahlia.*" She smiled. "I would like that."

London's throat felt tight, aching from things they wanted to say but couldn't find the words for.

Dahlia turned toward her door again. She put the key in the handle. Barely audible, she said, "I don't want to be small."

She walked inside without saying goodbye. London stared at the door helplessly as it started to close.

Suddenly, Dahlia turned and opened it again.

"Hey," she said, smiling. "You know what I like?"

"Rice Krispies treats?"

"Making you laugh. Your eyes disappear, and your face does this... thing." She waved a hand over her own face, not helping with this description at all. London had no idea what she was talking about. But for perhaps the first time in their life, they were exceedingly grateful for their face. For making Dahlia's own face look like it did right now. Like her previous monologue, like her divorce, had never happened.

"Can I see your phone?" London asked quietly.

Dahlia looked confused, but she handed it over. Quickly, they typed in their number, sent a text to themself. So they could check in on her tomorrow, make sure she was okay.

They handed it back and looked at her one last time.

"Good night, Dahlia," they managed to say.

Dahlia smiled. The door clicked shut.

London stood in the quiet hallway for a long time. They wished they could see through that door, to make sure she was still breathing, that she wasn't going to be sick in her sleep. That her chest was still rising and falling. That her bruised, so-far-from-small heart still beat safely inside her skin.

CHAPTER EIGHT

Dahlia awoke on Sunday morning with a deep case of the alcohol dooms.

She lay in bed, head pounding, as bits and pieces of the previous night came back to her.

She remembered dancing with London at the wedding.

She remembered talking to them about David, about her spectacular failure as a wife. *God*, why had she done that? Although she vaguely remembered London saying nice things. She remembered them being a good listener.

Maybe she had talked it out of her system, then. Maybe she'd stop thinking about the email now. Which she still hadn't responded to.

Maybe, too, Dahlia would be able to ignore all the birth announcements, all the ridiculous gender reveals, the proposals that seemed to pop up practically every day on her social media feeds. Maybe it would stop hurting, each reminder of how easily everyone she knew was navigating the path David wanted so badly, the path Dahlia couldn't give him. The path Dahlia just knew, in her gut, was one she couldn't walk.

And maybe, one day, she'd be able to ignore the way her mom looked at her, ever since Dahlia had told her.

Dahlia shook her head. And then groaned.

She couldn't even remember getting to her room. Jesus, she was a mess.

Her cheek pressed against something cold next to her pillow. It took her longer than it should have to realize it was her phone. She sat up, rubbing her eyes. There was a message from London from three hours ago.

Hey Dahlia, it's London... I made you give me your phone number last night so I could make sure you were okay today. So, are you okay today?

Yep, definitely didn't remember that.

Dahlia texted back a quick reply and then stood, stretching. While she wanted to stay snuggled under the covers, it was already ten thirty, later than she had slept in years. She felt godawful, and she knew from experience that wasting away the day in bed would only make her feel worse. She needed to get out, explore at least a small piece of LA while she had the chance.

After a hot shower and a detailed tooth brushing. With a side of ibuprofen.

Thirty minutes later Dahlia walked through the hotel lobby, feeling as refreshed as it was probably possible for her to feel. She was almost out the door when she saw Barbara sitting on a couch to the right, eating a blueberry muffin.

"Hey, Barbara." Dahlia swung her bag down and sat on a loveseat across from her. "How are you?"

"Dahlia, sweetheart." Barbara smiled. "You're looking better than I thought you would. I swear I don't actually live on this couch, by the way. You just have funny timing."

"Um. What?" Dahlia blinked at Barbara while something fuzzy scratched at her memory. "Hold up. Did I talk to you last night?"

"Yes." Barbara nodded. "But I'm gathering you don't remember."

"Oh my god." Dahlia rubbed her forehead. "I haven't been that drunk in a long time. Was I embarrassing? Did I do something dumb?"

"No, you were sweet." Barbara smiled reassuringly at her. Barbara probably would have smiled reassuringly at her even if Dahlia had vomited on her shoes, though. Oh god. "And you looked hot." Barbara grinned before taking a bite of her muffin.

"Babs!" Dahlia laughed, blushing. "Um. Thank you?"

"You two looked like you were having a good time."

"Yeah." Dahlia leaned back in the loveseat. It was surprisingly comfortable. "What about you? Are you having a good time here? I mean, not just on this couch. But on the show?"

Barbara looked thoughtful. "I am. It's been nice getting to meet so many different folks. Like you." She smiled. "It's definitely more work than I anticipated, though. I knew the challenges would be stressful, I never underestimated that, but I didn't know the filming times would be so long. I am absolutely tuckered." Barbara chuckled. "My kids are never going to hear the end of it for convincing me to do this."

Dahlia smiled. "I bet they're so proud of you, though."

"They are. To be honest, I thought I'd be one of the first ones out. All my recipes are kind of old-fashioned. But I've been lucky so far."

"If you know food, it doesn't matter if you're old-fashioned. At least, I don't think so." Dahlia didn't even know what Barbara meant by old-fashioned, other than *delicious and good.* "I tasted those dumplings you made on the first day! Oh my god. They were amazing."

"Thanks, sweetheart," Barbara said. "Still, I'm not up to par with you, or London. You're going to go far."

"Maybe." Dahlia looked out the wide front window to their left. It was a gorgeous August day, and she should get going before it got too hot. But she liked talking to Barbara. She was such a comforting woman. She radiated vibes of chicken noodle soup and weighted blankets.

"I thought I'd be one of the first ones to go, too," Dahlia admitted, feeling surprised that she wanted to say what she was about to say. "But now that I'm here and have made it through a few challenges…" Dahlia shook her head. "Why does it feel embarrassing, talking about things you want? But I want it, really bad. I want to stay."

Barbara smiled at her. "You looked good up there, when you won with your swordfish last week."

Dahlia blushed again. "Yeah. It felt good, too."

"You'll win more challenges, I'm sure."

"Maybe. Thanks, Barbara."

Barbara was quiet a moment. She looked right at Dahlia before she asked, "Pardon me if this is rude. But have you and London talked about what will happen when either of you get kicked off?"

Dahlia tilted her head. She didn't find this question rude, but it was odd.

"I assume I'll go back to Maryland and they'll go back to Nashville? Maybe we'll follow each other on Instagram?"

Barbara made a small *tsk*-ing sound under her breath before returning to her muffin.

Dahlia narrowed her eyes.

"Barbara. What are you saying? Did I do something embarrassing with London in front of you or something?"

"What I'm saying, Dahlia, is that it's clear they want to be more than Instagram friends with you. Ask anyone in this competition. When episodes start airing this week, I bet folks at home will be able to see it, too."

Dahlia's mouth hung open.

She couldn't think of a thing to say.

"Barbara." Dahlia fidgeted with her phone in her lap. She kept thinking something witty would come to mind to redirect this conversation, but she had nothing.

"You seemed rather cozy with them, too, you know, last night."

"I was drunk!" Dahlia protested.

"Mm-hmm."

"Barbara."

"And you were flirting with them pretty hard at the farm the other day, too."

"I...I was?" Dahlia felt truly bewildered now. "But all I did was make fun of them all day."

Barbara gave her a pointed look. "I know."

"But...no. Come on, Barbara, you saw all the stuff that happened to them with the cow! It was funny."

"Yes. But you know, Jacob stepped in a large pile of cow poo. Made quite a scene about it, too. Ayesha knocked over her bucket. Twice. There were other antics going on in the barn, but you were only focused on one."

"Well," Dahlia sputtered, "it's not my fault that Jacob is *boring*."

Barbara simply raised an eyebrow.

Dahlia sank back into the loveseat. She felt silly, anxious, like a little kid.

She hadn't pursued anyone since David, and even way back in high school, it had been David who'd done most of the pursuing. If Dahlia *was* flirting with London, she wasn't conscious of it, and shouldn't a person be conscious of that?

Dahlia remembered, suddenly, how naturally her hands had fallen to London's hips when they'd been dancing last night.

Oh god. She had no idea what she was doing. She felt like an idiot. Or a jerk. Maybe both.

"Dahlia," Barbara prodded good-naturedly. "You don't think they're cute?"

Dahlia tried to sink even lower into the cushions. Wondered if perhaps she could disappear into them. *Of course* she thought London was cute. The cutest.

She remembered how they had looked in their bow tie, that cute graphic button-up. What had been the pattern on the shirt? Giraffes, maybe. God, she had gotten too drunk.

Dahlia had to pivot this conversation.

"Okay. Wait. You said the episodes start airing in a week?"

Now Barbara laughed. "Have you not been listening to Janet shout about it? Yes. Less than a week, actually. The first episode airs Thursday night."

Dahlia breathed out. Less than a week, and everyone would see her trip and scatter her fish tacos all over the set. Less than a week, and everyone would watch London announce their pronouns on national television.

Dahlia realized she barely cared about the former now. But she had an awful sense of foreboding about the latter. People would be awful online. Maybe offline, too. It was so ridiculous. London only wanted to be themself, which hurt absolutely no one—in fact, London being themself was incredible, because it could only help everyone—and it was going to be the worst.

She bit her lip, feeling queasy. She needed food. The greasiest breakfast sandwich she could find.

Dahlia sat up.

"Thanks for, um, this chat."

Barbara nodded. "I'll chat with you anytime you want, Dahlia, you know. About anything. I'm in room five-ten."

"Cool." Dahlia nodded. She wanted to hug Barbara, badly, but she also wanted to sprint away from this hotel at top speed, and yes, breakfast would be good. "Bye."

And then Dahlia finally stepped outside and took a deep gulp of fresh air.

She found a perfect breakfast burrito two blocks away. Her first thought, before she could stop it, was, *I have to tell London about this place*, which made her freeze.

When, over the last two weeks, had *I need to tell London about this* become her first reaction? *Oh my god.*

And then her brain said, *You have their phone number; you can tell them about it right now.*

But she didn't. Dahlia pretended she hadn't been reaching for her phone at all.

Because...she was hungover. Because she felt weird. Because, as Barbara had so astutely pointed out, either of them could get kicked off the show any day now. They were just friends. London probably already had their fill of Dahlia Woodson last night. There was no need to bring *texting* into it. They were already together for, like, three-quarters of all their days. Texting meant they could contact each other during the other quarter, too.

Texting meant Dahlia could tell London Parker whatever she was thinking, whenever she wanted.

And the thing was, she knew they would always listen.

Still. London's text this morning had been thoughtful. Kind. She liked how it had been a proper little paragraph of text, all correct punctuation and capital letters. So London.

Dahlia threw away her burrito wrapper and stepped back outside. She put on her sunglasses and hopped on a bus.

She ended up in North Hollywood. She walked down Lankershim Boulevard, popping in and out of stores without buying anything. She texted a picture of a bar called the Idle Hour, which was shaped like a giant wooden barrel, to Hank, because she knew he would love it. He texted back seconds later in all caps: *DUDE!!* She smiled and wished he was there with her.

But Dahlia also felt a little proud to be there alone. *Look at me*, she kept thinking as she walked around this brand-new place, all on her own. *I'm doing it.*

But...it didn't feel quite right. It didn't feel like she'd hoped it would, when she was packing for this trip back on the East Coast. When she'd filled her head with affirmations and expectations about who LA Dahlia could be.

She had maybe felt like LA Dahlia last night. Wearing a sexy dress, dancing with strangers. Drinking with someone who only knew her as she was right now. Laughing by that fountain, under the muggy desert-city sky.

Dahlia sucked down an iced tea as she walked and wished she could feel like that again, right now, by herself. It felt close, *right there*, this new, carefree person she wanted to be, if only she could dislodge this pebble in her shoe that kept her from stepping into it properly.

She found the North Hollywood library, named after Amelia Earhart. She took a selfie in front of it and sent it to her dad. A university librarian at Johnson and Wales in Providence, her dad always dragged her and Hank to libraries wherever they went when they were kids, even when they were little neighborhood ones like this. He kept track of all of the ones they had ever visited in a tiny leather journal he always kept in his pocket to record such things. Dahlia loved her dad so much. She missed him.

Dahlia wanted to walk until everything that was mixed up in her brain—last night, David, her mom's sad and disappointed face, old lonely Maryland Dahlia, new confusing LA Dahlia—made sense.

Instead she just walked until her feet hurt, and she knew she had to go back.

Dahlia got out her phone while she waited for the bus. She bit her lip, staring at her messages, and then she finally typed it.

Hey, she wrote. *Sorry if I was weird last night.*

London's response came back immediately. *You weren't.*

And then, *You doing okay?*

Yeah. Thanks.

Dahlia stared at her phone for another minute, her head feeling dangerously empty and chaotic all at once. She wondered if she should say more. If London was going to say something else. What should she say? What did she want them to say?

Her bus came.

Dahlia stuffed her phone back in her bag and stared out the window on the ride back to Burbank. Her headache had reappeared, and soon she closed her eyes to block out the bright sunlight, the rhythm of the bus lolling her mind in and out of consciousness. Each time she jolted herself awake, she told herself to buck up. She was determined to not miss her stop. To be competent in this new, dazzling, overwhelming place. The land of palm trees and clean cars and blue sky.

And each time she drifted back into a half slumber, Dahlia allowed herself to think about London's face, annoying and cocky, telling her that her choice of wine was shit. London, fist to their mouth during the bar mitzvah challenge, shaking their head, because she had made them laugh. London's hands on her shoulders, a funny, surprising glint in their eye, inviting her to crash a wedding. London, listening to Tegan and Sara in their room, wearing a crooked pink bow tie. London's body next to hers on a sweaty dance floor, awkward but still full of joy, irrepressible even if they tried to hide it. London, trying to make her feel better about her fourth grade spelling bee.

London, who was an audio engineer. Dahlia didn't even really know what that meant, but she was pretty sure you could win an Oscar for it, which was more interesting than anything she had ever done. London from Nashville.

London, who was a better cook than her.

London, who had the realest chance of all of them, probably, of winning. London, who wanted to do good in this world, who volunteered their time doing farm labor just because, who wanted to make things better for queer kids. London, who came out to an entire table of strangers on their very first night in town.

London Parker was talented and brave and just irritatingly cute, and Dahlia could envision it now, crystal clear even as her head swam with blurry regrets. London, a few weeks from now, holding one of those ginormous replica checks in their hands. They were smiling for the cameras while confetti rained down on their strawberry hair. Sai Patel handed them a trophy, sparkling under the studio lights, and shook their hand with pride.

And Dahlia... She couldn't see herself. Was she there? Somewhere on the sidelines? Or was she in Maryland, begging for her old job back, figuring out which bills she could pay that month?

Or maybe she was simply a blank space, an empty canvas, atoms floating aimlessly across the landscape, each one trying to forget that foolish time she went to LA on a hope and a prayer, each one hopelessly trying to erase the memories of a person who wanted her to believe she could have it all.

CHAPTER NINE

London knew it. They'd screwed it up. They never should have invited Dahlia to crash that wedding.

She was being super weird today, in a way that was different from her other subdued moods. When they saw her in the morning at craft services before filming started, they'd asked how the rest of her weekend had gone, and she'd said, "Oh, good. Fine. Good. Yeah, you know, totally fine." And then she had forced a smile that looked like she had just tasted something gross but was trying to be polite about it.

She didn't ask how London's Sunday was. Which was fine, because their only answer would have been *staring at my phone wondering if I could text you again.*

Throughout the entire day of filming, through another Face-Off—London had been paired with Jacob, and they'd kicked that guy's ass—and another Ingredient Innovation, Dahlia kept looking at them. And then looking quickly away when London made eye contact. And then she'd look at them again, until the feel of Dahlia's eyeballs made London paranoid there was something on their face. She was...twitchy.

London should have let it go. But for some reason, they

found themself waiting for her to get out of the solo interview set at the end of the day. They didn't know if another attempt at normal conversation would work at this point, so they got desperate.

"Ay, mate." They jumped into step with her as she exited the set and walked toward the studio door. "Jammy day, eh?"

Dahlia stopped, so London did, too. She turned and stared at them.

"Uh…" London scratched at their neck. "How no yeez and me go, uh—"

"London," Dahlia interrupted. "What the hell are you doing?"

London frowned. "My finest Tanner Tavish impression, obviously."

Dahlia stared at them a moment more. And then, finally, *hallelujah*, she started laughing.

London pushed open the studio door.

"Tanner Tavish does not use whatever words you were just saying," Dahlia said, following.

"I know. And that's why I think he's full of shit."

"What do you mean?"

"That dude is not from Scotland," London said.

Dahlia laughed again. "And how do you know that?"

"His accent is all wonky. I doubt his name is even Tanner Tavish. I think his whole"—London waved their hand—"thing is an act."

"So you're an expert on Scottish people?"

London shrugged, stuffing their hands in their pockets as they walked toward the hotel. "Nah. Just an expert on eejits. And Tanner Tavish is most definitely one of those."

Dahlia shook her head, smiling. "He's a pretty hot eejit, though."

London frowned again. "He's not *that* hot."

Dahlia crossed her arms over her chest as they walked. London was feeling surprisingly grumpy about this *pretty hot* comment, but at least Dahlia was talking to them again.

"Do you think they always knew they wanted to be chefs? Tanner and Audra and Sai?"

London shrugged. "Maybe. Sai definitely; I watched a documentary about him a while ago."

"Yeah." A car driving by blared its horn.

"What did you want to be when you grew up, when you were a kid?" London asked.

Dahlia was quiet a moment, but finally she answered.

"A writer. When I was in elementary school, I filled notebook after notebook with these stories about girls at camp. My parents could never afford to send me to camp, at least a real sleepaway camp, not just, you know, summer classes at the Y. So I lived out all my camp fantasies in those books."

"What was the camp called?"

"Camp Sunnywood." Dahlia smiled, and London saw her shoulders relax. "Whenever I finished a story, I'd rip the pages out of the notebook and make a front and back cover out of construction paper, and tie it all together with purple yarn." Her smile grew. "I gave them to my dad to read, and he'd write blurbs on the back of each one. Like, 'Woodson's finest Sunnywood yet!'" She laughed, and London laughed with her. They were approaching the hotel now.

"Oh! Oh man. I definitely spent almost the entirety of fifth grade working on *Camp Sunnywood: Super Edition #1*. Tiffany and Molly got in a *huge fight* and tipped over each other's canoes and then Molly dumped Sunny D all over Tiffany's clothes."

London pressed the button for the elevator and looked down at her. Her eyes were so bright now.

"What a bitch," London commented as they stepped inside the elevator.

"No, listen, Molly was just going through some stuff," Dahlia said emphatically. "Her parents were going through a divorce, and honestly, Tiffany was acting real petty that summer. She never let Molly ride her favorite horse at the stables."

London realized they would be perfectly satisfied to spend the rest of the evening learning every single facet of Camp Sunnywood.

They also wondered when, exactly, Dahlia had given up her dreams of being an author.

"Okay, okay, I'm shutting up now," Dahlia said as they walked down their hall. "What did *you* want to be when you were a kid?"

London thought on it. There had been lots of things, including, for a while, a chef, but only one thing had been consistent.

"A musician."

"Really?" Dahlia looked over at them, eyes wide. "Oh my god, London, were you like, *in a band*?"

London huffed self-consciously.

"You are overestimating my coolness. I was in concert band, if that counts." They reached the door to London's room. London leaned against it, while Dahlia leaned against the wall, facing them.

"What did you play?"

"Trumpet. Still play, actually."

"Wait." Dahlia actually held out her hand in a *stop* gesture. "You play the trumpet? Like, currently. Just for fun. Or, *oh my god*, are you like, in a jazz quartet or something?"

"No." London squirmed, feeling embarrassed. "Just for fun." Although they shouldn't be embarrassed. Playing an instrument was a totally normal hobby. They had no idea why Dahlia was so amused.

"Huh."

"What?"

"Nothing." She smiled. "It's just, kind of sexy. Playing the trumpet."

London stared at her. "Dahlia, have you ever actually seen someone play the trumpet? It is not sexy."

This was true. It wasn't.

But London might have spent the rest of the night blushing in their room anyway, congratulating themself on graduating from *cute* to *sexy* in the eyes of Dahlia Woodson.

They walked home together on Tuesday night, too. After London won the Elimination Challenge, which had been about hearts. "*Ugh*, this is *disgusting*, of course you love cooking with hearts, you *heathen*," Dahlia had said to them, her face crinkled and adorable, back to her regular self.

Even though Dahlia did just fine with her own heart. Jacob, however, did not.

After he got the boot on Tuesday, Barbara shifted over

to take his place at Dahlia's station on Wednesday morning. When Janet made the change, Dahlia had literally jumped up and down and clapped her hands. London had pretended to write some recipe notes in their notepad, but mostly they smiled pathetically at nothing. Ahmed was totally onto them, and slugged their shoulder, which was embarrassing.

By the time Dahlia and London walked back to the hotel on Wednesday night, after another Face-Off and Ingredient Innovation day, London was starting to feel dangerously confident. At cooking on set. At making Dahlia laugh. At settling into this new routine.

But when the door to their hotel room clicked shut, they sank into the chair in the corner and took a deep breath.

London stared at their phone and tried to wipe Dahlia Woodson from their mind. There were two calls they had to make. Well, one, really, and they had put it off for as long as they could. It'd been at the back of their mind all day, niggling like an annoying itch. An itch they'd shoved away, purposely ignoring, ever since they'd been in LA. But *Chef's Special* season eight premiered tomorrow night. It was time now.

The other phone call was just for reassurance. That was the one London made first.

"London," Julie panted into the phone after one ring. "Thank god you called. I might die tonight, and you should know where to find my body."

"Julie." London frowned. "What the fuck are you talking about?"

"I'm in Percy Warner Park. On the—where the hell are we again?" Julie's voice faded away for a second. "The Mossy

Ridge Trail. I'm on the Mossy Ridge Trail in Percy Warner Park. Write that down, for the police."

"Julie." London rubbed their forehead. "I know where the Mossy Ridge Trail is. Why the hell are you in Percy Warner Park at"—London checked the time, calculated two hours ahead—"ten o'clock at night?"

"I know. We have an hour until the park closes. I hope you give a nice speech, at my funeral."

"Julie, I swear, if you don't just get to the—"

"Dearest Ben Caravalho is training to hike the Pacific Crest Trail."

"Yeah. I know. I talked to him last week."

Ben had been Julie's best friend since elementary school. London had been jealous of him for a long time, even though Julie had assured London they would always be her number one. The jealousy had been exacerbated by the fact that London had harbored an enormous crush on Ben all through-out high school, which had felt hopeless at the time, since Ben was super gay and London was still living under the illusion that they were just an awkward straight girl.

"Well, I've been trying to convince him what a horrible idea it is—"

"Julie! Why would you do that? Hiking the PCT is badass!"

"Yeah, and *dangerous*."

London smiled. "Ben will be fine."

"*Anyway*, he wanted to hike this dumbass trail in the dark to make sure he was prepared for night hiking. Which you apparently have to do in the desert in California, if you want to make the right amount of miles in a day, because it's too hot to hike all day during actual daylight. Did you even hear that sentence, London? Did you hear how *ridiculous* it sounded?"

"So you went with him to convince him how ridiculous it is."

"Exactly."

"Is it working?"

There was a pause. London could practically hear Julie's scowl.

"No. He is having a *great time*."

"Hey, London!" Ben shouted into the phone.

"You know what Ben was just telling me before you called?" Julie cut back in. "That we'll have to check for ticks when we get back in the car. *This* is why the best sports are played indoors."

While London had focused on music in middle and high school, Julie had been a star basketball player. She still refused to believe any other physical activity compared.

She was also over-the-top, exasperatingly protective of the people she loved.

God, London really missed her.

"You should probably go then, so you can get back to the car before the park closes. I can call later."

"Shut your face. We're like ten steps from the car. I can talk."

"So I *won't* have to report your missing body to the police."

"You know who hangs out in parking lots of creepy parks late at night, London? Creepy people. We're not safe yet."

London heard the beep of Ben's car door.

"Okay. So we're safe now. You know, unless there are ticks up my ass ready to give me Lyme disease. I'll keep you updated on that."

"Great. Can't wait."

"What's up?"

London sighed. They would actually be entirely pleased to keep talking about Ben's PCT plans, but they had to stop being a coward and talk about this.

"So the first episode of *Chef's Special* airs tomorrow."

It wasn't a good sign that they heard Julie sigh.

"No shit. But yeah, about that. Wait—you didn't get kicked off or something, did you?"

"I wouldn't be allowed to tell you, technically. But no, I'm still here."

"Of course you are. Good. Okay, so have you talked to Dad yet?"

London winced. "No."

"Listen, London, you should do that. Because Mom has sort of organized a big watch party at the house. She's having it catered and everything."

London groaned.

This meant that half of Nashville would be tuning in, together, in the living room where London was raised.

London shouldn't have been surprised. Of course their mom would organize a watch party. She loved her kids, and she loved an event.

London's family was privileged, but they weren't a dysfunctional level of privileged. The Parkers were close. Growing up, London's parents worked long hours. Their dad, in particular, traveled a lot. But their parents still always attended every one of Julie's basketball games, all of London's band and choir concerts. They had dinner together at the dining room table every night they could, and a big Sunday supper every week that included an open invitation to any cousin, uncle, aunt, neighbor, or family friend who wanted to come. London's childhood had been full of love and community.

"I've wanted to say something to Dad about it, to warn him, but…" Julie trailed off.

"No, I know. It's my responsibility."

And it *was* London's responsibility. To let their dad know that when half of Nashville showed up in their living room, they would all be witnessing London introduce themself as nonbinary on national TV.

London stared out the window at the lights of Burbank, the darkened sky.

They hadn't really known what to expect when they came out to their family three years ago. Their mom had seemed a bit confused, but she'd promptly done research, as her scientific mind usually did. And then she'd been fully accepting, even if she did have lots of intrusive Science Mom questions.

Their two older sisters, Jackie and Sara, had been on board right away, too. Jackie and Sara were seven and nine years older than them—Julie and London had been a double whammy of a surprise for their parents—and were out of the house by the time London was in middle school. But London still remembered how protective they both were of London and Julie when they were kids, and that hadn't changed.

Julie had been upset. Cried, even. At first, it was the most hurtful reaction London could have imagined. If Julie didn't accept them, of all people…Well, it would have been a struggle. But it turned out Julie didn't care about London being nonbinary; she was more upset that there was something so important about London she hadn't known.

Although, as their twin, of course Julie *had* known something. She grew up practically glued to their side, after all. She was there every time London threw a fit about wearing a dress, about getting dumb girl gifts every birthday and Christmas when all they wanted were new cooking tools and gift cards to the music store. She had been there when London had finally started questioning their sexuality in college, when they had come out as pan.

So when Julie had discovered, during their mom's grilling sessions, that London had already started microdosing testosterone, she had felt betrayed. London been annoyed at the time, thought Julie was being selfish, that she had unrealistic expectations, sometimes, of the whole twin thing. But looking back, London got it. They had been a little selfish themself, maybe. But maybe it was okay to be selfish with some things.

And it was a hard thing to explain. That they didn't want to be a man, but that they had never felt quite right as a girl. That they only started to feel really okay when they understood they could be their own thing. That they could exist in a space that was all their own, that they could shift and adjust until it felt right. They had settled on *nonbinary* feeling right for them, even though they knew others like them had their own names that felt right to their own experiences. And that was comforting, too. That each person could choose what brought them closest to belonging, the power in that. Knowing that one day, people might discover even better words for it. That there was only ever freedom in continuing to find new names for who we were, who we could be.

And so after more conversations, Julie had calmed down,

and things were as normal as ever between them. Maybe even better.

Their dad, though, had refused London's gender identity from the start. It had created friction between their mom and dad that London never remembered seeing before, which made them feel guilty as hell. They still didn't quite understand it. Sure, their father had rolled his eyes a bit when London came out as pan, which had been less than ideal, but London had never taken that as out-and-out rejection. It was like…it was like the nonbinary thing was the last straw for him. Like he'd had a lifetime of London being the weird one, and he'd had enough.

Julie, Jackie, and Sara had all tried to work on him, and London could only imagine that their mom had worked the hardest of all. But London's dad had never once used the correct pronoun for London in three years.

London worried that the longer their dad waited for London to get out of "this phase," the wider and heavier the fracture in their family would feel.

When London had said those few short sentences in the solo interview set over two weeks ago, it really had been easy. It had just been them, a quiet room, and Maritza's reassuring face next to the camera. They felt so far from Nashville, from reality. It had been important. Necessary. But right now, it felt a little bit foolish.

"London?" Julie asked quietly. She knew, of course, that London was going to be out on the show. They had talked about it before London left. "He should probably know before we all watch it."

"I know."

"You know how proud I am of you, right?"

Julie knew London better than anyone else in the world. She was always proud of them. But at this particular moment, it was what they needed to hear. For one second, London pushed their dad out of their brain. And they knew what they had done would be worth it: Viewers would view London as they were from the start. If they had the ability to see them as they were. The relief buoyed their entire chest.

"What about everyone else on the show?" Julie asked. "Are they cool with you? What about the judges? Oh my god, it would break my heart if Sai Patel was an asshole about you."

"No, actually, Sai Patel seems like a genuinely good guy. All the judges are pretty much exactly how they appear on TV. If anything, they take the competition even more seriously than you would think. None of it's an act. It's...impressive, actually."

London decided to not tell their sister about Lizzie. There was enough negativity brewing in the back of their head for one night, and they didn't need to worry Julie. And anyway, they'd been doing a pretty good job, if they said so themself, at ignoring Lizzie's existence.

"Thank god. Okay, so the other contestants, I need to know—are they assholes? Are there people I should be rooting for or not rooting for? Wait, ugh, don't tell me; I don't want spoilers. Wait until I at least watch the first ep and can put names to faces. And *then* you're going to have to give me all the details. Holy *shit*, London, I can't believe you are going to be *on TV!*"

London had signed up for this thing.

But they couldn't believe it, either.

London felt it in their bones on Thursday morning that they were off. And they weren't sure if even a whole day of cute Dahlia moments could cure it.

They had ended up texting their dad last night instead of calling. Because they were, in fact, a coward. They had typed and retyped the message at least ten times, trying for the most nonconfrontational angle, warning him they were out on the show, but ending it on a "miss you, love you" type of vibe.

It had taken their dad a half hour to respond. And when he did, it was with this:

Ok

Just the two letters. The worst possible response in the entire history of texting. London wanted to chuck their phone out the window. And yet, what else had they been expecting? Even this morning, they kept checking their phone like an idiot, as if some magical message might appear at any minute.

Hey kiddo, you know, I thought about it overnight, and I decided to stop being such an asshole and accept you! Sorry for all those times I didn't use the right pronoun and those three years I made you feel like you were fucking up our whole family! Super-duper proud of you now, though, buddy! Go get 'em!

London rubbed a hand over their face as they stood at their station. They hadn't slept well, and maybe that was contributing to how off-center they felt. Plus, it had been a four-day filming week, all long studio days, and while four days were better than five, it'd still been a lot.

They had a three-day weekend starting tomorrow, thank god. Clearly, they needed it.

In front of them, Dahlia laughed at something Barbara said.

There were eight of them left now. Single digits. As each person left, being on the show felt both more comfortable and more tense. They were all used to the production schedule now. They knew the crew, the pantry, the equipment, the tics of the judges and the producers. They knew each other better.

But as the numbers dwindled, the stakes felt higher.

Dahlia turned around, sensing London's presence. She was getting good at this, just knowing when London was there, when they wanted her to turn around and smile at them. Like she did now.

Then again, London wanted her to turn around and smile at them always. So maybe it wasn't a particular talent.

"Did you know I love Barbara?" she said brightly.

"Yes." London attempted a tight smile back.

"Hey." Dahlia tilted her head. "You okay?"

London nodded. Which meant, of course, that they weren't. Dahlia frowned, understanding this, but then Janet gave the signal, and the cameras started rolling, and she faced forward again.

She was wearing a floral-print dress today, hibiscus and plumeria and birds-of-paradise scattered around a black background. It was lovely. London wanted to collapse into it.

They focused on this, Dahlia's dress, the dark waves of her hair that swished over her shoulders, instead of the idea of everyone they knew showing up at their house tonight in Nashville to watch them on TV. Dahlia would put up that hair in approximately twenty minutes, London guessed. They knew her hair schedule by heart.

Moments later, the demonstration table was rolled out

onto the Golden Circle with a single appliance displayed at its center.

Dahlia bounced lightly on the balls of her feet, squeezed her hands behind her back.

A pasta roller.

London knew pasta was one of Dahlia's favorite things to make. She would do well.

The thought eased the tension in their shoulders slightly.

An hour later, though, things were not going so well for London. Things were not going well at all.

Their dough was too sticky, and then too dry when they tried to balance it, like they were an amateur who had never made dough before in their life. The contestants had a brief break in the middle of the cooking time to help the dough rest, during which London rubbed their sore arms and scowled a lot while Dahlia chatted with Cath. But even after their dough had rested, it kept getting stuck in the damn roller.

Sure, London had not worked with pasta a lot, but it was supposed to be simple. Soothing to work with, even. Why hadn't London practiced making more pasta before coming here? This was worse than the fish. They felt incompetent, flustered.

By the time their ravioli were on their plate, London knew it was far from their finest work. The filling was good, but the shaping of the ravioli was inconsistent, and there was too much sauce, which was too thin, but they didn't have time to fix it. Fuck.

"It's not that bad," Dahlia said, and London almost jumped when she put her hand over theirs, just for a second. They hadn't even known she was so close. But of course she was. This week, after Monday, Dahlia always seemed close by.

London was trying hard not to be dramatic about it, but the ten minutes they walked home in the dark had invariably turned into London's favorite part of the day. They wanted, at this moment, nothing more than to skip forward to that ten minutes today. Dahlia was looking up at them in concern and her eyes were like a hug, earnest and open. They were almost too much, today. Because she was being too kind when she called their ravioli not bad.

They had tasted Dahlia's Bolognese earlier. They had been surprised she would try to pull off Bolognese in only an hour, but of course she would, and of course it was ridiculously good. Rich and flavorful, but not too heavy. Her pappardelle were perfect, soft and chewy. Everything about watching her make it—from pounding the dough with her palms, to lifting the wide, delicate strands of pappardelle through her fingers, to how she constantly brought that wooden spoon to her mouth to taste her sauce—had all felt overwhelmingly erotic.

She told London, during a break, how her mom's side of the family was Italian. Her great-grandparents had immigrated to the US from a small town in the south of the country near Salerno. She said, with a small laugh, something about how getting pasta right was probably the only thing she'd ever truly done right by her mom's side of the family, and later, London would wish they had asked more questions about that. But at the time they could only think about how much of her skin was exposed in that dress, how much they wanted to touch it.

By the time judging started, London felt a riotous combination of frustrated, aroused, and disappointed in themself. They had failed today, and they knew it.

They were going to leave this competition without know-ing what Dahlia Woodson's lips tasted like, and it killed them inside.

Dahlia's judging went very well, as London knew it would. She smiled at London as she walked back to her station, like she always did when things went well. London simply stared at her, thinking of all the things they wanted to say that they might not ever get to.

London was not surprised to be in the bottom three.

They did not look at Dahlia as their name was called to the Golden Circle. But they could feel her eyes, how they never left them once. Their neck flamed with heat. They stood in that dumb circle next to Eric and Ayesha, and all they could think about were those two letters:

Ok

For a brief moment, London almost wished for Sai Patel to put them out of their misery. They pictured him looking at them, and just saying:

Ok

And London would know, and they would try to leave with dignity.

But Sai Patel didn't say that.

He and the other judges hated Eric's pasta more.

London's was bad, but apparently not the worst. Audra Carnegie called it "a shame."

"We were all surprised at your performance today, London," Sai said. "We expect more from you at this point. From here on out, you'd better step up your game."

London nodded, looked appropriately contrite, and walked back to their station.

They were going to make it to that three-day weekend after all. They would get another chance next week, to be better. They were grateful, and a bit in shock.

But, they remembered a second later, the first episode was still airing tonight. And London didn't know what would come after that for them, off set, back in the real world. It was like London's brain was a radio signal stuck between frequencies, constantly cutting out between LA and Nashville, and all they wanted was for the radio to shut off.

London hardly registered, moments later, that the cameras had stopped rolling, lost in their own head.

Until suddenly, stunning their brain into complete silence and snapping the radio dial clean off, Dahlia's arms wrapped themselves around their body.

"Oh my god," she breathed into London's neck, squeezing them tight. "I knew your dish wasn't the worst, but still. London, you can't go yet."

Amazingly, she kept holding on. London blinked, slowly comprehending Dahlia's body pressed completely against theirs, her hair brushing against their cheek.

All the other contestants had paused at their stations, staring at them.

Fuck it.

London moved their hands to Dahlia's back, touching lightly, cautiously. They shifted their head just an inch, allowed themself to breathe in her hair. It smelled like coconuts, rich and warm. Combined with the contrasting sharpness of her peppermint ChapStick, London's senses were overwhelmed. They only ever wanted to smell exactly this, coolness and warmth, all at once.

"Dahlia," they said, and then realized they had no other words.

She stepped back, took a steadying breath, and even though London *knew*, objectively, that that hug had been too long, too close, it didn't feel like enough. London's hands fell back to their sides. Their body felt cold without her.

"Let's go," she said.

They walked back to the hotel.

Today, they were silent. Halfway there, on an impulse they didn't overthink for once, London reached over and took Dahlia's hand.

Her fingers threaded through theirs immediately. London gave them a squeeze. Their head felt fuzzy. They meant to drop Dahlia's hand, after the squeeze, but Dahlia kept holding on, so they did, too. Her hand was soft and hot, and London swore they could feel her pulse beating in her pinky.

They both let go when they entered the lobby, as if the whoosh of air-conditioning broke a spell. When they got to London's door, London stuffed their hands in their pockets, looking past Dahlia's shoulder.

"Thanks," they said roughly, and cleared their throat. "For not wanting me to go. I don't want you to go, either. For the record."

Dahlia smiled. But it was small, close lipped. Not even a peek of those blinding teeth. "Yeah. I figured." She breathed out slowly. "Okay. Well. Good night."

London wanted to lean over and kiss her forehead. No, that wasn't right. They wanted to kiss her lips, feel her tongue on theirs. They wanted to kiss her neck, her shoulders. They wanted all of her.

And then they wanted to rest their head on her lap and tell her about their dad. How he really had been a good dad, before. How London didn't understand why he couldn't just get over it. How they didn't understand why they couldn't get over his not getting over it. How frustrated they were with themself.

If they stood any longer in this hallway, they just might reach out to her. They might just attempt any number of things.

But it had been a long week. A headache started to come on when London realized that, on Central time, the first episode of *Chef's Special* had probably already aired. It was done. The house party in Nashville had seen it, and there were probably strangers trolling their Twitter account as they and Dahlia stood there, staring at each other.

The hug had been nice. The hug had been more than nice.

The hug would have to be enough. Something about the air in this hallway felt reckless, and London didn't trust anything right now, most of all themself.

"Good night, Dahlia Woodson."

London put their key in their door, and they stepped into the cool darkness.

CHAPTER TEN

D ahlia knocked on London's door Friday morning. Her palms were sweating.

"Hey," she said when London opened the door. "Want to go somewhere?"

They looked at her, eyes bleary, blinking a few times. They looked awful, as she had worried they would. No, *awful* wasn't the right word. London was still in rumpled pajamas: a heather-gray T-shirt, green-and-navy flannel bottoms. That shock of hair on the top of their head pointed in several different directions. It was adorable. They were abso-freaking-lutely adorable, and maybe this was merely what they looked like at eight thirty in the morning.

But Dahlia worried that London was so disheveled not because they had accidentally slept in, but because they had stayed up too late reading the comments.

It had been immediate, after the first episode aired last night. She hadn't watched the episode herself—it would have been too cringeworthy—but she had scrolled social media feeds in her room, her stomach tense and queasy after saying good night to London. After holding their hand.

The commenters who weren't talking about her epic trip

were talking about London. She wished they were all talking about her.

Because almost everyone was being *nice* about her.

OH MY GOD I HAVE BEEN NERVOUS ABOUT A CONTESTANT TRIPPING WITH THEIR FOOD EVER SINCE I STARTED WATCHING THESE DUMB SHOWS, THIS POOR GIRL, MY HEART IS POUNDING FOR HER

Even the people who were laughing at her were simply laughing at her brief embarrassing moment. They weren't laughing at her identity, who she was at her core.

Dahlia was not surprised to see that her trip had been made into a gif. The first time she watched it, she had been horrified, but with each replay of the loop, it felt funnier and funnier to her. The surprised look on her face, the way the rice and tacos were suspended in the air. It was *funny*. It was totally gif-worthy, and she tried to process that her moment of shame would probably circulate on the internet for years. Surprisingly, she felt okay with it.

But Dahlia had underestimated how attached people were to the gender binary.

She had only been able to stomach it for an hour, before she put her phone facedown on her bedside table and picked up a book. A book she hadn't been able to concentrate on, not a single word, but it had helped her fall asleep.

Dahlia really hoped London hadn't read the comments, the threads, the hashtags. That they were smarter than her.

London scratched the back of their neck.

"Where would we go?" they asked eventually, their voice scratchy with sleep.

"Anywhere. The ocean, I was thinking. I still haven't seen

the Pacific even though we've been here three weeks now. It's an injustice, really."

A corner of London's mouth twerked up, just the tiniest bit, and a dash of hope leapt in Dahlia's chest.

"I was thinking we could rent a car," she continued. "There's a place right around the block, and it's probably not that expensive for one day and—"

"I have a car," London broke in.

"Really?" Dahlia hadn't heard them talk about driving anywhere. "Did you drive out here from Nashville? I've always wanted to do a road trip like that."

"No." London cleared their throat. "I rented one. I thought you sort of needed one, in LA. Even though I've hardly used it so far. It's in the hotel garage."

Dahlia tried to calculate the cost of a car rental for that long, when you weren't even using it, and gave up after a few seconds. She had gathered, from things London had said, that they had money.

"Let's go, then."

London looked at her for a steady moment, then looked down at their outfit.

"Give me a minute?"

Twenty minutes later, they walked into the garage. London tossed the keys in the air.

"Do you want to drive?" They looked over at Dahlia. "I feel kind of distracted, and—"

"Fuck yeah, I want to drive!" Dahlia snatched the keys from their hands. London smiled.

Dahlia backed them out of the garage, and they drove away from Burbank.

London had no idea how long they'd been in the car. It could have been twenty minutes; it could have been days. Who knew LA was so big? Who knew it had so much traffic?

Okay. Still. It was a really potent reality, when you were in it.

London was in a car, alone with Dahlia, with no real destination other than the beach. Dahlia had put Santa Monica in her maps app, but traffic in Santa Monica was almost worse than anywhere else. She had flapped her hands and said, "Too crowded," and kept driving up the Pacific Coast Highway.

London wanted desperately to be present. To be chatting with Dahlia about anything, enjoying the fact that they were on the fucking PCH and the sun was shining, the sky bright and clear.

Instead, they had spent most of the ride in total silence, other than the radio blaring. London leaned their head against the window, spacing out, the scenery rushing by them in a blur. They were aware of how mopey they appeared, but they were unable to stop it.

They felt strange. That was all. Strange. They hadn't watched the episode themself, but couldn't stop themself from looking at comments online. Social media was their life, more than they wanted to admit. Social media was what helped them figure out they were nonbinary in the first place. Social media gave them a community to be themself.

And they had received a lot of positive feedback from that community. Not just gifs on Twitter, but thoughtful DMs and texts.

OMG London! This is so amazing! Are you getting a lot of trolls? Take care of yourself, we'll shut them down for you <3 <3 <3 also you look super hot, you know this right

Look at you, casually mentioning your pronouns on national TV like it ain't no thing. You are a true American hero, London Parker

The thing about trolls was that London knew they were trolls. That you were supposed to be able to brush them off for what they were. Maybe London was softer than they should have been, but they'd never been able to make trolls' words stop hurting anyway. Even if they knew that was what the trolls wanted, even if they knew they were letting the trolls win.

Julie, Jackie, and Sara had all sent encouraging texts. Jackie lived in Atlanta now, Sara in Pittsburgh, so obviously they hadn't been at the viewing party in Nashville, but Julie said it had been a success. London had no idea what "a success" meant, but somehow they doubted it had been anything but awkward. Their mom had texted, too: *Your lamb really did look like perfection. We are so proud of you, London. I love you.*

There had been no texts from their dad. Obviously.

As the car wound through the hills, the ocean shining to their left, London felt their thoughts becoming not more present, exactly, but loosening, stretching as the miles passed. Why *were* they on this competition, really? Why was gender so easy for some people and not for others? Why did we care so much about other people's opinions? Why was Dahlia nice to them?

London looked over at her then. And their heart stuttered.

She had one hand on the top of the wheel. She was wearing

oversized sunglasses, a simple white V-neck T-shirt, short cut-off jean shorts. Her hair was down. And she was *beaming*. She was smiling through the windshield at nothing, while London curled against their seat belt in philosophical angst.

"You're happy," London said simply.

Dahlia's smile faltered. Her eyes darted over to them.

"Oh. Hi. Sorry. I thought you were sleeping, maybe."

"No. Just thinking."

She nodded. "I'm not happy about...you know." Another flap of her hand. "I've just discovered that I really like driving in LA."

"Yeah?"

"Yeah."

London grinned. "I'm glad."

"There are so many people, and everyone goes so fast. It's terrifying and thrilling," Dahlia went on, her skin flushing. London wondered if Dahlia was even real. A woman who could fillet a swordfish like it was nothing, who carried a Swiss Army multitool in her bag at all times, who reveled in LA traffic. She made them sweat. "I mean, traffic in DC makes you want to stab something, but this is totally different. This car is so nice, too. You should see the clunker I drive around the 'burbs in Maryland."

The rental was a Nissan. It was fine. London felt a little embarrassed about it, actually. It had been their mom's idea; she was paying for it. But they hadn't wanted to admit that to Dahlia for some reason.

They also didn't tell Dahlia that at home, they drove a Tesla.

"And look at this road!" Dahlia gushed. "I've never seen anything like it."

The road really was something. City traffic had faded away now. The highway curved into the hills, smooth and lilting and poetic, like a symphony in asphalt.

London wanted Dahlia to keep talking about traffic, about the road, about her car back home, about anything, really. Dahlia could sing the ABCs and it would help. London wanted to tell her that she was helping. But words were still feeling hard.

So London didn't say anything, and Dahlia stopped talking, and they drove for ten more minutes in silence. Until she pulled off the road randomly at an unmarked pull-off. She turned off the ignition and sat there for a second. Then she looked over at them.

"Hey, London?"

They unclicked their seat belt and met her gaze, raising an eyebrow.

"Fuck anyone who doesn't see you."

She got out of the car, slammed her door, and walked to the cliff's edge.

London watched her for a minute, listening to their heart beat in their ears. They wanted to crystalize this moment, however bittersweet it felt: Dahlia Woodson at the ocean's edge, wind blowing her hair, legs stretching for miles. Wanting to see them.

Feeling stranger than they had before, eventually London opened the car door and joined her.

They found a rickety set of stairs that led down to the beach. There was no one else there that they could see, which felt unbelievable after the chaotic mess of LA. Two majestic golden columns of rock jutted out of the waves.

"Look at this," Dahlia breathed. "This is the prettiest place I've ever been."

London agreed in silence. The water went on forever. The crash of the waves, the cry of the seagulls overhead. It forced the present on them. They couldn't ignore any of this.

They looked over at Dahlia to say something. To thank her for bringing them here. To thank her for what she said in the car. To tell her how wonderful she was.

But when their eyes landed on her, they puffed out a half-frustrated, half-amused burst of air instead.

"For crying out loud, Dahlia."

And before they could stop themself, they reached out and stuck both of their hands in her hair. The wind had made it wild, and it whipped around in every direction like a dust storm, obscuring her face. "Can you even *see* anything right now with this?" London tried to tame the dark locks with their hands, smoothing it away from her face, but the ends kept flying back, refusing to settle. "Seriously."

When London finally got enough of it in their fists to get a good look at her, they found her looking up at them, smiling, and everything crashed together inside of them, sharp and vivid: Their fingers tangled in the hair they'd been dreaming about for three weeks, their face inches from hers, the empty beach and the wind stealing their breath.

Dahlia leaned forward and kissed them.

London's brain barely had time to process the feel of her lips, soft and pliant and sweet, their fingers automatically curling even tighter through her hair, silky and strong, the touch of their noses bumping together, before they started to cough.

London backed away involuntarily, their hands letting

loose of their hold on her, choking on the tickle of a strand of her hair in their mouth.

Dahlia started to laugh. She pulled away too, yanking on the black elastic that perpetually encircled her right wrist. She dipped her chin, gathering the strands of her mane onto the top of her head. London stood still, heart pounding, fascinated at getting to watch this process up close, even closer than on set—stray pieces kept flying at their face as she worked on containing it—while disappointment dropped to their toes.

They were positive the moment had passed. They felt every inch of space between them. How could London have blown that so badly?

Although technically, it was her hair's fault.

But when Dahlia finally finished thirty seconds later, the longest thirty seconds of London's life, she closed the gap again. There wasn't even a beat of hesitation. Which meant the first time hadn't been merely a spontaneous fluke, the result of London rudely grabbing her hair in their hands. Their hands remained at their sides now, limp and useless, but Dahlia stepped toward them anyway. Close enough for London to smell coconuts.

Her hands cupped their face. Oh. Her hands were on their face. They were so soft. She was so soft.

London looked down at her for one second, saw the smile in her eyes before she closed them and leaned in. London didn't waste it this time.

They pushed into her lips so fervently that she stumbled back a step, and London quickly wrapped their arms around her, steadying her with their palm on the small of her back.

Their mouths opened to each other and there was her tongue, *finally*, hot and surprisingly determined, just like Dahlia, and the feel of it tugged at a string in their gut, a string that set everything else on fire.

The world felt right for once. They were anchored to the sand, to the earth, to the wind and sun and sky; there was no gender, no internet, no timelines—just skin and muscle and salt.

London could feel Dahlia folding herself into them, some-how, wrapping her hands around the back of their neck, her body inching as close as it was possible to be. It felt natural to hold her in this way, to become extensions of each other. Their body felt good, holding hers. God, Dahlia felt so good.

After an indeterminate amount of time, Dahlia's tongue disappeared from their mouth and London exhaled, their head drooping as Dahlia planted kisses along their jawline, up, up, until she sucked their earlobe into her mouth.

A strangled sound escaped London's lips.

Against every instinct, they broke away.

London and Dahlia stood staring at each other, cheeks flushed and mouths hanging slightly open, breathing heavily, while the waves crashed against the surf. London could feel the pulse of the sea in their chest, like they were connected, the force of the ocean pounding in an incessant rhythm against their rib cage, primal and wild.

They took another deep breath and wrung their hands through their hair.

The transcendent moment of peace and lust of mere seconds earlier began to shatter, reality smashing back into London's brain. Was this a pity kiss? Dahlia had read the mean things people were saying on the internet and dragged them to this beautiful place to try to make them feel better? And plus—

"Dahlia, are you straight?"

They had been trying to puzzle it out for a while now, but this kiss, the way she'd touched them—it was too much.

All they knew about Dahlia was that she had been married. To a dude.

Which, of course, didn't necessarily mean anything. But they also knew they were pretty masculine presenting, and... well, London didn't know anything, really, just then. Except for the fact that they knew they couldn't be some kind of experiment or fetish for her. They wouldn't survive it.

London wanted to explain all this. But Dahlia had just kissed them, and they had lost the ability to form at least eighty-five percent of the words they knew were in their vocabulary somewhere.

Dahlia looked at them, her eyes as clear and true as ever.

"Oh," she said. "London, no. I'm queer." She paused. "I... I guess I haven't mentioned that before."

London had to close their eyes. This was what they had wanted to hear, but irrationally, they felt like punching something. They wanted to grunt at Dahlia louder than they had ever grunted. "Nope."

"I'm sorry." She bit her lip, looking almost nervous now. "Although, I've only ever been with David. Before..." She waved a hand between them. "You're the only person I've ever even kissed other than David. Which... might be embarrassing. But I've known since college that... yeah, that I'm not straight."

Dahlia took a breath before stepping toward them again.

She reached for them, but then apparently thought better of it, sticking her hands in the back pockets of her shorts.

"London," she said, at the same time that London said, "Dahlia."

She looked up at them. "You first."

"This isn't a good idea."

It was the worst sentence that had ever twisted out of their mouth, this sentence. They watched as it deflated Dahlia's face, before she looked down and away from them, stubbing the top of her sandal into the sand. London's skin wanted to physically repel the words, take them back. They wanted to throw her down on the beach and never let her go.

Instead, they said, "You haven't been with anyone since your divorce; I haven't been with anyone since I came out as nonbinary. That's messy enough. But more than that, Dahlia... one of us could go home next week. And I can't..."

Now London looked down at the sand.

"Yeah," they heard Dahlia say, just barely, over the wind, her voice sounding so small that London could disintegrate into dust, right here. Disappear with the tide.

I can't, they wanted to say, *because even after that one kiss, I don't know if I can stand to be around you anymore. Because if you kiss me again, I will literally never be able to stop. I will take you right on this beach, I will consume you until I know every inch of you. Once I start with you, I won't be able to stop. I need you in a way that can't be temporary.*

Dahlia turned away from them, and she stared out at the sea.

London watched her profile, barely breathing.

They noticed, after a minute, that her hands had clamped into fists at her sides.

"I'm sorry," she said again. "I didn't mean to make things complicated for us."

"No, Dahlia—" London scratched at the back of their neck. "You didn't do anything wrong."

She swallowed and glanced over at them.

"We can still be friends, right? I don't know how to be on *Chef's Special* without you being my friend."

God, London really wanted to disappear.

"Of course," they said, and it felt like their throat was made of sandpaper.

Dahlia looked back out at the water. At length, she said, "I want to do something now."

London straightened. "Okay." Obviously, they should get the hell off this beach. If they didn't get off this beach soon, in fact, London's lungs might collapse. "We can—"

"You might not like it," Dahlia interrupted. "You can close your eyes if you want."

London blinked. "What?"

And then Dahlia Woodson took off her shirt.

London gaped at her as she quickly shed her shorts, too. She kicked off her sandals.

Dahlia didn't look back as she ran, full speed, toward the ocean, her heels kicking up sand as she went.

"Fucking hell," London said to no one.

Dahlia made a loud yip as the water hit her ankles, her knees, her thighs. London watched in a daze, unmoving, as she threw her body into the waves. Her head disappeared under the water, which was violently blue. They saw her gasp as she resurfaced, and then smile, the whites of her teeth unmistakable even from where London stood on shore.

She splashed around a while more, never going far enough as to make London truly nervous. The sun shone down on her head, on London's face. They could feel their skin burning. They would have to stop somewhere to buy aloe vera. Oh god. Dahlia and London had to drive all the way back to Burbank together after this.

Eventually, Dahlia made her way back to shore. She stepped slowly toward them, squeezing salt water out of her hair. London wondered, distantly, if they were perhaps having a panic attack, if they were hallucinating this whole thing. Dahlia's bra and underwear were a matching set, smooth, clinging, dark purple silk. Her bare stomach was liquefying London's insides.

She reached them, and she smiled, looking shy. London couldn't recall Dahlia ever looking shy. But then again, London had never stood in front of a Dahlia who was half naked and dripping wet. And London, try as they might, could not stop staring.

"The Pacific is fucking cold," Dahlia said, trying to sound breezy. Even as she blushed, her skin, her smile, were glowing, everything looking more relaxed than before, the edges that had been there soothed by the sea. She had legitimately never looked so kissable, and Dahlia looked pretty kissable most of the time.

"Okay, now actually close your eyes."

"What?" London asked again.

She leaned over and picked up her dry clothes from the sand.

"I'm going to change now. I can't wear this wet stuff in the car the whole way back. I'll chafe."

London closed their eyes, cursing silently over and over and over.

A minute later, they felt something cold and wet slap their hand. They almost screamed.

"I am *so*, so sorry, but can you hold this for me? I don't want it to get all sandy." London closed their fingers around the soaked underwire of Dahlia's discarded bra. The silent cursing in their head increased exponentially.

"All right, I'm decent. Well. Relatively, I guess."

When London dared to crack their eyelids back open to the world, Dahlia was in her shorts and T-shirt again, underwear in her hand. She was doing a weird little dance, squatting up and down.

"Huh," she said. "Unsurprisingly, this might chafe too, but it's not too bad."

"Dahlia," London said, pained. "Can you stop moving around, please?"

Their brain had been short circuiting for long minutes now, but watching Dahlia squat around the beach, testing out how her jean shorts felt against her labia, all while they still held her wet bra, was going to actually terminate the functionality of London's existence.

But when Dahlia did as they said and stood straight and still in front of them, hands on her hips, London knew they were wrong. They were ruined either way. Her soaked hair dripped from its melting bun onto her shoulders. Through her T-shirt, London could easily see her peaked nipples, the dark pink outline of her areolas. She was the most beautiful thing they had ever seen. London was head over heels for her, and they had just instructed her to not kiss them anymore, although they were having a hard time remembering why.

"Do you wanna go in?" Dahlia pointed her chin toward the ocean. "I won't look. It clears your head."

London could only meet her eyes for a second. "No, thank you."

Dahlia stuck her hands in the back pockets of her shorts, biting her lip.

"You're not mad at me?"

London shook their head. Even though they were unsure. If they were mad, and who they were mad at.

"Do you want to stay on the beach longer or do something else?" she asked.

The truth was that London both wanted to magically transport the hell off this beach at the same time that they wanted to stay here with Dahlia forever, away from TV sets and hotel rooms and responsibilities. There was still no one else around, like it had been meant for them, like Dahlia had known exactly where to go when she pulled off the highway. It could be their kingdom. They could live in a cave in the cliffs. They would cook over firelight. They would make love on the sand. They would come back to society occasionally, to text those who loved them to let them know they were okay. Julie and Hank would understand.

"Something else," London said.

"Okay." Dahlia took a deep breath and smiled, willing them both courage. She snatched her bra out of London's hands. Finally. She picked up her sandals. She looked at London, a sad corner of her mouth quirking upward, and said, "I know you won't do this. But. Race you to the car?"

And then she took off. London watched after her for a few long seconds before they moved their feet, slowly following her back toward the staircase up the cliff. She was right, of course. London would never try to race her. Dahlia Woodson was a firefly in the darkness, a humming-bird at your window. Maybe you got to see her brightness for a fleeting moment, but you couldn't chase her. She didn't deserve to be caught.

Back at the top of the cliff, she tossed London the keys.

"Do you mind? I'm feeling a little tired, all of a sudden."

As London navigated down the PCH, they wanted to rewind back to the drive up here, when Dahlia was in-candescent with joy about LA traffic, when the atmosphere between them still made sense, as opposed to the stuffy, clunky movements of the air around them now.

Or maybe London should rewind all the way back. They never should have rammed past Jacob to sit next to her on that bus to the bar mitzvah; they should have made their rugelach alone at a different table. They never should have invited her to crash a wedding. They should have stayed in their hotel room today. They should have focused on their cooking, kept their head down.

Sure, they would have wanted her regardless, but they could have done it quietly. Unexpressed longing was a skill they were good at. It would have been easier than knowing what she tasted like. Most importantly, she wouldn't have been hurt.

London glanced over at her to maybe say some of this, to

apologize. But then they stopped. Because Dahlia was asleep. Her sandals were on the floor of their rental car, her feet tucked up underneath the tan skin of her legs, inches from the gear shift, her head resting against the passenger side window, her underwear balled up in her hands.

CHAPTER ELEVEN

Dahlia had jumped in the ocean, raced up a rickety set of stairs alongside a sandstone cliff, and spent far too much money on ridesharing apps to solo sightsee around Los Angeles the rest of the weekend, all to get away from the feeling of London Parker's arms around her.

And then Tanner Tavish appeared first thing Monday morning and slapped them together again, because he was a bitter bastard, and Dahlia wanted to spit in his handsome face.

Their Face-Off was about tarts. So of course London was going to win it anyway. They excelled at dessert.

Two trays of individual, prebaked tart shells sat in front of each of them, along with an array of custards, fruit, and random flourishes. They had five measly minutes to fill as many tarts as beautifully as they could.

"This is so dumb," Dahlia heard London mutter next to her. "They already made all of the most important parts for us. Who can't fill a premade tart?"

Dahlia, apparently.

The first time she filled a pastry bag, she squeezed a bit too enthusiastically, and the gloopy custard exploded all over the rim of her first shell. Then she wasted a minute cleaning it up, because she didn't want London to see it. Even though she knew, because she kept glancing at them, that London wasn't even looking at her side of the table.

Dahlia felt more bitter than she expected that London was so cool and collected. Because she could *feel* them, their presence, crowding the space around them. It made the hair rise on her arms, prickled all the way up her spine, made her lungs feel tight.

Audra Carnegie hustled over and whispered, "Dahlia, who cares about the mess! You have no time! Keep going, keep going!"

Dahlia cared about the mess. London was neat and precise. They were currently methodically filling two rows of tart shells, boom, boom, boom, each application smooth and consistent. Perfect. Dahlia watched the muscles just visible under the freckled skin of their forearms, their flop of strawberry hair hanging over their eyes as they worked. It looked shiny and clean under the lights.

Of course Dahlia didn't have time to clean her station. She had two minutes and thirty seconds, exactly, to fill all of her pastry shells.

But she didn't want to be messy, sloppy Dahlia around London. She hated how much she didn't want that right now. Because ugh, why? Maybe she was a little messy. Who cared? What was wrong with her?

She glanced over at London with thirty seconds to go.

They were arranging nasturtium flowers along the edge of their tarts, bright and delicate and lovely.

Motherfucker.

By the time the clock ran out, Dahlia had filled eight tarts. She had plopped her assortment of berries right in the middle of each one, while London had elegantly placed them off-center. In all twenty of theirs. She was embarrassed beyond measure.

Tanner Tavish merely gave her a look when he got to their station. A look she deserved.

"Very nice, London." Tavish nodded. "Very nice indeed."

Dahlia could not wait for the cameras to turn off, to run to the restroom and scroll on her phone for cute pictures of puppies.

"Hey," London said, once the PAs gave the official signal, before she could run away to the digital comfort of floppy ears and soft fur. London wiped their hands on a dishcloth and turned to her, crossing their arms and bumping their hip against the table. Dahlia glanced at them quickly, noting, tragically, what a good look that lean was on them. "It's okay," they said gently. "We all have off mornings."

"Do we?" Dahlia snapped, grabbing one of London's picture-perfect tarts and chomping into it viciously before the crew came to whisk them away.

A corner of London's mouth turned up slowly. "Yes. We do." Then their mouth flattened and they cleared their throat. "Um. How was your weekend?"

Dahlia swallowed down the rest of the delectable tart and looked down.

"It was fine."

She closed her eyes briefly. She hated this, how awkward this felt. Her toes itched, wanting to run away more than ever. But if she wanted things to get back to normal between them, she had to try. So even though she didn't feel like it, Dahlia forced more details out of her mouth.

"I went to Venice Beach on Saturday. It was really crowded and smelled bad. I loved it."

London smiled fully at that.

"I went to the Griffith Observatory, walked around," they said. "I tried going down this trail that leads to the Hollywood sign."

Dahlia brightened a bit. She looked at them for real this time.

"Really? That's on my list. Was it amazing, seeing the sign up close?"

"I don't know. The trail was dusty and hot, and crowded as hell. I turned back after like a quarter mile."

Dahlia grinned. "You could hardly move on Venice Beach, there were so many people. You would have hated it."

London smiled back. "Probably." A pause. "Any time you want to use my rental car, on weekends or days off or whatever, you can. Just text me."

Dahlia hesitated. "Isn't that against your rental agreement?"

London shrugged and pushed off from the table.

"Consider us reckless rule breakers, Dahlia." They gave another small smile and walked away.

Dahlia ate another tart, one of her own. It might have been ugly, but it still tasted good.

It helped, just slightly, to cover the taste left in her mouth at the idea of driving London's car around Los Angeles, alone, without them.

And then she sat in a corner and looked at Twitter. It was full of people who were cooler than her, being more hip and charming than her, explaining news she felt guilty for not knowing enough about. She felt a little bit worse with each passing minute, but she kept scrolling anyway.

They were called back to their stations. Before the cameras started rolling, before Sai Patel revealed what the secret ingredient for their Ingredient Innovation would be today, Barbara reached over and squeezed her hand.

"You okay today, Dahlia?"

Dahlia looked down at their intertwined hands, at Barbara's fingers, weathered yet soft, clutching hers so confidently.

She didn't know why she had been so hurt by London's rejection on the beach. She just thought...Barbara had said...but no. She felt the way London had kissed her back. She knew the way they looked at her. Or, the way they had looked at her before today. Dahlia knew she hadn't made up the attraction between them, even if she had been slow on the uptake. Because apparently only ever dating one person for most of her life had made her inept at understanding flirtation.

Somehow, though, being slow on the uptake made it hurt worse. Because when it *had* hit her—how right it felt kissing London on that beach, how as soon as she did it, she understood she had wanted to do it for a long time—it was like a gut punch. All encompassing, shocking, air stealing.

It felt awful to know that London was right, that nothing about going beyond that kiss was a good idea, even if every cell in her body wanted to rebel against it. It was a bad idea because, like London said, they could get kicked off the show at any time.

As soon as tomorrow, in fact, Dahlia reminded herself.

There was another Elimination Challenge tomorrow. No matter how comfortable she had started to feel here, nothing was guaranteed.

But even beyond elimination, beyond the show… the truth was that London was an exceedingly stable person. A good person with goals and talents. They loved Nashville, a place Dahlia had never been or even seriously contemplated visiting, and they had no desire to leave it. They had a cool-sounding job they enjoyed. They were going to start a nonprofit that could potentially change lives, really make a difference. They had family and friends. London had a future.

Dahlia had a boring apartment in a soulless building in an average suburban town, the rent on which she had no idea how she was going to pay next month if she didn't win $100,000. She had credit cards with maxed-out balances and too-high APRs. Not only did Dahlia not have a job, but she had no idea what kind of job she wanted, or would start looking for, when she got back home. She had a dorky dad and a sweet brother who lived hundreds of miles away, who she didn't visit enough. She had a mom who was disappointed in her, who Dahlia didn't know how to talk to anymore. She wasn't even sure if she had friends.

Dahlia was a mess, and London deserved so much better.

Dahlia looked down at Barbara's hand in hers, tried to remember what Barbara had asked. Oh. Right. If she was okay.

"No," she said quietly. Because she always felt safe telling Barbara the truth.

"That's okay, love," Barbara said after a minute. "It's okay to not be okay sometimes."

Dahlia didn't let go of her hand until a PA gave the signal, and the cameras turned on once again.

London had never felt gratitude quite as pure as when Tanner Tavish announced the Elimination Challenge the next day.

Soufflés. One chocolate, one cheese. That was all they had to do. No embellishments or creative personalization. Just a couple of soufflés.

Soufflés made perfect sense to London. Egg yolks and egg whites. Melted chocolate; béchamel. Stiff peaks and folds. This might even be a short filming day. People were intimidated by soufflés, for some reason, but they were really quite simple. They were much simpler than, say, figuring out how to handle their heart around Dahlia Woodson.

On set yesterday, they focused harder on the challenges than they ever had before. They planned on doing the same today, and the next day, and the day after that. And maybe off set, when London stared at the ceiling of their hotel room for hours on end and thought about Dahlia, standing in front of them in her underwear on a lonely stretch of paradise, or Dahlia, dancing in that black dress on a sweaty dance floor, or Dahlia, cooing over godforsaken cows that she had named Margaret—well, maybe they would eventually drive themself mad.

But on set, that misery might just drive London to a focus so steadfast they would have to win the $100,000. Which was what they had flown to LA to do.

So all in all, an even trade.

Halfway through the cooking time today, though, that focus was interrupted by a panic-stricken whirl of dark hair.

"I don't know what I'm doing wrong." She was turned around to face them, her hands gripping the sides of London's station, her face twisted. London felt a strange sort of relief that she was turning to them for advice at all. Even if she looked miserable. She had asked for their advice on set all the time, pre-Malibu, and this was the first moment since then that actually felt normal. "They're hardly rising at all."

"You didn't mix the egg whites in too much, right? You just folded?"

"Yes, London, I fucking folded," Dahlia hissed, moving her hands to her hips, staring anxiously back at her oven, and London had to bite back a smile. Now *that* felt normal. Dahlia cursing at them felt absolutely fantastic.

"You still have time," they said. "Do as many ramekins as you can; they don't all have to be perfect."

"What if none of them are perfect?" Dahlia distractedly blew a stray hair out of her face. There was a streak of flour on her cheek. "Yours are going to be perfect." She was freaking out.

London hesitated. Then they reached over their station and put a hand on her forearm. They only kept it there for a second. Still, they felt it, the feel of her skin under their fingers, tingling all the way to their scalp.

"You'll be okay."

Dahlia stared at where London had placed their hand. And then she said, "Okay," and turned back around. London swallowed.

Dahlia wasn't okay. And both she and London knew it.

Typically, the timed cooking portion of each challenge

flew by. It was the judging that followed that took entirely too long, especially during Elimination Challenges. That was where all the dramatics came in, where things were shot and reshot to look exactly right. But today, every second of watching Sai Patel's furrowed brow, Audra Carnegie's concerned eyes, and Tanner Tavish's peevish face blurred by in London's anxiety-riddled mind.

London's body brought their soufflés up to the judges, but it was like their mind was stuck in a wind tunnel. They could barely hear what the judges said, although they thought they were smiling.

When it was Dahlia's turn to bring up her soufflés, their smiles disappeared.

That was when London truly started to panic.

This must have been how Dahlia felt when London had nearly been kicked off with those horrible ravioli. Maybe, if Dahlia got kicked off, they could volunteer to get kicked off instead. Just a little switcheroo. Like Katniss in *The Hunger Games*. That was acceptable, right? That could happen? God, what had been Katniss's sister's name again? Why hadn't London tried out for the Hunger Games instead of this? *Chef's Special* was the worst.

London realized, as the judges huddled together for their fake deliberations, that they were losing control of their thoughts. They needed to focus. They needed to—

London, Ahmed, and Khari were called to the Golden Circle.

Top three.

"Congratulations, London." Audra smiled at them. "Another stellar performance."

Ahmed cuffed them on the shoulder with a grin.

London's mouth tasted like chalk.

Tanner Tavish announced the bottom three.

Dahlia, Barbara, and Cath.

The top and bottom three switched places, and London could only watch with dread.

They were all such excellent cooks, Dahlia and Barbara and Cath. It didn't make sense. What had happened? Maybe there was something wrong with the power in Barbara and Dahlia's station, something haywire with their stoves—

Cath was saved. She walked back to her station, puffing out her cheeks on a deep sigh.

Barbara and Dahlia remained on the chopping block in that horrible, awful circle. They moved closer together, held hands. Barbara rested her head on Dahlia's shoulder.

As London gripped the edge of their countertop, they tried to recall what had happened to the contestants who had been sacked already. They walked off set and then...London never saw them again. The producers must really ship them off back home right away. It made sense. No reason to waste money on unnecessary hotel rooms.

Suddenly Barbara and Dahlia were hugging each other. They were crying. Wait. What the hell just happened? London hadn't heard what happened. They couldn't hear anything. Why were they so bad at existing right now? Numbly, they saw Barbara say something in Dahlia's ear, squeeze her arm, give a reassuring smile.

And then Dahlia walked back to her station. She didn't look at London. Her head remained down as Barbara walked off set.

But Dahlia was still at her station.

The cameras stopped rolling, but London's heart was still pounding. Dahlia was immediately called in for a solo interview, her shoulders tense as she walked away. Janet hustled over to London, told them to wait, that they'd be next.

They assumed Janet would ask about winning the challenge. But instead, when they were shuffled into the solo interview set—Dahlia had disappeared, and all London could think about was where she had gone—Janet asked instead what it felt like to see Barbara and Dahlia and Cath in the bottom three.

She asked about all of them, but London knew instinctively that Janet wanted to see their reaction to Dahlia. And then London knew that Janet knew. Maritza gave them a sad smile from behind the camera. They all knew.

London deserved an extra prize from *Chef's Special*, no matter when they ended up getting kicked off. They were making for some excellent TV, and they wanted to throw up.

London said a few words that were hopefully part of the English language, and then they ran out of the studio. They looked around wildly once the cool night air hit their lungs, like they were a detective in a TV show ready to jump over moving cars to find the criminal.

"Your girl took off a few minutes ago."

The voice was unmistakable. London twirled around to look at Cath, leaning against the building, dragging on a cigarette.

London hadn't smoked since they were a dumb teenager in high school, but suddenly nothing had ever looked so appealing.

"She's not my girl," London managed to say, willing their heart to beat less frantically, to look less pathetic in front of Cath, who was undeniably cool. They stared at the smoke curling expertly from her lips, trying to not think about Dahlia walking home alone. Without them.

Cath just raised her eyebrows and took another deep drag. She had on the backward baseball cap that always appeared as soon as filming was done, and the brim tapped against the concrete wall of the studio.

"All right," she said, not judgmental, necessarily, but kindly dubious.

London kept standing there like an idiot, suddenly desiring some wise butch lesbian advice from Cath. Or for her to smack them and tell them to stop being such an emotional basket case, or something.

After a moment, Cath said, "That hug she gave you the other day was so sweet it just about broke my goddamn heart."

London looked away then.

"She's never been with anyone like me before. And..." All the words fell away in their head, the reasoning that had seemed so solid on the beach. Or maybe it hadn't seemed solid then, either, but they knew it was at least rational. To not fall in love with someone on the set of a reality TV show. "Fuck, I don't know."

They could see Cath nod, out of the corner of their eye. "Yeah." Another quiet beat. "She seems like a good one, though. It was a tough day today. She and that old broad seemed close."

God, all London could think about was Dahlia, but of course Dahlia was going to be devastated about Barbara.

Cath clapped London roughly on the shoulder as she pushed herself away from the wall and ground her cigarette under her sneaker.

"Sometimes, you just gotta do what you gotta do. But listen...take care of yourself, all right?" She gave another nod and started to walk away.

London stood for a few moments longer, outside of the surprisingly boring façade of the studio, watching Cath go, breathing in and out as the daylight bled out of the sky.

And then they ran until they reached Dahlia's door.

CHAPTER TWELVE

Dahlia opened the door immediately, sighing a little. She said, "I was waiting for you."

"Dahlia." London took a step inside. Distantly, they heard the door click shut behind them. Dahlia's room was messier than theirs. They tried not to look at the discarded clothes, the books, the crumpled receipts. Tried not to imagine Dahlia stuffing everything back into her suitcase. "When I saw you up there today—"

London was out of breath from running over here, and they didn't know how to end this sentence. They paused, gaping like a fish, while Dahlia stood three feet away, hands in the back pockets of her shorts. Her eyes were soft and sad, and she wouldn't stop...*looking* at them. Like she was waiting for something. The air felt heavy in London's lungs, their hair prickling at the back of their neck.

"London," she said simply.

Their feet took a step closer to her of their own accord, as if pulled there by her voice, by her stare, and the rest of London was helpless to stop it.

They took one step more, closing the gap between them.

Dahlia looked up at them, imploring. London had gotten their breath back, but now it felt trapped in their throat. Was this what they had wanted to happen, when they ran over here? They no longer knew. Or maybe there had never been a plan. There had only been panic, and now there was only Dahlia's face.

"Please," she whispered.

London cupped her face in their hands, ran a thumb down her cheek. She closed her eyes, leaning into their palm, and released a sigh that was so small and vulnerable it cracked whatever defenses London still possessed.

They kissed her.

There was no roar of the ocean here, no wind whipping at their faces, no salt in the air. There was nothing to detract from the realness of her, the taste of her, the noises of relief and want in her mouth.

After a precious moment of tenderness, Dahlia kissed London back with an intensity that surprised them, that almost knocked them over, and they steeled themself against her. She pushed her tongue into their mouth at the same time that she brought her hands to their neck, squeezing against their throat.

London's heart roared, but their mind quieted.

Dahlia's body leaned fully into theirs with another little sigh of heat and need, and London dropped their arms to sneak around her back, to press into the base of her spine, to press her closer, closer, until there was nowhere else to go. The coconut smell of her hair filled their senses; they could not imagine breathing air without it.

Then, suddenly, that irritating, instinctual alarm in London's brain went off again, forcing them to step back, disentangling limbs, inhaling fresh air into their lungs, whipping their hands away from Dahlia to rub their own temples instead.

"Wait," they said.

London was so very tired of breaking away from kisses with Dahlia. It was starting to feel like a horrible habit.

"You're upset. It was an upsetting day. We need to talk, to—"

"London." Dahlia stepped toward them again. "No. This isn't just about today. Don't tell me how I feel. Okay?"

She brushed the back of her hand against their cheek, and it reverberated down to London's fingertips. She bit her lip, looking like she wanted to say more. London wanted to trust her, more than anything else they'd ever wanted. They wanted to give in.

Dahlia stepped back and took off her shirt.

"God, Dahlia." London curled their fingernails into their palms. "You keep doing that."

She was wearing a necklace, a thin chain attached to a solid gold bar. London blinked at it, resting above her lavender bra. It heaved slightly, in rhythm with her breathing. She was staring at them with determination now. God, she was gorgeous.

"Wait," London said again, but their blood was thrumming so loudly in their ears they could hardly hear themself. They desperately thought of the notes on their phone. They had made a list, on Sunday night when they couldn't sleep, of things they didn't know about her. It had felt like a particularly sad exercise at the time, but it seemed important now. They didn't want whatever was going to happen to be impulsive and fleeting. They wanted to be grounded in her.

"Dahlia. What's your favorite movie?"

"What?" She frowned.

"Your favorite movie. What is it?"

Dahlia shook her head and moved toward them again. She put her hands on London's hips. Pressed fingers into the soft, lumpy skin there they hated, before she leaned in and nipped at their neck. Jesus, her teeth. London felt their skin heating, becoming hypersensitive.

"I hate those kinds of questions. I can never think of a favorite anything. Too much pressure," she said.

"Except for Rice Krispies treats."

She laughed, her breath floating over their ear. "Yes. Never any question on that."

London swallowed. They attempted one last valiant effort.

"Okay. Favorite song."

Dahlia groaned, and the noise was too much for London. Their arms returned to the small of her back like they belonged there. Their thumbs rubbed circles on her now-bare sides, her skin so smooth under their calloused hands, and they felt her shiver, even as she opened her mouth to protest.

"That question is even worse, and you know it. It depends! Genre? Time period? Mood?"

London tilted their face, sank their nose into her hair. They did know it. They were being ridiculous. She was answering the question exactly as they would.

But as she talked, her body was loosening, the real Dahlia returning in her voice, and London settled along with it. This wasn't just scared, vulnerable Dahlia, but the one who talked too much, who made London laugh, who didn't hide when she was annoyed with them.

"But," she added, her body giving a slight jerk as London's fingertips made their way around to her stomach, "if we are being purely objective, Fleetwood Mac's 'The Chain' is probably the best song ever written."

London paused. "Hm," they mumbled into her hair.

"Is that not a cool answer? I should probably note that my dad raised me on a pretty steady stream of seventies rock and seventies rock alone, so I don't really know if—"

"No," London interrupted, pulling back to look at her face. "It's perfect. You're perfect."

Dahlia rolled her eyes and shoved London lightly on the shoulder. "Shut up."

"You shut up," London said, smiling now. They pulled her closer again. They rolled a thumb over her nipple, through the sheer fabric of her bra, and she made a whimpering sound, her head falling forward.

London felt her hands slide under their T-shirt, inch up their back, touching skin no one else had touched in years.

"Is this okay?" she asked quietly. "Is there anywhere I can't touch you?"

London's eyes floated closed. "No. You can touch me anywhere. But, Dahlia..."

London searched for self-control one last time. They knew her first kiss hadn't been out of pity for them, that this, tonight, wasn't out of pity for herself. They knew that. That this was simply what Dahlia wanted.

But London also knew that if this happened, they would be all in. They wouldn't be able to be casual about it. They wouldn't be able to say goodbye to her—tomorrow, whenever they got kicked off the show, ever.

Dahlia brought her hands to London's face. Made sure they were looking her in the eye.

"I need you. Okay? And I need you to need me back."

London sucked in a breath.

"You have no idea," they said.

"Then okay."

She kissed them, hungry, hard, wet, and London let themself go. It felt like a physical release, letting go, something they had to work for, but they did it. They forgot about the notes on their phone. They pushed *Chef's Special* out of their brain. The only thing that mattered, they decided, was this human in front of them, her skin, her hair, her very big life that she was, miraculously, letting them be a part of.

London's mouth traveled to Dahlia's neck, sucking, licking, chasing those sounds in her throat, wanting to feel them against their lips. Their fingers returned to her nipples, pinching harder, and she rewarded them by pushing her pelvis into theirs and releasing a gasp that went straight to London's gut.

In a smooth motion, London unhooked Dahlia's bra, slid the straps down her shoulders, and gently, finally, pushed her onto the bed.

London was starting to feel heady now. Some part of their brain told them to slow down, but as they followed her onto the bed, knees straddling her thighs, her peaked nipples called to them. The way her body writhed when London took them into their mouth was addicting. She was so reactive to everything; it made London feel like a magician. A thrill licked through them at the curse she released when they engaged the slightest pressure of teeth against the puckered, sensitive skin.

London's hands tracked down her sides as their mouth

worked. They heard the uptick in Dahlia's breathing, sensed the slight arching of her back with each touch. They felt almost disconcertingly wild with power.

At length, London backed away to take a breath, to study her, take her in. She stared back, eyelids heavy and dark.

"Seriously, though," London said, lightly trailing fingertips down her belly. "You're perfect."

Dahlia froze. After a second, she propped herself up on her elbows. Her eyes cleared.

"I had really bad acne in middle school. I still have scars, all over." She motioned to her face. "Not perfect."

London's frown matched hers. They leaned in to examine Dahlia's face, to show her they weren't being dismissive. There was some scarring. Maybe they had noticed it before. Maybe they didn't care.

London shook their head. "Still looks pretty fucking perfect to me."

Dahlia growled in frustration. She flopped back down on her back, smacked a closed fist against her hip.

"Don't do that."

London crawled farther onto the bed, resting at her side.

"Do what? I'm not lying. You really are perfect to me."

"Perfect isn't real," Dahlia said, exasperated. She turned to face them. "I don't want to be perfect, because I know I'm not. I want this"—she touched London's chest—"to be real."

London stared at her for a beat. They had never looked at Dahlia's eyes this close up before. They tried to stop their brain from categorizing them as perfect. They failed.

London wondered what *real* meant for her, how it was even a question that this was.

They knew Dahlia hadn't been with anyone other than David. That being with someone else was probably scary, or strange. Maybe...maybe she'd thought things were perfect with David, until they weren't, so now she didn't trust perfect anymore.

But Dahlia had to know this was real.

London needed to convince her, they decided, how real this was.

London stood up from the bed and removed, as rapidly as possible, every single item of their clothing.

Dahlia returned to her back, propped up on her elbows, and watched, a slightly amused yet attentive look overtaking the uncertainty that had been on her face.

"You are very not perfect," she said when London was naked in front of her. "And I like you very much."

London had been about to leap onto the bed and rip off Dahlia's shorts—the removing of their own clothing was meant to be efficient, not a striptease—but suddenly they stopped. They comprehended Dahlia staring at them, studying them, what they had just done. They had been so focused on Dahlia, on what she was feeling and what she needed that it was like their brain went to another dimension, and now...oh. Now they froze, self-consciousness crashing back on them like a wave.

This was it. This was possibly why they had not slept with anyone since they came out. If Dahlia was scared to do this, she had no idea what scared was. They were baring their body to her, this body that had never felt quite right London's entire life.

But it felt better now, due to time and education. Internet friends. Courage and testosterone.

And maybe, London realized, they hadn't wanted to share that with anyone but themself.

They knew their clothes didn't exactly hide the way they looked underneath, that Dahlia shouldn't be surprised by anything she was seeing now. A binder only did so much. But there was still this fear, pounding in London's temple, that things would be different now. That Dahlia would see them differently.

"Hey," Dahlia said softly, moving to kneel at the edge of the bed, the amused look on her face gone. "You okay?"

London managed a nod, their throat dry.

Dahlia looked at them a moment longer, but she was only looking at their face this time.

"Is it okay if I tell you what I like most?" she asked quietly.

London met her eyes and attempted a small smile, trying to act normal. "All my imperfect things?"

She nodded seriously. "Yes."

London swallowed. And eventually, they nodded back.

"These patches of freckles." Dahlia reached out both hands to smooth over London's shoulders. "To die for." She ran her hands, flat and smooth, touching London from palm to fingertip, across their collarbone and down the middle of their chest. "And I like this."

London glanced down to where her hands rested. They suppressed a grunt.

"You like my pudgy stomach? I call bullshit."

"Yes. Although I don't like the word *pudgy*." She tickled her fingertips over it, and London sucked in a breath. "It's soft and lovely. This whole area, really—" Dahlia grabbed London around the hips with surprising aggression, "it's like, *mmmph*. Meaty and strong and I *like it*."

London stared at her, not knowing how to respond to any of this.

"And then, of course, there's your face." Dahlia lifted her hands from London's sides to gesture randomly in the air. "And I can hardly even talk about your forearms." Dahlia flopped herself back onto the bed, flinging her arms out to the sides dramatically. "They are ridiculous."

This broke the spell.

London knelt at the foot of the bed, blushing, and picked up one of Dahlia's petite feet. "Meaty," they repeated before bringing the foot to their mouth and kissing her arch, fingers kneading her heel.

"Is that not an acceptable descriptor? I said I liked it."

Dahlia looked down at London caressing her feet for a moment before closing her eyes, her hands absently touching her stomach. She liked this. London liked that she liked this.

"It is…interesting," London said. "Imperfect and meaty. There are better descriptors, probably."

They brought her big toe into their mouth.

"Fine," she said, breath hitching. "You are very much sexy, and I am incredibly attracted to you. Better?"

London picked up her other foot. "Yes."

"Boring," Dahlia muttered.

When London moved on to her ankles and a happy hum escaped her lips, they grinned.

And as they inched onto the bed again, between her legs, as their mouth and hands moved up to her knees, her thighs, as they unbuttoned her shorts, as they slid off her underwear, London did slow down. They let themself truly absorb all of this.

Because they realized that maybe they had still been unsure. Not about how they felt about Dahlia, but about how Dahlia felt about them. That kiss on the beach had been… spectacular. But even a legendary kiss was different from this, from bare, awkward bodies—London's body—from skin on skin in a quiet room.

London was in the habit of trusting people when they told you who they were. They hoped, one day, the universe would extend this courtesy back to them, or at least for the next generation. That one day people could just say *This is who I am* and not be greeted with disbelieving puffs of breath, with *What do you mean?*

So they trusted that Dahlia was queer.

But the fact that she had only been with David…London knew, as they pressed kisses onto Dahlia's stomach, as they moved their mouth to her breasts again, that they had still been paranoid about being an experiment. Part of London had been worried that if it came to this, this level of closeness and reality, she'd change her mind. She would be embarrassed, and feel guilty about it, but London would accept it, and then it'd be over.

But every noise Dahlia released, every shiver of her body was an affirmation. London kissed the shiny smooth spaces underneath her breasts, ran their hands down her sides. And as Dahlia's breathing grew heavier again, as she said, "Oh," and "Fuck, London," and traced her hands over their back, they let themself believe it fully. That she hadn't blinked when London had disrobed in front of her. That she wasn't just trying to be cute when she listed the parts she liked. That she didn't see them differently now.

That Dahlia had, in fact, always seen them for exactly who they were.

And that she wanted them.

London dragged their lips to her neck, moving aside her thick hair for better access.

"Oh," she said, her voice sounding deliciously drugged. "I meant to ask." She cleared her throat, blinking, and struggled to sit up. London pulled back. "I know my hair is like, a thing for you."

"Well," London said, almost wanting to laugh at being called out like this, "it is rather inescapable."

"So do you want it up or down for this?"

London looked at her. Dahlia stared steadily back, and her eyes were bright. Happy. Not uncertain or embarrassed at all.

"Up," London decided finally. "Better access to your neck."

Dahlia reached for the elastic on her wrist.

"God." Heat pooled in London's stomach as Dahlia's fingers worked through the dark strands, arms moving over her head. Her forearms weren't bad, either. "I love watching you do this."

Dahlia glanced at them as she finished the final few twists of her wrist.

"You love watching me put my hair up?"

"Yes," London said solemnly. "You normally do it fifteen minutes into a challenge, on set." They leaned forward to speak into her ear. "It turns me on every time."

Dahlia exhaled a breath that London thought might have been a laugh, but that ended up sounding like a strangled, high-pitched wheeze instead.

London moved their lips back to her neck, but Dahlia pushed them back again, lightly, her fingers pushing into their shoulders.

"Okay, wait." Smiling, she licked her lips and took a steadying breath. She wiggled her hips, sat up straighter. "So what would happen if, say, one day I happen to wear a particularly faulty elastic, and after I put it up, this happens?" Dahlia yanked out the elastic suddenly, and her mane cascaded around her shoulders again. "And then," she said dramatically, enjoying this, "I'll just have to try again, and—"

Her attempt to sweep up her hair again was interrupted by London pushing her back onto the bed.

"You," they whispered into her lips, "are a very not-nice person."

They pinched her nipple and kissed her jaw and her smirk turned into a whimper.

So it turned out Dahlia's hair stayed down after all.

They kissed her again, fervent and lazy all at once, and London felt now like they had never quite belonged anywhere as much as they belonged right here, with their tongue in Dahlia Woodson's mouth, their body fully on top of hers. Dahlia's fingernails ghosted up and down their back, lightly at first and then pressing harder as the kiss deepened. London loved it, the undeniable sharpness of it, the slightest hint of pain.

When Dahlia wrapped a leg around one of their own, London stopped thinking completely. There was no teasing now, no more questions. London wanted to feel all of her. They wanted to make her come undone.

They kissed down her neck to her collarbone. Her skin was

heated, tacky. They shifted themself to move further down her body.

"Wait," Dahlia said. London paused to look up at her. "Come back." She motioned vaguely but urgently, and the breathlessness in her voice made London comply immediately.

London spoke into her ear again, gently this time.

"I was hoping to go down on you. Do you not like that? It's fine if you don't, of course, but"—they kissed the skin just under her earlobe—"I am very good at it."

Dahlia released a noise in her throat that London couldn't interpret.

"Next time. I just…I want you here."

She wrapped her arms around London and pressed them even tighter into herself, to demonstrate. London let their weight fall fully onto her chest, providing the pressure and closeness she needed, letting the words *next time next time next time* sink into their skin.

They had to lift themself slightly, though, to slink a hand between their bodies and between her legs.

"Fuck." Dahlia said this so loudly that London stopped again to look at her in concern. Had the touch been too sudden? They thought they'd been gentle, but maybe she needed more warning? "Sorry," she said. Her neck flushed as she bit her lip. "You just touched like, the exact right spot right away. Jesus."

Well. London could work with that.

They maintained eye contact as their hand reconnected with this exact right spot, warmth spreading through their gut as they watched her pupils dilate, her focus growing hazy.

"So this is real enough for you, then?" London tried not to sound too smug.

"Fuck you," Dahlia managed to say before she broke their stare, leaning her head back into the pillow. Her eyes closed as London's hand started to move in a wider circle. A second later she added, more softly, "Yes."

London tried to keep as much of their skin pressed firmly against Dahlia's as possible, as she wished, while their hand found its rhythm. "Is this okay?" they asked, their fingers sliding further down her folds.

"Yes. Uh-huh. Please," she breathed, eyes still closed, and London smiled into her shoulder. Carefully, slowly, they moved their middle finger inside her, her hips shifting forward as they sank in to the knuckle. Their mouth dropped back to her sternum, tongue tasting everywhere it could reach while their finger worked deeper inside of her, the base of their palm rubbing against her clit.

"Can I do more?" they asked.

"Huh?" Dahlia's eyes flitted open but just barely, her voice scratchy and confused, like London had asked her a question in a language she didn't understand. God, she was breathing hard. God, London felt good.

They spoke more deliberately this time.

"Can I put another finger inside of you, Dahlia?"

"Oh." Her eyes closed again, and she licked her lips. "Oh. Um. No. No, that's all right. This is good."

London smiled, drawing back their finger before plunging it in again, applying more pressure on her clit. "Just good?"

She groaned. *"London."* London angled their finger upward, biting lightly on her shoulder, and she whimpered and said, "You are the worst," followed almost immediately by *"Oh,* that feels so good," and London felt like they were flying.

She didn't form many coherent phrases after that, but nothing had ever mattered to London like the noises Dahlia was making right now. The first time London had ever had sex, they had been practically silent, embarrassed by the feelings and sensations, but Dahlia didn't hold anything back, and that was the sexiest thing they had ever experienced. They felt like her gasps and moans were a part of them, that her sighs rushed through their own lungs. They felt every single blessed sound between their legs.

London knew she was close, her walls squeezing in on their finger, her leg clenched around London's thigh. Her brow was furrowed, her jaw clenched almost like she was in pain.

"Dahlia," they breathed, increasing the speed of their hand, the essence of everything good in this world spinning on their fingers, in the space between Dahlia's ragged breaths.

And then she was suddenly silent, silent and shaking, mouth open, hands clutching at their back. London watched her face in awe, damp and wild looking and still so devastatingly pretty.

They were both still as Dahlia calmed, foreheads together, their chests rising and falling. Slowly, London removed their finger. She whimpered once more and then weakly pushed them away, laying an arm over her eyes.

"I...I didn't..." she started to say, but as London moved their weight to her side, giving both of them more space to breathe, she never finished her sentence.

"You okay?" London asked softly, running a hand over her stomach.

Dahlia didn't answer, or move her arm. London started to get concerned. They wanted to see her eyes. They watched her breathing, attempting to be patient. Her hair splayed across the pillow, small dark strands pasted to her neck.

Finally, she removed her arm. She stared at the ceiling.

"You were so good at that," she said. "What if I'm not good at touching you?"

London reached out and took one of her hands. They brought it in between their legs, sighing when Dahlia's fingers reached their destination.

"Dahlia," they said, "no matter how you touch me, I'm going to come in approximately thirty seconds."

That made her smile at least. She turned on her side, so they were face-to-face.

"But you like it like this," she said softly, her fingers moving beneath London's instructive hand. They lifted one leg to lay on top of her thigh, to open themself more for her.

"Yes," London said, and they contemplated taking away their hand, to let her take over. But then they didn't.

They liked this, telling Dahlia's fingers where to go, feeling her feeling them. They liked being in control.

When they looked at her, their faces inches apart, she was staring down at their joined hands, and London's skin prickled with the awareness of being studied again. After a moment, she looked up to meet their gaze.

"Hi," she said, and it made London laugh, but only for a second, because their lungs didn't have room for it, their airways already overwhelmed by the other sensations racing through their body. Maybe it would take them more than thirty seconds to come, but it wouldn't be long. They felt weightless, a simple animal paired with another, all warmth and need and instinct.

It really had been so long since someone had touched them. They had thought it could only ever be a fantasy that the someone could be Dahlia.

London kept eye contact for as long as they could while their fingers moved together, until they felt the pressure building and they had to close their eyes, forehead pushing forward into Dahlia's again. They dimly heard her whispering encouragements, *I got you, I got you,* that were so earnestly sweet London's heart felt drunk with them, even though part of them wanted to laugh and protest, *actually we got me,* and then they were truly gone, their brain frozen, their insides spasming. With a final, dizzy gasp, they held her hand tight and still against them for as long as they could stand it before releasing her fingers, their leg falling from her thigh, rolling onto their back to fill their lungs with air.

London wasn't sure, exactly, how many seconds or minutes passed while they caught their breath. Eventually, they gathered together enough pieces of shattered consciousness to turn their head to see Dahlia, still on her side, a hand under her head, watching them. She smiled and ran her fingers through London's hair, smoothed it off their forehead again and again.

"Thank you," she whispered.

London closed their eyes as Dahlia's fingers ran down their cheek. Their limbs felt heavy, their muscles deeply relaxed, their mind already slipping into darkness.

They let Dahlia Woodson cradle their face as they fell asleep, felt her stomach settle against their arm as she cuddled in closer, and at least right then, in that moment, both of their bodies felt, if not perfect, then real, wonderfully so. London's and Dahlia's bodies were meaty and scarred and warm, and they leaned against each other: just right, exactly how they were supposed to be.

CHAPTER THIRTEEN

Dahlia woke up far before London, while the sky was still dark.

She stared at them, how their eyelids twitched occasionally, their eyelashes brushing against their freckled cheeks, which looked ghostly in the dim light. She listened to the steady cadence of their breathing, smelled their skin, stared at their slightly open lips.

And then she started to feel creepy about it and flopped over to pick up her phone from her shorts, crumpled next to the bed.

Dahlia looked through Instagram blankly, liking every single post, even the boring ones, even the ones she probably shouldn't be liking, from people she probably shouldn't be following anymore, that she should have cut off after the divorce like they had cut her off. She imagined them looking at their phone in surprise when they saw her likes, pinging in at this ungodly hour. Dahlia wondered how many of them even knew she was here, that she was on *Chef's Special*.

No, of course they would know. That kind of gossip wouldn't go unheard. She wondered what their old friends were saying.

Yeah, she left David high and dry, and now she's flaunting herself on national TV? Seriously. The audacity.

Dahlia threw her phone onto the bed. She watched the sky begin to lighten through the gauzy white curtains. She contemplated getting up, taking a shower. But she didn't want London to wake up and think she had left them. She wanted to be there when London woke up.

She looked over at them, still so silent and content and innocent looking, and she held back a scream, fisting her hands in her hair.

She had had sex with London Parker for two reasons.

One: She had wanted to. She had really, really wanted to. And LA Dahlia did what she wanted.

Two: She'd had a horrible day on set, and she thought sex would make her feel better.

It had, she supposed. She certainly didn't give a fuck about soufflés anymore.

Now Dahlia just gave far too many fucks about everything else.

When she thought of the kiss on the beach, when she thought about the way she caught London looking at her sometimes, she had thought the sex would be fast and dirty. Raw and satisfying. She hadn't anticipated that London would kiss every single inch of her, slow and studious.

Although in hindsight, of course she should have anticipated this. She'd seen London cook. She knew how attentive, how detail-oriented they were.

And of course sex would mean a lot to London, too. They had just told her they hadn't slept with anyone since they came out as nonbinary. The look on their face, when they got undressed in front of her. She had wanted to wrap herself around them forever. Was she even worthy of that kind of trust?

No. She wasn't. She knew that intrinsically.

Dahlia curled up on her side, staring at her messy room. At London's soft T-shirt, thrown across the arm of a chair. She loved London's T-shirts.

God. She slapped a hand to her face. They were literally just plain T-shirts. They were probably nice, expensive T-shirts, not the $5 Target specials she wore, but still. What was wrong with her?

What was wrong with her was that she hadn't expected the sex to unhinge her so completely. Just thinking about it sent a rush of heat between her legs. It was barely six a.m. and she was completely turned on. She wanted to shake sleeping angel London awake so she could jump on top of them, say "Hey, you can go down on me now," and then bite their freckled shoulder.

She squeezed her eyes closed and tried to take a yoga breath.

Sex with David had been exciting back in high school and college. Or at least, she was sure it must have been. But ever since they got married, started jobs, jumped headlong into their adult lives...she couldn't remember exactly when it had stopped being good. They were just so *tired* most of the time, after long days at work and long commutes. They still had sex, sometimes, although increasingly less as time went on.

For the last year especially, when their fighting was at its worst, sex almost made Dahlia cry. Because the sex wasn't giving David what he wanted. She wondered if he even wanted it anymore, or if the act only reinforced his disappointment. It was all she could think about the last few times. *I am sorry*

I can't let your sperm penetrate one of my eggs and implant on my uterine wall. She began to think of her body as a vessel, full of emptiness and pain, one she had chosen to hijack from the world. It might be an empty vessel, but it was hers.

Surely she hadn't completely forgotten that sex could simply be about pleasure, right?

There had certainly been no toe sucking with David. Or nipple pinching, or neck licking. Every second that London was touching her clit, or slipping their finger in and out of her, they were touching something else, kissing her somewhere else, and it made everything feel so much more intense, like firecrackers going off all over the place until her body lost track, and all she could think was *Oh yeah, this is why people like sex* and *God, how can one solitary digit feel so good in there* and *Why is this person being so nice to me* and *I think I forgot I have so much skin* and *Fuck fuck fucking fuck.*

And when London had held on to her hand while they got off, holding her to them ... it was surprisingly sexy. David always pulled away when he came; she liked how London had leaned into her instead, pressed their foreheads together, so that she witnessed every emotion on their face, inhaled their breath. She wanted them to guide her hand all over their body so she could learn every funny spot that felt good.

Every single thing about last night had been different from anything she'd ever experienced: softer, hotter, more tender. It wasn't just pleasure; it was ... closeness.

Of course, it was when Dahlia was ruminating on this that London woke up.

Which they did with a throaty groan. And if Dahlia wasn't already wet, well.

"Hello," Dahlia said, hoping this sounded like a normal hello, and not a you-have-fucked-me-all-the-way-up hello.

London rubbed their eyes before looking at her.

"Have you been awake for a while? You look awake."

"Maybe."

They stretched their arms above their head. "You are totally a morning person, aren't you."

"Maybe."

She totally was. Even though that wasn't why she'd woken up so early today.

London groaned again. "Of course you are." And they sounded so irritated that it delighted her right down to her toes, breaking her reverie, and she couldn't help it. She smiled so hard her cheeks hurt.

"What time is it?"

Dahlia glanced at the clock on the bedside table. "Ten to six."

London sat up. "Are you serious? Dahlia, we have to be on set at six fifteen! Dammit. I have to do my hair!"

London rolled out of bed, furiously tossing on clothes.

"You have to do your hair?" Dahlia repeated, trying to keep the laughter out of her voice.

"Yes."

"That's what they have hair and makeup for, on set."

"They don't do it right!" London shouted.

Now Dahlia did laugh.

"I hate you," London said, stepping into their pants.

"No, you don't."

"Yeah, that's true. Are you going to get dressed now, or what?"

Dahlia got dressed while London ran to their room so they could throw on fresh clothes too. When she stepped into the hall, London was waiting for her, looking harried and adorable, and they hustled to set, London holding Dahlia's hand the whole way.

Except that wasn't exactly right. London wasn't holding Dahlia's hand; they were *gripping* it, holding on for dear life. Like they were trying to tell her something.

They only dropped it when they opened the door to the studio. The moment Dahlia and London walked inside, Janet appeared in front of them.

"Dahlia Woodson, did you walk through a tornado on the way here?" She patted the top of the lumpy bun on Dahlia's head, frowning. "Hair and makeup, *stat*. And both of you"— she pointed at them in turn, giving a look over the rims of her glasses, tortoiseshell today—"if you make it a habit showing up late and disheveled like this, get ready for a PA to be stationed outside your doors with an airhorn at five o'clock sharp. Seriously. I have airhorns. I will use them."

Janet shook her head and turned around to stalk away, muttering, "I swear, nasty business, every single season," under her breath.

Dahlia had never felt more grateful to be scolded by Janet. It made her feel calm, somehow. She had to fight the urge to chase after her. Ask her to yell at her some more. Maybe, if she could arrange it, Janet could be a dear and dump some ice water over Dahlia's head.

Of course, Janet didn't do that, because life was cruel, but Dahlia still had a moment of peace at hair and makeup, away from the lust-and-feelings cloud of London Parker. It was only as Mack was yanking on her hair that she comprehended the last thing Janet had said as she'd walked away.

Nasty business. Every single season! *Oh my god.*

Who had been doing nasty business every other season?

Was it Chloe and John? From season five? Dahlia had always thought something was up with them. Or *wait*—Dahlia almost gasped out loud—was it Patrick and Tony, from last season? Their hatred for each other had been evident, but maybe that hatred was actually just *sexual tension.*

Dahlia had to talk to London about this.

It took Dahlia longer than it should have to remember why her cooking station felt so empty.

Barbara.

Dahlia had forgotten, momentarily, in her sex haze, that Barbara was gone.

"Finally." Janet appeared in front of her, staring down at her phone. "Y'all are ready. London, up here."

Dahlia's hands froze, halfway through tying her apron behind her back.

A beat passed. Janet looked up.

"Parker," she snapped, glaring beyond Dahlia's shoulder, and then pointed. "You're taking Barbara's spot. And make it snappy, for crying out loud."

Janet hustled away then, muttering under her breath. But before she left, her eyes caught Dahlia's, for just a second. And Dahlia saw it.

Janet was smiling.

Dahlia swallowed.

Her eyes remained focused on the station in front of her, her cutting board, her beautiful shiny knives, but she sensed London's presence next to her when they finally moved.

"Well," they said. "This is fine."

Dahlia allowed herself the briefest glance their way. London's jaw was tense.

"Right," Dahlia said, smoothing her hands down her apron. "Fine."

"I mean, it's fine that this isn't the station I've become used to cooking at for the last month," London continued. "And that I was just thrown up here without warning and my hair looks bad and now I can't stare at your butt when I'm anxious, and we're filming in like two seconds. Everything is great."

Dahlia looked over at them, a startled laugh caught halfway up her throat. But if London was freaking out, then Dahlia couldn't freak out. This was helpful.

"Your hair looks fine," she said. Because it literally looked the exact same as it always did. The morning she'd knocked at their door before their road trip to the ocean was the only time she'd ever seen it even slightly askew. And, well, last night when she'd swept it off their forehead, and it was sweaty and—

"Wait," she said. "You stared at my butt?"

"No, mostly your hair. I don't know why I just said your butt. I stared at your butt sometimes."

Dahlia shook her head, smiling.

"You can still stare at my butt if you want. Just tell me when you need it."

London let out a burst of nervous giggles, which was so

hilariously out of character, and Dahlia felt comforted that perhaps they were *both* losing their minds.

As the cameras started rolling, though, the lust-and-feelings fog settled hard around her again, every cell in her body aware of London next to her, their arms, their neck, their hips, their hands. She had consciously ignored Jacob's presence in the beginning of the competition; it was easier to focus that way. And then Barbara had been so nonintrusive, so pleasant, that cooking next to her had been a breeze.

But now all of Dahlia's brain power was attuned to making sure her elbow did not brush London's elbow. She barely heard the judges telling them about today's challenge. Until she remembered with a start that she'd almost gotten kicked off yesterday.

She blinked, grinding her teeth. She could get through this. She *had* to get through this. She refused to go home now.

Dahlia took out her tiny notebook from her back pocket, with its polka-dotted cover and weathered pages, as the six remaining contestants gathered around the familiar demonstration table that had been wheeled onto the Golden Circle. A large plucked raw chicken sat on top. London stood beside her as Tanner began his demonstration of how to properly break the chicken down. Their cotton T-shirt brushed against her arm, just so soft and wonderful, and seriously, didn't London want to go talk to Cath or something? Dahlia needed to focus.

And after a few minutes, she did. As Dahlia watched Tanner slice a boning knife with authority into the chicken's flesh and bones, instead of the panic and uncertainty that had flooded her during some of the first challenges, she now took notes and thought, *I can do that.*

And *that* was why she was here.

She was paired against Ahmed for the Face-Off, a perfectly neutral party. They smiled at each other before the timer began, and Dahlia felt okay. Or closer to okay. She took apart that chicken like a boss. Her hands were steady. She felt almost herself again, mind-blowing sex almost forgotten. Dahlia's deconstructed bird was clearly better than Ahmed's, and when all three judges confirmed it, her chest filled with pride.

"Dahlia, Cath, Khari—you'll find out your advantage before the Elimination Challenge." Audra smiled at them. "Now, get ready to take that confidence into the Ingredient Innovation."

When the cameras turned off for a break, Dahlia returned to her station. She had thrown her notebook on the counter and was getting ready to rinse her hands when London approached. They didn't say anything, but their hand brushed against hers before they wrapped their pinky around her pinky for a quick squeeze.

And then London kept walking without looking back.

Dahlia looked down at her feet, attempting to hide her dumb grin. Maybe she could do this, working next to them. Maybe she deserved a pinky squeeze after doing a good job.

The secret ingredient for the Ingredient Innovation today was passion fruit, "a very common and popular fruit in other countries, but less so in America," as Sai Patel explained. While Dahlia had consumed her fair share of passion fruit–flavored things, she had never worked with the fruit itself: a plum-colored shell with a surplus of seeds inside, covered in gelatinous bright orange pulp. It was, altogether, an extremely strange thing. Dahlia loved extremely strange things. They reminded you that Earth was full of surprises.

Dahlia leaned over the countertop before heading into the pantry, pen poised over her notebook. She decided to make a passion fruit coulis, because she had never made a coulis before. Maybe it would top some simple but decadent cheesecake cups, which would be easy to do in forty minutes. A crunch of crushed graham crackers on the bottom, creamy richness in the middle, the sweet but tart coulis on top. She had no idea if it would be too simple, but she already had an Elimination Challenge advantage. She would feel good about trying something new, at least.

But twenty minutes later, she was less sure.

The coulis *tasted* good, but was the consistency right? Should it be thicker?

She turned without thinking. "London." They looked up from their pile of passion fruit seeds. "Can you taste this?"

Dahlia held a spoonful of the coulis up to London's lips, her other hand balanced beneath to catch any falling drops.

London's eyes caught hers for just a second before they opened their mouth and accepted the spoon.

As soon as Dahlia's fingertips brushed London's lips, she realized her error.

Contestants were allowed to give each other advice. Tasting each other's food was acceptable.

But spoon feeding it to each other, so close your fingers brushed your competitor's lips, your other hand hovering dangerously close to your competitor's chin, tempting your thumb to run itself down your competitor's throat—well, that probably wasn't normal.

Dahlia lowered her hands away from London's face, blushing. London's eyes were steady on hers as they swallowed, and Dahlia felt helpless to do anything but stare at the muscles of their jaw, their throat, working in alluring ways. Slowly, unnecessarily, London brought out their tongue to swipe along their lip, damn them, and Dahlia felt her heartbeat thud behind her rib cage, the calm she'd worked all morning to achieve shattered once again.

It had felt so natural, to turn to London and ask for advice this way, to bring her spoon to their mouth. She had done it without thinking.

A vision swarmed into her mind. Her and London in a kitchen, a real one, not an industrial-sized one on a Burbank TV set. She pictured London's eyes on her as she pounded out fresh pasta dough. Flicking flour onto their nose. Bringing her wooden spoon out of her sauce to their tongue, again and again, for their approval.

They would eat the meal fresh, standing hip to hip by the kitchen island, while they drank wine straight from the bottle like they had done in the hotel courtyard that night. Dahlia would roll her eyes while London made fun of her sauvignon blanc, and she would call them pretentious for their overpriced pinot noir. There would be a window above the sink, fogged from the boiling water, and London would nuzzle the back of her neck while she did the dishes, slightly tipsy, occasionally splashing soapy water over her shoulder at them.

And after the dishes were done, London would push Dahlia up onto the counter, where she would hop happily, wrapping her arms around their neck and opening her legs and—

"I wouldn't change a thing."

Dahlia snapped her mouth shut. She hadn't realized it had been open. She brought her gaze up, away from London's lips, where she also hadn't realized she'd been staring, to their eyes, which were crinkled at the sides, barely containing a naughty grin.

"About the coulis," London supplied. "It's really great."

Dahlia swallowed. "Right. Thanks."

"Could I perhaps have a taste, too, Ms. Woodson?"

Dahlia almost stumbled backward at Tanner Tavish's booming voice, right beside her. When she looked over, she noticed the two cameras behind Tavish's shoulder, pointed straight at her.

"Of course." Dahlia twirled around and stepped back to her side of the station, cheeks flaming.

The cameras had probably filmed the whole interaction. They were standing so close to each other. Barbara's voice echoed in Dahlia's ear: *Ask anyone in this competition, and they'll tell you London wants to be more than Instagram friends with you. When episodes start airing, I bet folks at home will be able to see it, too.*

Dahlia wondered, briefly, if Janet had seen her nasty business hair this morning and hustled over to the rest of the production team to say, "You know what we should do? Move Parker up next to Woodson. Keep a close eye on those two, okay? The audience is going to eat that shit up."

Dahlia didn't want to believe Janet would do this.

But TV was a business, after all.

A wave of nausea rolled through her stomach.

Trying to ignore it, she returned to her coulis, back to the comfort of food and her own mind.

Her mind, which had just done a funny thing.

There were many nonsensical facets of the fantasy Dahlia had just had, before the cameras had ruined it. There was the fact that she and London were both currently living in a hotel, clearly lacking in cozy, steamy kitchens. And that when they did return to their respective kitchens, away from *Chef's Special*, one was very much in Nashville, while the other remained in Maryland. As they had established. As had been established, since the beginning.

And anyway, Dahlia had already proved she was spectacularly bad at domestic bliss. Had she learned nothing? The idea of letting down London like she had let down David—if London wanted domestic bliss, too—made her stomach sink into her toes like a stone.

Plus, they had slept together *once*. Her brain really must have been addled. She thought this morning she had just been overwhelmed by how good the sex was, but now here she was, mentally decorating their imaginary kitchen. She needed to calm the fuck down.

Except London, apparently, wasn't very calm either.

As soon as the crew called them off on a break after the cooking portion of the Ingredient Innovation was done, London waited until all the other contestants had walked off stage, toward craft services or the bathrooms, before grabbing Dahlia's hand and yanking her away into an alcove behind the solo interview set.

They pushed her against a wall, their hands running down her sides, forehead pressing into hers, and it was all very fast and surprising and awesome. No more covert pinky squeezes, then. Dahlia tried to hold in her quivery sigh at the sudden sensation of all of London pressed against all of her again.

"Tell me what you were thinking about earlier," London said, lips inches away from hers. "When you had me taste your coulis and your eyes went all glassy."

"I don't want to." Dahlia cringed at how childish this sounded.

London dipped their head to the side to suck on Dahlia's ear, while rolling their hips ever so slightly forward. *Fucking A, London.*

"Tell me." Their breath tickled her cheek.

Blood thundered in Dahlia's ears. She swallowed.

"You're very authoritative and sexy right now, you know that? Seriously, impressive stuff. A-plus work."

"Dahlia."

She tried to whisk the cooking-with-London-in-our-cozy-home daydream out of her mind, but honestly, London's whole deal right now was only enhancing it. The things they could do to her against that imaginary kitchen island…

"I was thinking about what we could do," Dahlia said after a moment, mind racing, "with food."

This was not technically a lie.

Even if the implication in her voice wasn't what had been in Dahlia's head at all.

But she was totally down with the implication that had just fallen out of her mouth, too, so, whatever. Nice save, brain.

London froze. "I'm going to need more details there, Woodson."

"Well. Whipped cream is a little cliché, right? So maybe something else."

London was quiet a moment.

"I don't know," they murmured into her hair. "If it's home-made whipped cream, it might be worth it."

Dahlia shook her head, feeling steadier now.

"Nah, that involves way too much whisking. I'd prefer you keep your wrist strength for other things."

A bolt of laughter exploded from London's throat, and Dahlia smiled, relaxing further. God, she loved making London laugh.

"Maybe honey. Or caramel," she said. "Except those would get pretty sticky, probably. We'd mess up the sheets."

"I'd say anything we're thinking about here is likely to get pretty messy, Dahlia. Luckily, we're living in a place that employs a housekeeping staff to help with that."

Dahlia frowned, pushing away a few centimeters.

"Is that kind of rude, though? Housekeepers have a hard enough job."

"They have to clean the sheets anyway."

"I guess so."

"Dahlia. What's your favorite fruit?"

"Blueberries," she said automatically. London laughed again. "What?" she asked defensively.

"I'm just picturing dumping a tub of blueberries over you and having them roll everywhere. Doesn't seem very... efficient. Name another fruit."

"Honeydew melon."

London considered. "We can work with that. Even though, Dahlia, that is a horrible fruit."

"Okay, Fancypants. What's your favorite fruit?"

"Nectarines."

"Oh. Good choice."

"I have very good taste."

Dahlia leaned up to kiss them just as the sounds of other contestants shuffling back to their stations hit their ears, too close.

"Want to take a trip to Vons after we're done filming?" London asked. "You can drive."

Dahlia took one of London's hands and planted a kiss on their palm. "It's a date."

CHAPTER FOURTEEN

L ondon dumped the Vons bags onto the small table in
their hotel room.

"So we should make a plan." They started unloading their
wares. Dahlia laughed.

"Is this the type of thing you plan? Shouldn't it be sort
of...spontaneous and messy?"

London tried not to feel annoyed. Dahlia was the one who
had implanted this whole idea into their heads, but she'd
spent half their trip to Vons giggling and blushing. Which
had been cute, on one hand, but London was also tired and
ready to get down to business.

And *obviously* the sex would be better if it was planned.

"Fine," they huffed, crossing their arms. "So where do we
start?"

Dahlia took out the can of whipped cream, popped off the
top, and squirted a stream straight into her mouth.

"Getting naked," she said, muffled through her full mouth
of sugar and chemicals.

She was truly insufferable. And dammit, London was
going to take off her shirt this time.

Funnily enough, their irritation faded with each item of clothing they shed. There were less nerves, less fuss this time, but if anything, the tension in London's body was even greater. They knew what she felt like now. Their body was already learning how to best crave it.

Having to stand next to her all day had been torture. The most exquisite kind of torture.

Within a few minutes, they were tangled around each other on the bed, knees and thighs pushing between the others', chest to chest, Dahlia's tongue so sweet in London's mouth. It was satisfying as hell to feel how slick she already was as she rubbed against them. They thought again about that look on her face when she'd asked them to taste that coulis, and they wondered, with a thrill of sensation prickling up their spine, if she had been this wet for them all day.

"Okay." They pulled away suddenly, before either of them got too far out of control, to grab the can she'd left on the bedside table. "Let's do this."

"Oh," Dahlia said, biting her lip. "We don't have to *actually*—I mean, is this—"

London interrupted by pressing down on the nozzle once, twice. Two perfect bursts of whipped cream for two perfect boobs.

She exploded in laughter and punched London in the arm. "Jesus."

"You're the one who didn't have a plan. This is my plan." They leaned down and licked one nipple clean. Even as they felt her stiffen, her breathing uptick slightly, she was still giggling. London leaned up, can still in hand, and plopped a large poof of cream on her nose before returning to her other breast. "Stop laughing."

But she didn't. Dahlia was practically out of her mind by the time she was screaming about the melon, which London had picked out of the bag next, being too cold. And while it was indeed entertaining, London was sliding fast back toward annoyance. They leaned back on their heels.

"This was your idea, you know."

"I know." Dahlia caught her breath. "I know." She swallowed, trying to stifle a grin. "I'm sorry. I'll be better. Try something else."

London leaned over the bed and sifted through the shopping bag, extracting a nectarine.

They had felt, at the grocery store, how soft and ripe these nectarines were. Which was rare, for the produce section of a chain supermarket, where the fruit normally arrived hard as a rock, preserved for a longer shelf life. As London held the stone fruit in their hand, its skin as supple as Dahlia's underneath them, they felt, truly, blessed.

They took a big, messy bite. They let juice trail down their chin, feeling a bit feral. They squeezed the fruit the tiniest bit in their fist, felt another trail of translucent juice slide down their arm. Dahlia's mouth twitched as her grin softened, fading away. After a second, her lips parted slightly.

"Oh," she said.

London rested the open wound of the nectarine onto Dahlia's skin. They started at her side, the soft curve that stretched out from her belly to her hip, before trailing it over her stomach. They had been straddling her hips, but now moved themselves farther down, their knees resting on the sheets between her legs, which fell open even wider for them. They trailed the nectarine down the inside of her right thigh and then her left, getting teasingly close, before tracing the fruit down to her calves, watching each twitch of her body, listening to each of her deep, raspy breaths.

They crawled back up over her torso, concentrating on steadying themself with one hand and grazing the juicy orange flesh back up her stomach with the other, until they were face-to-face again.

Dahlia was not laughing anymore.

Her face was slack, mouth open, but her eyes were wild, even darker than normal, two black pits of desire. Feeling entirely pleased with themself, London took another noisy bite of the nectarine.

"Fuck," Dahlia said. "London, fuck me."

London didn't move for a moment, chewing, letting the sound of Dahlia's demand wash over them.

"London," Dahlia said again. She grabbed the nectarine from their hand and chucked it at the wall. They heard it hit, first the closet and then the ground, with two dull thuds. "Fuck me now." She licked her lips, and then slightly softer: "With your mouth."

And now London was fully feral.

They kissed down her stomach, following the trail of the discarded nectarine, and as the sweetness of its juices melted with the salt of Dahlia's skin, a delicious swirl on their tongue, London decided this was the best idea Dahlia had ever had. They were very grateful to be sleeping with a genius.

After they settled in between her legs, they paused, massaging Dahlia's thigh. She was trembling.

"Hey," London whispered, trying to cool their own mounting adrenaline. "You okay?"

"Nope," she said, and London looked up to find her arm slung over her eyes again. "Not even a little bit."

London frowned. "Do you want to stop?"

She shook her head vigorously underneath her arm.

London massaged her thigh a bit more.

"I need a verbal confirmation, Dahlia."

She sighed dramatically.

"It'd be nice to see your face, too," they ventured.

Her arm fell away, but her eyes remained focused on the ceiling.

"Can you kiss me?" she asked. London bolted up to comply.

"Sorry," she said when they hovered over her mouth. She rolled her eyes a bit and made funny gestures with her hands that London saw out of the corner of their eyes. "I just..." London waited for her to complete her thought, never taking their eyes from hers. "Feelings," she eventually finished. And she sighed.

London kissed her lips, softly, with what they hoped was all the tenderness they felt for her right then. It was fascinating, watching her be messy and vulnerable like this. Understanding she didn't have the right words, exactly, because sometimes there were no right words, but knowing that she was feeling something big, and stopping to recognize it. Dahlia was perhaps the most emotionally honest, perceptive person London had ever met, and it bruised their heart to know she didn't think this was an admirable quality. London had never admired anyone more.

When you were around someone who felt everything, it

made you feel like you could feel everything, too. Like the depths of the world were suddenly limitless.

"Okay." Dahlia broke away, nodding. "I'm ready to be awed by your talents, or whatever."

London smiled down at her. They kissed her one more time. And then they resumed their position between her legs, where they started with more soft kisses, pushing her legs up and apart further still, rubbing their thumbs along the tender creases of her thighs and her backside, before they used one hand to spread her lips and lick her where she deserved to be licked.

The whimpers she released made London less inhibited with their own moans, pressing close so she could feel the vibrations of their lips, their tongue on her most sensitive places, before starting a steady circular rhythm around her clit.

"London," they heard her murmur.

They looked up at her then, never pausing the activity of their mouth, and saw her looking down at them, lazily fondling one of her breasts.

London maneuvered a finger inside her.

Dahlia's head fell back, her eyes closing. "Can you do more this time?"

When London moved in a second finger, they felt something shift within her, somehow. Like she was loosening herself for them, inside and out.

"One more, maybe," she breathed.

London had to lift their mouth, to make sure they were being careful with her.

"Tell me if it doesn't feel okay," they said, adjusting their fingers inside her to make way for a third. Dahlia's eyes remained closed, but her mouth opened silently when London felt their way inside. They paused, waiting for her to adjust.

"Yeah," she said breathlessly a moment later, nodding. "That's good."

With that confirmation, London's tongue got back to work, and with a moan, Dahlia let herself go completely. She pushed her hips up at them, and London worked with her, to find the perfect rhythm of fingers, mouth, thrusts.

When London glanced at her again, she had both arms cradled above her head, her teeth digging in to her bottom lip. It felt like the opposite of her body language last night, when she'd needed London close, their body trapping hers, keeping it safe. Tonight... it was like she was letting her body be free. This was her pleasure, and London was simply lucky enough to witness it.

She tasted good in London's mouth. She felt good in London's hands. But London felt like she felt good to herself, too, tonight, and it made none of this feel dirty at all. It felt beautiful.

They sat back on their heels, after Dahlia had come undone, and watched her. She didn't cover her face this time, but let her head fall to the side, one hand on her chest, feeling her own heartbeat. London ran a gentle hand down her thigh. Their head felt heavy, their throat thick, everything in them full and warm.

Finally, she moved her cheek away from the pillow. She looked up at them and reached out a hand toward their face. London leaned into it, lowering their cheek onto her palm.

"London," she said softly. "What do you want?"

London thought on it. They looked at her damp skin, her hazy eyes. She looked so content.

Did they need anything more than this? This felt like enough. This felt like more than they had ever been able to imagine.

"Can I lie on my stomach?" they asked after a minute.

Dahlia moved herself out of the way so London could take the center of the bed.

"My back." London motioned with a hand once they settled. "Just...go to town on it."

Dahlia did not laugh, or make a comment, or do anything other than what London asked. She reached over the side of the bed, rustled in the shopping bag. And then London felt something drip between their shoulder blades, viscous and cool. Its path continued down their spine, to their tailbone, sending a shiver down London's arms, the back of their legs.

And then Dahlia started to knead.

London's eyes were closed, their head facing away from her as they breathed onto the pillows, but they could picture everything about her. They had been watching Dahlia use her hands for weeks. When the heels of her palms dug into their skin, they pictured how she had looked pounding out the dough for her pappardelle. The fingers that lovingly spread olive oil and spices under chicken skin were the same fingers that now massaged their shoulders and their sides with strength and care.

London had always found cooking to be a form of art, of therapy, an expression of love and intent. Without all of their nanny's cooking lessons, their kitchen warm and humid from hot stoves and boiling water, London's childhood would have been a far lonelier landscape. Even today, cooking lent London a sense of control that they often lacked in the rest of their life. They couldn't control their father, or how their genes had been configured in their brain, or the breathtaking inequality of the world.

But they could make soufflés, and cakes, and the most tender steak. They could make anything they wanted.

It made sense to London that cooking had helped Dahlia through her divorce. Of course it had. They had watched how it calmed her, whenever she had a knife in her hands, a set of ingredients in front of her, and a plan in her mind. It calmed them in much the same way. They understood each other in this, an understanding London had never quite shared with anyone else.

And so as Dahlia's hands worked on their back, as she spread what they thought was melon along their skin, they knew, without having to see it, the look of concentration that was on her face, relaxed and focused all at once. Ever since they had seen Dahlia Woodson gut a fish, they had wanted to feel those hands on them, peeling back their own prickly layers. Perhaps Dahlia had been uncovering their scales, sneakily, one sharp edge at a time, bit by bit over the last month, until this very moment, their body pliant and smooth in her hands, when they finally felt fully washed clean.

Dahlia leaned down and used her mouth. She started at the back of their neck, making her way along their shoulder blades, down their sides. She made a satisfied hum.

"London," she said. "You taste delicious."

London smiled. "This was a good idea."

Dahlia's hands had lulled London into an almost medi-
tative state, but her tongue reawakened other sensations in
London's core. After a few blissed-out moments, they spread
their legs apart.

"Touch me."

London raised their hips off the bed to give her better access.
Dahlia's fingers touched them, just right, while her tongue
continued to caress their back, their shoulders, her nipples
grazing against their spine, and it was all London needed,
everything they wanted, to start spiraling inside, tighter,
lighter, until the sensations condensed into a column of heat.
They blindly shot an arm behind them, pressing Dahlia to
their back. She kissed the spot where their neck met their
shoulder, murmuring their name, and they thought, through
the heady haze of their mind, they could hear themself saying
hers in return.

And then London crashed, curling suddenly off their
stomach into a ball, and she fell onto her side with them,
sliding her arms around them, holding them tight, the skin
between them still sticky and sweet.

Dahlia stood under the hot flow of water for a final second
before, with reluctance, she leaned over to shut it off.

Brushing aside the shower curtain, she gazed at London in
front of her, vigorously rubbing a towel over their head before
wrapping it under their armpits. They looked at her, that
damp bit of strawberry hair sufficiently mussed and lovely,
their skin red and dewy from the hot steam.

"Hey." London smiled. And then, their eyes narrowing an inch, they said, "You okay?"

Dahlia grabbed the towel they handed her, wrapping it protectively around herself.

They were always asking her that, at the precise moments when she had no idea how to answer.

The night before had been, alternately and sometimes simultaneously, the funniest and most erotic thing she had ever experienced. She had loved every single second of it. Every moment with London was a new experience in letting herself go. An exercise in being vulnerable. A trial run of true, exhilarated happiness. Last night, she had felt... free.

The only logical course of action when they woke up with tangled limbs akimbo in very messy sheets had been a hot, thorough shower together. And while Dahlia had at first thought this could be an equally sexy venture—she had always wanted to try shower sex!—both of their bodies had been too exhausted to contemplate it.

Instead, the scene in the shower ended up being almost embarrassingly gentle.

London had washed off every square inch of Dahlia's skin in the confines of the shower, bending down awkwardly to get between her thighs, behind her knees, the bottom of her heels and between all of her toes. She kept yelling at them, worried they would fall on the wet tile and smack their head, but then they'd touch her with such reverent attention that she'd go speechless again.

There were patches of herself, sore from how determinedly London had sucked sticky sweetness off of them, shocked at being seen and adored, that she wasn't sure she had even been aware of before.

She had attempted to return the favor, scrubbing down London's back and shoulders, all of their hidden crevices, wanting to make them feel clean and renewed and cared for.

And now, as she stood dripping in the shower, watching London dry themself off and brush their teeth, such ordinary, intimate things, Dahlia felt frayed at the edges. Like she felt too big for her body, suddenly, like she didn't know how to proceed without her limbs falling apart.

"I'm going to need another towel for my hair," she said eventually, motioning limply to her head. "This is a two-towel affair."

"Of course." London handed her another towel and she scrunched her hair in it, grateful for a practical, normal action.

"You didn't answer me," London said as they watched. "Are you okay? You seem...a little shaky."

Dahlia twisted the towel on top of her head.

"I'm...tired. You are exhausting me, London Parker."

A grin jerked up a corner of their mouth.

"I would apologize, but you know, I don't really feel sorry."

Dahlia shook her head, but she grinned too. Smug, sexy London was too much.

"I think I need a night to catch up on sleep," she said. "Is that okay? We can collapse in our own beds tonight, and pick this back up tomorrow?"

The more she thought about it, the more she knew she needed this. A breath of bittersweet relief coursed through her.

"That sounds very reasonable and healthy. I mean, I don't

love it, but sure, if you're into that kind of thing." London took a step closer to the shower. They leaned down and kissed her shoulder.

"Thank you," she said. And then she stepped out of the shower to start preparing herself for the day.

It was only later, when they walked onto set, about to film another Elimination Challenge that could result in either of them being sent home, that Dahlia realized her mistake.

She had suggested a night off. That they pick this back up tomorrow.

Like another night was guaranteed.

Like tomorrow was a promise.

CHAPTER FIFTEEN

Dahlia!" Janet's hand landed on Dahlia's shoulder. "Let's head to hair and makeup. Parker, you're good."

Dahlia gave London a small shrug of her shoulders, which they returned, before she followed Janet down the hall. When they reached hair and makeup, Janet plopped into one of the black chairs next to Dahlia, swiveling a bit as Mack untwined Dahlia's still-damp hair from the clip she'd thrown it in.

"Morning, love." Mack smiled softly at her, as he always did. Mack was gentle, reassuring.

Janet, on the other hand, seemed hyped up. She was always intense, Janet, but in this controlled, intimidating way. Today her leg bounced on the silver ring at the bottom of the chair, a slightly wild grin perched on her face beneath her chunky, magenta-framed glasses.

The fact that she was sitting here at all, next to Dahlia, instead of hustling around set, preparing everyone for the day, was...odd.

Really odd.

Oh god. Anxiety started to army-crawl inside Dahlia's gut.

Janet seemed weirdly happy, but maybe she was trying to cover for something, preparing Dahlia for a blow. Was something wrong? Had something happened to Hank? Her mom or dad?

"Janet? Is something wrong?"

"Hah!"

Janet's exuberant outburst startled Dahlia so much she jumped. Mack frowned.

"Sorry." Janet cleared her throat, lacing her fingers in front of her. "No, Woodson, for once, nothing is wrong. In fact, season eight is going incredibly *right*."

Janet leaned forward in her chair.

"Dahlia, you must know *Chef's Special*'s ratings have been tanking the last few seasons."

Dahlia breathed in deeply through her nose. Her heart felt tender from last night, the whole ruckus of the last few days, and all she wanted was to get through another's day cook and then curl up in her bed for ten hours. She did not give a flying fig about ratings, and she had no clue why Janet was talking to her about them.

"There are so many cooking shows now, on every single platform," Janet continued, waving a hand in the air, "on Netflix, every other random streaming service that seems to pop up every month these days, even YouTube. *Chef's Special* is old hat now. We've been losing viewers left and right. But." Janet leaned back in her chair, a satisfied grin on her face. "As I predicted, London Parker has changed all that."

Dahlia's neck swiveled toward Janet so quickly it hurt. Mack *tsk*ed under his breath.

"London? What do you mean?"

"Well, you know, there's the whole Team Lizzie versus Team London thing—"

"Excuse me?"

"Oh." Janet's eyebrows raised, seeming genuinely surprised. "I figured you'd be following it." She dug her phone out of her pocket and did a quick search before handing it over.

The anxiety in Dahlia's gut changed shape, transforming into something closer to a ghost, whispering up into her lungs as she read the headline open in Janet's browser.

Chef's Special Fans Take a Stand: Are you #TeamLizzie or #TeamLondon?

Dahlia scanned through the article, disbelieving. Her mouth gaped open.

"But…but Lizzie and London hardly talk on set. How do people even know they don't like each other? That Lizzie has a problem with London?"

For the first time since she'd greeted Dahlia ten minutes ago, Janet looked uncomfortable.

"On the first episode, when the judges were praising London's lamb. One of the cameras caught Lizzie rolling her eyes. And then…Lizzie said some things, in one of her solo interviews."

"What?" Dahlia looked up from the phone. She felt like she kept talking in all caps, but there was no other way to respond. "What did she say?"

Janet scrunched her mouth to the side, like she'd tasted something sour.

"That's not important. Nothing…nothing that would surprise you, or London."

She leaned forward, placed a hand on Dahlia's knee.

"Anyway, that's not why I wanted to talk to you. You know we're all Team London, right?"

Janet glanced meaningfully toward Mack. Who looked visibly uncomfortable but nodded at Dahlia in confirmation.

Dahlia felt like she couldn't breathe.

If Janet was truly #TeamLondon, she would have demanded they edit out that fucking interview.

If *Chef's Special* was #TeamLondon, they wouldn't be using London as a pawn.

"The London-and-Lizzie tiff brought up our viewership right away. But then"—Janet beamed, her hand still on Dahlia's knee—"there was *you*." She leaned back in her chair again. "I expected some extra media attention when London informed us they would be out on the show, but I didn't expect you."

Janet smiled, eyes bright.

"Your heroics, rushing to London's side when they cut themself with the fish. And then there's the way they look at you... The internet is only mad that it's hard to make a good ship name out of London and Dahlia. Believe me, our team's working on it, but we're coming up short, too. When next week's episode airs and everyone sees you two being all giggly during the bar mitzvah, my *god*—"

Janet's phone, which Dahlia had still been clutching, dropped out of Dahlia's hand, meeting the floor with a tinny clatter that felt too loud in her ears. She was going to vomit. If she did, she'd aim it at Janet's face.

"Dahlia," Janet said, leaning over to retrieve the phone

with a frown. "You must have seen some of the comments online, right? I know people are blowing up your Instagram. You and London are very lovable."

"You're looking at my *Instagram*?"

"Of course we are," Janet said, matter-of-factly, like this shouldn't be a surprise.

But it was. It felt like Dahlia had entered an alternate reality *Chef's Special*. One where she was the star, but for none of the reasons she wanted. Reasons that had nothing to do with her cooking abilities.

She hadn't seen the comments online. Ever since the beach last week, after the first episode had aired and she'd seen all the horrible things people were saying about London, she'd turned off all notifications on her phone. Just like she'd advised London to do.

And she had been...busy. With other things. Like deluding herself into believing she had entered into a private relationship, apparently.

She swallowed back bile, while Janet sat, tilting her head with an odd look on her face.

Dahlia bit her lip, mentally shaking herself. No...She knew. She knew that she and London were on national TV. Barbara had warned her. Her own brain had told her, yesterday on set, when she slipped up and acted too intimate with London and saw the cameras closing in. Janet had seen, and commented on, Dahlia's *nasty business hair* just yesterday. None of this should be a surprise.

But it all felt like too much, suddenly. This conversation. The last two nights with London. Everything.

"Why are you telling me all this?"

Janet leaned in.

"There's going to be an opportunity today on set. It's all worked out perfectly. You and Cath and Khari have the advantage from the Face-Off yesterday."

The Face-Off? Dahlia could barely remember it. Yesterday already felt like so long ago.

"You're going to get to save another contestant. You'll get to choose between London or Lizzie. Or Ahmed, but he's not really important here." Janet waved a hand. "So this is what I'm thinking," she went on, grinning, like this was genuinely fun for her. "Khari and Lizzie are tight, so I imagine he'll want to fight for her."

"Khari and Lizzie are *tight*?" Dahlia was so thrown by this that it cut through her temporarily shut-down brain.

Janet rolled her eyes. "You and London wouldn't know it, but yes, other contestants have made friends with each other, too, Dahlia. So anyway, I imagine Khari will fight for Lizzie. And it'll be *your* opportunity to really fight for London, explain why they deserve the advantage more than Lizzie. A classic Team Lizzie–versus–Team London setup, with some romance thrown in. It's gold."

Janet sat back in her chair.

"I thought I'd warn you so you're prepared when you're up there, so you can maybe think of some real good zingers about Lizzie or something." Janet snorted. "*I* could think of some good zingers about Lizzie."

Dahlia opened her mouth, but Janet was still going.

"The beautiful thing?" Janet smacked the side of her chair, shaking her head. "Is that Lizzie and London are both such strong competitors. I can see the finale being Team Lizzie versus Team London for real, and man, that would probably be our most watched finale ever."

She paused, her smile faltering again for a moment.

"Again"—she reached a hand toward Dahlia—"we're all totally Team London. Right?" She looked up toward Mack again. "Right?"

"Right," Mack muttered, putting the final touches on Dahlia's hair, looking disgruntled.

Even with how foggy Dahlia's thought process had felt over the last fifteen minutes, something seeped through the cracks now. A slow, viscous hurt, like a honey without any sweetness.

Was there any possibility in Janet's mind? That it could be Dahlia in the finale instead?

Was anyone Team Dahlia?

Or was her only purpose here to be a cute anecdote, the funny klutz, a supporting role for Team London?

Being with London had made her feel more alive, more connected to another person than she had perhaps ever felt in her life.

But in that very moment—a confusing contrast to how fully she also wanted to be Team London, how violently she had wanted to defend their honor moments before—Dahlia suddenly felt acutely alone.

"I thought..." she eventually got out, swallowing. "I thought *Chef's Special* wasn't scripted. How do you know who'll be in the finale?"

"Oh!" Janet's eyes widened in surprise. "No, no, I was just spitballing about the finale. Even though I do tend to get these things right, after doing this for so long. But sorry, you're right; I'm getting a bit carried away. It's been an exciting morning, getting the latest numbers and everything. But no, Dahlia." Janet's serious producer face settled in again, the one Dahlia knew, the one she had previously found comforting. "If I've made you question the integrity of our judges for even a second, I'm sincerely sorry. Everything Sai and Tanner and Audra do on set is legit. Nothing's predetermined. They take this competition very seriously. As do I. *Chef's Special* has been my life for eight seasons now. I love what I do, and I'm good at it. The judging is always authentic, but it's my job to make sure people actually tune in for that judging. You know?"

A PA stuck their head into the doorway.

"Hey, Janet. We ready to go soon? The contestants are getting antsy."

Janet gave a curt nod. "Five minutes."

Dahlia had no idea how she was going to walk back onto set after this. She wanted to crawl into a dark hole.

Janet stood. She brushed invisible dust off of her pants.

"You're going to do great today, okay? We're all so glad you're still here. Go get 'em, Woodson."

After giving Mack a nod, Janet smacked Dahlia on the shoulder and smiled before walking away. As if this had been an inspiring huddle before the big game.

Dahlia blinked, listening to the fading patter of Janet's footsteps, the rhythm matching the lonely beating of Dahlia's heart.

London frowned.

"You sure you're okay?" Not for the first time today, they held the back of their hand up to Dahlia's forehead. She swatted it away, eyes darting around the set.

"London, seriously, I'm *fine*," she hissed.

"You're pale. And...damp."

"Thanks for the confidence boost. Focus on your cake, okay?"

She turned back to her own work, furiously smashing raspberries in a small ceramic bowl, her lips a thin line. London frowned deeper but did as they were told.

The Elimination Challenge today was all about cakes, and London, too, was all about cakes. They were having fantastic sex with a fantastic person. Everything about today should have been awesome.

Except for the fact that Dahlia looked like she was going to pass out. And was barely talking to them.

Still, everything was going relatively smoothly with London's cake preparations—coffee, flour, sugar, chocolate, and peppermint, measured and folded and mixed—until the clock stopped unexpectedly. Right in the middle of the Elimination Challenge, the red numbers at the judges' table came to a sudden halt with exactly forty minutes left to go.

Sai Patel called for their attention. The six remaining contestants' hands paused in place at the edge of their baking sheets, on mixer stands, wrapped around spoons inside bowls of icing.

"Dahlia, Cath, and Khari," Sai continued. "Please make your way to the judges' table."

London attempted to flash Dahlia a reassuring smile for

whatever this was. She wiped her floury hands on her apron, face grim, and didn't look back once.

Sure. Dahlia was obviously just fine.

"Let's switch things up. Will the three of you please take a place behind the judges' table?" Sai gestured behind him to the dramatic front table with the frozen clock. London watched Dahlia assume Tanner Tavish's spot, flanked by Cath and Khari on either side of her. London couldn't help but smile. She might be refusing to admit she'd come down with the plague or her appendix was about to burst or something, but Dahlia still looked good up there.

"You know…" Sai strolled casually across the Golden Circle, steepling his fingers in front of him. "Having the responsibility of making *all* the decisions gets tiring sometimes. The three of you won an advantage in yesterday's Face-Off. And this time, it's a big one. Right now, you will pick one person out here"—Sai pointed to the remaining three contestants at their stations—"one person you choose to save, right now. They can stop baking this second and leave set to rest up until next episode, safe and sound."

Sai turned back around to face the judges' table.

"You will also choose one person to put at a disadvantage. They will have to finish their cake fifteen minutes early."

London's eyebrows lifted. Damn. That was an intense disadvantage.

Baking was all about timing. They were told they'd have sixty minutes to bake. There was literally nothing you could do if your cake wasn't already in the oven.

"That seems harsh, boss," Cath voiced out loud.

Sai smiled good-naturedly. "Perhaps. But if you had timed

things well, you would have already planned to take your cake out of the oven fifteen minutes early to allow it to cool before applying your icing. This disadvantage will simply require some creative thinking. You have three minutes to decide."

Sai made a big show of setting a timer on his smartwatch. "Go."

Khari and Cath huddled toward Dahlia. She didn't say anything at all for the first thirty seconds, her face a strange blank while Khari and Cath talked heatedly around her, their voices a low murmur. London was contemplating calling for the medic. There was clearly something going on with Dahlia.

And then she frowned, deeply, crossing her arms in front of her chest, and jumped into the conversation. She looked pissed. London very much wanted to kiss her.

"Ten seconds!"

Dahlia rolled her eyes and sighed, drooping to the back of Tanner Tavish's chair.

"Aaand time is up!" Sai snapped his fingers. "Judges' table, we're ready for your decision. Khari, who has fifteen minutes less to bake today?"

"Ahmed," he said.

Ahmed groaned and hung his head.

"And, Dahlia, who's the lucky soul who gets to take the rest of the day off?"

Dahlia closed her eyes briefly. When she opened them, she looked to the side of the set, off camera. London glanced in the direction of her gaze, confused. Who was she looking at? Janet?

Dahlia opened her mouth. And it wasn't until her tongue lifted to roll out an *L* that London even thought about what she was going to say. It wasn't until she finished it with *izzie* that London realized they'd been positive she'd say something else.

It sounded wrong. It *felt* wrong, in London's gut, hearing that name come out of Dahlia's mouth.

London knew it was only a silly advantage for extra drama. That this was just a TV show. But they also knew they would have fought to save Dahlia, if the situation were reversed, to give her extra peace of mind if they could. They never would have gone along with saving Lizzie.

Who was currently gasping, behind them. London turned around to watch her clench her hands to her heart.

"Congratulations, Lizzie! You can put away your apron for the day and go rest your feet." Sai Patel flashed his award-winning smile.

"Oh!" she trilled. "Wow! But..."

London thought they saw Sai Patel's mouth twitch.

"Do you mind if I finish the bake anyway?" Lizzie asked. "I'm already halfway through; I'd hate to see a good cake go to waste!"

"Oh, good lord," London muttered.

But Sai Patel allowed it. Dahlia, Cath, and Khari were released back to their stations.

"London," Dahlia said urgently as she retied her apron. "I'm sorry, that was—"

"The clock's running again," London said. "You should work on your ganache."

They sensed her pause next to them, the heaviness that had settled over their station.

London smashed apart peppermint sticks with perhaps a smidge more force than was necessary.

Yet it was satisfying, seeing Dahlia jump with each loud crack of their hammer. Watching a solid confection break into sharp shards.

As Dahlia worked on her cake beside them—chocolate sponges with layers of raspberry jam, topped with decadent ganache—London knew, somewhere in the logical part of their brain, that there was no way Dahlia had wanted that to happen. Cath, too. Khari must have pushed to save Lizzie.

Like many of the other contestants—everyone who had sat in awkward silence during that meet-and-greet dinner weeks ago—London hadn't ever been sure where they stood with Khari. No one else had stomped off that night like Lizzie had. But that didn't necessarily mean anything. Maybe Khari thought they were an abomination, too.

Either way. Dahlia should have fought harder for them than Khari fought for Lizzie.

London felt good about their cake; they weren't worried about elimination. They didn't need the advantage.

But when Dahlia said Lizzie's name, everything Lizzie represented was brought from the depths of London's subconscious into the forefront of their brain. Painful, present, impossible to ignore.

The truth was that London had gotten very good at pretending Lizzie didn't exist on set, but they were only pretending to pretend. Like they pretended with their dad. Like they pretended almost every hour of every day that they were in public.

The fact that London would always be surrounded by people who either didn't approve of their identity or didn't understand their identity was not a fact that could simply be ignored. London could push it away in order to exist. But it was always lurking in the shadows, making London on guard for how they should act, what they should say in front of other human beings.

They had become so used to this mode of existence that they only truly comprehended the depths of it when they imagined what the opposite would feel like. If there was a society where everyone rejected the binary, where gender norms didn't exist at all, where bodies were just bodies, every one real and valid and equally human, and you didn't have to worry about what people were assuming or not assuming about you.

The idea made London feel so light and free that it was only then that they fully felt the weight of the invisible stress they carried, compacted in their bones.

Except they didn't feel that stress when they were with Dahlia. When London was alone with Dahlia, their subconscious could let go.

And when Dahlia said Lizzie's name, it was like London's stress brain jumped forward into London's Dahlia brain and ran around inside with muddy feet, leaving dirty stains on the floor.

When the sixty minutes were up, London glanced behind them again. They were extremely pleased with their cake, but Lizzie's, which London had heard her tell the judges was called Strawberry Lemonade Afternoon, was stunning. The icing was perfectly scraped around the sides, offering artistic peeks of the lemon-yellow cake beneath. It looked airy and decadent all at once. The sugared strawberries on top were plump and bright. Lizzie had cut herself a piece and sunk a forkful into her mouth with a satisfied hum.

With Lizzie's existence now more pressing in London's consciousness, they also had to accept how excellent she was. Lizzie was a true contender.

Lizzie could win it all.

And wouldn't that just be fucking typical.

"Damn," Tanner Tavish said when London brought up their cake. He tapped the tines of his fork against his mouth. "That is a good cake."

"I agree." Audra nodded. "The flavor combination here is stellar. The richness of the chocolate and coffee really come through, but then your tongue finishes on the freshness of the mint. And your decoration of the smashed peppermint around the sides is so well done. It could've looked messy, but you've made it look sophisticated. Really lovely."

"You knocked it out of the park," Sai said.

This would have been a good day, London thought.

Dahlia did well, too. She looked shocked to be in the top three, but the judges had really liked it.

"The ganache is smooth as velvet," Sai said. "The cake is rich, but the tartness and sweetness of your raspberry filling balances it out perfectly. Sure, the flavors could have been more creative, but this is a well-executed dessert. Nice work."

London won the challenge. But for the first time all day, Dahlia's glow reappeared.

She was so pretty when she was happy.

London's chest hurt.

And then Ahmed was kicked off.

Creative thinking had not apparently helped Ahmed's

cake, which didn't have enough time to finish baking, which was too hot for his icing to even attempt to adhere to.

Once the cameras turned off, London walked over to him to say goodbye, feeling ready to punch something.

"Hey, London."

Ahmed actually smiled at them. In fact, Ahmed was almost beaming.

"Look, that was shitty, Ahmed. I'm sorry." London crossed their arms over their chest and shook their head. This disadvantage had been unfair.

"It's cool. It's a competition." Ahmed shrugged. "If anything, it surprised me they thought I was enough of a threat to give me the disadvantage. Almost made me a little cocky there for a second."

London tried to smile. They realized, with clarity, how much they liked Ahmed. Ahmed had smiled at London during the meet-and-greet dinner. Ahmed and London were not friends, necessarily, but Ahmed had always been cool with them. London had been really lucky, they knew, getting Ahmed as a tablemate for so much of this competition. His acceptance had let London feel comfortable, had given space for them to cook at their best.

One more person London could slot into the *You can relax* side of their brain. And now he was leaving.

"Listen, London, don't feel bad about me. This is the longest I've ever been away from my wife and kids, and honestly, I've been losing my damn mind. The fact that I even made it this far will definitely be my coolest dad moment ever, so I'm good."

London held out their hand. Ahmed glanced down at it.

And then he pulled in London for a hug.

"Take care of yourself, London," he said near London's ear. "Don't let the bastards get you down."

Ahmed stepped back and patted London on the shoulder with a genuine smile. And then he walked away for his final solo interview.

London turned back around. Dahlia waited for them with nervous energy, shifting from foot to foot, twisting her hands.

"Hey," she said. "Let's go."

She turned on her heel and hustled under the wooden archway toward the exit briskly, with purpose. London had to jog to catch up with her.

They headed in the direction of the hotel in silence, the muggy night air filling London's lungs.

"Good job," London said after a few minutes, deciding to take a neutral route of conversation instead of *What the hell is going on with you?* "I know you get nervous about desserts. Hopefully this made you realize you shouldn't."

"London," Dahlia said, stopping in the middle of the side-walk. She dropped her head into her hands. "I know you're mad at me about the Lizzie thing, and you should be. I am so, so sorry."

London rubbed the back of their neck. They hated being mad at her. They hated being mad at their dad. They even hated being mad at Lizzie. Being mad took up so much space. Being mad was exhausting.

"It's okay," they said eventually. "I'm more worried about whether you're okay."

"Khari really pushed to save Lizzie, for whatever reason,"

Dahlia said in a rush, ignoring London's last sentence. "And give you the disadvantage. I just wanted to make sure you didn't get the disadvantage. And I was so flustered being up there, and tired, and I couldn't—"

"Dahlia." London reached over and took her hand. They suddenly didn't want to talk about this anymore. It had been a small, dumb thing. Dahlia was right; at least they hadn't gotten the disadvantage, which could have been disastrous. They pushed Lizzie away again, back into the recesses of their mind where she belonged.

"It's cool, okay?" they said. "We both made it through another elimination. We're both still here. That's all that matters."

And this had been a big elimination to survive. It was Thursday now; they had a three-day weekend ahead of them, and the next Elimination Challenge wouldn't be until Tuesday. They had both just earned themselves five more days of being together.

And London still wanted that.

London still wanted to fall asleep next to her tonight.

"Do you think Ahmed's pissed at me?" Dahlia asked. "I meant to apologize."

"Nah, Ahmed's good," London answered. "He's happy to be heading home to his wife and kids."

"Yeah?" Dahlia's shoulders visibly relaxed. "That's good."

"Yeah."

"London, do you think...?" Dahlia bit her lip. "Do you think being on this show is worth it?"

London frowned.

"What do you mean?"

Dahlia looked away, hugging her elbows to herself and shivering a bit, even though it was warm out. A long moment passed.

"Never mind." She shook her head before smiling at them. But it was such a small, forced smile, the most un-Dahlia-like thing London had ever seen.

She turned and kept walking toward the hotel, the now familiar sounds of this city filling in the silence. London followed, trying to think of some way to bring her back to them.

"You deserve part of my win, really," London said as the hotel came into view. "You were the inspiration."

"But..." Dahlia frowned. "I don't even drink coffee."

"Yeah, which makes no sense. The coffee part was me. But—" London cut themself off, feeling a bit embarrassed now. But they needed to fill the space between them somehow, with something good and true, before they went back to their room alone.

"You taste like peppermint."

"What?" Dahlia's mouth cracked into a real smile this time, one hundred percent Woodson, and warmth flooded London's chest.

"Oh my god," Dahlia said. "You made me a cake."

"One of my best, if I say so myself."

Dahlia stopped once more, yanking on London's arm. They stumbled back toward her, and she wrapped her arms around their neck, reaching up to plant a kiss on their mouth.

London could feel her playful smile under their lips. They grabbed her hips and pulled her closer, changing the intention of the kiss, pushing her mouth open, wanting to feel her tongue, her hot breath.

This was uncomplicated. This was glorious. This did not involve thinking, and London wanted more of it.

They pulled away just an inch. "You sure you still want a night off? We can sleep in tomorrow morning, you know." They ran their knuckles up her side.

"Yes," she said, but her voice wavered with the effort. "I think if I even kiss you one more time, I *am* going to pass out. We need some space to breathe, London."

London sighed and pressed a firm kiss to her temple. They stood there a moment, holding each other, breathing in the night air: half jasmine, half engine exhaust.

"All right, Woodson," London said eventually, releasing her, and they walked into the glow of the hotel. "Let's go breathe."

CHAPTER SIXTEEN

The sky outside Dahlia's window was hazy and pale when she woke the next morning, and it matched the color of her emotions, bright and muted all at once.

It felt strange, being alone.

Even though, prior to her *Chef's Special* life, Dahlia had become quite accustomed to being alone almost all the time.

She wondered what London was doing. Drinking coffee in their pajamas with their cute bed hair? Walking to get a breakfast burrito from that place around the corner? Still snoring under the covers? Except London didn't snore. Which was weird. Who didn't snore? Were they reading a book? What did London like to read?

Even if Dahlia didn't know what London was doing at this exact second, the strange thing was that she felt them anyway. Two nights in their arms and it was like her skin had memorized them, could feel the weight of them still, a ghost taking up space in her bed. Knowing they were down the hall, a few rooms away, only made it worse.

She ached for the comfort of their proximity.

But she had to sort out her head first. Because the last twenty-four hours had made *that* an absolute mess.

Ever since she'd talked to Janet yesterday, her mind had felt...twisted. Like she was looking at her own memories through a contorted looking glass.

Dahlia flipped onto her other side, away from the window.

The conversation with Janet would have been enough to ruin the day, but then there had also been that whole dumb advantage. It had been awful, saying Lizzie's name. As Janet had predicted, Khari *had* fought for Lizzie to walk free and for London to get the disadvantage. Cath had tried to play the peacemaker, making the compromise that Lizzie would get the advantage but London wouldn't get the disadvantage, and then time had been up.

But a part of Dahlia wondered. If she would have fought even a little harder. If she would've said London's name anyway, when Sai called on her, defying the group's decision. If she didn't know, now, that saying Lizzie's name would be going against the narrative. That it would make Janet surprised. And Dahlia wanted to leave Janet surprised.

Because Dahlia didn't want to be a pawn, either.

She curled into a tiny ball, shutting her eyes against the daylight.

As the day had gone on, Janet's words had all sunk in a bit more. Most of it eventually felt less shocking than merely mildly depressing. This was a reality show. Of course there would be hashtags, small manipulations.

Except with each day that passed with Dahlia still in Los Angeles—with each new day spent with London—Dahlia had started to forget. That none of this was normal.

And there were certain things Janet had said that refused to sink in. That kept bouncing around Dahlia's head.

I can see the finale being Team Lizzie versus Team London for real, and man, that would probably be our most watched finale ever.

And right before she had walked away:

We're all so glad you're still here.

It had felt patronizing. Like…it was a surprise that Dahlia was still here.

Dahlia wasn't delusional. She had been reminding herself, every day, how this could all end any moment. And she knew there were several strong competitors left. London. Cath. And—ugh—Lizzie. God, Dahlia didn't know if she'd ever truly forgive *Chef's Special* for airing whatever Lizzie had said about London.

Still. Dahlia could feel her cooking skills sharpening with each challenge. She was in the Top Five. *Five.* More than halfway to the finish line.

That had to mean something.

It wasn't completely ridiculous, right? To want to keep fighting?

She remembered what Barbara had whispered into her ear, before Barbara had left the Golden Circle forever that day, that day that was only a few days ago but felt like so much longer:

You deserve more than you think you do. Go and get it all.

Dahlia liked to think that by *get it all*, Barbara had meant she believed Dahlia could win $100,000.

Even though in her heart of hearts, Dahlia knew Barbara was talking about more than just that.

And right now, thinking about more than just that—actually getting it all—only felt overwhelming.

She hadn't expected so much of this when she flew to LAX from BWI a month ago. She had always wanted to win the

$100,000, there was no question about that. She wanted to hone her cooking skills. And she had had dreams about LA Dahlia, about maybe having some fun adventures on her way to the prize.

She hadn't expected London.

And she hadn't expected LA Dahlia to sink into her bones so completely. *Actually* feeling like a different person, a person she would like to be friends with, maybe. Settling into a dry, overpopulated land, feeling comforted by smoggy skies. Feeling seen by palm trees.

If she *did* get kicked off the show…Dahlia didn't know where she'd even go from here now. How she would say goodbye to LA Dahlia.

How she would say goodbye to London.

I do tend to get these things right, after doing this so long.

No.

Dahlia shook her head and finally rolled herself out of bed. She paced the length of the room, past the window, the dresser, the chair in the corner full of dirty clothes. This little, sterile space that almost felt, in its own funny way, like home.

Because Dahlia had been here for so long.

Janet might get a lot right. Maybe she was a really excellent producer.

But she didn't decide Dahlia's fate.

No. Dahlia wasn't going to say goodbye to any of it. God, she had been on the verge of a breakdown all day yesterday and still baked the best cake of her life. She had earned this.

Who cared if the only other member of Team Dahlia was Barbara.

Grandmas were smart as hell.

Dahlia stopped her pacing, a sudden thought hitting her.

There was at least one other member of Team Dahlia, too.

She picked up her phone from the bedside table and dialed the number of the person she missed the most.

"Bay. Bee. *Girrrrrrrrl! How does it feel to be famous?*"

"Hank. You almost broke my eardrum." Dahlia's voice was scratchy from using it for the first time this morning, but her face broke into a grin.

"Are you at work?" she asked. "Can you talk? And/or scream?"

"Of course I'm at work and of course I can talk. My boss will understand that I'm talking to my very famous baby sister. Someone else can tell people to restart their computers for a while."

Hank worked in IT for a hotel group in Boston, where he'd been for years. Like their dad, he had always been an affable nerd, and Dahlia couldn't imagine him doing anything *other* than IT.

"Hank, you are one year older than me, and I am not famous."

Hank snorted. "Whatever, baby sister."

Dahlia jumped back on the bed, stretching out her toes. "How is work, though?"

"How is *work*? Oh my god, *boring*, Dahlia; shut up and tell me about LA! How the fuck are you! Is Sai Patel a total dreamboat in real life? Are you killing it? Because we just watched the second episode last night, and I have no idea how this all works and when you actually filmed that shit, but in case you've already forgotten, let me remind you that you *killed it*."

Dahlia laughed.

And then an odd thing happened.

Her laughter turned into a sob.

It was a laugh-sob. Fat, salty tears hurtled down her face, at the same time that she couldn't stop giggling.

It was possible she was still a little sleep deprived.

And it appeared that all the things that had changed in her life over the last four weeks hit her the hardest, somehow, when she heard her brother's voice. The voice that had known her before LA Dahlia. Who would love her no matter which Dahlia she was. She wished he were here in person, could wrap her in one of his rib-squeezing hugs. Help her meld this new version of herself with all the old ones. Promise her it would all work out, that being Team Dahlia wasn't just a pipe dream.

There was a pregnant pause on the other end of the line.

"Um, Dahlia? You all right?"

"Sorry," Dahlia mumbled through her snot. She grabbed a tissue, let out one last weak laugh. "I, uh. I was calling because I wanted to hear exactly what you just said. So... thank you."

"You're welcome. I think? Have you come down with a case of the sads? I mean, I can only imagine the stress you're under, baby sis. It's understandable."

"Actually." Dahlia sighed. "I'm... I don't know."

"Ah. The I-don't-knows. Those can be even worse. Well, thank god you called. Hold on a sec."

Dahlia heard rustling and muffled voices in the background.

"Okay." Hank came back on the line. "Gonna take my lunch break. I'm walking and talking here. You got a notebook?"

"Yeah. Somewhere. Let me find it."

Dahlia put Hank on speaker and stood up, looking around her wonderful disaster of a room. She tossed clothes around, searching on the floor. She could tell, from the increase in background noise on Hank's end, the moment he exited his building and walked into Copley Square.

"Ugh, there are a lot of tourists around today. I'm going to try to find a quiet spot by the library. Let me know when you're ready."

"Aha!" Dahlia spotted a notebook underneath the bed. This notebook was regular journal size, and served a different purpose from the small notepad she carried around set. The notepad was for food; the notebook was for feelings. "Got it."

"Good. So I am obviously concerned you have the I-don't-knows, and you will tell me why you have the I-don't-knows later, if you want, but I have to say I am rather excited that you called. I've been storing up some truly killer ideas for a *while* now."

"Fantastic. Go for it."

Dahlia settled back onto the bed, leaning against the headboard.

"Top ten Britney songs, 2001 or earlier only."

Dahlia rolled her eyes so hard she was positive Hank could hear it.

"Hank. We have done Britney before. Like five times at least."

"But we keep leaving off key tracks! I realized we hadn't included "I'm Not a Girl, Not Yet a Woman" on any of our previous top tens, and it's just egregious."

Hank and Dahlia had been crafting top ten lists to combat

the sads—or, apparently, the I-don't-knows—for well over a decade now. It started during their parents' divorce, when Dahlia was in fifth grade. Dahlia had a particularly hard time when their dad moved out, and one night, when Hank heard Dahlia crying, he came into her room and sat on her bed, combing her hair with his fingers until she calmed down. And then he asked her to list her top ten *Lizzie McGuire* episodes.

Dahlia had sat up in bed immediately, taking the task so seriously that she eventually had to find a notebook to scribble her thoughts, crossing out and rewriting until she had her perfect ten episodes. Then Hank had asked her to write down her top ten lunches from the New Bedford Intermediate School cafeteria.

Looking back, Dahlia was still floored by Hank's genius, still didn't know what made him ask her those things at that moment. But by the time Hank left her bedroom that night to return to his own bed, Dahlia felt significantly less sad. She fell right asleep.

"No more Britney. How about…" Dahlia tapped her pencil against a blank page. "Top ten cheeses."

Now Hank laughed. "No way we haven't done that one before, too."

"I swear we haven't! I know we've done ice cream several times, but we haven't done cheese."

"Fine." Hank sighed. "Number ten. Swiss."

"Blech." Dahlia stuck out her tongue at her phone. Her tears had dried completely now. "Let's do Havarti for number ten."

Hank groaned. "This is why I don't do food lists with you anymore."

"Hank! Havarti is not that snooty!"

"Dahlia Woodson, I literally have no idea what Havarti cheese tastes like."

Dahlia smiled and listed numbers one through ten in her notebook. She wrote Havarti on the tenth line.

"I'm assuming you wouldn't support American cheese for number nine."

Dahlia chewed on her pen cap before answering.

"No, let's do it," she said. "American is delicious."

As she wrote it down in her notebook, she grinned, imagining what London would say. They would stare at her list in dismay and then gesture wildly with their hands. "American cheese *isn't even cheese*, Dahlia," they would say. And then she would kiss them.

Hank and Dahlia finished the cheese list. She was just getting ready to suggest a top-ten-times-Dad-locked-his-keys-in-the-car list when Hank swiftly changed the subject.

"So what's going on, baby sister? Did you get kicked off the show?"

"Oh," Dahlia said, her system feeling confused at the sharp turn back to reality. "I signed an NDA so I'm technically not allowed to tell you. But I'm, um, still in LA."

Dahlia stood and walked to the bathroom, filling a glass with water.

"So..." Hank waited. "What's wrong?"

Dahlia stared at herself in the mirror above the sink, at the shadows under her eyes.

Her mouth asked the question before her brain had even truly known it needed to ask it.

"Would you be disappointed? If I don't win?"

She heard Hank cluck his tongue. "Dahlia," he said. "Come on."

"Mom would be disappointed, probably. I feel like I'm always disappointing Mom."

"No shit." Hank snorted. "For the record, she was hard on *both* of us, you know. You don't hold exclusivity on disappointing our mother."

"You didn't get divorced from her, like, favorite person because you didn't want to give her grandbabies," Dahlia retorted.

"You didn't come out as transgender in your mid-twenties," Hank countered.

Dahlia paused. "Okay, fair. Mom was pretty great about that, though."

"I think she's okay about your divorce, too. You just can't see it."

Dahlia sighed quietly and walked back into the main room. Hank didn't know how excited their mom had been, whenever she visited Dahlia and David at their house in the 'burbs, the way her eyes lit up when she talked about grandkids. The way that light had been extinguished when Dahlia broke the news about the divorce.

"She's really proud of you, Dahlia," Hank said after a moment. "You have to know that."

"I don't believe I do."

"We all watched the first episode together, you know. You should've seen how upset she was when you tripped."

"Oh god." Dahlia flopped heavily back on the bed and put her head in her hands. "How is that being proud of me?!"

"Because she got all protective. She sat up on the couch

and said, 'They shouldn't have shown that. They're laughing at her.' She was so pissed."

"That sounds like she was embarrassed, Hank."

Now Hank sighed audibly into the phone.

"She wasn't. Dahlia, you know Nonna and Nonno were hard on Mom, too. Having high expectations is just how she was raised."

"Yeah," Dahlia said weakly, even though she knew this was true. Dahlia and Hank's grandparents on her mom's side had been loving but hard people. Dahlia had been slightly terrified of them as a small child.

"Just…maybe, I don't know, try to talk to her more," Hank said. "I know talking to Dad is easier for you, but if you're feeling all sad and weird about Mom, reach out and tell her stuff. See what happens."

"I talk to her about stuff," Dahlia said defensively.

Hank snorted again.

Fine. Point taken.

"And you know we're all going to love you just as much no matter what happens on the show. I don't care if you get kicked off on the third episode and you've just been bumming around LA since then. Okay?"

Dahlia was quiet for a long moment.

"Okay," she said. "Top ten Sandra Bullock movies."

She picked up her notebook and sat down again, jiggling her foot.

"Easy," Hank said. "Number ten, *The Proposal*."

After they fought for a while about whether *While You Were Sleeping*, *Miss Congeniality*, or *Speed* was more deserving of the number one spot, Dahlia put her pen down.

"Your lunch break has to be up soon," she said.

"Maybe," Hank said noncommittally.

She wanted to tell him about London. She knew Hank would be on her side about so many things. Like the fact that Brussels sprouts definitely *did not* count as comfort food. Like the fact that London Parker was simultaneously the cutest and sexiest person who had ever existed.

She wanted them to meet one day, so London could tell Hank anything he ever wanted to know about Nashville.

She wanted to tell Hank everything.

But that was for another day.

Maybe right now the assurance that after all this, even if she didn't get it all, she'd still have Hank, was enough.

She took a deep breath.

Okay.

Okay.

Team Dahlia, ready for liftoff.

"You are a really amazing brother, Hank."

She could hear his smile. "I never get tired of hearing you say that."

"Okay, go back to work before you get fired."

"They would never fire me. I send all the best memes. Place would be a total killjoy without me."

"I love you, loser."

"Love you too, baby sister."

CHAPTER SEVENTEEN

L ondon, as a certified pushover when it came to all things
Dahlia Woodson, really thought they'd be the first to
break. They felt a little proud of themself, actually, that they
had gone a full twenty hours without texting her or, alterna-
tively, knocking down her door.

It had been easier than London might have expected.
Because anytime the pining got close to being too much,
London would simply picture Dahlia sitting in Tanner
Tavish's chair, saying Lizzie's name.

And London would deflate, just a tiny bit.

But when this text came through at four o'clock on Friday
afternoon—

hi i miss you

—London's chest filled all the way up anyway. Just like it
had when they'd kissed her last night.

London probably needed to get their head checked.

They probably also should not have spent the last eight
hours lying in bed and watching rom-coms. Now they really
had no perspective on reality.

London picked up their phone.

London: Are you breathing better now?

Dahlia: much

Dahlia: what are you up to?

London paused. They glanced at the TV.

They could lie. They should probably lie.

London: I . . . . am possibly watching Mamma Mia

Dahlia: OH

Dahlia: MY

Dahlia: GOD

Dahlia: ONE OR TWO LONDON

London: . . . . two

Dahlia: OH MY GODDDDDDDDDD

Dahlia: ARE YOU IN YOUR ROOM

London: Yes.

Dahlia: HERE WE GO AGAIN!!

London's phone was still backlit from this last text when a fast, hard knock on their door cracked through the room thirty seconds later. Jesus. London glanced down at themself. They were wearing their flannel pajama pants, their binder thrown on the floor, and their T-shirt still had a stain from the burrito they'd eaten for lunch. And their hair was probably—

Another impatient knock.

Grumbling, London crawled out of bed.

"Oh no," Dahlia said when they opened the door.

She was wearing her raspberry sweatshirt and shorts. Her hair was down, slightly wet, like she'd just taken a shower. Which meant now London was picturing her in the shower. She bit at the sleeve of her sweatshirt, bunched up over her hands.

"What?" London asked, hand still on the door handle, confused about the *oh no*.

"I forgot how cute you are," she said.

And then she was in their arms, her mouth on theirs, tasting fresh and clean and soft, and London had to bite back a moan. A rush of warmth filled their system, having her solid against their chest again, the door clicking shut as they pushed their fingers into her back, their head light and fuzzy and—

"Okay." Dahlia pushed back, walking into the room. "Where are we at?" She gasped, looking at the TV. "Oh my god, it's almost over! Cher's almost there!"

She leaped onto London's bed and got under the covers. When London joined her, she immediately cuddled up next to them, shoving her head under their arm like a puppy and resting her head on their chest.

This was what London wanted. Every goddamn day of their life.

A laugh burst from Dahlia's throat when Cher came on-screen.

"Have you ever seen anything so over-the-top? God. This must have been so fun to film."

London turned their head to nuzzle their nose in her hair. They breathed in deep. God, it felt good, having her next to them like this. It felt good, letting the weirdness of yesterday slip away.

"Want to watch something else?" London extracted themself from Dahlia once the credits started rolling, digging around in the sheets for the remote.

"Sure." Dahlia sat up.

As London scrolled through the Netflix menu, they felt her shift next to them, draw up her knees to her chin.

"London?"

They looked over at her.

"Yeah?"

But she just bit her lip, not saying anything. London pressed Mute on the remote.

It was peak Dahlia Thoughtful Face. London could practically feel the thoughts swirling underneath her skin. But she only sat there, silent.

She jumped up suddenly, opening the drawer on London's bedside table, pulling out the generic hotel pad of paper inside.

"Let's make a list." She sat back down, crisscross applesauce, on the bed.

"A list?"

"Of things we want to do before we leave LA. Top ten."

Something twisted inside of London's gut when Dahlia said that phrase. *Before we leave LA.* She started scribbling something down, in that messy, loopy handwriting.

"I want to go to Hollywood and take a selfie with Dolly Parton's star on the Walk of Fame, for Hank," she said before looking back up at them. "What about you?"

London just stared at her. They couldn't think of a single thing, other than simply being with her. Staying on *Chef's Special* for as long as humanly possible. Sleeping next to her. They didn't want to think about leaving LA.

"Maybe we could go to Universal Studios?" London said eventually, racking their brain for things that were in LA. "Or Disneyland?"

Dahlia smiled before she caught herself and shook her head.

"I've always wanted to go to Disney. But no, too expensive."

"I could pay," London offered. "I don't mind."

"No," Dahlia said immediately, sharply. "No. Actually, pretty much everything on this list has to be...cheap. Or free. I sort of blew my budget already on rideshares, when I was sightseeing last weekend. Anyway, there are a ton of free things to do in LA," she said, voice business-like now, like she was a travel agent giving a PowerPoint presentation. "I want to go to the Last Bookstore. Oh, and there's another one I read about that's devoted completely to romance novels."

She wrote *Bookstores* next to the number *2* on her list.

"Okay, what's something else you want to do?" she asked. "You have to contribute at least one thing to the list. Please," she added.

"There's an art installation outside some museum," they said after a moment of thought. They had seen pictures on Instagram. "A bunch of lampposts all together. It's supposed to look cool at night."

Dahlia nodded emphatically and wrote it down.

"Want to go tomorrow night?" She looked up at them, her eyes full of a cautious hope, almost like she was nervous.

Almost like she was...asking London on a date.

"Sure." London's stomach flipped.

"Cool." She smiled, face relaxing, and looked back down at the list.

"And I want to go back to that beach with you," London said, their mind racing now to what they truly still wanted to do in LA. "In Malibu. I want to make out with you for real there. Like, flat out on the sand, full-body making out. Like, you'll-have-sand-stuck-in-your-hair-for-days level of making out."

Dahlia laughed, and it was the most magnificent sound. Maybe it hadn't even been a full twenty-four hours since they'd been apart, but London had missed it anyway.

"That sounds...rather unfair to my hair."

London shrugged. "It's what I want."

Dahlia stuck her thumb between her teeth, grinning.

"I can't see engaging in full-body making out with you that doesn't result in full-body sex."

"All right then," London said. "Write it down."

Dahlia wrote next to the number *4: Sex on the beach*. And then, *maybe*.

"Excuse me!" London scoffed and reached over to grab the pen from her hand, scribbling out that last word. "You can't *maybe* your own suggestions!"

"I just!" Dahlia sputtered. "All I'm picturing is sand in the vag, and doesn't that seem uncomfortable?"

"We'll bring a towel," London growled, and Dahlia laughed again.

"Okay, okay. Oh, and I want to go to Koreatown," she said smoothly, like this transition made sense, and London was tempted to check off number four right now, beach or no beach.

"Taco trucks," they said, to get their mind out of the gutter. "Those are cheap," they added.

Dahlia wrote it down.

They came up with four others—Santa Monica Pier, the Getty, Grand Central Market, Sunset Boulevard—and then Dahlia put down her pen, smiling.

"Know what else is cheap? Ice cream. We definitely need ice cream before the next movie." She stood. "Let's do an AM/PM run."

London looked down at themself again.

"I can't go out like this."

Dahlia rolled her eyes.

"To the gas station? Yes, London, you can."

And just like that, she was dragging them out the door.

A half hour and a shared pint of Chunky Monkey later, Dahlia's body was curled next to London again, and they were a quarter of the way through *Always Be My Maybe*. London had attempted to slide their hand under her shirt ten minutes ago and she had slapped it away, saying distractedly, "Stop it; I've never seen this before," her eyes glued to the screen.

Having now spent nine hours watching movies, London's own eyes felt dry and sore. The heat of her body next to theirs made them sleepy. They were fine with a simple night of movies and cuddling, they supposed. Mostly.

They ran their fingers through her hair.

"That could be you, you know," they said, referencing Ali Wong's celebrity chef character on the TV screen.

Dahlia shook her head against their chest.

"No. That should be you."

London was quiet a moment, fingers still in her hair.

"I don't want that," they said.

"Me neither," she murmured.

A few minutes later, she hugged London's torso tighter.

"What am I going to do, London? After this."

London tried to look down at her. "What do you want to do?"

"I don't know," she whispered.

They placed their lips on her forehead.

"I think… the dreams we have when we're kids matter."

London had been thinking about this, too, almost subconsciously, since they'd been out here. They were going to make more of an effort when they got back home to get into a music studio. There were a ton of people these days who were more passionate about podcasts than they were. London wanted to be around guitars, drums, pianos. They wanted to feel bass lines reverberating in their bones. They wanted to spend their days filling their guts with music.

"Maybe you should write."

Dahlia released a breathy half laugh.

"About what? I hate to break it to you, London, but my dad was wrong; Camp Sunnywood was in fact not worthy of a Pulitzer."

"Well, first of all, I doubt that." London moved their hand to rub her back. "Write about what you know." A moment later, they added, "You could write about food."

"Writing about anything won't pay my bills," she said.

"You're going to win $100,000, though," London said. "You won't have to worry about bills."

She didn't answer. But she gave their body another soft squeeze.

London was sad that Dahlia's breath was already growing heavier, stretched out, by the time they got to the Keanu Reeves dinner scene. Dahlia would love this. But they were pretty sure she was already asleep.

Then they heard her mumble something into their side.

"What?"

"I'm going to disappoint you," she said. Her eyes were closed.

"What?" London asked again.

"I disappoint everyone."

"Dahlia," London whispered, nudging her shoulder.

What did that mean, she disappointed everyone?

But she was already asleep.

London frowned, running their fingers through her hair a moment more.

Carefully, so as not to wake her, they reached for the side table, fingers fumbling for the remote. But before they could turn off the movie and follow Dahlia into slumber, before they could further analyze what Dahlia had just said, their phone buzzed.

London, srsly, was our dad always an asshole? And we just didn't know?? Because he was our dad?? I can't stop thinking about this

London blinked.

Before they could think of what to say in response to this, Julie kept typing.

But our mom is so baller

And she wouldn't be married to such an asshole, right?

But sometimes people in relationships do weird things

Ugh

London finally found the remote and shut off the damn TV. They stared at their phone, the only sound in the room now the loud thud of their heart.

They had been waiting for these texts, at least subconsciously. For weeks, Julie had sounded off, dodging relatively normal questions from London like, *Hey Jules, how was*

Sunday supper? And Julie wasn't one to dodge, wasn't the kind of person to give vague, one-word answers. Julie Parker usually told a person everything that was on her mind, whether they wanted to know or not.

Yet suddenly, everything back in Nashville, according to her, was *fine*. Fine fine *fine*. London was starting to hate the word.

But now that Julie was finally sounding like herself again, London felt queasy.

Julie, they typed, gathering their courage, *What's going on? What did Dad do?*

And then, of course, she was silent.

They extricated themself from Dahlia, rolling her gently toward the other side of the bed. She went willingly, making a little humming sound.

London turned onto their side, took a few deep breaths.

Julie? They tried again.

Ugh, sorry London

Ben gave me tequila; he will be punished tomorrow

Ignore me

Everything is fine here

Love you

London stared at the phone for long, useless minutes, wishing their twin's ruthless honesty would magically reappear, even though they knew it wouldn't.

Because the other thing London knew to be true about Julie was that she'd do anything in her power to protect those she loved.

Sighing, London threw the phone onto the side table, rolling back over toward Dahlia, pulling her close. They wrapped an arm around her stomach, finding her hands, twining their fingers together. More indistinct murmurs rumbled from her chest as she wiggled her butt into them, and they couldn't help but smile into her hair.

London knew, deep down, that they didn't need Julie to put two and two together for them. They didn't like that she was hiding the details, but London could guess well enough. That having your child parading around in an identity you didn't agree with, on national TV, no less, probably wasn't an easy thing for a proud man like Tom Parker to swallow.

They just didn't know what to do about it. What it would feel like, when they went back home, when they had to face their family and everyone they knew again. They'd outed themself to millions of strangers. They knew there would be fallout.

It was just so easy to ignore reality when they were on set. When they were here, next to Dahlia. London tucked their face into the warmth of her neck and closed their eyes, trying to calm their pulse.

Maybe Dahlia and London had more in common than just cooking. They still didn't know exactly what Dahlia had meant, before she'd fallen asleep. But maybe London knew a thing or two about being a disappointment.

CHAPTER EIGHTEEN

Dahlia squeezed London's hand on the way back to the hotel from the set Monday night. They grinned at her. She grinned dumbly back.

The past weekend had been... incredible. Dahlia had decided to shove any lingering doubts about *Chef's Special* out of her mind, and for this one, magical weekend, just be. No hashtags, no anxiety about eliminations. No cameras. She let herself have it all with London, one memory at a time.

Everything had felt carefree and fun, exploring LA together, filling their stomachs with tacos and bubble tea and laughter and wine.

And today the magic had continued, even with the returned pressure of being back on set. They had worked together on a special group challenge, along with the other remaining contestants, cooking a meal for the *Chef's Special* crew. It felt so *right*, cooking side by side. Dahlia loved watching London work. Their plating skills were impeccable, so precise and beautiful.

They were an artist. All the best chefs were.

For her, she had helped make several rounds of the

most delicious pork tenderloin. It had been a rush, working on so many plates at once, and the crew had raved. It was so satisfying, cooking for someone other than the judges. It filled her belly with pride, cooking good food for good people.

They had another Elimination Challenge tomorrow. But as they walked into the hotel lobby, Dahlia didn't feel nervous, full only of a restless kind of energy.

They walked toward the elevators, but Dahlia paused, tugging on London's arm as an idea sneaked into her brain.

They quirked an eyebrow but followed without question, until Dahlia paused before two massive doors.

"I think it's empty."

Dahlia held her ear to the ballroom doors for another second before trying a handle. To her delight, it swung open. She pranced inside, light on her toes. She turned to London once she reached the center of the dance floor, now completely devoid of wedding revelers.

"We missed the slow dance, last time we were here."

London ambled over to her, scratching the back of their neck.

"I don't think we're supposed to be here right now."

"That didn't stop you last time." She smiled. A bubble of laughter escaped her throat as a flash of memory lit up her brain.

"You should have seen the panic on your face when that slow song came on. I had to steal that wine for us to save you."

"It was a bad song anyway." London dug their phone out of their back pocket. "Do you have a better one in mind?"

She shook her head. "Your choice."

London was quiet a moment, scrolling through their phone.

Dahlia bounced on her feet, fine with waiting. Fine with stretching out this night as far as it would go.

"That dress you wore that night…" London glanced up at her for a second. "That dress was rude, Dahlia."

"I had never worn it before."

"Really?" London's eyebrows raised a smidge, a corner of their mouth lifting. They were pleased, she could tell, that they were the only one who had seen her wear it.

"Yeah. I bought it as a bit of retail therapy one day, before I flew out. I had visions of maybe making a new friend in LA who might want to go out on the town one night." She smiled. "Turns out I got you."

London finally made a selection and placed their phone on the ground.

Dahlia moved to put her hands around their waist but paused at the deep frown on their face.

"What? You don't even want to slow dance with me when we are literally the only people here?"

"No, no, not that. It's just…" London waved their hand in the air angrily. "The sound quality of this phone speaker is atrocious. It's an insult to Sam Cooke, honestly."

Dahlia reached around their waist and squeezed, shoving her face into their chest. "I'll take it."

"Wait," London said. "Aren't I supposed to have my arms around *your* waist? I don't know what to do with my arms now."

She pulled back to look at them. "Isn't that pretty gender role-y?"

"No. I'm taller than you. You put your hands around my neck, I put mine on your back. That's how it works."

Dahlia settled her face back into their chest, squeezing their torso even tighter.

"Too bad. I'm comfy here."

She felt them shake their head, but their arms wrapped around her shoulders, their fingers brushing the back of her neck.

It was more of a slightly swaying hug than it was a dance, but that was how she liked it. She closed her eyes, resting her forehead against their shoulder.

"London," she said quietly after a minute of listening to the lyrics. "I think this is a sad song."

She felt them kiss her hair. "All the best love songs are."

Dahlia didn't know what to say to that. So she just held London Parker through another sweet, sad song.

In the middle of the third song, London trailed their fingers up the nape of her neck, reaching into her hairline, massaging her scalp. Her eyes fell closed.

"My dad has never used my pronouns," London said.

Dahlia's eyes popped open.

She tilted her head back to look at them, every other thought dropping out of her brain.

"What?"

London's eyes were unreadable.

"I don't know why I wanted to tell you that just now. But...there it is."

"So he doesn't..."

"Yeah. He thinks I'm going through a phase, or something. A three-year-slash-lifelong phase."

Dahlia extracted an arm from their back, ran a finger down their cheek.

"London. I'm so sorry."

"Julie has texted me some vague things about him recently. I think…" London's forehead creased. "I think me being out on the show has caused some drama, maybe."

"And you hate drama," Dahlia supplied.

"I really do."

"The rest of your family…?"

London nodded. "Yeah. They're okay."

"Good," Dahlia whispered.

"Anyway, I don't really want to talk about it. I just wanted you to know."

"Okay." She rubbed their neck.

"Will you talk to me more about…stuff that's ever bothering you, too? Family stuff or life stuff or anything."

London's eyes were searching, serious.

Dahlia swallowed.

"Yes," she said. Although feeling mopey about never being able to please her mother seemed like a small thing, just then.

"Okay." London took a shivery breath. And then, "Enough of that."

They leaned down and picked up their phone. "Let's get some air."

Dahlia followed them through the ballroom, toward the door that led to the courtyard.

It felt like she was walking through jelly.

Rage seeped through her system with each step, with each second that London's words tumbled through her brain. He hadn't used London's pronouns once in *three years*? She had turned from a purring cat inside London's arms to a hulking lioness. She wanted to roar, to sink her talons into London's dad's chest, watch him writhe in pain.

Dahlia and London stepped out into the early evening, into the courtyard with the lit-up, shimmery fountain under a purple sky.

"It's weird no one else is ever out here," London said. "It's beautiful."

Dahlia nodded, barely hearing them, feeling weirdly short of breath.

London turned to look at her, their mouth turned up in a half smile.

"Maybe it's just for us."

Dahlia caught their eye and had to look away.

Suddenly, Dahlia really couldn't breathe.

Oh god.

She had known this for a while, probably. Maybe she didn't know it the last time they were out here in this courtyard, but at some point after that. Maybe the first time she'd actually pressed her lips to theirs. Maybe that morning in the shower, after the food sex. This weekend, probably, when they'd gone to bookstores and museums and London had gotten a slight sunburn and she'd been happier than she could ever remember being.

But right now, as London took a step toward her and she could already anticipate how their lips were going to feel in a few seconds, she knew. When London had asked her, a few minutes ago, to tell them things, anything that bothered her, she knew they meant it, and she knew she wanted to tell them. Anything and everything. When London had told her about their dad, she felt an urge to protect London with her life, to battle anything that ever caused them harm.

Because she loved them.

London pressed her back against the concrete wall, her bare shoulders scraping against its cold, unforgiving surface. She was wearing a loose summery dress, navy dotted with small light purple hearts. Sleeveless and high necked, a small ruffle around the collar. She had her hair up; the ruffle didn't work otherwise.

This dress wasn't tight and revealing like the black one had been, last time they'd been here, but Dahlia still felt pretty in this one.

She knew London always thought she was pretty. But it felt better when she felt it, too.

London leaned down and claimed her mouth. Her lips parted automatically for them, wanting to be claimed. Wanting London to swallow her whole.

London's mouth moved to her hairline behind her ear, their hands traveling up the outside of her thighs. Dahlia gazed over their shoulder at the hazy sky, orange hues blasting through the purple and pink. A picture-perfect smog-enhanced twilight. It blanketed the courtyard in warm light, making even London's pale skin look golden. Their hair shone like fizzy champagne.

"London," she said, her voice strained. "Can you fuck me hard and dirty? Right here?"

They lifted their head to look down at her.

"Yeah," they said after a moment. "I can do that."

The breeze kissed the skin of her thighs as London shifted up her dress with their palms. It was still warm, even though the sun was almost gone, that warmer-than-it-should-be late-summer evening feeling, heavy and intoxicating.

Dahlia sighed as London's fingers smoothed over her underwear once before yanking them down completely, and Dahlia barely had a second to kick them off before London was pushing her back against the wall again, pushing their lips into hers with bruising force, while their hand slipped back under her dress and found her clit.

She moaned against their lips. She wanted this to last forever, hoped against hope that if London just fucked her hard enough, this sensation could somehow solve things. Sex felt easier than talking, than telling the truth.

Because the real truth, Dahlia knew, hiding right underneath the surface like a sad, slow song, was that no matter what happened next, one of them would be leaving soon.

And maybe they were both too scared to talk about it.

Dahlia preferred this truth: the way London's hands always knew exactly where to go, the way their mouth always unlocked her favorite sacred spaces.

As if hearing her thoughts, London moved their lips to her neck and shifted their fingers until they were inside of her, two digits sharp and deep. Dahlia sank down onto them, shoving her body closer to their hands.

"I love how wet you always are for me," London breathed into her neck, while their thumb found its way back to her clit.

She groaned, head falling on to their shoulder. "That's good. Keep talking like that."

Dahlia tried to focus on how exciting this was. They were outside, in public, the sounds of the street just beyond the courtyard walls loud in her ears, the unlocked door back to the ballroom and the hotel literal inches away. Dahlia had never done anything like this before. There was also the fact that London was fully clothed. While her dress was hitched up around her waist at the moment, Dahlia essentially was, too. She knew London was going to get her off and that it was going to be good, all while they wore those skinny jeans and that faded lavender T-shirt. Dahlia didn't quite understand why this was so sexy, but it was.

London paused, withdrawing from her, stepping back an inch.

"Is it possible for you to move up a bit? The angle isn't right."

They shifted their stance and Dahlia hooked a leg around their thigh, arching up as much as she could, anchoring her shoulders against the wall. London gripped her hip, securing her against them. Their other hand reached up and tangled in her hair, pulling slightly. The slight pressure on her scalp made her want to scream.

London leaned down and bit her neck.

"Fuck," Dahlia said, half in surprise, half in pleasure. London's tongue reached out to massage where their teeth had just marked her, its wet pressure both soothing and increasing the pain.

"Touch me again," she said, achingly aware that London's hands were still occupied elsewhere.

"Not until you promise to stop holding back," London said into her ear. "You're normally much louder than this."

"Well." Dahlia tried to gesture around them with her chin. "The street is, you know, just beyond that wall."

"Your point is?" London nipped at her jaw. "Let them hear you. Pant for me, Dahlia."

Their fingers found their way between her legs again, and she did as asked. London was right. It felt better when she was uninhibited. It felt better when she let her body release what it needed to.

London circled around her clit, slow and tortuous, until Dahlia groaned.

"Faster. Two fingers in," she huffed.

"Like this?"

"Oh, *fuck*."

London was correct. The angle was much better this time.

"Ride my hand, Dahlia." London's voice was low, rumbly against Dahlia's cheek. Perfection.

She wrapped her arms around their neck, clutching at their back, and did just that.

"Dahlia," London groaned, their teeth nipping at her ear. "God. You're so…"

Dahlia bit her tongue, feeling herself starting to slide away, just like London's words. And she didn't want to yet. This had to last forever. It had to.

She released a heavy breath while she slowed the motion of her hips. London licked down her neck.

"Yell for me, Dahlia."

"Make me."

In one smooth motion, their fingers never slowing inside her, London dropped to their knees.

When she felt their mouth on her, she did yell. She shoved a hand into their hair and hung on tight.

"London," she breathed.

She couldn't stop. She was reaching that pinnacle now, the point of no return, where everything felt so good, and then she'd crash back to reality and why, why couldn't this keep being reality? Why did they have to be on a dumb TV show, why didn't they live in the same city, why couldn't she keep having just this, this, this—

"Oh, *fuck*," she cried, shoving London's face to her, fingers clenching in that wonderful strawberry hair. She had never come so hard in a standing position before, and before she knew what was happening, her legs gave out and she crashed, inelegantly, to the ground, to London's waiting arms.

They wrapped themself around her as she trembled, still coming down, their hands smoothing down her back.

Their voice was soft and gentle.

"Dahlia," London breathed onto her temple. "My Dahlia."

Something cracked open in Dahlia's chest.

Tears sprang to the corners of her eyes.

Her arms, which had been limp at her sides, came to life then, wrapping themselves around London's torso, her fingers curling in the soft cotton of their T-shirt.

They sat on the hard ground under a heavy Los Angeles sky, and they held each other until they found strength enough to stand again.

CHAPTER NINETEEN

The next day, their Elimination Challenge was based on the theme of seasons.

Dahlia was assigned autumn, which was perfect. Fall was her favorite.

She loved the comfort food feel of it, the tastes of the season as important as scarves and cozy cardigans and falling leaves.

The best time for soup.

A pumpkin and black bean soup, to be precise, with roasted pepitas and fresh, crusty spiced croutons. It was hearty, filling, flavorful. It was something Dahlia would actually make for herself to eat at home, and there was something about that that felt right. She adjusted the seasoning over and over to ensure that it was sweet and creamy but also had savory depth, a bit of kick left on your tongue. She knew the cameras and Janet's watchful eye were following them closer than ever, but she had less control today. She had London taste it no less than fifteen times. One, because she honestly wanted their advice. Two, because she loved brushing her fingers against that mouth so very much, watching them smile and nod their approval.

London had been assigned summer, and was making a

blueberry lavender galette with a lemon meringue topping. It was pretty and light, the opposite of Dahlia's, but she liked working on different things together: London confirming she'd used the right amount of chili powder, her assuring them the blueberry filling wasn't too sweet.

Dahlia wished, later, that it hadn't been such a lovely day. That she hadn't been so pleased with herself.

It would have made the fact that the judges hated her dish far less crushing.

"It's not that it's bad, Dahlia," Audra Carnegie said. "But we're getting closer and closer to having to decide who's going to be in the finale. You really have to step up your sophistication level at this point, and I'm not sure if this soup does that."

"It's ugly," Sai Patel said, bluntly. "It tastes okay, but it's an ugly dish."

"This soup is *fine*," Tanner Tavish said. "But we're not looking for fine. This is a dish for moms on Pinterest, not contestants on *Chef's Special*."

Dahlia had no idea what she said in reaction to these judgments, if she said anything at all, or how she got back to her station. But she was there, staring at the stainless steel countertop, during the interminable amount of time it took to judge the other contestants' dishes. She focused all of her energy on not looking at London.

She didn't hear what the judges said about their galette, but she was sure they liked it. It was beautiful. Everything London made was beautiful.

She kept thinking about that trip on her first day on set. How her tacos had flown through the air. How mortifying that had felt.

But that was silly, a meme. She hadn't known how much worse this would feel.

Dahlia thought she'd get kicked off after she truly messed up on something, when she floundered in a set of skills she didn't possess. Like how to make a great soufflé.

She didn't think she'd get kicked off on something she loved.

When she stepped into the Golden Circle for her final judgment, something funny tickled the back of her throat when she realized the other contestant in the bottom with her was Lizzie.

Had Janet orchestrated this? She could picture the head-lines: *London's Enemy versus London's Lover.* The cameras must be laser-focused on London right now, editors itching behind the scenes to soon splice in their reaction shot.

Lizzie stood next to her, chin raised, proud, while Dahlia barely held it together. Lizzie knew she was getting into the next round. She'd get into the next round, with London, and Dahlia was sick with jealousy and anger.

She felt like she was outside her body, watching it play on her own TV screen back on the East Coast, when Lizzie dropped away back to her station and Dahlia heard Tanner Tavish say her name with a sigh. She felt herself nodding and handing her apron to Audra Carnegie, who smiled sadly at her and squeezed her hand. Audra's hands were slightly rough—calloused, working hands—and something about that felt reassuring to Dahlia's skin. Maybe one day she could have hands like that, too.

She turned, eyes focused on the archway at the back of the set. Made her feet walk underneath it for the last time. She did not turn to look back at her station.

Team Dahlia was done.

Janet caught her lightly by the arm at the back of the set for the last time. They exchanged a wordless, curt nod. Right. Time for her last interview.

"It's okay that I'm going home," Dahlia said into the camera, trying to keep her voice steady, feeling numb. Because it wasn't okay. It wasn't okay at all. "I've learned so much from the judges and the other contestants, and I feel so grateful. I've met the most amazing people."

She stopped. Maritza tilted her head, wondering if Dahlia would continue.

"I'm sorry," Dahlia said. "That's all I've got."

Maritza nodded, eyes kind.

Dahlia looked behind her, at the thick turquoise glass she'd sat in front of so many times for these solo interviews. She knew everyone sat in this same exact set for these things, but it almost felt personal, a safe haven where she'd somehow become comfortable sharing thoughts in front of a camera. The turquoise glass was so pretty. She wondered how she could replicate something like it in her apartment, and knew she couldn't. It looked expensive.

"Keep your phone on," Maritza said gently. "I'm sure Janet will let you know your flight info back home when the PAs get it to her. It'll probably be in the morning sometime. And hey, Dahlia? You did a great job here. Get some rest. You should feel proud."

Dahlia nodded and stood. Part of her wanted to give Maritza a hug—she had really enjoyed the time she spent with her—but her body didn't quite know what to do, like it was functioning on low battery. She hesitated behind the closed door, dread pooling in her stomach about what she would find outside of it. Would London be right there, waiting, their eyes full of pity and disappointment? Why hadn't she planned what she wanted to say to them?

What *did* she want to say to them?

A tiny sliver of luck must have been granted to her by a sympathetic god, because when she finally opened the door— or when Maritza eventually opened the door—London was clear on the other side of the room, talking to Cath. Their hands were stuffed in the pockets of the loose army-green chinos they wore so much. They were the prettiest thing she'd ever seen.

She turned on her heel and fled out of the studio, not taking another second to look back.

Her luck did not last long.

"Dahlia. Dahlia, what are you doing?"

London wrapped their hands around Dahlia's wrists.

Dahlia closed her eyes at the contact. Her sprint here had afforded her a few extra moments to herself, to unearth her suitcase from the closet, to breathe. But she hadn't been able to ignore the knock on her door she knew would come. Now, inevitably, London was in front of her, eyes panicked and pleading. And her mind remained as foggy as it had been in the solo interview set. This was going to be the worst.

"What it looks like, London." Dahlia swallowed, trying to keep her voice calm. "I'm packing. My flight leaves tomorrow morning."

"But you—" London sputtered. Their face was pale, dotted with splotches of red. They looked unhinged. "You can't leave, Dahlia."

"I don't think I have a choice."

"Sure you do!" London released her wrists and threw their hands in the air. "Say you don't need the ticket. Just wait with me. Wait until I go, too. Then we can—"

London stopped. Understanding that they had never talked about it, how to end that sentence.

"You're not going to go, London," Dahlia said, trying to sound proud, not sad, but she knew she was failing. "Not until the end."

"Then stay until the end!" London begged, eyes wide. "Please. Please, Dahlia. Don't leave me. I...I can't do this without you."

Dahlia felt a chill advancing down her spine. Sadness morphing into a touch of anger.

She didn't want to be angry at them. She wanted to hug them and have them squeeze her tight for the next eight hours, and then kiss her sweetly before she left. She wanted them to soothe her, tell her it would be all right. And then they could both look back at all of this with fondness.

But their desperate panic was causing all of her frayed, embarrassed nerves to snap, to seethe, angry and hot, under her skin.

They were missing the point. They didn't get to be upset here. They were going to win; didn't they see? They were going to get the $100,000. They were going to accomplish their mission.

And she was happy for them. She was.

But right now all she was capable of understanding was that she had lost.

Just like Janet always knew. Just like everyone watching at home probably always knew.

She had lost it all.

"God. You'll be fine."

Dahlia huffed out a breath, waved a hand in the air. The anger bloomed like a virus in her chest, unwanted but thriving anyway.

She turned and continued flinging clothes into her suitcase. If she kept moving, then maybe she wouldn't cry. Silence ticked away as she worked, London unmoving behind her.

She could feel them, though, even without seeing them. The tension in their body, the pinched stress in their face weighed down on her shoulders, a load she didn't know how to handle.

"I quit my *job*, London," she said eventually, twirling back around to face them. Dahlia knew her failures weren't London's fault. But she needed them to at least bear witness to them here. To acknowledge the difference between them and her. "I don't know if I'll even be able to make rent next month. Fuck. *Fuck.* I am a fucking idiot."

"Come to Nashville." London stepped toward her, reaching for her hands. "Dahlia. You don't belong in Maryland. You're not happy there. Come to Nashville. You'll love it, I promise."

Dahlia stepped away, an icy feeling filling her chest.

"London. No. You don't get to tell me where I do or don't belong, okay? This is my life. I'm in charge of it. The whole reason I tried out for this thing was to see if I could be good at something, on my own. To follow you home like a lost puppy…" Dahlia shook her head, squeezing her eyes shut for a moment. "It would be even more of a failure than getting kicked off *Chef's Special*."

London looked wounded.

"I don't think trying to be with me would be a *failure*, Dahlia," they said softly, the hurt in their voice evident.

But something about that hurt slotted inside Dahlia's brain, felt right in a sickening way. She wanted London to be angry, too. It was so lonely, being angry alone.

"You don't understand, London. I know you have money, okay? I bet you could probably start that nonprofit no matter what, even without the prize money. But I *needed* it. You have no idea how humiliated I am right now. That I finally have to face it, what a mess I am."

"Dahlia," London said, an edge finally entering their voice. "You're not—"

"*Stop.*"

Dahlia needed London to stop lying.

"Okay." London dropped their hands and took a deep, shaky breath. "I'm sorry. For trying to tell you where you belong. What if…what if I come to Maryland?"

"What?" Dahlia shook her head, shuddering at even the idea of that. Why couldn't they get this? She had lost. She *was* lost. But they…they were going to shoot their shot. They had so much good ahead of them. She'd go back to her life, try to reshape it again, and they'd start their nonprofit in Tennessee. If they threw that away for her, she'd never forgive herself. Or them. "No. No, London. I don't want that."

London stared at her, the color that had been in their

cheeks fading away until they looked pale and gutted. It was the worst thing Dahlia had ever seen.

"London." She put her hands on her hips, looking down at the floor. Tried to be the voice of reason, focus back on the here and now. "I have to go, but you have to stay. You can't let Lizzie win. Okay?"

"Dahlia." London scoffed. "You have to know that I don't give a shit about Lizzie right now."

Dahlia needed to keep moving. She'd been standing still too long.

She was running out of things to say, things that could keep this overwhelming sadness at bay. Nothing was working, and a pressure was building behind her eyes. She knew if this conversation didn't end soon, or get better somehow, the tears would start. And she didn't know, if she let them start, if she'd be able to make them stop.

She picked up a book she had started three weeks ago and never finished, and tossed it into the suitcase.

"Although maybe that was how this all was supposed to shake out in the end anyway," she muttered, half to herself. The effort to keep it together was starting to make her feel half-delirious. "Lizzie wants to start a bakery, right? Isn't that why people normally try out for this awful show? To actually start a career in food? Why'd they even the let the two of us on here? God. Maybe we are just two idiots."

Dahlia slammed a bra on top of the book.

"I don't..." London's voice wavered. "I don't think you mean that."

She didn't. She barely understood what she was saying at this point. It did seem kind of funny to her, though, now that she thought about it. That neither of them fit the narrative of this show, how it was supposed to be. That they had both somehow found their way here anyway.

"I don't think we're idiots at all," London said quietly, after a horrible, awkward minute of silence as Dahlia looked under her bed for missing socks. "But I do think you're acting like an idiot right now."

Ouch, Dahlia thought. At the same time that she thought, *Fair*.

The pressure was prickling at the corner of her eyes now. *Danger zone.* She stood, spinning in a circle, seeing what else in the near vicinity she could throw into her suitcase.

"Dahlia," London said, frustration ringing in their voice now. "Can you please stop fucking packing and *look at me*? Show me I mean anything at all to you? I don't...I don't understand why you're being like this."

Dahlia ran a shaky hand through her hair. She needed them to go, now. It was too much.

She turned to face them.

With David she had learned what it felt like to break your own heart slowly, torturously, fight after fight, month after month.

Now she knew what it felt like to break it all at once.

"London." She licked her lips. "We knew this would happen. You don't even know how grateful I am for...you, for every-thing, but now we have to both go back to—"

"Don't do that." London took a step closer. "Don't you dare fucking do that. What are you saying, that this was a *fling*? You're just declaring it over? Don't I get a say?"

Dahlia couldn't look at them. She stared just past their

shoulder, at the door, at a loss for what to say. She wanted
to explain it all better somehow. Explain what they actually
meant to her, what this had all meant. She knew she was
saying all the wrong things, but all she could hear was Tanner
Tavish saying her name for the last time. Maritza, with
her kind, sad eyes, telling her a PA would bring her plane
ticket soon.

They should have talked about all of this before, she and
London, but they hadn't, and now, when she should have been
telling them how much she loved them, all she could taste was
her own bitter loss.

"Dahlia." London tried again, gentler this time, and the
audacity of them to be gentle at all with her right now, when
she knew she was being awful, was just gut-wrenching. "Don't
run away. Wait with me. Be with me."

She swallowed.

"You're braver than this," London whispered. "Don't run
away."

Dahlia closed her eyes. There were so many things she
could have said.

I'm not braver than this.

I love you.

But what she said was "I think you should go."

London froze. They stared at her for too many beats, each
second feeling too long. Waiting for her to take it back.

"Please, London," she whispered, the pressure in her head
painful now. "I want you to go."

Their face changed then. They clenched that beautiful jaw
and looked down at the floor.

"Fine." London sighed, and finally, finally, in that heavy

puff of air, Dahlia heard *goodbye*. "Your self-fulfilling prophecy has finally come true. Congratulations, Dahlia. You've disappointed me, too."

Dahlia blinked.

Her bones felt hollow, like a bird's. On the verge of breaking, pulverizing into dust.

London took a step back. They shook their head one last time.

"Have fun rooting for Lizzie."

No, she wanted to cry. *That wasn't—*

London walked toward the door.

Frantically, she tried to compartmentalize this in her brain, the last time she would see London Parker. But all that flashed behind her eyes were error messages. Everything felt wrong.

London didn't look back. The door closed behind them, the softest of clicks. Of course London Parker would not slam doors. They would not shout.

They simply walked away, quiet and steady. Dahlia stared after them, the sudden silence of her hotel room crowding her brain, suffocating and vicious, until her legs gave out and she slumped to the floor, finally alone with her sloppy, half-packed suitcase.

CHAPTER TWENTY

Dahlia's first thought, when she entered her apartment, was that she should cancel cable.

She'd been thinking about doing it forever anyway.

The entire plane ride from LAX to BWI, her brain had been stuck on a loop of memories. Eating ice cream and watching movies on London's bed, dancing with them at that wedding, ocean breezes streaming through her hair in the car while they rested in the seat beside her. And then a new frame would cut in: the way London looked at her last night. The click of the door when they left. Rinse and repeat.

She had shed all her tears between the time London left her room and the taxi took her to the airport. Time to cut off the loop now. Start a new frame.

Maybe she could apply for deferment for her student loans. It wasn't a great financial decision, but it would only be for a little while. Everyone did it. Maybe she could get her old job back, or apply for something else at the paper. She had been a solid worker. Maybe they would take her back.

Dahlia's suitcase slapped the floor as she dropped it next to the door. She walked into her tiny kitchen. Faced its empty cabinets.

For the last few weeks, Dahlia had cooked with the finest ingredients in the world. She had almost started to feel like it was normal, having an endless pantry full of food of the highest quality. It was so bizarre, this experience Dahlia had just had, that standing in her barren kitchen now, she wondered if it had even happened. If she had hallucinated the last month of her life entirely.

Dahlia walked into her bedroom. She curled into a ball on top of the covers without taking off her clothes. She tried to make herself small, as small and unnatural as she felt.

When she woke hours later, all she could think about was how much she missed the hotel.

Eventually, Dahlia got up. She changed her clothes. She would get through this. She just needed to make a plan.

She found a spoon and a half-empty jar of peanut butter in the kitchen and sat on her drooping Ikea couch. Okay, she *had* missed this rug. Sinking her toes into its high-pile luxury had been the best part of her day, sometimes. It was probably the nicest thing she had bought for herself after the divorce. She'd let David keep almost all their old furniture.

She walked to the window. Her apartment looked out over a highway, the boxy gray roofs of shopping plazas, occasional canopies of trees. Sometimes, at night especially, she liked watching the lights zipping by on the highway, so many people on their way to somewhere.

Her apartment was okay. She had been proud to have a space that was all her own.

It was acceptable, she told herself, to admit that this was hard. To admit that returning here confirmed it. That although this apartment had been an important step for her, for a little while, it still didn't feel like home.

And Dahlia suddenly, achingly wanted a home.

You don't belong in Maryland. You're not happy there.

Dahlia turned back toward the living room, clutching anxiously at her neck.

Building blocks. Taking things one step at a time.

There was a U-Haul store around the block. She would go and get boxes. She would pick up bread and milk on the way back. Steps one and two.

Dahlia picked up her phone. Step three.

"Hey, Dad? Hey, yeah. So, I'm back in Maryland. I got kicked off the show. Yeah, it's okay. Don't tell anyone else. No...no, Dad, I'm all right. But I was wondering...How would you feel about having a visitor for a while?"

London squinted into the sun.

It was barely ten o'clock, and this day had already felt a million years long.

They had no idea how they were going to survive this weekend.

The last two days had been tolerable. Sure, London had been living in a state of excruciating purgatory, but at least they'd been able to cook. They'd had tasks to complete on set, things to occupy their hands and their mind.

After the fight with Dahlia on Tuesday, London had lain in bed, unsleeping, staring at their phone for hours, willing a text to come through. Or maybe a knock at their door. Sleep must have overtaken them at some point, and they woke to Janet banging down their door.

"I didn't have the heart to bring the airhorn," she'd said, when London had finally opened up. "But you gotta get going, honey."

And by that point, Dahlia was gone.

Had someone been there to pick her up at the airport? London couldn't stop thinking about that. Hank and her parents were in Massachusetts. Dahlia hadn't, now that London thought about it, mentioned many friends back in Maryland, other than some old coworkers. Maybe she had called them. Maybe she wasn't alone. The idea of her being alone made them want to set something on fire.

Even though thinking about the way things had ended between them on Tuesday night made them want to set something on fire, too.

London would be happy with an inferno right about now. Just burn everything clean. Spark new growth.

But they had followed Janet back to set on Wednesday morning. They had completed the challenges that day and the next, watched Khari get kicked off on Thursday. Listened to the judges congratulate them, Cath, and Lizzie on being the top three.

And felt absolutely numb about all of it.

Now they had a three-day weekend, before one last Elimination Challenge next week that would determine the final two contestants of season eight, who would then head to the finale.

London had no idea how to fill three entire days without Dahlia.

So they were doing what they'd done the last two nights, after they'd returned to their hotel room after filming and realized they had no desire to do anything but punch things.

They walked.

London put on sneakers, left the hotel, and walked. They walked even though they were already exhausted. They walked until their feet hurt.

Eventually, they'd call a Lyft back to the hotel.

They knew they should probably return their rental car. They weren't going to touch it, obviously. It reminded them too much of her.

London pulled out their phone now as they walked and checked for new notifications. They had muted everything the last few weeks, after the first episode aired. It was too hard, trying to filter out the trolls from the encouragement, too time-consuming blocking everyone who said something shitty. London knew they were out of touch with the world, but frankly, they'd been too infatuated with Dahlia Woodson to care.

Ever since she left, they'd plugged back in. London was dumbstruck at the amount of followers they had now. They'd connected with all their online friends again, who had been freaking out and were thrilled to hear from them. It felt good, talking to people who actually wanted to still talk to them.

The encouraging messages that had been pouring onto their timeline and into their DMs now felt important enough to filter through the trolls for. They drowned out the #TeamLizzie versus #TeamLondon bullshit. London had been checking their phone obsessively these last few days, during breaks on set, at night when they couldn't sleep. They tried to skim through the worst of it. They clicked through to the Block button as fast as they could.

And then they slowed down for the rest. Made sure they read every word.

I can't tell you how much it means to me that I get to watch a nonbinary person on TV. On this week's episode, Sai and Tanner were discussing your dish, and they kept saying "their dish" and "their skills" and I almost couldn't believe it, these two famous people using your pronouns like it wasn't a big deal. It's made me picture a better world for myself. Thank you.

My child came out to me this week as nonbinary. We watch Chef's Special together and I can't help but make the connection. Thank you so much for being you.

Are you seeing anyone? Because I am available, all hours of the day. Just so you knooooowwwww

I know you're from Nashville—do you have any advice for a trans kid living in a small town in Kentucky? It's like we're neighbors but we're not…I've been daydreaming about moving to Nashville and hanging out with you and things being okay. But I'm just in high school and don't have money and don't want to leave my mom, but things don't really feel okay.

My previously kind of transphobic sister totally has a crush on you and it is HILARIOUS. She keeps saying "They are just a really good cook!" but WE ALL KNOW and she says THEY!!

She even makes us watch all the episodes LIVE, like in REAL TIME, and who even does that? I am obsessed with it. You are rocking worlds out here, London

Hey London, love watching you on Chef's Special! Was just wondering if you could RT this thread? It's full of assigned-male-at-birth nonbinary folx, and honestly it feels like a lot of people don't even know we're out here too. Thanks <3

I had never heard the term nonbinary before, but my grandson helped explain it to me. He is also helping me send this message. I just want to say I am so impressed with your generation. I know a lot of people probably give you a hard time, but you young people are always teaching me new interesting things, and I wonder about how many people of my generation could probably never be themselves, and how many of us are feeling better, even as old geezers, seeing you change the world. Thank you for teaching me. I hope you win.

London hadn't been able to respond to all of the messages, often because they simply didn't know what to say. But they boosted and retweeted all the ones from other trans people. They had sent a line to that Kentucky kid. Told them they could hang out with them in Nashville anytime they wanted.

They had been thinking about that kid in Kentucky a lot.

The messages were also a balm against London's increasing anxiety about their family. They hadn't heard from their father since that lonely *Ok*. And Julie hadn't texted anything real since that night a week ago. The Parkers were still "just fine."

London stopped to watch a group of kids running around the yard of a YMCA. Their screams had pierced through London's headphones.

They watched them tumble down slides, hang like monkeys from a play structure. They chased each other in zigzags, tagging the backs of elbows, giggling furiously.

London continued walking after a minute. An idea was forming in their mind.

By the time another few blocks had passed, London almost felt...excited.

A summer camp for LGBTQ+ kids. A cooking camp, to be specific. London would find a place in the woods and teach queer and trans and gender-nonconforming kids of all ages how to cook.

Telling marginalized kids that they were loved, that it would get better, was all well and good, but it didn't necessarily change their realities. Giving people a skill, on the other hand, making them feel like they were good at something, was useful and empowering.

This was what their nonprofit would be.

They could reach out to other LGBTQ+ nonprofits that already existed when they got home, other city programs that already ran for underprivileged children in the summer. Hopefully their name recognition from the show could encourage some type of partnership. It wouldn't have to be all on their own.

London's mind was racing through everything they should do first when their phone rang.

The noise made them stop, take stock of their surroundings. They had no idea where they were.

"Julie? Is everything okay?"

"Sure, other than the fact that you have been *ignoring all of my texts* so I just wanted to, you know, make sure you were *alive*."

London rolled their eyes. Had they been ignoring her texts? They didn't honestly know. Their memory was blurry these last few days.

"You didn't even respond to the video I sent where I tried on Ben's hiking backpack and promptly fell backward on my ass."

London laughed. They *had* watched that, and it had been hilarious. They must have forgotten to reply. That backpack had to be seriously heavy to knock Julie over.

Between this sudden burst of laughter and the adrenaline in their system about the cooking camp, London almost felt halfway alive again.

"I'm sorry. I did watch it. I've been distracted."

"Did something happen? Did you get kicked off the show?"

"No." London spotted a coffee shop across the street. They stabbed at the button at the crosswalk, waited for the orange hand to change. "Again, I'm not really supposed to tell you anything. But I'm in the top three."

"Holy shit, London. So you just have to get through one more challenge and you're in the finale?"

"Yeah." London hurried through the intersection.

"Oh my god. Oh my *god*, London, you're going to win."

"Eh. Probably not. Hold on, I'm going to go order a coffee and I'm not going to be that asshole talking on their phone at the counter."

"London—" they heard Julie shout, but they were already muffling her against their chest, walking up to a sleek black counter to order their Americano.

"Okay, so what's up?" London cradled the phone between their ear and shoulder after they'd gotten their drink, adding milk from the carafe station before walking back outside. "Did you really just call to yell at me about not answering your texts?"

"Why don't you think you're going to win?" Julie demanded, ignoring the question.

"There's this woman Cath, she's really good. Better than me probably. I wouldn't be upset if she won. And then there's—"

London stopped midstep and midsentence. They still didn't want to tell Julie about Lizzie. They didn't want to even have to say Lizzie's name. So they didn't.

"And then there's who? Who's the last contestant? Is it— wait. Wait, London, is the last contestant Dahlia?"

London sat down on a bench.

"No."

"Oh," Julie breathed. "So...she's gone?"

"Yeah." London kicked at a piece of trash on the ground. "Left Tuesday night."

London had told Julie some basic details about Dahlia last week. Even if they hadn't, turning their notifications back on had alerted them to the fact that everyone in the world apparently knew about them and Dahlia.

Almost every hour, London got more likes on the dumb photos they had posted last weekend, running around LA together, eating at taco trucks and taking selfies in front of tourist traps. And because they were a glutton for punishment, they couldn't make themself delete them.

"Wait," Julie said. "So what's happening? Are you going to do long distance, or—"

"No." London opened their mouth to explain more, and faltered. They were still so confused about what the fuck had happened this week that they didn't have words for it. "It...appears not."

"Oh," Julie said again, soft and concerned. "Oh, London." A pause. "Why not?"

London took a long drink of their Americano.

"She doesn't want to."

Julie guffawed into the phone. "I highly doubt that, London. That latest picture you posted, where you're eating ice cream and she's looking at you and laughing, I swear to god I have never seen anything so pure and—"

"I asked her to refuse the show's plane ticket back to Maryland, to stay with me and then come to Nashville, or I would go with her, whatever, and she basically told me to go fuck myself, so yeah, maybe you should believe it."

London huffed out an aggravated breath.

Maybe Dahlia hadn't used those exact words. The more time went by, the more London could barely remember what either of them had said, exactly.

But...well, it had felt like she said that.

Julie was quiet for a long moment.

"I mean...did you ever talk about what would actually happen? If either of you got kicked off?"

London racked their brain. As they had been doing all

week. They were positive they must have, at some point. After all, that was why London had rejected Dahlia's kiss in Malibu in the first place. Because they had been thinking things through. They had...

They had raced to her room a mere few days later and slept with her and then never looked back.

London ran a hand over their face. They assumed their silence was answer enough.

Julie sighed.

"Okay," she said. "So you just assumed Dahlia would move to Nashville? For you?"

London's defenses kicked in immediately.

"No. I said I would go to Maryland, too, but Julie, Dahlia hates Maryland, okay? The only reason she moved there was because of her ex-husband. She quit her job before she started the show, so there's literally nothing keeping her there. *Of course* she should come to Nashville."

"Right, but like...did you ask her what *she* wanted? If she *is* unattached to Maryland, maybe there are other dreams she had instead. Maybe she wanted to move to like...Colorado, or something, if she had been planning to move at all, and Tennessee wasn't exactly in her plans."

London stood up and threw their empty coffee cup in a trash bin. They didn't have a response to this. But it was annoying that it felt like Julie wasn't on their side here.

They had also been drinking too much coffee and eating too little food these last few days.

It was possible this was affecting their mood.

After a few moments of silence, Julie continued.

"London, you know I don't want you to leave Nashville. It

would be lovely if Dahlia moved here. Seriously, I support it one hundred percent, if it's her choice. I just feel like you two should have talked about this."

"I tried to talk about it, I swear, but when I got to her room that night, after she was kicked off...she was just throwing stuff into a suitcase and...I don't know, it was like she was a different person."

"Well, yeah, London, she'd just been *kicked off the show*. She was probably freaking out."

London stopped walking again, pinching their nose and taking a deep breath. They knew, suddenly, that they were going to cry, and they didn't want to, and they hated this.

"I wish we had at least gotten closure. It was the worst, Julie." London leaned their forehead against a pole, struggling to keep their voice even. "I...I don't even know what I'm doing here anymore. I just want to go home."

London heard Julie sniff. They almost laughed, knowing she had likely started crying the second she heard London's voice warble. She felt other people's emotions too easily.

"Anyway, thanks for letting me vent, Jules," they said quickly, wanting to backtrack so Julie wouldn't be sad. "I'm okay."

"No, you're not, you big jerk." Julie sniffed again. "God, I hate that I'm not there. If I was there, I would have made you dumbasses talk about this long before Dahlia got kicked off, and everything would be fine."

Now London did choke out a laugh.

"I don't know what I was thinking, coming to Los Angeles without you."

"You're damn right," Julie said. "It was foolish."

"It was also your idea."

Julie scoffed. "We were drunk that night, London. I didn't think when I dared you to get on the show that you would actually, like, *do it*."

London smiled. "Sure you did."

She sighed. "Yeah, you're right. Okay, but back to the show. I know you're upset about Dahlia, and I'm sure you miss home, but no more I-don't-know-what-I'm-doing-here talk, okay? Or eh-I-probably-won't-win bullshit. You're in the top three, London. I've watched you cook since we were babies, practically. I know how much you deserve this."

London stood back up and walked through another crosswalk, taking a steadying breath. They felt uneasy about the idea of *deserving* anything. Dahlia had deserved $100,000. So did Cath. So did anyone, really, who worked hard and tried to be a decent person.

"If you say so," they said.

"I do say so. I believe you can win this more than I've ever believed anything in my life. And hey, if you get into the finale, they invite families to come watch, right?"

They did.

They invited back former contestants, too.

But Dahlia probably wouldn't come. Probably.

Not that London had even made it into the finale yet.

They definitely weren't thinking about this.

"So hopefully, I'll be out there in less than a week to help cheer you on. I've already told work I might be taking a few days off."

London's whole body sagged in relief at the idea of seeing their sister again. Whether they got to the finale or not, they'd get to see her again soon.

"It'll be so good to see you, Julie. I'm glad you believe in me. It means a lot."

"Oh my god, you are positively sappy over there. The West Coast *does* make you soft."

"To be fair, I am extremely exhausted and haven't been eating properly. My brain likely isn't functioning right."

"You haven't been *eating properly*?" Julie's voice quickly escalated to a screech. "London, you know you are on a *cooking show*, right? God, you really do need me out there."

London smiled and rubbed their eyes again. It was especially hot today, and their binder was irritating them. They were calling a Lyft as soon as they hung up with Julie. They'd watch a movie while the caffeine wore off, and then maybe take a nap.

"And hey, London?"

"Yeah?"

"Don't give up on Dahlia, okay? Because…you shouldn't give up on yourself, either. And I worry that's what you're doing. Sometimes people make mistakes, especially when they're stressed. But…not everyone is like Dad, you know? Most people own up to their mistakes if you give them some time."

London stopped walking. They stared up at the wide, high branches of a palm tree, wondering if they should make Julie expand on that Dad comment.

"Okay," they said after a minute.

"I have a meeting in ten minutes, so I should go. But please, call or text me as much as you need to get through the next few days, okay? I love you."

"Yeah, okay. I love you, too."

London requested a ride and stuck their phone in their

back pocket. They kept staring at the palm tree while they waited, remembering how much Dahlia had liked them. Wondering if things would've been okay between them if they had talked about what was going to happen post–*Chef's Special* like Julie said.

After the things Dahlia had said Tuesday night, though, it didn't feel that easy.

In the universe London previously understood, where they truly meant something to each other, Dahlia would have fallen into their arms when they opened the door. She wouldn't have brought up Lizzie, in any capacity. London would have known what to do, been equipped with the right things to say.

They wouldn't have broken apart from each other at the first roadblock.

The shadow of the palm's heavy fronds gave London shelter while they rested, watching for a silver Toyota, ready to escape the unforgiving heat, the harsh brightness of the August sky, and the unanswered questions taking up too much space in their tired mind.

At the end of her third full day back in Maryland, Dahlia realized the last person she had talked to was the cashier at Food Lion two days ago. The apartment was already three-quarters packed. Maybe she'd be ready to drive to Massachusetts as early as this weekend.

And there wasn't a soul, other than her dad, who knew it was happening.

She poured herself a bowl of cereal and sat on her couch.

She was exhausted from packing, couldn't concentrate on any book she cracked open. Only one thing left to do.

With a sigh, she turned on her TV and opened up her DVR.

Chef's Special: 3 New Episodes

Dahlia prepared her psyche for seeing London.

But the first thing that threw her after she pressed Play, funnily enough, was herself.

It was strange. Dahlia looked at herself every day in the mirror. But she had never seen this much of herself, from a perspective like this. Once the cooking actually started, she looked…good. Competent. Strong.

The camera panned behind her to London.

The screen cut away to their introduction in the solo interview set. Dahlia catalogued every detail of their face, highlighted so perfectly by the studio lights: the freckles, the intriguing flecks of rich colors in their hazel eyes. How their smile tilted slightly up to the left.

Her chest ached.

It was fascinating, watching London work, now that she knew them. That first episode, when they had seemed so grumpy to her, she now recognized the tension at the corner of their eyes, in the set of their jaw. They were stressed. She wanted to reach through the screen, across space and time, and retroactively caress that jaw, press a reassuring hand into the small of their back.

London's stressed face was two shades away from their hyper-focused game face, which Dahlia was delighted to discover when she moved on to the second episode. It prickled at senses that had been asleep since Dahlia had landed in Maryland.

So serious. So talented. But Dahlia knew all the softness hidden underneath. What it felt like to have that game face focused on her.

She wanted to feel their mouth on her skin.

Dahlia blinked, shifting on the couch. She lay on her side and tried to quiet the vivid memories, the heating of her blood.

She focused instead on how sweet Barbara was in these challenges, how often she giggled at herself while she was cooking, how often she patted her tablemate Ayesha reassuringly on the shoulder. Dahlia missed her too.

Dahlia had been intimidated by so many of these people when she first arrived on set. But by the time she'd left, only a few actually left a bad taste in her mouth. Jeffrey. Khari. Lizzie. The rest were just people.

The camera inevitably scanned back to London, their forehead wrinkled in concentration.

Dahlia wondered if Julie got a similar look on her face, whenever she and London played board games, or wrestled in the backyard, or whatever it was competitive twins occupied themselves with.

She longed to see a photo album of the two of them growing up, all gangly limbs and freckled faces in Southern sunshine. Were London's eyes always so serious, even as a child?

It was silly, of course. Wondering these things. If she and London did meet again, would London even want to talk to her? She was the one who'd pushed them away. She didn't get to wish for childhood photographs now.

Watching these episodes at all was clearly a bad idea. But she told herself that wallowing was part of the grief process.

She'd been so good these last few days, trying to forget everything.

So she let it bleed back, for just a little while. She forgot that she was surrounded by boxes containing all of her worldly belongings. She forgot that her back ached. Instead, she seeped back into this *Chef's Special* world, the life she had been so fortunate to live for a few weeks.

Dahlia was fascinated by the postproduction work, how all those hours on set were condensed into a neat sixty minutes, how the music and cuts made it all feel so much more dramatic. And it already felt pretty dramatic, honestly, during filming.

But mostly, Dahlia couldn't stop staring at herself. At how much joy was in her eyes. At London, how handsome and good they were. It made her body feel overly full.

And then someone knocked at her door.

Dahlia jumped, heart thrown into her throat. She pressed Pause on the remote and took a second to calm herself. Who would be knocking at her door anyway?

She stood frozen in shock a minute later, her hand clenched on the doorknob.

The person on the other side of the door cleared their throat, adjusting an overnight bag on their shoulder.

"Hello, Dahlia."

"Mom?"

CHAPTER TWENTY-ONE

Dahlia wrapped yet another bowl in newspaper and placed it in the open box in front of her.

She glanced over at her mother, wrapping up mugs on the opposite counter.

Why had Dahlia decided to pack the kitchen last?

Everything was heavy and awkwardly shaped, and there was simply *too much* of it, and Dahlia was cranky.

She was going to have to get more boxes.

Dahlia hated boxes.

She especially hated boxes when packing them in uncomfortable silence next to her mother.

Guilt chipped away at her as she moved on to the plates. It had been late when her mom arrived last night. Dahlia had found extra sheets from a previously packed box and made up the couch for her. They hadn't talked much.

But when her mom first stepped into the apartment, she'd said this: "Your dad told me you're moving home. Since it sounds like you're staying with him, I thought I'd help you pack. I'd like to be useful somehow."

And Dahlia had immediately felt like shit.

She hadn't even thought to ask her mom.

Not that every parent's dream was to have their grown daughter move back in with them. But she hadn't even sent a text telling her mom she was coming.

Horrible wife, horrible girlfriend, horrible daughter. Mediocre chef.

They had gone out to breakfast this morning, and Dahlia had attempted to make up for it. She'd prattled on about the show, which challenges had been her favorite, breaking her NDA left and right in an attempt to make her mother smile. Her mom, in turn, filled Dahlia in about changes in New Bedford, the latest updates about family acquaintances. It had been perfectly pleasant.

And then they returned to Dahlia's apartment, and awkward silence had descended once again.

They were an efficient team, though. With her mother's help, Dahlia might be ready to move back to Massachusetts within a day.

And she still wasn't exactly sure how she felt about it.

But, Dahlia reminded herself, life wasn't simply about feelings. Sometimes, being an adult meant accepting facts. And the fact was that Dahlia had lost *Chef's Special* and couldn't afford to live here anymore, and taking a breather back in New Bedford was the only real option. She'd look for copyediting jobs in Boston. There was a lot of publishing work there, and her old boss from the paper would write her a stellar recommendation. It would be nice to be close to Hank. Maybe she'd sleep on his couch for a while as she rebuilt her savings, paid down some of the scariest bills.

Dahlia taped one box shut and moved on to another that was half full. She could fit her immersion blender in there, some ladles and wooden spoons.

Something caught her eye as she riffled through it, trying to rearrange things for optimal space utilization. She reached into the corner to pull it out, its cover soft and smooth against her fingertips.

Dahlia's heart gave a small flutter.

Had she really tossed this in a box without a second thought earlier this morning? Or maybe her mom had.

The notebook was bigger and fancier than the small notepad she'd always used on set. Dahlia ran to her bedroom, suddenly wanting that one, too. It was on her dresser, where she'd tossed it her first night back, untouched since.

Back in the kitchen, she pushed aside boxes and newspaper on the counter to make room. She stood, hands on hips, studying both notebooks in front of her.

The smaller one was messier, prone to more spillage during the frantic timed cooking stints on the show. The larger, neater Moleskine she'd just unearthed from the box had lived in her own kitchen, where she could take her time—hours, most nights—to figure things out. To practice, to experiment, to taste and try again.

Her mom came to stand next to her.

"I sense these are important?" she ventured.

Dahlia handed her the Moleskine. Her mom opened it, turning carefully through the pages.

"The first half are recipes I found online or in cookbooks. I only copied them in there when I had adjustments I'd figured out that I wanted to remember." When she had replaced an ingredient, or altered the seasoning, or added something new to the mix.

"The last half," Dahlia told her mom, "are my own."

Nothing compared to that first recipe, about halfway through the notebook, that she had made herself.

It had been exceedingly simple, just a rice dish with random ingredients thrown in, a casserole essentially, but Dahlia had still felt nervous while she was making it. Choosing all of her building blocks, on her own, for the first time. Certain it would be a mess.

But then it had tasted good. Really good.

Tanner Tavish's voice popped into her head.

This is a dish for moms on Pinterest.

She laughed silently to herself now, that he thought this was such an insult.

Moms on Pinterest made some delicious food.

An idea burst into Dahlia's mind, refreshing and bright, like a crocus after a long winter.

"Hey, Mom, do you mind if I pop over to Food Lion?"

Her mom looked up from the Moleskine.

"Want me to come with you?" she asked.

"No, that's okay. I'll make us lunch when I get back."

Dahlia rustled through her bag for her keys. This might be one of the last times she drove her old clunker before she sold it. She already had some decent offers online; it would help offset the cost of the U-Haul.

"Sounds good," her mom said, her face turned back toward Dahlia's notebook.

Dahlia might not have a car or an apartment soon, but as she grabbed the few ingredients she needed at the store, she knew she had those two notebooks. Those notebooks were her, sloppy and real and full of failures and successes. A testament that Dahlia Woodson could learn new things, by herself, just because she wanted to.

Handing that Moleskine over to her mother to look through had been another attempt to make up for things. It had felt like handing over her heart.

Dahlia laid the ingredients out on the counter when she got back. On the show, she'd gutted and pureed an actual sugar pumpkin, but she didn't need to be that fancy now. She would have soaked her own black beans overnight too, if she was a proper chef, but oh well. Dahlia had no shame in the canned food before her.

Her mom helped her find the things she'd already packed that she needed: her good pot, spices, some olive oil.

"Can I help?" her mom asked, almost hopefully.

Dahlia studied her ingredients and shook her head, but she smiled.

"No, I'm good. You can just relax. It won't take long."

Dahlia put on some music, and she got to work.

The movement of her hands, the smell of spices filling the air. The rhythm of stirring, the patience of waiting, the magic of ingredients melding themselves together all on their own.

For the first time in days, Dahlia felt right in her body. She almost cried at the relief of it.

Once the flavors had simmered enough, she brought two steaming bowls over to the couch.

Her mom smiled after she took her first sip. Dahlia did, too. It was both sweet and spicy, warm and comforting in her belly, full of the promises of turning leaves and golden light.

It would be September soon, and Dahlia was glad. It would be easier, somehow, she thought, to be sad in the fall.

"This is delicious, Dahlia," her mom said.

Dahlia stared into her bowl, still smiling.

"This was the dish that got me kicked off the show," she said.

Her mom's spoon rattled against the side of her bowl.

"What?"

"I made this soup. And I guess it was too boring and ugly," Dahlia said, swallowing another spoonful. "But I like it."

Her mom put her bowl down on the coffee table with a loud clatter.

"Is it okay?" Dahlia looked over at her, smile faltering. "Too hot?"

And then, with confusion, she realized her mom's eyes were wet.

"I'm not mad that you divorced David," her mom said.

Dahlia froze with another spoonful halfway to her mouth.

"Uh," she said, lowering her spoon. "Okay."

When her mom simply worried her lip, not adding to this odd and shocking statement, Dahlia joined her bowl of soup with her mom's on the table.

Dahlia turned, propping an elbow on the back of the couch.

"Mom," she prompted.

"Hank might have said something vague to me, about something you told him."

"*Ugh.*" Dahlia smacked her forehead with her palm. *Hank!* What a big mouth. Dahlia should have known.

"Dahlia, I know you think I was mad at you. Or upset, or something. And I *was* upset. You have no idea how hard it is to see your child in pain." Her mom frowned. "And yes, I was excited about grandkids. Okay?" She flashed a quick eye roll. "So sue me."

Even though so far this conversation was *confirming* Dahlia's fears, something about her mom's eye roll, this splash of open honesty, so unusual for her mom, made Dahlia want to laugh.

"But I was never mad at you," her mom continued quickly. "I was . . . jealous, maybe."

"Jealous," Dahlia repeated dumbly.

"Yes. I was jealous when I understood that the divorce had been your idea. That it was what you wanted. But I also wasn't surprised. You've always known what you wanted, Dahlia."

Dahlia opened her mouth to interrupt, but her mom kept going.

"And even more than that, you follow through on *getting* what you want. It's a quality not many people have, you know. Definitely not one I've ever possessed, as much as I wish I did."

Dahlia's brain was working on overdrive to process all of these . . . feelings from a woman who rarely talked about feelings. Her mom looked downright wistful right now.

None of this made sense.

"You think . . . I know what I want?" Dahlia asked incredulously.

Dahlia threw her arm out, gesturing at the room full of boxes.

"Mother. This is not the apartment of a woman who knows what she wants. This is the apartment of a woman who's almost thirty and moving back in with a parent."

"Exactly," her mom said passionately. "Please, Dahlia, if you truly *wanted* to stay in this apartment, you would make it happen. As someone who has known you for all of those almost thirty years, trust me, you would. But you know you need a fresh start, and so that's what you're making happen instead. Do you think I would have been able to tuck my tail between my legs and ask my parents for help when I was in my twenties? No, because that's not how I was raised."

Her mom's eyes flashed with something akin to...anger? Regret?

"I would have found a job I hated and been absolutely miserable, as long as I was keeping up appearances."

Dahlia sank back into the couch, not knowing what to say.

Her mom took a deep breath, regained some composure.

"What I mean to say, Dahlia, is that my whole life, I've tried to do what I was supposed to do. I never allowed myself to listen to what I actually wanted. I am so, so proud of you, that you do that, that you always have."

Dahlia knew she should be soaking this in, letting it absorb all of the hurt inside of her, turning that hurt into something better. But instead, she just felt confused.

And a little angry, too. That apparently her mom had always been *so, so proud* of her but was only actually expressing that right now.

"So you're not...disappointed in me?"

"No, Dahlia," her mom replied immediately. "Of course not. I'm sorry if..." She trailed off, seemingly lost in thought.

"It's like, since I always kept my head down," her mom started again, "never listened to my instincts, sometimes I feel like my whole adult life has been surprise after surprise. I was surprised when you told me you were getting a divorce. If I acted poorly, that's why. I'm sorry. But I had no idea, and from what you said, things hadn't been good for a while. I know I'm not your dad, I know we're not... friends, but a mother should still know when her child is unhappy. So I was upset at myself. And then, like I said, after I realized you were the instigator of the divorce, that you went through this horrible, scary thing because you believed in your own happiness..."

The moisture in her mom's eyes reappeared then, with force, threatening to spill. But ever the queen of composure, she sniffed, wiping it away.

"I was jealous. Proud, but jealous. Which is a selfish thing to feel. I'm sorry."

"But... Mom... sorry, I don't get it. You went through that horrible, scary thing, too, yourself."

"Yes," her mother said simply. She sat stiffly, smoothing her palms over her jeans. "My divorce was different. But it isn't appropriate to talk about that with you."

Dahlia blinked at her. And suddenly, she got it.

Her parents' divorce hadn't been what her mom wanted.

Her parents' divorce must have been another surprise.

"I've been going to therapy," her mom said swiftly, moving past this. "I know I can only control my own reactions to things, and no one else's, even my children's. But I suppose I... wanted you to know more about my reactions. In case I have not explained them well in the past."

Dahlia's jaw hung slack in shock.

"Mom," she said after an awkward pause. "You're going to therapy?"

"There's nothing wrong with therapy," her mom chirped.

"I know," Dahlia said immediately.

"But yes. It wasn't just Hank that inspired me to come down here." Her mom studied her fingernails, a sly, funny hint of a smile growing on her face. "Nonna and Nonno would be rolling in their graves, probably."

"Maybe not," Dahlia said. "You never know." And then, "What else took you by surprise? You said your whole adult life was surprise after surprise."

Dahlia was trying to picture her mom as a person now. Not as her mom, but a regular person with insecurities and doubts. It was like the puzzle of her mother was suddenly coming together, piece by piece, and Dahlia wanted to see all of it.

Her mother shook her head quickly, as if she'd already said too much.

But then she said, "I can tell you one thing that took me by surprise. You." She looked up, eyes twinkling, staring directly at Dahlia for the first time. "Being on TV." She gestured to the dark, quiet screen opposite them. "And flourishing on it."

"Really?" Dahlia bit the inside of her cheek to try to quiet the smile that had exploded on her face at approval from her mother, approval she was actually tempted to believe.

Another win for Team Dahlia.

Attempting a tone of cool calm, she asked, "You think I flourished on it? Even with falling on my face?"

"Of course," her mother said. "You're so full of life on-screen, Dahlia. You're a natural."

Her mother reached over and picked up her soup. Finishing the conversation.

Silently, brain reeling, Dahlia shifted in her seat and reached over for her own bowl. It was still warm.

"Speaking of the show," her mom said, "I never got to watch the latest episode. Do you have it saved? Would it feel strange to watch it together?"

Dahlia shook her head slowly.

Her mom had interrupted her *Chef's Special* marathon last night after the second episode. Dahlia hadn't watched the third one either.

Dahlia picked up the remote.

"Hey, Mom?" she said. Her mom looked at her.

"I'm really glad you came down."

And when she said it, Dahlia realized it was true. Not only because of everything her mom had just told her, but because packing up everything she owned by herself had been so very lonely. And because she hadn't been quite sure, exactly, how she was going to navigate her furniture by herself into the U-Haul. And even though Dahlia liked to think she could drive a U-Haul hundreds of miles by herself, it would still be nice, knowing her mom would be following behind, making sure she was safe.

Dahlia and her mom hadn't hugged once since her mom had shown up at her doorstep the night before. But the smile Dahlia's mom gave her now felt close enough.

Dahlia pressed Play.

It was the first Real World Challenge at the fire hall. The bar mitzvah.

Dahlia finished her soup. She placed the empty bowl on the floor and hugged her knees to her chest.

She and London were standing so close to each other. No one else stood that close to each other. Barbara and Janet had been right. It really was obvious.

They didn't air her and London talking about torturing Jeffrey, but as expected, they did air when Tanner yelled at her. Dahlia winced.

"What a jerk," her mom said with a scowl.

Dahlia allowed herself a small smile.

And then the camera shifted to London.

Dahlia didn't remember seeing London's reaction in that moment. She'd been too busy getting back to work, trying to act serious.

She had missed that London openly glared at Tavish. Flushed cheeks, that clenched jaw, eyes like knives. Like London wanted to punch him. For her.

Dahlia paused the episode, heart hammering.

She opened her mouth, feeling slightly wild. Maybe her mom had inspired her. Dahlia could speak surprising truths into the air, too.

"That person there? London?" Dahlia said, her chest squeezing when she said their name out loud. "I'm in love with them."

Her mom released a small gasp, brought a hand to her mouth.

"Oh," she said. "Oh." And then, after a beat, "And they're...oh."

"Yeah." Dahlia inferred her meaning. "I'm queer. I guess I never told you that."

"No," her mom said. "No, you didn't. But thank you for telling me now."

Dahlia laughed suddenly, a funny croaking sound, like it came from deep in her gut.

"And Hank said I never tell you things! Take that, Hank."

Her mom released a small, nervous giggle of her own but sobered quickly, her hand now resting on her chest.

"Thank you, Dahlia," she said again, "for telling me."

Dahlia picked up the remote, but her mom quickly snaked her hand out to cover hers, telling her to wait. Dahlia glanced over. Her mom's face looked puzzled, like she was working something out.

"Dahlia," she said. "You've barely touched your phone since I've been here. You haven't called or even texted anyone."

"Way to rub my thrilling social life in my face, Mom."

"No, no." Her mom waved a hand at her in irritation. "Dahlia. I am honored and a little shocked that you just told me this, but... have you told *London* that you're in love with them?"

Dahlia stared down at her toes.

The excuses she had made to herself back in LA seemed to wither. She knew none of them would make sense if she said them out loud to her mother.

"No."

Dahlia's mom crossed her arms over her chest.

"Well. Dahlia Grace Woodson, if you don't take that whole speech I just gave you and put it to some good use here, I *will* be disappointed in you."

And then Dahlia actually laughed.

You've always known what you wanted.

And even more than that, you follow through on getting it.

Dahlia chewed her lip.

Could she...?

Would London...?

Oh, god.

Oh, god, she was going to try anyway.

She stood, feeling halfway like she might pass out, halfway like she could run a marathon. Or, all right. At least a 5K. "Okay," she said. "I think I might have an idea."

"Of course you do," her mother said smoothly.

Dahlia walked to the door and shoved her feet in her shoes.

"So...I'm going back to Food Lion. Yeah. Okay. That's what I'm going to do." She nodded, her confidence inching higher as she talked to herself, slowly but surely. "I only need a few more ingredients."

Dahlia found her sunglasses and car keys and gestured to the TV.

"Feel free to keep watching, if you want. I know what happens."

"Dahlia?" her mom called when she was already halfway out the door. Dahlia turned on her heel.

"Yeah?"

Her mom stood and searched through her purse before shoving a twenty-dollar bill in Dahlia's hands.

"Would you mind picking up a bottle of wine? It's been quite the day."

Dahlia smiled.

"Sure, Mom."

And then she was gone.

London flopped heavily onto their bed, face-first, upon returning to their hotel room Monday night. They screamed dully into their pillow.

Today, in short, sucked.

It had sucked hard.

They had been so ready to get back to set this morning. It was the only place London felt any semblance of normal now. The challenges had started to feel almost easy, now that there wasn't anything left on set to distract them.

So easy that London was sailing right into the finale. The Final Face-Off.

They only had one competitor left to beat.

And it wasn't Cath.

London had already been picturing it, they realized. Two misfit queers who could cook for all they were worth. Now *that* would be a *Chef's Special* finale to look forward to. An openly nonbinary pansexual and a woman as obviously gay as the day was long? Invite Carly Rae Jepsen and hang rainbow flags from the rafters.

But Cath had been kicked off today.

They couldn't believe Cath had been kicked off.

Bitterness descended into London's system.

This was the way it was meant to be, wasn't it? The producers had likely planned it from the beginning. It hadn't truly bothered them until now. Team London versus Team Lizzie, right? What a great TV moment.

London slid off the bed. They had been in their room for less than five minutes, and they couldn't take it. They had actually contemplated asking for a new room this weekend. One where they hadn't slept with Dahlia.

They grabbed their key card and left.

When London stepped back into the hotel lobby almost

two hours later, that blast of air-conditioning still a shock every time, Hugo at reception called out to them.

"Hey, London! Glad to catch you. Got something for you."

London had gotten to know a lot of the hotel employees over the weeks. Hugo was one of their favorites.

"I was going to leave it outside your door, but I got worried someone would take it."

"Yeah, thanks, man." London took the package from Hugo's hand with a nod. They walked over to the elevator, wondering what their mom had sent them now. Although it was sort of weird. Their mom, along with the rest of their family, was flying in tomorrow. She probably could have just waited to give London whatever this was in person.

It was only when they were inside the elevator, on their way to their floor, when they looked down and saw the loopy, messy handwriting on the front of the box.

The elevator doors opened. London almost let them close again, stuck against the elevator wall in dumb shock.

Somehow, they made their way back to their room. They set the box on their bed. Stared at it for a few long moments.

And then they dug around their entire hotel room, looking for something sharp. She had taped the hell out of this thing. With a half laugh, London thought about how they should invest in one of her Swiss Army multitools. She would have been prepared, if she were here.

Eventually, they jammed their rental car keys through the tape enough times to get a ragged rip going. Their heart was going to pound straight out of their chest.

As soon as London had the box opened, they staggered back. Holy shit.

The smell.

London knew exactly what it was, and they covered their mouth to both escape the scent and hold in a laugh. With the tips of their fingers, they lifted the offending Tupperware and went back into the hall, down to the trash, where they dumped the whole thing inside, silently apologizing to anyone who walked through the hallway and had to endure it. Brussels sprouts, roasted with garlic and butter, and then left to fester in a package mailed across the country.

Back in their room, with slight trepidation now, they examined the other contents of the box. One other Tupperware, and a note.

London sat on the edge of the bed and opened the folded paper.

I know. I know. I hope it doesn't smell too bad. I tried to tape the container shut really well but I'm nervous. I couldn't afford refrigerated packaging. If it's awful, you only have yourself to blame.

I'm so sorry, London. You don't know how sorry I am.

You're the only chef I'm rooting for.

See you soon.

xoxo

London opened the other Tupperware, gave it a sniff. It didn't seem like the Brussels sprouts had infiltrated it too much. They moved the empty cardboard box to the ground and lay on their side, propped on a pillow, chewing the Rice Krispies treats. They read the note, over and over. Pictured her writing it, scribbling the first part fast, then stopping, biting her lip, fiddling with the top of her pen.

See you soon.

London ran their fingers over the paper, the creases where her fingers had been.

They closed their eyes. They felt more fractured than ever, in a strange way, their tendons and ligaments taut and fragile.

But then they started to laugh. They laughed by themself in their lonely hotel room until they could barely breathe, and each shake of their shoulders, each wheeze of their lungs brought their body closer to resetting itself, new cells stretching over wounds, trying their best, nudging each other on, not giving up on these weary bones yet.

CHAPTER TWENTY-TWO

H ey, asswipe." Julie clocked London in the arm. "Maybe put your phone away and enjoy some quality time with your family that you haven't seen in over a month."

"Julie," their mother clucked from across the table. "Seriously. Language."

"Fine, Mom. *You* tell London to stop texting their girlfriend and actually hang out with us. Their flesh and blood, who flew all the way across the country on a red-eye flight—"

"I'm not texting her," London interjected. But they stuffed their phone in their pocket anyway.

Had they been obsessively staring at their phone ever since they received that package, waiting for a text, wondering whether they should send one first? Yes, yes they had. Maybe they were, in fact, being an asswipe.

Dahlia just felt so close now. All of *Chef's Special*'s former contestants, from current and previous seasons, were invited to attend the finale tomorrow. London had never felt certain, until they were chewing on Rice Krispies treats last night, that Dahlia would be there. And now…now Dahlia's note with her big joyful handwriting was in their back pocket, and for all they knew, she could be back in LA right now, as they and their family ate dinner at this fancy Italian restaurant. Was she unloading her suitcase at the hotel? They could be breathing the same air again. London was practically vibrating with it.

"So you admit she's your girlfriend, then," Julie said, a satisfied smirk on her face.

"I hate you," London said.

"My, how I have missed you two squabbling every second of the day," their mom said, lifting a wineglass to her mouth. Which was curved up in a smile.

London's own mouth couldn't help but mirror hers. They had missed it, too.

Even if they had no idea if Dahlia Woodson was actually their girlfriend or not.

God, they wanted to talk to her. They wanted to kiss her, and talk about all the things they should have talked about before she left.

But first, selfishly, they wanted to go over their menu with her, for tomorrow. London had already gone over it in depth with Sai and Tanner and Audra; they knew they had done all they could at this point. But talking with Dahlia about food calmed their nerves. She would assure them they had made the right choices, that they could do this, that they'd be better than Lizzie, that—

"Okay, listen. I've tried to keep my mouth shut here, but I have a question now."

London's smile fell, whisked away by the gale force wind that was their dad, lumbering forward to rest his elbows on the white tablecloth.

Since their family had arrived at LAX that morning, London and their father had barely exchanged ten words. Tom Parker had simply sulked into the background all day, as moody and detached as a teenager. It felt...weird, and not like their dad, and there had been an underlying tension in their mother's face all day that London was trying to ignore. Their sisters had helped. Julie, Sara, and Jackie had been babbling all day, clearly overcompensating for whatever the hell was happening with their family, and London had gone with it. The note in London's back pocket had been helping, too, a silent comfort.

They just had to get through the finale, they told themself. And then they would summon the mental capacity to deal with whatever this Parker family cloud was.

But Tom Parker had been drinking tonight. Heavily. And apparently, he was ready for the thunder now.

"All right, Dad." London sighed, leaning back in their chair. "Let's do this."

His dad's eyes lasered onto theirs.

"Are you a lesbian now, or something?"

"Dad," Julie said, but their dad held up a dismissive hand, silencing her.

London's jaw clenched, but they didn't move.

"I'm pansexual, Dad, like I told you in college. And—"

"You just always brought home boys, in high school," their dad continued, waving another hand as he interrupted them. "But now, apparently you have a girlfriend."

London had brought home exactly two boys in high school. One, they dated for five months. The other lasted two weeks.

London never knew their father had become so attached.

"I dated other people in college, Dad." London took a sip of their water, in an attempt to show that they were calm and collected. "I just didn't bring them home to meet you. I wonder why."

London's mother cleared her throat. London glanced at her, their heart dropping at the tortured look on her face as she folded and refolded the napkin in her lap.

"Tom," she said, in a lethally quiet way.

But her husband ignored her.

"So you and this Dahlia person," London's dad said now. "You're dating."

"I…" London's face flushed. *I'd love to know the answer to that question, Dad. I'll let you know if I figure it out.*

But London's dad didn't seem too concerned with the actual answer here; he barreled on over London's hesitation.

"And you're comfortable calling her your girlfriend. But what, pray tell, does Dahlia call *you*?"

London's heart started to thump, insistent, pounding against their rib cage.

"What do you mean?"

"If you're not Dahlia's girlfriend? Are you her *partner*?"

"Dad, stop it," Julie said.

London glanced over and, with horror, saw that Julie was crying.

"Hey." They took her hand and squeezed. "It's okay, Jules." Even though it wasn't.

They looked back at their dad.

"I don't fucking know, Dad. Okay?" Out of the corner of their eye, they saw their mom flinch. They swallowed and kept moving. "We haven't talked about it yet. But yes, I would be damn grateful to be Dahlia Woodson's partner. I think being partners with the person you love is a pretty reasonable goal to strive for."

Julie released a small gasp, her fingers still clenched in theirs.

"London," she breathed, and London ripped their eyes away from their dad's to look at her. "You *love* her."

"Yeah," London said, blood rushing in their ears, making them light-headed. "I do."

Julie's eyes were still wet, but she grinned. "Good."

"Are you quite done now, Tom?" London's mother asked, and when London looked up, they saw her eyes were like daggers, pointed at their dad's throat. "It had been such a nice evening until you decided to open your mouth."

And it had been, was the thing. Even with the weirdness clearly surrounding their family, being around them had still been grounding today. Familiar.

London sat back in their seat, taking another sip of water. Godspeed to anyone who had to suffer the wrath of Charlotte Parker when she looked like that.

London's dad was undisturbed. He brought his wine-glass to his mouth once more. After a big slug, he shook his head.

"Of course. I'm always the bad guy. Fine. Someone has to be. I'm just trying to look out for you, London. You've always been so flighty. If it's not one thing, it's the other, and you're far past the age of *finding yourself*. You need to grow up one of these days."

"That's rich," Charlotte muttered.

London looked at their dad one last time. Part of them wanted to feel sorry for this man, drunk and childish, so deeply thrown by the slightest deviation from societal norms. And they would have, if they were sitting across from Lizzie, or Khari, or someone else who didn't matter. But this man had held London in his arms when they were a baby. This was the man who had gleefully kicked London's ass at Trivial Pursuit during family game nights, year after year, ruffling their hair and smiling with his whole face when he said "Better luck next time." This man had shared late-night hot chocolates with London on nights when neither of them could sleep. They had watched rom-coms together in the den; their dad always pretended they didn't make him cry, that his allergies were just flaring up. This man had come to every major event of London's life.

And he wasn't going to ruin this one.

"Okay," London released Julie's hand to push themself back from the table. "Time to go." They drained their wineglass before they stood but left their half-eaten tagliatelle on the table. It wasn't as good as Dahlia's pappardelle, anyway.

"London, honey"—London's mom reached over to grab their hand—"please. Don't go like this."

"Can I come with you?" Julie asked, throwing her napkin on the table.

"No, no." London attempted to give her a reassuring smile, attempted to pass it around to everyone else at the table, to Sara and Jackie, who were both staring at London, frowning, concern etched into their brows. London couldn't make themself look at their mom. "It's okay. I promise. I just have a big day tomorrow."

London patted the top of Julie's head, a gesture that had always pissed her off ever since sixth grade, when London went through a growth spurt that officially left them two inches taller.

"I'll see you soon. Thanks for dinner."

They took a deep breath once they were back in the driver's seat of the Nissan, allowing themself one forehead thump against the steering wheel. They wished Dahlia were here. They weren't much in the mood for driving.

They pulled their phone out of their pocket. Sixty new Twitter notifications since the last time they'd checked. Thirty-nine from Instagram.

No new texts.

They put the car in reverse and drove out of the parking lot.

London couldn't sleep.

The finale was in ten hours, and every anxiety-ridden thought London's brain had ever possibly conceived since flying to LA over a month ago was now parading through their brain.

London was proud of the visibility they'd achieved for their community on *Chef's Special*.

But right now, in the dark, the clock ticking away until the moment they would step onto that set for the last time with the world watching, that visibility felt heavy on their shoulders.

They knew that those who didn't like them would discredit them either way. If they lost, they would have had it coming. If they won, then it would be rigged in favor of political correctness.

But what if London lost in front of everyone who wanted them to win?

How would that trans kid in Kentucky feel?

Quietly, London got to their feet. Their habits of the last week were still ingrained in their system. Their body was itching to walk.

They would just go get some of that awful green tea from the lobby they'd drunk too much of this week. Walk around the corridors for a bit.

But London didn't even make it as far as the tea station. Because when they walked through the lobby, they were stopped short by a familiar short profile, a dark bob of hair with a streak of silver, sitting at the hotel bar.

Automatically, London walked toward her. They sat down next to their mother.

"What are you drinking there?"

Her eyes widened in surprise, and then lowered again. Her creased forehead smoothed, and she smiled.

"A hot toddy. If I consume any more wine tonight, I'll be passed out for your big day tomorrow. Please." She pushed the warm glass along the counter toward them. "Drink it."

A hot toddy actually sounded perfect right about now. London took a sip.

"So you're in love, huh?" Charlotte Parker asked.

London choked on the rum. Once they had recovered, they cast her a sidelong glance. "We're just jumping right in then, huh?"

"Will we be able to meet her anytime soon?"

London ran a finger along the countertop.

"Hopefully."

They took longer sips of the toddy. It slid down their throat, warm and comforting.

A moment passed, and then Charlotte sighed. She reached up a weathered hand and rested it on London's cheek.

"Oh, baby," she said softly. "I'm so sorry."

London put down the glass. They stared at the rings it had left on the counter.

"I just don't get it," they said eventually. "He's had so long. I don't...I don't know why it's such a big deal."

Their mom ran a hand through London's hair and looked at them for a long moment. They closed their eyes, wanting to lean on her while they could.

She dropped her hand and stared forward again, focused on the rainbow of liquor bottles along the wall.

"No matter how many times we all told him, I think he really did think it was a phase," she mused. "And you being yourself on the show has made him realize he was wrong. Your father does not deal well with being wrong."

Boo fucking hoo, London thought.

"It feels like..." London fiddled with the curved handle of the hot toddy glass. Knowing how pathetic this was going to sound, but needing their mom to hear it anyway. "Like he doesn't even love me anymore."

Charlotte brought a fist up to her mouth. She kept it there a long moment, and London grew disturbed that she was taking so long to disagree.

"He loves you, London. He does. Even if he has forgotten how to show it. He's..." Charlotte sighed again. "He's built his whole life around the four of you. Every single place he goes, he talks about what his girls are up to. And now...He doesn't know what to say, I think. Now that he can't say 'my girls.'"

London cursed under their breath.

"It's not that hard," they said, annoyed. "He can talk about his *kids*, then. His children. His offspring, I don't know, whatever! I've taken one word away from him. Cry me a river."

"I know, London, I know. I'm not making excuses; I'm trying to understand it, too."

"Sorry, the cry me a river was directed at him, not you."

"Yes, I gathered that."

She shook her head.

"I've never seen him act like he did tonight," she said. "And before your big day. I am...appalled. I don't know what to do anymore."

Charlotte Parker rubbed her eyes and looked lost, a level of exhaustion and vulnerability London had never seen in her, and it felt like the world as they had always known it was collapsing. Their head felt heavy; their throat clogged.

"Mom," they choked out. "Are you going to get a divorce because of me?"

She jerked toward London suddenly, as if remembering they were there. She turned on her bar stool to face them. She took London's face in both of her hands, smelling of the Chanel perfume she had worn for as long as London could remember.

"My serious, sensitive, beautiful London," she said with a watery-eyed smile. "If my husband can't get his head out of his ass about this, that has nothing, not even a single iota, to do with you, and everything to do with him. Do you understand?"

London tried to swallow, but it was like their tongue had become lead inside their mouth. They managed a small nod.

"No matter what happens with your father, I love you exactly as you are, exactly as you will ever be, and I am so proud of you I can barely even begin to express it. Okay?"

They sat like that for a moment, looking at each other, scared hazel eyes searching wizened, gentle brown and finding nothing but the truth.

London's tongue dislodged enough to allow them to whisper, "I love you too, Mom."

Finally, Charlotte released London's face and sat forward again, stealing a sip of the toddy as she did.

"London," she said after a few moments of comfortable silence. "Do you want your dad at the taping tomorrow?"

London looked over at her. She was studying them carefully, but without judgment.

"I'll make sure he doesn't come, if you don't. Don't feel guilty, either way. It'd make sense to me if you wanted him there, and it'd make sense if you didn't. But it's your choice."

London stared into the almost-empty glass in front of them.

They had never even considered that could be an option. That London could tell their dad no. About this, about anything. That London could be in charge.

They felt childish, suddenly, that this hadn't occurred to them.

They still wished . . . they wished this wasn't an option they had to consider at all. It still seemed unfair. But having some power in the equation felt marginally better.

"I want him there," London decided. "I want him to see me win."

Charlotte brushed their cheek with another sad smile. "That's my London."

She reached over and drank the last dregs of toddy.

"Speaking of. I believe we both need our beauty sleep if we're planning on stunning the cameras tomorrow."

They slid off their stools and left the dark bar.

Charlotte weaved her arm through London's, leaning slightly on their shoulder as they walked toward the elevators.

"I just hope we all get through tomorrow without Julie assaulting anyone," Charlotte said as she pressed the silver button on the wall. "You should see your sister when she watches you on this show. I swear, she has turned *Chef's Special* viewing into a full-contact sport."

London laughed as they stepped inside the elevator, the jittery nerves that were gaining speed in their veins again marginally offset by a hazy warmth.

"Sounds like her."

The elevator dinged at their mom's floor.

London smashed her into their chest in a slightly awkward, half-drunken hug before she stepped away from them.

"London?"

Charlotte turned once she'd stepped into the hallway.

London looked down at her expectantly. She smiled.

"You got this, baby."

And then the doors closed.

CHAPTER TWENTY-THREE

The set was a mob scene.

Not in the suffocating staging area where London and Lizzie had been waiting for what felt like hours. London could do with some more chaos back here.

But they could see out onto the main floor from a crack in the temporary walls set up around them. Their pulse pounding in their ears, London watched everyone pour in.

The set had been transformed to make way for a live audience. All of the cooking stations had been removed, with the exception of two mega stations for London and Lizzie, which were situated directly across from each other. They'd made the judges' table even higher and more grandiose, so all three could loom over the cooking process for the entire three-hour cooking period.

And behind the two mega stations, black risers had been installed to seat the family members and former contestants. London watched Ahmed walk in now, talking with Ayesha. With a pinch in their gut, they saw Cath. Jacob. Jeffrey.

London's eyes scanned around the room. She had to be here soon.

They were ninety-eight percent positive she would be here soon.

Lizzie sat quietly in the opposite corner, as she had been all morning, studying notecards and apparently practicing some type of inner Zen.

Good for fucking her.

London scratched at their neck. The white chef's jacket that was adorned by contestants only during the Final Face-Off was itchy as hell.

There.

London stopped breathing.

London's family walked in with Dahlia. Dahlia was laughing with Julie until she saw Barbara, at which point she zoomed across the floor.

A flurry of expletives ran around London's mind like foul-mouthed bunnies on speed. How was she laughing and smiling with Julie? When had they even been introduced to each other? Holy mother of pearl. She was here. She was smiling. She was wearing a black-and-white-striped top, off the shoulders, and this flouncy black tulle skirt with Chucks, and she looked so hot even from here that London felt like their skin was going to melt off.

With a loud, awkward gasp, air refilled London's lungs. Lizzie looked up, a quizzical look on her face.

Fuck Lizzie.

London jiggled their leg. *Okay. Breathe.* They couldn't focus on Dahlia right now.

They watched their family settle into the front row.

London wasn't supposed to leave the staging area, but they had decided, at some point between last night and right now, that there was something they needed to do. They slipped out the back door, and they searched for Janet.

"Parker, you're supposed to be waiting for the final call," she said with irritation once London tracked her down not too far away.

"Please," they said, knowing she was about to punch them. "I need you to do me a tiny favor."

"Are you serious right now?" Janet stared at them over the top of her skinny violet frames. "You know how many balls I have in my court at this very moment? Yours, for one."

"Do you see that guy out there? Standing near Cath?" London rushed out. "Tall, hair the same color as mine?"

"The dude who looks just like you but old. Yeah, London, I see that dude."

"I need to talk to him. Can you send him back here for just, like, five minutes? Please?"

Janet gave London a dead stare before promptly walking away with nothing more than a shake of her head. Even after six weeks of taking direction from the woman, London still wasn't certain if this was a yes or a no.

But two minutes later, their dad stood in front of them.

His hands were stuffed in the pockets of his khakis, and he wore a chagrined look on his face. A hungover look. London didn't care.

London had to spit out these words now, before they lost their nerve. If they didn't, they worried they'd accidentally swallow them forever.

"London," their dad started. "Look, I'm very—" And then he stopped. He sounded startled when he asked, "Are you wearing *makeup*?"

London closed their eyes. Which were adorned with green eyeshadow, eyeliner, and mascara. They had convinced some PAs to let Julie come on set with them, early this morning, to do it the way they liked.

And they would not let their dad distract them.

"Just...stop. Don't say anything." To London's own shock, their voice sounded steady. "I'm talking now, and you're listening. Okay?"

Their dad shut his mouth. To London's relief, he nodded.

London inhaled deeply. They briefly shut their eyes.

They could do this.

"Dad, you start using my pronouns or else I'm done. You don't see me anymore."

Their dad frowned, let out a small disbelieving huff. "Now, London—"

"I don't come over for Sunday suppers," London continued. "You won't be allowed in my apartment. I won't see you at special occasions. I know we live in the same town, and we might run into each other occasionally. But you've had three years, Dad. And every single time you use the wrong pronoun, what I hear is that, even though I feel better about myself than I have my whole entire life, you don't respect me. You don't see me. Sometimes, it feels like you don't love me. And yes, people slip up with pronouns all the time. It's natural to make mistakes. But every time you misgender me, it's purposeful, and it fucking hurts."

London took a breath. They found that they couldn't look directly at their father's face, so London wasn't quite sure of his reaction to any of this. They were staring somewhere in the vicinity of the right shoulder of their dad's blazer instead.

But they were still doing it. It was terrifying, but they were saying the words. And they were almost done.

"No matter what happens, whether I win or lose, don't find me after the show. I don't want to talk to you again until you decide. And I want you to take your time, take this as seriously as I am. So."

London faltered for just a moment, feeling suddenly dizzy. But they pushed on.

"I'll see you back in Nashville, Dad. Or I won't."

And then they turned and walked away, back to the claustrophobic staging area they were now desperate to get to.

London threw themself in a chair and covered their face with their hands. Which were shaking terribly.

Lizzie did not ask if they were okay. Lizzie did not even look up.

"All right, kids." Janet popped her head into the small temporary room. "Ten minutes until the judges go on stage. You'll be called up shortly after that. Prepare yourselves."

London smoothed their palms on their pants.

They closed their eyes and thought about Brussels sprouts. They thought about barbecue. They thought about sitting on a hard bench in a small quiet courtyard with Dahlia Woodson, drinking from bottles of wine. They knew they had just done the scariest thing they would ever do. Scarier than losing to Lizzie. Scarier than cooking a meal in front of three judges that they'd already cooked for so many times before.

And they were calm.

London and Lizzie were called to the edge of the set.

Maritza looked over from behind her camera and winked. The PAs gave a nod.

The studio lights always seemed bright, but when London walked to their station for their last cook on the set of *Chef's Special*, they were more blinding than ever before. When London glanced behind them at the audience, all they saw was darkness punctuated by bright stars.

But even though they couldn't see her, London knew Dahlia was there. Along with their sisters and a mother who loved them fiercely. And that was all that mattered.

"Welcome, one and all, to the Final Face-Off of season eight."

Sai Patel held his arms wide with a smile of triumph, inviting the audience to raucous applause.

Tanner Tavish stood next to him, his face set in a conceited, serious stare.

Audra Carnegie looked a treat.

It was time.

Dahlia gripped Barbara's hand.

She had been thrown when she walked onto set this morning. It looked so different.

When she'd seen Barbara, it was the perfect distraction from the nerves pummeling her stomach.

"Babs," she had said, "I have so much to tell you."

Dahlia sat sandwiched between her and Cath now, and it was the funniest, most perfect sandwich. It gave Dahlia the strength she needed to get through this.

She could tell from the moment she saw London at their station that they felt good. That they weren't too nervous. Their face only had that steady, focused look instead.

Well, fine, Parker, she had thought. *Guess I'll just have to swallow down enough nerves for the both of us then.*

It was taking everything in her to not tap her feet against the floor, to not crush Barbara's fragile grandma bones, to not grab Cath's hand too, to not bite straight through her bottom lip.

They were only on the fucking appetizers.

The judging was *excruciating.* Had those three fools ever taken longer to contemplate two baby bird bites of food?

And then, when they finally stopped being ding-dongs and made a pronouncement, the judges liked Lizzie's appetizer more.

Dahlia's head flopped into her hands.

Holy hell.

She wasn't going to make it.

Barbara rubbed her back and made soothing noises.

"It's cool, Dahls," Cath said. "London will kill the main course. And you know there's no way Lizzie will beat them on dessert."

"Cath," Dahlia said, looking at her. "Lizzie wants to open a fucking bakery."

"Yeah," Cath said calmly. "And there are a ton of mediocre bakeries. London's better."

Dahlia sat back up. Nodded. "You're right."

"I always am, Dahls," Cath said.

Dahlia's nerves started to settle slightly during the main course, mainly just because it took a long time, and her nervous system probably would have imploded if she hadn't calmed down a smidge.

Plus, the more she watched London cooking, the more turned on she got. So there was also that. She hoped it wasn't too obvious, the fact that all of the blood in her body was rushing toward specific places. It felt like it had been ten years since she'd last seen them. Damn, it was hot in here with these lights. She was certain they had installed extra lights today.

It seemed like the judges liked London's duck. A lot.

But they also liked Lizzie's lamb.

"I'm going to die," Dahlia whispered.

Barbara gave her hand a squeeze. Cath was leaning forward in her chair now, backward baseball cap on. She was silent, too, but gave Dahlia a quick nudge with her knee.

London swiped the back of their hand over their forehead as they walked back to their station to start prepping for dessert. They looked tired now. Dahlia wondered if anyone would mind if she just popped down, real quick, to kiss them.

London was making a coconut key lime pie. Lizzie was making macarons. Dahlia was worried. Macarons seemed more technically advanced, more impressive. Dahlia sat up straight and made sure she was breathing from her abdomen. She focused on this, inhaling and exhaling, and watched.

She could tell when it was done that London was pleased. They even smiled a bit. They plated three perfect slices, sprinkled on toasted coconut and an extra dollop of whipped cream for presentation. They stood back from their station, hands on their hips. Their hair flopped down over their eyes. They needed a haircut, Dahlia thought absently.

And then she realized they were done.

London had officially finished their last meal on *Chef's Special*.

Dahlia's heart started to swell when Audra took an extra bite of London's pie. And then Tanner took an extra bite of his.

Sai Patel ate the whole slice.

The judges left the stage to deliberate, and London and Lizzie had a break.

"Don't you want to go down there?" Barbara asked as London walked over to their family.

Dahlia watched Julie jump out of her seat and hug them. She reached up and yanked on London's hair and said something. Dahlia smiled, wondering if she had just told them to get a haircut.

Then Julie ran her finger near London's left eye.

Dahlia could make it out slightly, even from a distance. Maybe some eyeliner action? London with makeup. God, it was sexy as hell.

"Not yet," Dahlia said to Barbara. She watched Charlotte run a reassuring hand along London's shoulder.

She had met them all this morning, in the lobby of the hotel. It felt...strange, meeting them without London, but Julie had pulled her into a death grip hug as soon as she'd seen Dahlia slinking by. So Dahlia had hugged her back, and then hugged all of them, and it had felt good.

Well, she hugged everyone except for London's dad. Who remained seated now.

And then London looked up at the rest of the audience, put a hand over their eyes, squinting.

Dahlia's stomach *swooshed*.

They found her. Dropped their hand.

And slowly, adorably, they grinned.

Dahlia smiled back so fast and so hard that her cheeks hurt.

And then Julie smacked London on the back of the head. London turned to her, mouth moving quick, and Dahlia saw Jackie and Sara's shoulders shaking with laughter.

Janet ran over and dragged London away, probably for a solo interview. Dahlia sat back in her chair, a hand on her chest, and attempted to slow her pulse. She tried to reassemble her face into a more normal expression and found she could not.

Beside her, Cath chuckled. Barbara cleared her throat.

Dahlia glanced between them.

"Shut up."

Cath laughed harder. Barbara simply reached over and squeezed her hand.

After what seemed an eternity, the finalists and the judges returned. London and Lizzie were called to the Golden Circle.

Sai prattled on for a while about what a fantastic season it had been, what an amazing finale, how close it was, blah blah blah. Dahlia squeezed her knees together. She had let go of Barbara's hand, finally, to grip the corners of her chair.

When Audra Carnegie said it, Dahlia didn't feel surprise, just relief that this entire thing was over now. She could breathe. God, she really had to pee, but she'd been too nervous to move for the last three hours.

Julie jumped out of her seat and threw a clenched fist in the air, like she'd just made a three-pointer.

Their dad stood and clapped.

And then Lizzie turned and stomped off the set.

Barbara gasped. "That bitch," she breathed.

Dahlia couldn't even take this in, how unprecedented and awful it was, because all she could see was London. London, smiling, shaking the judges' hands. London, covered in glitter falling from the ceiling. Oh dear. London hated glitter.

London, turning toward the audience as their family ran to them. London, looking over the heads of Julie, Jackie, Sara, even as they hugged them. London, looking for her.

Barbara nudged her. "You're really not going to go down there?"

"Yeah, Dahls," Cath said. "Give the people what they want."

Dahlia laughed, just a little, through her tears. Oh. She hadn't realized she was crying.

"No," she said. "This should just be for them." She sniffled, wiped her eyes. And then she gave Cath and Barbara a hug in turn.

"I have to go," she said. "Thank you both for being you."

And Dahlia hustled down the risers, away from the blinding lights.

CHAPTER TWENTY-FOUR

J ulie took the flute of champagne out of London's hands.

"But that's only my second one!" they protested. Surely, winning *Chef's Special* warranted more than one and a half flutes of champagne.

Rolling her eyes, Julie dragged London out of the crowded bar. She didn't let go until they reached the parking lot.

London frowned. "Where are we going?" They gasped. "Julie, do you have *weed*?" They hadn't sneaked away from a family gathering to smoke together since college.

"No, London, I do not have weed. God, how much champagne did you actually have?"

"Not enough. It's just the endorphins. From, you know, winning *Chef's Special*."

"Dear lord." Julie stopped in front of the Nissan. "You are going to be positively insufferable now, aren't you?"

London grinned. "Only around you."

"Get in, asswipe."

"Wait. Where are we going?" London asked again, but they were already clicking in their seat belt.

Julie glanced at her phone before tossing it in the cup holder.

"You're needed back on set for something."

"What?" London threw their head back with a groan. "I thought I was done with that place! They better have cleaned up the glitter. Wait, are you taking me back there just to torment me with more glitter? It's weird, but also feels like something you would do."

Julie shook her head, eyes on the road.

London turned in their seat. They squinted at her.

"Why are you being so quiet? What secret are you hiding?"

Julie bit her lip.

London squinted harder.

"Hmm. Everyone in our family knows how bad you are at hiding secrets. So who would...?"

London gasped. And smacked their twin sister in the arm.

"Ow!" she shouted, rubbing her bicep. "Jeez, London. Don't kill us before we even get there."

"It's her, isn't it? I saw you talking to her this morning. Are you like, *friends* or something? What the *fuck*."

Julie just smirked.

London faced forward again, rubbing their temples. Their stomach flip-flopped.

She had disappeared, after the cameras turned off and they could finally look for her. It had left them feeling unsettled, disappointed, but then Ahmed was hugging them, and Cath was smacking them on the back, and they were being introduced to all the former winners of *Chef's Special*, and their family was whisking them away and plying them with champagne.

Julie came to a stop outside the gate to the studio lot. She turned to smile at them.

"Go get her, London."

Their hands shook as they undid their seat belt. They were halfway out the door when Julie called out to them again. London looked back.

"Yeah?"

"She seems cool. Don't be a doofus."

"I hate you." They slammed the car door shut. And leaned back inside the open window. "But also, you know I love you, right?"

"Oh my *god*," Julie waved an arm. "Go!"

So they did. London sprinted through the gate, down the sidewalk, past jacaranda trees, fizzy champagne bubbles coursing through their veins, until they reached sound stage three. They ripped open the door. Ran until they reached the wooden archway where they had first met.

They paused, wheezing slightly, leaning over to catch their breath. Finally, gathering themself, they straightened, and for the actual last time, stepped onto the set of *Chef's Special*.

And that was when time stopped.

The pause in the universe allowed all the remaining bruised, healing pieces inside London to rush together again, until miraculously, their entire body relaxed, and they felt whole.

Dahlia let out a small squeak. She tried to quickly pull off her dirty apron, although of course it got stuck in her hair, which was up in its signature bun. After a moment, she untangled herself, the bird's nest on her head only thrown slightly askew, and she threw the yellow apron to the side. She nervously patted down her skirt.

See you soon.

She stood in the middle of the Golden Circle in front of the judges' station, which was now graced with a dollar-store

CONGRATULATIONS! banner, the metallic colors of each letter glinting under the studio lights.

London could see, even from the back of the set, that Dahlia's knuckles were white as she held them in front of her, worrying the black tulle of her skirt.

London stuffed their hands in their pockets.

They made their way between the two mega stations, still set up from the finale.

They tried not to smile too hard, but the champagne and adrenaline still in their system were making it difficult.

Dahlia twirled around before they could reach her. She jumped behind the judges' table, moving plates and utensils.

London stopped when they got there. They looked down at her spread.

London was never going to forget this day.

"You made me barbecue."

"Stop smiling like that," Dahlia snapped. "You don't even know if it's good."

London smiled harder. "What a ridiculous statement. Of course I do." They examined the dishes closer. "You made my favorite sides. How did you know my favorite sides? I don't think I told you."

Dahlia plopped herself in Audra Carnegie's seat and waved an impatient hand.

"Julie comments on all of your posts. I know how to use the internet. It wasn't hard."

"And we're sitting at the judges' table. That seems bold."

"I thought…" Dahlia swallowed. "I thought you deserved the best table." She picked up her glass of white wine and then put it down again without taking a drink.

London glanced at the glass of red placed next to their plate.

"You know, we should really be drinking beer with barbecue, not wine."

"I don't know what kind of beer you like, and I'd already bugged Julie about too much stuff! And…I've never seen you drink beer!" Dahlia shouted, her voice on the verge of hysterics.

She closed her eyes and took a breath. London almost felt bad. Maybe they were being mean. They were too happy to have any sort of perspective. They loved that she was snapping at them while trying to pull off this nice thing. How had she even pulled this off? She must have been here ever since the finale finished. She had a streak of barbecue sauce on her cheek. She was so, so pretty. London had missed her so much.

"Are you going to sit down, or what? The food's getting cold."

London sat down.

"So I obviously didn't have a lot of time to marinate or smoke the ribs, although I did start them earlier, back in the kitchen at the hotel, but still, they might not be as good as what you're used to. And when I asked Julie *how* you liked the mac 'n' cheese, she just said, 'I don't know dude, it's mac 'n' cheese,' which was really not helpful at all—"

"Dahlia," London said.

"I'm sorry," she whispered, her shoulders suddenly sinking. "I'm so sorry I left. For everything I said. I wish I could…I—"

London was at her side immediately.

"You already said sorry," they said. "With the Rice Krispies treats. Thank you, by the way."

"Did the package smell bad?" She was still whispering.

"So bad." London smiled. Dahlia smiled a little then, too, but her eyes were wet at the edges.

"Dahlia, I'm sorry, too."

She shook her head. "You didn't—"

"Dahlia. Let us both be sorry. Let's be very sorry people eating barbecue. Okay?"

She bit her lip, the skin around her eyes creased in concern. London drew a finger down the side of her cheek until it landed on those worried lips.

Automatically, as if she couldn't help herself, Dahlia opened her mouth and bit down, the grip of her teeth on their fingertips so sharp and gentle at once that London visibly shivered.

Removing their hand, they made themself lean back into their own chair again and look at the food. She had clearly worked hard, and none of it would get eaten if there was any further action of lips and teeth. Their system was already starting to spiral.

"Dahlia, I don't know what to say. I don't know that I even deserve this."

"London," Dahlia said, sounding exasperated. "Seriously, you won *Chef's Special*. Just . . . fucking eat."

And then she laughed again, at herself. It sounded better this time, more real. London picked up their fork. They were about to dig in to the mac 'n' cheese, or the potato salad, when they spotted another dish on the table.

"Oh my god." They reached over and grabbed a perfectly fried ball of cornmeal. "You made *hush puppies*, too?"

"Yeah . . ." Dahlia winced. "Sorry, I know they're more of a Carolina thing—"

"Dahlia," London interrupted before stuffing it in their mouth. "Never, ever apologize for hush puppies." And then they groaned.

And realized they were starving.

London tucked into the potato salad and then some greens, and they were just about to pick up a rib when Dahlia stomped on their foot.

"Ow!" They laughed, their mouth still full.

"Stop making all those noises! It's..." London looked over and realized Dahlia's cheeks were flushed. "It's unfair."

London grinned. "Well, if I'm about to watch you eat ribs and suck sauce off your fingers, which I'm *pretty* sure I'm about to do, I'd call us about even."

Dahlia blushed even harder. "God, I can't wait to kiss you."

London stopped in their tracks.

She was right. They had eaten some of the food now. Kissing was obviously in order.

They dropped their fork and stood from their chair. Thank god these judge's chairs were ridiculously oversized, like three seats made for kings. It made it surprisingly easy to slide onto Dahlia's lap, to straddle their knees next to her hips.

Dahlia let out a small, shaky breath. It was the sexiest thing London had ever heard.

They took her face in their hands.

Her eyelids fluttered on her cheeks, her focus shifting to their lips.

London ran a hand around Dahlia's neck, slinking a hand into her hair, stretching out their fingers, feeling the silky strands between each one. She closed her eyes fully and leaned her head back into their palm, releasing a soft whimper.

"Dahlia." London leaned forward, pressed a kiss in turn onto each of her eyelids. "Dahlia." They sighed into her cheek. "I missed you so much."

And then a timer went off.

Dahlia's eyes blinked open. "Oh, shit!" She shoved London to the side, and they stumbled off the chair. "I almost forgot!"

She ran around the judge's table and over to London's station, where a stove was beeping. She tugged on an oven mitt. After London had recovered from their seduction being so rudely interrupted, they joined her and stared at what she had just unearthed from the oven.

"Did you make me *sweet potato pie?*"

London didn't want this night to ever end.

"Yeah?" Dahlia said nervously. "Julie said it was your favorite. But it was sort of hard to tell, over DM, if she was just messing with me or not. If you don't—"

"No, no, Dahlia. I love it."

London looked at her a second more and then pushed off from the countertop.

"Hey," they said. "Stay right there for a minute. Seriously, don't move."

Dahlia gave them a funny look. "Okay."

London walked behind her.

They took a few steps to the right. Considered. Yeah, this was about right. This was about where their old station would have been.

They looked at her hair, at the back of her neck. Her shoulders were tense, uncertain. Like she was waiting to be called to the Golden Circle. But her cooking tonight had been perfect. She should already know she'd blown the competition away.

London made her wait a minute more.

"This is where I fell in love with you," they said.

Slowly, she turned. She was smiling, no teeth, almost shy.

"And this is where I fell in love with you."

London smiled back. "But you were facing away from me. You couldn't even see me."

"Yeah," Dahlia said softly. "But I always knew you were there."

London made a quick assessment of their surroundings. The station where they had cooked the meal of their life earlier today, where she had just cooked hers, was an absolute mess, dirty pots and pans everywhere, along with a cooling sweet potato pie.

They stepped forward and shoved it all away. Except for the pie, of course. A pan clattered loudly to the floor and Dahlia gasped. London took her by the waist, twirling her around, pushing her back against their countertop. And then they did something they'd secretly wanted to do for weeks. They picked her up and shoved her on top of the table, in this place where they had cooked and pined for her and loved her. They stepped between her legs, which she immediately wrapped around them, and, at last, they leaned in and kissed her.

Dahlia kissed them back, cupping their face in her palms, tasting like peppermint, smelling of coconut and barbecue, everything striking and precious and *her*. For once, she was taller than them, and it felt strangely thrilling. But her tongue pressing against theirs was so familiar, the sighs in her throat the soundtrack London had been missing, her lips tugging at the most alive places in their body, the places they had already pushed so deeply away in her absence, that were thrumming back to life.

"Wait." Dahlia broke away, pushing lightly on London's shoulders. She took a big, shaky breath. "I was so nervous when you walked in here I could barely think. But now I have to say some stuff. Please."

London dropped their hands to Dahlia's sides. They pushed a thumb into her hip.

"You were right." Dahlia swallowed. "I was disappointing, that night."

She lifted a hand to London's cheek.

"Honestly?" London said. "I think we both were."

"Maybe." She smiled, but it looked a little sad. "I should have handled myself better, though, talked things through with you. I was just so, so scared, about so many things. I'm still scared, to be honest. I still don't really know what I'm doing with my life." She swallowed again. "I might disappoint you again, in the future. So. Fair warning."

London looked at her.

"The future," they said.

"Yeah." Her thumb grazed London's lower lip. "If…if you want that."

London kissed that thumb, and then her wrist. They kissed up her bare arm, tan and lightly dusted with dark hair, her shoulder, the heavenly spot where her shoulder met her neck.

"I want that," they said, and felt her exhale. "Do your worst, Woodson. Let's be scared together."

They kissed up to her jawline, smiling when they got there. They could feel her pulse, fluttering fast in her neck.

"Really," they murmured, "I blame Tanner Tavish."

Dahlia laughed, a bit breathless, tinkling delightfully in London's ear.

"What?"

"For kicking you off in the first place."

"London. I think it was a joint decision."

"Yeah, but I really want to blame that guy for something."

Dahlia hummed in amusement against their cheek.

"I suppose," London said on a slight sigh, "I can't give anyone on *Chef's Special* too much shit anymore, considering they're giving me $100,000. Well, minus all the taxes."

"London." Dahlia pushed them gently away from her neck, so she could beam at them. "Your nonprofit."

"Oh yeah." London found themself beaming right back. "I've had some ideas. God, I have so much to tell you."

Dahlia blinked, her eyes suddenly misty.

"I can't wait," she whispered.

"Dahlia." London shook their head, still smiling. "You are so tall right now." They ran a thumb over her cheek. "It feels funny."

Dahlia released another puff of laughter, release and relief and joy wrapped together in the small, wonderful sound.

"I know," she said, sounding so much more like herself. "I can't believe you walk around like this all the time. I feel drunk with power."

And then, as if to prove it, she wrapped both of her legs around London's hips, pulling them as close as they could possibly be, and kissed them so hard and deep that London couldn't even control the growl that came out of their chest.

Their brain blanked, all the pressure and excitement of the day wiped away, replaced with nothing but white heat and pleasure, spirals of comfort and contentment radiating into their limbs. Their heart beat, steady and solid in their chest, *yes, yes, yes* with each thud.

Dahlia tore her mouth away, but London wasn't letting her get away this time. They hugged her tighter, moved their lips to her earlobe, sucked it into their mouth through their teeth.

"London." She dropped her legs from their waist. "I hate to stop this, but... the food's getting cold. And if I worked so frantically on all of this without it getting eaten, I'll cry." She pushed lightly against their stomach.

"Fiiiine."

London admitted defeat and stepped back.

Dahlia hopped down from the counter. And stumbled.

"Whoa there." London grabbed her elbow.

Dahlia put a hand to her head, hunched over, not moving or responding for a troubling number of seconds.

"Dahlia. You okay?"

She straightened.

"Sorry. Got dizzy. It is... possible that before I flew here yesterday, I might have driven a U-Haul from Maryland to Massachusetts. And watching that finale almost gave me a panic attack. I am, maybe, just a tiny bit, running on fumes. But I'll just shut up now, because *you*, you probably had to get to set today at like, what, five a.m.? And then cook three whole courses and—"

London stepped in front of her, holding her shoulders. "Dahlia. Breathe."

"Yeah." And she did. "I'm good now."

London kissed her once more, softly, on the lips.

"So"—they ran a hand into her hair again—"we're going to start with the barbecue, but then you're going to tell me much more about this whole U-Haul thing."

She nodded.

"Deal."

"All right, Woodson." London squeezed her hand and picked up the sweet potato pie. "Let's eat."

EPILOGUE

Three months later

Dahlia gripped London's hair in her hands.

"Oh, fuck," she said. "London. I'm close."

London pulled back to grin up at her.

"I know. You're rather obvious about it."

"Just..." Dahlia groaned, exasperated, before she pushed London's cheeky face back between her legs. "I need you to—*oh.*"

Several dizzy, stars-blinking-behind-her-eyelids moments later, London crawled back up Dahlia's body, leaving kisses along the way.

"Good morning," they whispered into her lips, haughty and beautiful, before rolling off the bed, leaving her boneless in the depths of their voluminous white duvet.

Dahlia really did love Nashville. But she swore London had tricked her into moving in with them with this bed. The mattress was heavenly. Dahlia did not want to know what it cost.

She had sublet a room when she officially moved to

Nashville two months ago. But after only a month, London convinced her she was losing money on it, being that she was always here anyway. After Dahlia insisted she would pay rent, which London noncommittally consented to with an eye roll, she agreed.

And so Dahlia had moved in to London's apartment in 12 South, with its exposed brick walls, its high ceilings and minimalist furniture, and its proximity to Jeni's Splendid Ice Creams.

Dahlia had been shocked that London never told her that her favorite ice cream in LA had a location here, too.

So maybe it was actually Jeni who tricked her.

In either case, Dahlia and London were still in negotiations about the rent.

They were in even more heated negotiations about a dog.

"You sure you don't want me to do something for you?" Dahlia asked with a yawn.

London shook their head from the bathroom, already brushing their teeth.

"No time." They rinsed. "And anyway, that was more than enough for me."

"I suppose it was a decent way to wake up."

"I still can't believe you're not going with me." London walked back into the bedroom, rolling the cuffs of their shirt.

"Believe me, I want to traipse around New York with you, too." Dahlia snuggled even further into the sheets. "But Hank's had his ticket booked for two months. And I have a ton of stuff to do before he gets here."

"I know, I know." London sighed. "But what if they ask me dumb questions? And I get cranky? What if I'm not good enough at talking about being nonbinary, or I say something wrong, and people get mad at me on Twitter? *Blerrrgh.*" London took a break from folding clothes into their suitcase to hang their face in their hands.

"London." Dahlia struggled to sit up. "Trust in Hoda. It'll be fine, okay? Remember, you'll get to promote the nonprofit. You'll be amazing. But...maybe promise me you won't look at Twitter for at least an hour after it airs?"

"Promise."

London unplugged their phone charger from the wall, sighing.

"I can't wait to watch it." Dahlia smiled. "I can't remember the last time I actually watched the *Today* show. Me and Max are going to have the best time, relaxing in our PJs and gossiping about how hot you are."

London paused, carefully folded underwear in hand. "Max?"

"Oh, yeah, you know, the dog I'm going to get while you're away. I've decided to name him Max."

"I hate you," London mumbled, searching around the room for their nice shoes.

Dahlia stretched her arms above her head and grinned before finally shifting the covers away.

"Stay in bed." London frowned. "It's still the crack of dawn."

"Nah." Dahlia pulled a ratty Belmont sweatshirt over her head. Being that it used to belong to London, it was huge on her. She supposed it still belonged to London. Technically. But it was her favorite. "I'm up now. Maybe I can finish my review for the *Source* of that new barbecue place after you leave. It's always easier for me to write in the morning. And then I'll have plenty of time later to finish editing my latest video and get it posted before I get ready for Hank."

Dahlia swung her hair into a bun and went into the bathroom to wash her face.

"Always hustlin'," London said. They zipped up their suitcase.

"The millennial dream, baby."

London leaned against the doorframe of the bathroom, looking at her.

"And maybe you'll post another entry on the website too?"

Dahlia blushed slightly as she brushed her teeth. But she nodded.

Her restaurant reviews for the *Nashville Source* were challenging and thrilling. Her YouTube videos were more work than she had anticipated, but they were rewarding and fun. It was a lot more enjoyable, she'd learned, being on camera without judges and a team of producers watching. She liked sharing cooking tips, the recipes that had helped her find herself again. Connecting with people through food—but in her own way this time, without a ticking clock.

Dahlia's website, though, she had waited to launch until last week. When the finale finally aired, and all the secrets of season eight were finally revealed. Because she'd had to hide what the title of her first post was going to be. She'd written it weeks ago.

The Recipe That Got My (Not So) Sorry Ass Kicked Off Chef's Special.

It was about divorce, and hard work, and taking chances, and surprises. And soup.

Hank said it made him cry. Which didn't count for much,

considering the things her brother shed tears for, but Dahlia had still appreciated it.

It was exciting, getting paid to write for the *Source*. But writing her personal stories and recipes on her website was what she was proudest of. It was vulnerable, and scary.

But *Chef's Special* had taught her she could do vulnerable, scary things.

When Dahlia wasn't writing or creating videos, she had a part-time office job at Vanderbilt University, where Julie worked too. That was what actually paid Dahlia's bills. But Dahlia liked it, the office job, the hustling on the side. Maybe the hustles would turn full-time, someday. Her YouTube channel was already more successful than she had even hoped for. But for now it turned out she loved having a bunch of eggs in a bunch of different baskets, this chaotic life she and London had fallen into. She felt challenged, creative. Stable, but wonderfully alive.

It helped, of course. Knowing that London would be at her side, no matter what she wanted to try next. London had been different from David from the start, but Dahlia was committed to being different this time, too. More honest. Admitting earlier when she wasn't sure about something. When she was insecure. When she was scared.

But the truth was, she didn't feel scared very often these days.

Most of the time, she was too busy simply feeling excited.

Most of the time, she let herself feel proud.

London rolled their suitcase out of the bedroom, Dahlia following close behind.

"You have everything?"

London sighed and nodded, calling a rideshare on their phone. "Yeah, unfortunately."

"Aw, come on, it'll be fun. You'll get to see Sai again. Oh! You should ask him for nonprofit advice! Doesn't he have, like, ten?"

"Yeah, and I'm sure he has a hundred assistants to deal with all the boring stuff I'm dealing with now."

Work on the nonprofit, tentatively called Camp CookOut, had been slow going and complicated, and it included an amount of paperwork that left London disgruntled. But Dahlia had full faith they'd make it happen, and that it would be incredible.

"Ask him anyway," she insisted.

"Yes, dear."

They paused by the door. London let go of their suitcase to cup Dahlia's face in their hands, placing one last pillow-soft kiss on her lips. Dahlia's eyes lingered closed after they pulled away. She put two fingers to her mouth, a small burst of melancholy suddenly pulling at her. It really would have been fun to trot around New York City together.

"You okay?"

London put a finger underneath her chin, forcing her eyes to meet theirs.

She smiled. "Yeah."

Next time.

London kissed her nose.

"It's just a few days. You know the studio needs me back by Monday anyway."

London had started at the music studio a month ago, around the same time that Dahlia had moved in. Dahlia had never witnessed London more hyped and more on the verge of having a nervous breakdown, all at once. She had found it impossibly adorable.

"I love you," they said.

"I love you, too."

"Tell Hank I'm sorry I wasn't here to officially welcome him to Tennessee for his first visit. But that I'm excited to see him when I get back."

"I will."

"And make sure you get the cinnamon bread at Dollywood."

Dahlia rolled her eyes. "I know. For the tenth time."

London hesitated.

"Dahlia?"

"Yes?"

"Please don't get a dog while I'm gone."

Dahlia laughed and shoved them out the door.

"Go!"

The door clicked closed behind them.

Dahlia walked to the window, to make sure London made it down the steep stairs of their building safely to the street. They turned when they reached the sidewalk, squinted up into the slowly lightening sky, and waved at her, three floors up. Dahlia waved back, a little flutter in her stomach at the silly sweetness of it. She watched them step into their ride, waited as the car drove away down their tree-lined city street Dahlia loved so much. The street that had felt like home, from almost the first moment Dahlia saw it.

And then, a different flutter landed in her stomach at the knowledge that she had the place completely to herself for the next twenty-four hours, until Hank arrived tomorrow.

She turned and walked straight into the office, determined to do what she had said and get some work done.

The office used to be London's old roommate Eddy's room. He had moved out when Dahlia had moved in, which she had felt horrible about. London assured her Eddy was trying to move in with his own girlfriend anyway. Dahlia hadn't felt too bad about it for long, though. It *had* been a relief to return to as-loud-as-Dahlia-wanted sex, wherever and whenever they wanted to have it.

She dug her toes into the high-pile rug she'd placed in the center of the office. She hadn't brought many things with her to Nashville from New Bedford, but she was glad she'd brought this, a little bit of good from her old life to mingle with the new.

Her eyes drifted to a photo on the desk while the computer loaded. It was of London's family on the set of *Chef's Special*, soon after London had been pronounced the winner. Glitter was still falling from the ceiling. Julie was clinging to London's arms, with Charlotte, Jackie, and Sara leaning in close by and smiling wide.

London's dad was in the photo too, at the very edge, his hands stuffed in his pockets.

Dahlia was excited for many things this weekend: having alone time today, introducing Hank to her new home. But she was also intrigued to attend Sunday supper at the Parkers'. London had assured her she didn't have to go while they were in New York, especially since Hank was visiting. But Dahlia wanted to. She loved Sunday suppers; Sunday suppers were loud and happy and fun. Plus, she was convinced Hank and Julie were going to hit it off immediately.

But she also maybe had a secret mission this weekend. She just wanted to make sure. That London's dad would still use the right words, even when London wasn't around.

Tom Parker had chosen the right side of London's ultimatum upon returning to Nashville. The *Chef's Special* finale had apparently been the wake-up call he needed, and he was working on atonement. Things were still awkward, at times, but London was feeling good about it, so Dahlia tried to be supportive. Meaning, she smiled at their dad now when they were all together. Sometimes.

But if he showed his true colors without the pressure of London being in the same room, Dahlia was prepared to awaken the lioness.

When the computer loaded, Dahlia opened the draft of her review of the new barbecue place in Germantown. She read approximately two sentences before her brain went *pppffffffitt. No thank you.*

Dahlia pushed back from the chair. New plan.

Sustenance first.

She padded into the kitchen over the hardwood floors. She knew they had a decent amount of assorted leftover veggies, and London got the prettiest local eggs each week from the co-op. And, she remembered as she opened the fridge, London had picked up that fresh bacon this week, too.

Damn. This was going to be a good frittata.

Dahlia heaved the cast iron skillet onto the stove.

She wondered if London was at the airport yet. If they were listening to music and letting themself relax.

Her heart felt back to normal as she assembled ingredients. She was especially looking forward, she realized, to cooking by herself this weekend. Dahlia loved cooking with London. But she had missed this, too.

She put on some music, already starting to sway her hips to it as she worked. She studied the food in front of her. Started to plan her building blocks.

There was something essential missing, though.

Dahlia opened the fridge again and rummaged through the vegetable drawer. Ah, there. All the way in the back. She grabbed the onion and brought it over to the cutting board, its papery skin already starting to unravel.

And then she picked up her knife.

ACKNOWLEDGMENTS

If you had told Little Me about the last few years of my life, I think I would have been overwhelmed—not necessarily about the actually-getting-to-publish-a-book thing, but about how many kind, fascinating, wonderful people I would somehow find to help get me there. (And if you had told Little Me that my first published book would be a sexy book about queer and nonbinary people falling in love, I probably would have turned beet red, crawled into a hole, and promptly passed out. For all the other Little Anitas out there: Life is a ride!!)

Thank you so much to my agent, Kim Lionetti, for falling in love with London and Dahlia and always having my back. Thank you to my editor, Junessa Viloria, for truly understanding London and Dahlia from the get-go, and guiding them to their best selves with such care. This journey has been a delight because of both of you, and my gratitude is never-ending.

Hattie Windley, thank you for a cover that took my breath away, and for making my people look so effing hot. Everyone on the Forever team who helped make this thing an actual, real live book, you are my heroes: Beth deGuzman, Amy Pierpont, Leah Hultenschmidt, Daniela Medina, and

Tareth Mitch. Thank you, too, to Lori Paximadis, and all the Muppet applause, always, for Estelle Hallick.

Thank you, Rosie Danan and Meryl Wilsner, for everything. I am so blessed that you chose to love not only London and Dahlia but, even more importantly, me. You changed my life. Your continued support means the world to me.

Thank you to Cat Knight, the first person to ever read this manuscript, and to Manda Bednarik, my oldest friend and reader. I love you both so much. Fanfic forever. Thank you to Kate Cochrane for your longtime writing support and encouragement, and thank you especially to Piper Vossy, whose comments make my writing better every time, and whose energy makes this world better.

Thank you to Emma Osborne for your kindness, and to Kate Shannon and Mari Levine, forever honorary cousins, for your foodie fact-checking!

Thank you to my Fork Family, without whom I would not have survived these last few years. Thank you especially to Kate, whose publishing knowledge and wise logic have guided all of us, to Kaitlyn for being the absolute funniest and living through debut anxiety with me, to Hugh for being Hugh, to Amanda for reading this book in a single night, and to Angel for being an angel. Please know I am punishing myself with a flaming penis emoji for not naming every single one of you, but I promise, you all fill my life with so much joy on the daily. You are truly family.

Thank you also to the Thirstiest for your endless supply of thirsty gifs and support, especially Jen St. Jude, one of the smartest people I know.

For Anita Box: Thank you for letting me borrow your

name. I hope Anita Kelly can bring the world even a fraction of the compassion you showed everyone you ever met. Thank you for making those around you feel like they could do big things.

Thank you to my family, especially Mom, Dad, Jeff, and Sara, for raising me with love, good food, and good books, and supporting me through all my various weird pursuits. The same goes for my aunts, uncles, cousins, and in-laws: I love and miss you. Thank you for making life so fun. Let's all pretend you never read my sex scenes.

Thank you to all of the romance writers and the romance community who have made me feel so welcome and changed my life for the better. I was late to the HEA game, but now I'm never leaving.

In a way, everything I ever write is for the queer and trans teens I have been lucky enough to work with, who make me laugh and constantly rediscover myself. For everyone who has ever been brave enough to be themselves, even when the road is long, winding, and full of brambles: Thank you for shining your light in an often dark world. You help remind me, on my bad days, that the trolls will never win.

And for Kathy: Thank you for being the best partner in all things, and for always telling me my food tastes good, even when it doesn't. I love you.

Don't miss Anita Kelly's next irresistible novel!

Coming winter 2023

ABOUT THE AUTHOR

Originally from a small town in the Pocono Mountains of Pennsylvania, Anita Kelly now lives in the Pacific Northwest with their family. A teen librarian by day, they write romance that celebrates queer love in all its infinite possibilities. Whenever not reading or writing, they're drinking too much tea, taking pictures, and dreaming of their next walk in the woods. They hope you get to pet a dog today.

To learn more, visit:
   AnitaKellyWrites.com
   Twitter @daffodilly
   Instagram @anitakellywrites